LAURENCE I
approximately 52.5 per cent of his total life expectancy on the
Falls Road, where he currently lives with his fiancé and
young children. A geek before geek-chic was chic, he's been a fan,
follower and writer of sci-fi and fantasy most of his life. The first
novel in the *Folk'd* trilogy was published by Blackstaff in 2013.

Folk'd Up

LAURENCE DONAGHY

BLACKSTAFF PRESS

First published in 2012 by Last Passage

This edition published in 2014 by Blackstaff Press
4D Weavers Court
Linfield Road
Belfast BT12 5GH

With the assistance of
The Arts Council of Northern Ireland

Typeset by KT Designs, St Helens, England

Printed and bound by CPI Group UK (Ltd), Croydon CR0 4YY

A CIP catalogue for this book is available from the British Library

ISBN 978 0 85640 922 6

www.blackstaffpress.com

This book is dedicated with love to my boys, Laurence and Adam,
whom I've watched go from being helpless and cute to helplessly cute.
As their father, I shall be granted a merciful death
when they rule the galaxy with an iron fist.
That's more than the rest of you will get.

The Future

The mother smiled. 'I'm not a mind reader,' she said as, with a stray thought and a wave of her hand, she levitated the blankets then tucked them in more securely around her daughter. 'I had no idea you expected to get the whole story in one night. And besides, we had reached a natural end.'

'But, Mummy...' the child pleaded, wide-eyed, excited and clearly reluctant to sleep.

The mother looked down at her daughter and despite the lateness of the hour, despite the fact she'd been looking forward to going downstairs and spinning her wheels doing precisely nothing for the rest of the night, she couldn't help but feel a surge of love.

Still, it wouldn't hurt to make her work for it.

'So,' she said, 'what do you make of the Origin so far?'

Her daughter sat up and adopted a pose of deep concentration. 'It's ... not what I expected it to be,' she said eventually.

'How so?'

'Well, it's got a *lot* of cursing in it.'

Colour bloomed on her mother's cheeks. 'I forgot about that. I'll take it out,' she said. It would require a small change to the mix–

'Do you have to?'

'Well, yes. It's very bad language, love. It's not for little kids.'

The child stared at her with the sort of naked curiosity that only children can conjure. 'How is language bad, mummy?'

She was floundering now. She knew it, but somehow she was compelled to keep trying. 'Language isn't. Just some words are.'

'Why?'

'They're not nice.'

'You use them. Daddy uses them. You're nice.'

'Thank you.' she said uncertainly, not knowing what else to say. They said if you stared at a word for long enough it lost all meaning. She was beginning to feel the same way about this particular conversation. Besides, what was the point of the Origin, if not to tell the young how this world they lived in had begun?

'Okay,' she said reluctantly. 'The cursing stays. But if I *ever* hear those words coming out of your mouth, little lady …'

Her daughter made a play of zipping up her mouth but, unfortunately, she must have visualised this a little too enthusiastically, because a real zipper now existed where her mouth had been, closing off her face even as the child's eyes widened in alarm. Her mother smiled and wiped a hand across her daughter's features, erasing the zipper as quickly as it had appeared.

'So apart from the cursing,' her mother prompted, 'what do you think of the story?'

'It's not like I thought it would be,' the child confessed. 'I thought it would be a love story, but Danny and Ellie don't seem like they love each other.'

Her mother smiled a little at that. 'Because they fight?'

'Because they only really got together cos Ellie was pregnant with Luke.'

'And that's bad?'

'It's …' her daughter paused, 'kinda sad. And it's not very magical, so far.'

'We'll get there,' her mother promised, starting to re-create the necessary story bubbles. To create the Origin the bubbles had to be mixed and it required quite a lot of concentration. Plus, she needed permission from the others involved in the stories to use their memories, so there was always a slight tug of delay as she asked a question and received the answer.

'Danny is silly,' the little girl said suddenly, vehemently.

'Why do you say that?'

'He's angry that he's a daddy. Does he think he's a bad daddy?'

'I'm not sure it's that,' her mother said, now quite lost in contemplation herself. 'He was very young, remember, to be a daddy, and he had lots of plans for what his life was going to be like and then all of a sudden there's a baby and he can't go travelling and see the world any more. All of his plans went up in smoke –' and as she spoke, all of the story bubbles she had created did promptly that. The mother cursed and began the creation process once more.

'But he had a lovely wee baby,' her daughter said. 'That's better than travelling.'

The mother paused, thinking of a way to explain this that the child would understand. 'You want to be a Flier, don't you? When you grow up?'

Her daughter beamed. 'Yes! I want to go to Olympus and race the Harpies and the Furies, and I want to go to Asgard and study at the Halls of the –'

'What if you couldn't, because you had a baby?'

The child's smile wilted. She faltered. 'But I wouldn't. I'm not going to have a baby until …' and then, in a moment so laden with metaphor that the bedroom light overhead (a particularly needless device in a land with two hundred and sixteen suns in the skies above) actually switched on, realisation dawned on her daughter's pretty little face. 'Oh,' she finished.

'That's how Danny felt.'

'Then why didn't he like his other life the faeries gave him? All his world changed, and he wasn't with Ellie any more and he didn't have Luke,' her daughter sighed, perplexed. 'He was grumpy when he had Ellie and Luke, he was grumpy when they went missing, and he was even *grumpier* when he woke up in the other life where he never had them. Now Danny's trapped in Eriu – I mean, what did they call it back then?'

'The Otherworld,' her mother supplied.

'Ugh, yes, trapped in the Otherworld – without a clue what he's going to do. He doesn't have a magic weapon or anything. This isn't at all like the old bedtime stories you used to tell me, Mummy, about Setanta and Odysseus and Thor.'

'Because of the cursing?' her mother teased. The story bubbles were ready. She moved them together and a thunderclap resounded throughout the room, such was the power of the story they now contained.

'No, because it doesn't make any *sense*. It's so complicated and

4

nobody really seems to know what they want or who they want. Is this what all grown-up stories are like?'

The Origin bubble touched the child's hand and burst in a silent explosion. The girl tumbled gently backwards, but was caught by her mother's thoughts and lowered with endless care to the pillow, where her eyes softly closed and her mind was thrown open. The mother clasped her daughter's hands in her own, as the room itself seemed to inhale and exhale in perfect synch with the child's breathing.

Leaning forward, she kissed her daughter on the forehead.

'My little angel,' she said wryly, 'you have *no* fuckin' idea ...'

The Meeting With the Goddess

THE OTHERWORLD, NOW

Someone sniggered.

He was going to have to open his eyes, he decided, because the sound of the sniggering had coincided rather neatly with the memory of being sucked into the earth through a portal in what had once been his front garden. When something like that happened to you and you found yourself alive, tasting grass and being sniggered at, you at least owed it to yourself to open your eyes.

It was a crow. A crow, perched on his shoulder, as if crows perching on your shoulder was the done thing. And every so often it would lean forward and peck him with its hard little fuckin' beak, right in the crook of his neck, not hard enough to draw blood but hard enough to penetrate right through his unconsciousness and make him emerge into the waking world. What the fuck was a bird's beak made of anyway? Diamond?

'Get the fuck off, ya fucker!' he said, jerking his upper body – forcing it to take off in a *phutphutphut* of wings – and pushing down with his palms so he was no longer lying facedown in the ... *where the almighty fuck was he anyway?*

He got to his feet and squinted in the moonlight, shielding his eyes from the glare until his brain reminded him that, generally speaking, moonlight was not something people had to shield their eyes from. So, ignoring the crow, which had landed a mere six feet or so away, he looked up.

Generally speaking, the moon wasn't usually that fuckin' big, either. It was hanging so low and so huge that if there really was a Man in the Moon Danny could have told him if he'd something trapped in his teeth.

He dropped his gaze to the crow, which regarded him with equal interest. For a moment man and bird simply stood there, watching one another with intent, on a lonely hilltop in the middle of a great plain lit by the glow of an impossible moon. Danny was the first to break the silence between them.

'You laughing at me, ya big feathery cunt?' he asked it evenly.

'Shouldn't I?' the crow replied.

Talking crow. Danny was vaguely aware that he should be going through all the clichés of disbelief and fear, but right then and there, after the parallel universe and the amazing vanishing baby trick the cosmos had pulled on him, he had very little disbelief left.

'You're not gonna talk only in poetry or somethin' are ya?' Danny demanded. 'If I sniff so much as a whiff of iambic pentameter comin' outta that beak –'

The crow hopped a few feet sideways. Insofar as birds could have facial expressions, this one looked decidedly patronising. 'I assume you've never talked to a Creature of Omen before?' it asked.

'I've been very drunk in some very dark clubs,' Danny offered. 'Chances are I've done more than *talked* to some Creatures of Omen, mate.'

'Ignorant mortal! I am a crow! Harbinger of the battlefield! Kings and chieftains would await my appearance and the portents for good or ill that I would bring!'

Danny sat on the grass, because he needed a moment to take stock, and as he sat, he gave this news all the grave consideration he could muster, using all his years as a Belfast native to come up with an appropriate riposte.

'So?'

Expert linguists have agreed that the Belfast 'so?' is unique among all retorts contained in all dialects of all the world's languages. There exists no counter-move. Said properly, with exactly the right amount of disdain and nonchalance, coupled with a sneering contempt and flavoured with a soupçon of aggression, the most reasoned and logical statement simply falls apart when confronted by it.

Had it been said to Moses when he presented the Commandments from Mount Sinai, Christianity would have crumbled there and then and everyone would have filed off sheepishly to see if manna could indeed be rolled up and smoked.

'So?!' the crow spluttered, which for a thing lacking lips was not an easy thing to do. 'For millennia the crows served as mystical portents of doom, divining the chaos of the battlefield and choosing from its infinite variations an unerring picture of the future! My magics were ineffable! My conclusions unchallenged!'

'So?' repeated Danny.

'So? So? SO?' the crow thundered and Danny knew he had the wee bastard.

'Yeah, so?!' he concluded, and then sealed the deal. 'And what? What'dja want, a fuckin' medal?'

The crow fluttered up and down a few times, looking for all the world as if were hopping with rage. 'Have you any idea who you address in such a way?'

'No,' Danny said, switching tack, ladling the infinitely wide-eyed patience on with a trowel. 'I thought that's where we came in?'

'I am The Morrigan!'

Danny flashed immediately on the name; back to Mr Black's office, to the on-hold narration playing. The Morrigan ... some sort of warrior goddess. Beyond that, and the obvious fact they shared a surname (surely not a coincidence ...), he didn't know much.

'You have the talent,' the crow said, as if sensing the flash. 'It's true, then.'

His thoughts were not his own. Danny felt his mental guard go up, even as he burned to ask more questions. Remembering. That was meant to be his gift, wasn't it? Some gift. It wasn't exactly a double-bladed lightsaber or crimson eye-beams. He was unlikely to threaten the pantheon of the great action heroes with a talent like that.

'You're meant to be The Morrigan?'

'I am The Morrigan!'

'You're a fuckin' crow!' he exclaimed. 'What's your great power – shittin' on your foes from a great height? Stoppin' them gettin' any sleep by sittin' in a fuckin' tree all night cawin' like a cunt?'

'Crows are a form of the goddess Morrigan, an aspect of her whole,' the crow explained, in a tone that suggested it was flabbergasted at his stupidity.

'So where's the rest of her?' Danny asked, deciding to forgo the temptations presented to him by the phrase 'aspect of her whole' but making a note of it for later.

The crow didn't answer. 'You have the talent,' it said instead. 'Because of that, I'll choose to ignore your staggering lack of respect.'

'Ach thanks,' he said. 'I appreciate that so much. Mind if I ask you a few questions?'

'I shall allow it,' the bird said graciously, unruffling its feathers and turning its head away in a somewhat haughty pose.

That was when Danny lunged.

The bird never saw it coming. It squawked, a proper bird *aaaaawwwwrrrrkkk* and it tried to launch itself up and away to safety, but Danny's attack had been timed to coincide with the bird turning its head and that crucial fraction of a second had been enough for him to clamp his hand firmly around the bird's meagre little body and prevent its escape. The crow went crazy, pecking him this way and that, until Danny was able to pinch that wicked little beak shut with his free hand.

'My question is,' he said, ever-so slightly out of breath, and starting to bleed from a few shallow puncture wounds on his right palm, 'why shouldn't I break your scrawny fuckin' neck?'

What do you think you are doing?

He nearly released the bird from sheer shock. The words had come at him in his own inner voice. It was like hearing your own subconscious rebel against you, and for a moment he actually wondered if he had finally, somewhat understandably, snapped under the strain.

No. No, the voice wasn't his own, despite coming from inside his head; it smelt different. It smelt of dirt, and blood, of this strange place he'd found himself in.

'I'll tell ya what I'm doin',' he replied, vocalising because it was easier to structure his feelings that way, 'I'm getting sick of all this shit that's been happenin' to me this past week, and you were just the talkin' crow that broke the camel's back.'

I am trying to help you. You have no idea what sort of place you're in. No mortal has been here in—

'Aye,' he broke in, 'hundreds of years. Inexcusable magics or some shit. Blahiddy-blah fuckin' blah. And I have some sorta talent. So you said. Whoo-pee-fuckin'-doo. Look. All I wanna know is how I make this all stop. How I go back to the way things were. That so hard? That so much to ask, aye?'

There's so much you don't know. So much you don't understand.

The voice was almost pitying now. He felt like squeezing his hand around the little black body he held in his fist until it exploded. If one more person pitied him, just one more—

The landscape around him turned blood-red so quickly and so completely that he was stunned by the speed of it. He looked up, and saw that massive overhanging Moon had changed to crimson, just like – and he felt his blood run cold at the memory – just like the one in his dream, moments before the...

The same howl came forth, as he had known it would. Terrifying, ear-splitting, like every wolf in the world howling at once.

The goddess in his palm promptly crapped herself all over his hand.

Let me go. Let me go now.

He complied, not quite knowing if he did so willingly or because the crow had some power of compulsion. The bird fluttered up and away, but it didn't abandon him; it hovered about twenty feet above his head. Crows were particularly ungainly things, he could see that now. Little wonder they'd earned a reputation as grim eyeball-guzzling harbingers of death. They radiated menace.

'Something's coming,' the crow called down to him. 'One of their soldiers. One of the elites, by the look of it. Behind you. Look.'

He rotated and from his vantage point on top of the small hillock he saw it almost immediately, lurching across the plains toward him. It moved like the crow flew; in a way that looked clumsy, but was filled with power. It came at him across the red-tinted grass in a stop-start way that put him in mind of those scary fuckin' skeletons in the *Jason and the Argonauts* movie he'd loved as a kid.

'Well! Don't just...! Do something then!' he shouted up at his airborne companion.

'Who? Me?'

'Yes you!' he said, his voice hoarse with terror, as the thing began to rumble on the upward incline, now no more than two hundred feet away. 'You're the fuckin' Morrigan aren't ye?'

'Should I shite on it? Or wait till tonight, perhaps, and keep it up all night cawing like a … what was it …?'

He glared death at the crow. The crow, who had evolution on its side, did the same and won. 'What do I do?' he cried out, taking one step backward, then two, testing the surface beneath his feet, trying to judge how quickly his feet would spring off it, estimating the running speed of the thing moving at him. Knowing it was moving faster than he could ever hope to. There was no getting away, no escape.

'You fight,' said the crow, and flew upward and away from sight before he could say another word, leaving Danny alone with the oncoming nightmare.

He had dreamed of this thing. He had seen it before, when he'd talked with his da in the dream – his da had fought it, had shown some surprisingly good warrior moves for a guy who suddenly sprouted a set of crow's wings. Crow's wings. How had he ever forgotten a dream like that? His mind raced. He had forgotten it, but he had remembered it. *Remembering is your power.* Great. A wolf the size of a barn with teeth the size of meat cleavers was bearing down on him, and he had all the powers of anecdote at his disposal.

He was still moving backward, his steps turning to bounds turning to almost full-out backward jogging, because the one thing worse than seeing this fucker coming at him would be turning and running from it knowing that it would be closing on him, closing and gaining, then pouncing and sinking its teeth into his soft, yielding flesh. A glance up overhead. The crow was gone. Fucker. Same couldn't be said for the wolf-thing. He could hear it now.

The ground shook with every step it took. Danny was well down the far side of the hill, and for a few moments the beast slipped from view. But now it was coming for him, gravity assisting its descent. It wasn't going to slow down to talk to him or to impart some cryptic message, it was going to keep bounding until it went right through him and scythed him neatly in two.

There had to be something he could do, something he could use. After all, there was always something, wasn't there? Some spear or some sword or some piece of the landscape that came to the rescue. He'd seen these movies before. He was the hero, right? He'd just been dropped in the magic world, yeah? He wasn't gonna get eviscerated within half an hour of arriving. Not unless he had two younger brothers who'd get progressively better results than him.

Stop. Stop thinking about this like it's a fuckin' story.

The thing was about forty feet away from him now. Thirty feet. Twenty. He could see the muscles in its shoulders ripple. It must have been fifteen feet long from nose to tail. Fifteen *feet*. Each leg was as big as a large dog, and the head was all red eyes and a bobbing jaw line revealing a thin white line of teeth, though he knew that the brief glimpse of those teeth was like seeing the one-tenth of an iceberg visible above the surface of the sea.

Fuck it. Danny spurned his final chance to turn and run. No magic sword was going to appear. No hitherto unknown superpower was about to present itself. If he was going to survive this, he was going to have to save himself. He planted his back foot in the soil, stopped his retreat and made his move, the single solitary gambit he could think of.

'Here. Stall a wee minute,' Danny said.

It was all in the voice. Ninjas may take years to hone their skills with shuriken. Danny Morrigan had talked his way out of trouble his whole life. His voice was his bow, and the tone was the arrow. If he sounded like a man pleading for his life, he knew, beyond all doubt, that this thing wouldn't stop, it would just plough through him and his intestines would end up as interesting geometric shapes on the grass.

His voice was icily calm. It was conversational. It was 'can I borrow a fag?' outside a pub, 'sorry mate d'you have the time?' on a street corner. There wasn't a trace that the speaker had the slightest inkling he was in danger.

On hearing him, the single-minded head-down killing stance the wolf-thing had adopted dissolved. The creature tripped over its own legs and went to ground in a tangle that Danny had to quickly sidestep, lest the creature accidently achieve its original objective of cutting him down. His heart was pounding in his chest but he exuded an aura of calm as the thing unwrapped its massive legs from underneath itself and stood up on its haunches barely a few feet from him, red eyes glinting.

'Y'all right?' Danny said, and managed a cursory nod. His chest was a pinball table and his heart was racking up a high score, but outwardly he radiated nothing but slightly rumpled geniality. He may have lacked crimson eye-beams, but right now he was projecting Danny-ness at high intensity.

'Aaaaallllllriiiiiighhhhttt?' it echoed, snapping at the air as if wanting to bite the word itself.

It hadn't been meant as a response, but Danny treated it as one.

Taking it to the next level, he sat down and gave a little sigh. 'Ach aye, not so bad. So what's the craic with this place then? This the Netherworld is it? Fuckin' Nether Regions more like, am I right?'

The wolf-thing reared back up, then shook its head violently, a move which if it hadn't been for the size and ferocity of the fucker would have reminded Danny of a sodden dog trying to dry itself. 'Sssssttttooopppppp tttttaaaallllkkkkiinnnngg!' it said angrily.

He cocked his head and frowned. 'Stop talking?' he echoed. 'Sorry I don't mean any offence like but I didn't really catch ye,' and he snapped his fingers. 'Tell ya what. Try saying the words a wee bit quicker. Try movin' from one letter to the next a wee bit faster. How's that work?'

The thing's breathing was incredible; it was like hearing two dragons go at it doggy-style. 'Llll … liii … likeee thhhhiss?'

Danny clapped his hands together once and grinned. 'Now you're cookin' wi' gas! Now, don't suppose ya could direct me to the oul …' he looked around and gestured, '… palace or hideout or secret dungeon or whatever it is?'

'I ammm tooooooo eattt yooou?' it replied, and that slight querying tone in its voice, that note of puzzled bafflement, was Danny's only hope of coming out of this alive.

'Nah,' he said. One word. Keep the big lies short. Keep them simple.

The wolf-thing paused to mull this over. 'Nnooo?' it said.

'Think about it,' Danny kept on quickly, not giving the thing a chance to stop and dwell on anything he was saying, knowing he was balancing his life on a knife-edge, 'I'm the first human to be here for fuckin' *ages*, aye?'

'Cennnnturies!'

Danny snorted. 'So what's the use in eatin' me? Doesn't it sound more likely you should bring me to the boss and let them decide what's to be done? That's what they're for, isn't it like? Imagine they says to ye, "well, what was the craic out in the oul endless wastes of eternal despair tonight, same oul shite?" and you were all like, "no, I saw an actual livin' human danderin' about the place, so I ran at the fucker and ate him." They'd be ragin'! They'd be sayin', "fuckin' hundreds of years we've been waitin' on somethin' different happenin' and you go and eat the fucker!" Then what'd happen? You'd be in the shit, that's what'd happen. Not that it'd be your fault like. Sure we all know what the bosses are like. Heads up their fuckin' holes most of the time.'

If he'd had a cigarette he would have offered it ceremoniously.

He'd struck a nerve with that last sentiment. The wolf-thing nodded its massive head in enthusiastic agreement. 'Theyy instructtted us we couldddd no longerrrrrrr consummme our own offsssspring!' it said, adding a mournful little *awwwrrrlll* at the end for emphasis at the depth of this injustice.

'Bastards.'

All business. He had to keep being all business. It was like walking through an office with a clipboard; you could walk through just about any office in the world unmolested and unchallenged so long as you looked like you belonged there. He stood up – fighting an urge to stamp out his imaginary cigarette – walked right up to the wolf, giving it a companionable thump on the side of its midriff, where he imagined its shoulder muscles might have begun.

'Right, c'mon, let's be away then,' he said. And he rolled his eyes in an exaggerated way. 'Wouldn't wanna keep the mucky-mucks waiting now would we? Tch.'

To his everlasting relief, the thing squatted down on the grass, flattening itself to the surface. He hesitated for only a second before quelling his fear and hopping up onto its massive broad back, swinging his legs over. The thing raised itself up and he could feel himself settle in between two groups of muscles that formed a makeshift saddle.

The wolf's head swung back, teeth glinting in the crimson moonlight. It was every nightmare he'd ever had, all rolled into one. 'I am gladdd I did not consummmmmee you,' it rumbled, and then they began to move off, Danny swaying forward and back rhythmically as the creature began to lope in that start-stop motion across the Otherworldly landscape.

He held on grimly, his fingers grabbing onto the loose fur matting on the thing's back, but it didn't seem to mind (or likely notice) his tight grip. His balls were being banged around a little bit, but apart from that it wasn't too bad. Of course, he was currently riding a living, breathing killing machine which was taking him to the headquarters of probably thousands of even scarier fuckers. What in the name of Jesus fuck was he going to do when they reached the 'boss'?

Some suicidal impulse made him feel a sudden kinship with the creature he was conning into giving him a lift. There was every chance that whoever called the shots around here would not be pleased that Danny hadn't been sliced into tiny little pieces on sight, and he suspected his new mount would pay the price for its gullibility.'What's your name?' he called out.

'I am withoooooout naaaaaaaaame. Itttttt isssssss not considerrrrrrred necesssssssary.'

'Typical,' Danny grunted, packing as much disgust as possible into his tone. 'Well we'll soon fix that. How bout ... Wily?'

They stopped so abruptly he was almost pitched forward and off the wolf-thing's back, and he thought that he'd made some sort of horrible *faux pas* by naming his unexpected new proletariat sympathiser. Maybe he wouldn't have the chance to worry about his fate upon reaching Thing Central after all. But it swung its head back to look at him and when the teeth flashed this time, it almost looked like a smile.

'I liiiiiike it,' said Wily, and they set off again.

Danny pitied the Road Runner that fucked with *them*.

With a disorganised flurry of wings, his erstwhile guide the crow landed on Wily's back, appearing so suddenly that Danny wondered whether it actually needed to fly anywhere or if it simply materialised into being. 'You!' Danny hissed with unconcealed hatred. 'You wee cunt!' He wished he could let go of his handholds to lunge forward and wring that little neck.

'Me?' the crow said innocently, keeping its balance with no apparent effort. Wily, for his part, seemed not to have noticed the extra weight settling on him.

'You left me!'

'You seem to be doing okay. Better than okay. Naming a soldier faerie and turning it into your own personal mount? Not exactly what I had in mind when I said to fight it, but I have to give you points for originality. What's next? Get it to form a union and loiter outside some standing stones howling "We Shall Overcome"?'

'You seriously wanted to me fight it?' he said. 'Are you out of your fuckin' mind?'

'Am I out of my mind? Yes. I am. That's what an "aspect" is. Isn't that where we came in?'

He narrowed his eyes and studied the bird. *Make the connection. See past the surface.* Since stepping on that tablet, doing that seemed easier. 'You're stuck, aren't you?' he said. 'Trapped as a crow.'

Wings fluttered. 'Astute. And accurate.'

'Who are you?' he asked. 'Who is "The Morrigan", I mean? I need to know, I mean really know, what all this is about. What I'm gettin' into. What I need to do. All of it, the truth. Or I'm gonna be dead in about two seconds flat and I think,' he said, fixing those little beady eyes with a level stare, 'that'd be as big a disaster for you as it would for me.'

You really want to know?

'Yes.'

It'll be quite the journey. Unlike anything you've ever taken before. Be warned.

He didn't break the stare. Didn't speak. *Show me.*

The crow hopped forward. He felt a wing brush his face …

The world exploded into fire, and oil.

GRIFFIN STREET, BELFAST, 12 YEARS AGO

With an angry hiss, the hot oil began to bubble and sizzle, heating the captives that just been dumped into its midst to hundreds of degrees in seconds.

'Ma?'

Linda Morrigan didn't have time to look back to where her son sat. The chips had gone on. Right, that was that done. She'd a few minutes before they'd need to come out. She wished they'd been able to afford one of them deep-fat-fryers that had the wee bleeper instead of this Poundstretcher special. The bread was frying on the pan; she flipped it and it sizzled angrily.

'What is it, Danny son?' she said, affording him as much of her attention as she could. He was only ten, God love him, and he hadn't yet learned when was a good time to try and attract his ma's attention and when, for the sake of his digestive system and its continued health, he should let her get on with things.

'What does my da do?'

She did glance back at that, only because of the unexpectedness of the question; truth be told she'd expected it to be about whether Steve could stay the night (yes, so long as the TV stayed off Channel 4). 'He works for Ordnance Survey, love,' she said. 'He's a cartographer ... am ...' she fumbled for a term that he'd probably find more descriptive, '... a map-maker. Sure I thought ya knew that?'

Danny looked a bit dubious at that. 'But like ... hasn't all Ireland been discovered already?'

Taking the grill tray out to inspect the bacon, she couldn't help but laugh as she turned the rashers over. God love him. 'He's not going anywhere people haven't been already, son. He goes around with a wee special camera and he ...' she struggled here, because she'd never really taken a blind bit of notice of what Tony did for a living, so long as it brought in the wage (which it had) and paid the bills (which it did),'... well he measures distances and heights and stuff. And they make wee maps from it. Or big maps. You know that big map of Ireland you have on your bedroom wall? The lovely big one? He helped make that!'

'Oh,' Danny said. He seemed deflated by this. She supervised the chip basket removal, divided the fried bread and the bacon and shovelled his share onto his plate. He grabbed it and was about to troop out when she called him back. 'In the kitchen tonight, love. TV can wait.'

'Ach ...'

'Ach nothin. Get yer arse back here. 'Mon, we'll have a wee chat. You and me.'

He flumped down as if to his last meal prior to execution. She sat across from him at the kitchen table, the smell of the fried dinner thickening the air between them. For a few minutes they ate, because he didn't eat enough for her liking and she wanted to make sure he had a good few mouthfuls before she started, and start she meant to.

'So,' she said, when she thought he had eaten a good bit of the meal before him. 'What's brought all this on about yer da?'

He shrugged. 'Dunno. Nothin. Dunno.'

'Danny ...' she said, giving him a sharp look. 'I'm yer Mummy amp'ten I? How many years now have you seen yer da go here and there, and then outta the blue tonight I get the questions?'

Again he shrugged. 'I dunno,' he said. 'I just ... like, he just seems a bit ... have you noticed him bein' a bit ...'

She frowned. 'A bit what?'

A third shrug. 'Bit, I dunno. Bit grumpy,' he said, and then promptly filled his mouth with food in what seemed to be part embarrassment and part dread that he was going to get in trouble for saying what he'd just said.

Linda felt the fuzzy amusement she'd been feeling about her son's curiosity dissipate. Danny was serious, she could see that. She paused, going through the last few days, weeks, even months in her head, scanning them for any signs of odd behaviour from her husband of these past fourteen years.

To say Tony Morrigan wasn't a verbose soul was an understatement. She hadn't married him for his scintillating conversational skills. He'd been young and dashing, and there had been rumours around the place that he was a bit dangerous, which in this place usually meant you were mixing with a certain band of eejits, but in all the years she'd known him he'd never once demonstrated the slightest sign of interest in religion or politics.

The 'dangerous' side of him had never surfaced, but she'd been glad, because he was a devoted partner and a kind, good-hearted man, and he doted on wee Danny. His wee Miracle Baby, he called him. So if her son thought his da was being a bit off with him, something was wrong, one way or the other.

'What makes ya say that, son? I'm sure your da's fine ...'

Danny's head was still turned down towards his plate. When he spoke it was in the mumble of a child saying words he didn't want to say but, as is sometimes the way with children, when the tap was turned on it was turned on full blast.

'Just that when he comes back from a trip, like, he's usually dead pleased to be back and he would take me out for a wee dander round the place or if it's night, like, he'll sit and talk to me for ages about how school is and Steve and all that oul stuff but for the last few months he's been, like, quiet and even when he came back last week from that one away down south he never came to get me from school and I waited about for him and he was here paintin' the house and I know that's like important but when I says to him can I help ya a wee bit he just got a bit angry or somethin' and said no and then he came up to see me later on and said he was sorry and that yes I should learn to paint cos ya never know what skills ya might need to learn and it was a bit weird cos he hugged me and like I could sorta see that he mighta been cryin' and I was talkin' to ones in school about what made their da's act a bit strange and they said maybe it's his work is gettin' him, like, maybe he's gettin' paid off and he hasn't told ya or yer ma yet.'

He paused and took a breath but didn't look up, which was just as well because Linda's mouth had formed a large 'O' of astonishment and seeing that would have derailed him entirely. The effort of the last outburst had seemingly drained him, because his next few words barely formed a sentence at all.

'That's what happened Steve's da,' he concluded, and went back to his food.

'Ach, son,' Linda said, and did the worst thing she could have possibly done. She got up and gave him a big hug, which made him determined never to talk about his real feelings ever again if his reward was going to be getting a 'Mummy Hug Of Doom' and having to watch her pretend she didn't have tears in her eyes. 'Ach Jesus … you're imagining things. He's probably just had a bad headache or somethin'; he gets them sometimes, sure as God. And sure didn't he come and show you the paintin', and a brill job yous two did of it an all! Place looks grand!'

'Mmmf,' Danny agreed, with a faceful of cardigan. At that point he would have agreed to substituting the ketchup for strychnine had it meant release.

She let him go and sat back down, wiping her eyes. 'And sure he'll be back tomorrow night. He's away in Meath, I think he said, looking at some hills or somethin' or other. Do you want me to give him a wee shout and let you have a wee word with him? I have the number of the B&B he's at.'

'Have a wee word with him?' Danny echoed, aghast. 'And say what?'

'Tell him you're worried about him and that you love him and miss him.'

Danny's jaw dropped. 'Tell him *wha?*' he choked. 'He's my da fer Jesus' sake!'

'Danny!' she snapped.

'Sorry,' he mouthed, and gulped down half a slice of fried bread like a frog swallowing a bluebottle. 'Can I go now?' he pleaded. 'I'm finished, look. I'm all done. Can I go?'

'Aye go on. You sure you're–'

The kitchen door had already closed, leaving her alone with her thoughts. She pottered away with the dishes for a while, stopping when she heard him tramping about upstairs. It wasn't even 9 p.m., but he'd obviously decided to take himself off to bed, and she knew he could be trusted to get his teeth done. He was a good boy, was Danny. He'd make some wee girl very happy one of these days.

She went back to splashing around with the dishes but as she washed, dried and put them away she found that her gaze kept drifting to the phone resting on its cradle in the kitchen.

A few seconds later she was holding a scrap of paper in one hand and dialling the number of the B&B with the other . Danny might not want to talk to his da, but after all that emotion (all hers, but even so) she could do with hearing his calm voice. And it'd do no harm to suggest that he take his son – and in all likeliness that big lig Steve as well – along to a wee football match or somethin' at the weekend. Fellas loved their football, she knew that as sure as sure. Football'd see them right.

'Tony Morrigan's room please?' she said.

'I'm sorry madam,' the musical Irish voice came back. She'd always been a bit jealous of the Southern Irish lilt; her own Belfast twang sounded like someone gargling with razor wire by comparison. 'We don't have anyone by that name here.'

'Are you sure?'

'Quite sure, madam.'

She hung up, frowning. That was strange. Tony always used that B&B when he was down that neck of the woods, which, come to think of it, seemed to be often enough. There must be precious few bumps there that he hadn't triangulated within an inch of their lives.

She shrugged. Maybe she'd get him one of them mobiles when the prices came down another fair whack. He'd phone tomorrow and she'd tell him about it then and ask him what had changed his plans.

Going to bed, some time and some soap operas later, she saw

Danny's closed bedroom door. The 'Mummy' instincts inside her screamed at her to go and check he was sound asleep, maybe adjust his covers just a wee bit, even if they were perfectly set upon him; after all, it was just about giving them a wee touch, just to let yourself know you'd contributed in some physical way to their peaceful slumber.

But he was ten years old, and if he wasn't asleep, his oul mummy coming in was sure to send him into an indignant tizzy and he'd only end up asking for locks for the door, and then they'd be through the looking-glass and either Steve would never get staying again or she'd have to wage a non-stop one-woman reign of guerrilla warfare until Channel 4 was shut down for good.

So she restrained herself, feeling proud, and went in to sleep, trying not to think about the unoccupied half of her own bed.

In his room, Danny heard the creak of his mother's body settling into her mattress and opened his eyes. In the almost-darkness of his bedroom, he could make out the outline of Ireland on the map affixed with sturdy Blu-tack to his bedroom wall. All he could discern was the thick black outline of the coast; the interior seemed dark and featureless. It was his da's job to change all that, apparently.

He went to sleep thinking there were worse things to do.

*

Danny looked down at the things on his plate. The chips were black, the egg burnt beyond repair, the beans covered in third-degree burns. It looked like a nice wee peaceful fry had been the victim of nuclear terrorism.

'M-Mummy?' he said.

'WHAT?' Linda snapped, her back to him.

He lifted his fork, speared a few of the beans. 'Nothin,' he said, and shoved them into his mouth. They tasted as good as they looked.

It had been six days. He knew two things.

She was crying again, that was the first. He could see her shoulders shaking, and he wanted to tell her it was okay, but he was a million miles from possessing that kind of ability. So he sat there wallowing in the embarrassment of being present during another human being's collapse and he ate the dinner that she had prepared for him out of some robotic need to do something approximating normal life.

It was his fault. That was the second.

He wasn't gonna tell his ma that, of course. Ever. Cos he'd tried to in this very kitchen six days ago, and look where that had got him – nowhere except hugs and whispers that he was being silly and that hadn't stopped her being wrong, had it? He'd seen it a mile off; his da had just wound down – stopped doing things with him because he wanted to and started doing them because he had to, because he didn't want to feel guilty or feel like a bad da for not doing them. Even then Danny could tell when his da thought he'd spent enough time 'Being A Good Father' and when that happened, he'd call a halt to proceedings, retreating back into that quiet shell.

His ma hadn't seen it because … well. He was only ten, and he loved his ma dearly and couldn't imagine any reason why he wouldn't always do so – it was somewhat hard to hold a grudge against anyone who'd armour up *Rambo*-style and waste a hundred people without any qualms if she thought any of them had so much as looked at him crooked – but he already knew he wasn't about to hold any all-night debates with her about complex world issues (beyond what that tart in *Coronation Street* was doing floozying off with yer man when she knew rightly he was a proper cunt).

Her snapped response hung in the air between them, but just as he'd known would happen, she was now murdering herself with guilt. She tottered toward him, her face empty with grief, demanding he come to her and give her a big hug and let it all out and he did so, he went to her and he hugged her but tears didn't come. Fuck tears. Tears did no fuckin' good, didn't stop anything bad from ever happening.

He ripped the map from his bedroom wall that night, ripped it down and tore the bastard into wee tiny bits and filled the bin with it and then put somethin' on top of it so his ma wouldn't see and know what he'd done. When he was done doing that he got into bed and shamed himself by crying anyway, unable to look at the empty patch of wall where the map had hung for as many years as he could remember.

*

The next day, he'd found the letter, lying on the doormat. His ma was upstairs asleep – the first time she had really slept in days – and the envelope was addressed to her

It was from his father.

He held it in shaking hands. This was it. This was the note that would explain where his daddy had gone. He'd been called off on some mission to somewhere far off, somewhere without a phone and this was the fastest way for him to get a message to them. He should call his ma now, wake her up. She'd want to be the one to read it, he knew.

He got halfway up the stairs before he stopped, and turned, and sat down, and ripped that envelope apart as carefully as he dared.

Reading it blew his world apart.

GRIFFIN STREET, BELFAST, 2 DAYS AGO

Tony Morrigan's world was falling apart.

Last night, watching Danny try and cope with Ellie and Luke's disappearance, he had come close to telling his son everything. The only thing that had stopped him was the thought that there might, just *might*, be a mundane explanation for all of this, that there was a hope Ellie really had just thrown up the head and taken the baby away somewhere for a few days to calm down after some fight. He glanced at his wife, currently busying herself doing absolutely nothing in the kitchen cupboards. Anything to take her mind off her son's woes. If he left her much longer he was going to find her alphabetising the spaghetti loops.

The awful truth was that Tony longed to tell his son everything, but he knew it wouldn't solve a damn thing. In what world would Danny hear what his da had to tell him and nod and say *that explains a lot, Da* and both of them would set off to kick some faerie arse together? Danny would either punch him in the face or never speak to him again. What little remained of their relationship would be gone. He couldn't face that.

He knew Linda had hardly slept a wink all night. He had fallen asleep only once, and had been glad to wake up, because his dreams had not been kind.

Tony and Linda moved carefully about the kitchen, avoiding each other. Things weren't a fairy tale between the two of them, God knew; fucking off for a decade on your wife and son tended to put a bit of a crimp in a marriage.

Sometimes he wished she hadn't decided to take him back, because there were times – they'd be watching TV, or out on a drive, or doing any one of a million ordinary, everyday things – when he would look at her, the woman he loved, and he would practically see a veil come down behind her eyes as the memory of his betrayal reared its head. It broke his heart to see it, especially since she always found a way to force the memory away again.

If she hadn't taken him back, though it would have been worse.

'Cup of tea, love?' he said.

'Aye, yeah, thanks,' she replied, not looking at him as she spoke. She had barely looked at him at all since Ellie and Luke had disappeared. She was watching her son go through abandonment all over again. He would be a fool to think it wasn't bringing back memories. 'I'm gonna get on me and then head over to Danny's, see if he needs me to mind the house while he heads away out.'

'Yeah,' he nodded, his throat dry. 'He'll appreciate that.'

'You coming?'

'Of course I am,' he said, a little more sharply than he'd meant to. Linda hadn't meant it as an accusation.

'Maybe the police will have some news. They seem to be taking it seriously anyway,' she said.

'They have to. Bad enough Ellie is missing, but the wee man too? It's not something they can ignore.'

Linda set her cup down, and for the first time since she'd stepped into the kitchen, she looked directly at him, a puzzled expression on her face. 'Wee man?' she asked.

Tony felt a wave of nausea wash over him as the truth hit, all the worse for how sudden and how undeniable it was. All of the faint hopes he'd been clinging to that there was some safe, boring, sensible explanation for all this, were all fucked, in the space of two words from his wife's mouth and a puzzled frown written all over her face.

'I just meant … that it's just as well,' he said, feeling as though he were speaking in slow motion, 'that Danny and Ellie don't have any children.'

Linda's eyes filled with tears. 'Do you think that's part of this?' she said. 'It's been almost a year since the miscarriage. Do you think they've argued and it's upset her?'

Right, you cunts, Tony Morrigan thought grimly. *That fuckin' did it.*

'I don't know,' he replied, this time his curtness deliberate. 'Listen love, I'm gonna be no fuckin' use sitting moping at Danny's, am I, and let's face facts, he doesn't want me there anyway. I'm gonna head into town. I can drop you off at Danny's on the way if you want.'

She gaped at him. 'You're going to *what?*' she said eventually.

He repeated himself. This only seemed to irritate and upset her more and before he knew it, she was dressed and wearing her going-out coat. She marched past him, almost through the front door when he turned her around and kissed her, unapologetically. He hadn't kissed her like that in over a decade.

'I love you,' he said.

'You think that makes up for it?' was all she said.

The door slammed shut a few seconds later, and he was alone. Tony Morrigan's shoulders straightened. His jaw set. For half an hour or so, he was a whirlwind of activity, gathering things his wife knew nothing about from around the house, gathering supplies. And, as he worked, his anger, his sense of outrage and injustice, only grew. There had been an agreement in place. He had honoured his side of it, and they had done this regardless. Well, fuck 'em. Their actions had just set him free. He would get to the bottom of this, then he would go to his son and tell him everything. He'd fuckin' well *make* him believe.

There was a crash from outside. Startled, Tony glanced out of the window and saw one of his roof-tiles had fallen, smashing itself into pieces on the porch below. The sun was shining behind his house, casting a silhouette of the rooftops on the street outside.

Part of the shadow extended itself, grew … and scuttled, scrabbling for purchase on the sloping tiles. A similar movement must have caused the tile he had just heard smashing to fall. As he stood, unmoving, not breathing, he heard a much softer thud from the direction of the back yard and without even having to check, he knew it was the sound of something large, heavy and four-legged vaulting from the back alley.

There was a wolf at his door, and a spider on his roof.

No one was there to witness Tony Morrigan's savage smile.

COUNTY ANTRIM, 247 BC

All things considered, Danny decided – as he clawed his way back to consciousness with a headache that felt as though Thor's hammer was slugging him repeatedly between the temples – when it came to methods of travel through supernatural planes, he preferred being dragged through the bowels of the Earth to psychic transportation.

'Welcome back,' a voice said softly. It sounded like the crow. He tried to get up, or at least to open his eyes and focus, so that he might get on with the task of wringing the little bastard's neck, but it was obviously too early to try to do something so complicated. He groaned like a poltergeist faking orgasm and slowly lay back on the cool surface.

Something was touching him now. Not feathers. Fingers, locking around his wrist.

He felt himself pulled upright and, panicked by the sudden movement, he swung wildly with his fist. On meeting nothing but empty air, he teetered and the fingers removed themselves from his arm …

Amazing how grass could feel like concrete if you hit the fuckin' stuff wrong.

'Let's try that again,' the crow's voice said, sounding amused. Cool fingers wrapped around his wrist once more and he was pulled effortlessly to a standing position. 'Quickly. There's something I want you to see.'

The pain in his head had subsided a little so he risked opening his eyes to try and get his bearings.

He was standing on a grassy hill, close to the coast. Salt stung the air around him and he could see where the lush greenery had stopped, and the landscape turned to golden dunes which rolled down to the long flat beach.

There was not a red moon or strange wolf-thing in sight. Instead a yellow sun hung overhead – it was low-set, not long past dawn. All of this he noted, in some back section of his mind, because most of his processing power was being taken up by something else.

He was standing beside a goddess.

'Something wrong?' the woman before him asked, in the voice of the crow. His tormentor, his supposed guide, the scrawny little bird whose neck he'd tried to wring.

'You've grown,' he understated magnificently. He put her at six foot five if she was an inch, easily taller than he was, and broad-shouldered with it. Her dark, almost-black hair spilled in every direction, finishing just shy of her hips. She was barefoot, clothed in a white skirt that whipped around her calves and a light green tunic of some sort that was fastened with four big gold buttons down the front.

Danny had a mate from university, Flan, who was into his comics and had a talent for sketching; she looked like the figures Flan would idly doodle in the margins of his notes, Amazonian, impossibly lithe. Of course, she wasn't currently orally pleasuring

Homer Simpson or Rupert the Bear, so she wasn't *totally* like Flan's sketches.

Danny thought, not for the first time, that he had some odd friends.

'How's the saying go? Take a picture, it'll last longer?' the Morrigan said, noticing his ruminations.

'Have you got bullet-proof bangles?' he asked, unable to help himself.

She fixed him with a glare. '*Up* your bullet-proof bangle.'

'Lasso of truth?'

'You'd better hope not, buster. Especially with that hidden folder on your desktop you think Ellie doesn't know about. One more Wonder Woman crack and I'll make myself a lasso out of your lower intestine.'

He grinned. 'Ach c'mon. It's not every day I find myself standing in the Otherworld talking to Xena's big sister.'

'This isn't the Otherworld,' she corrected him.

'It isn't?' he said, surprised.

'No. This is Ireland. The North Antrim Coast, to be exact. That's Rathlin Island over there.'

She pointed. He looked. Something clicked. He started looking around, running short little distances to check out different views from different directions. When he ran back to her, he was excited. 'We're near Ballycastle! Aren't we?'

'It's about a mile in that direction,' she nodded, pointing east. 'Well … it will be.'

'Will be?'

'In about fifteen hundred years time, yes.'

He sagged a little. 'My cousin had a caravan here,' he said sulkily. '*Will have*. Whatever.'

'Everyone's cousin has a caravan in Ballycastle,' the Morrigan replied dismissively. 'It's the law.'

Danny looked out at the beach, at the waters roaring up the shore. 'We used to go and stay in it sometimes durin' the summer. Me and my ma and da. It pissed with rain every fuckin' day, like, and I spent most of my time walkin' round the town and goin' into the same five shops over and over again thinkin' somehow they'd have got somethin' different in by the time it had taken me to do the lap of them all, while my ma and da argued like cat and dog cos they were fuckin' sick of the sight of each other. My ma wanted to come back after he left, but I couldn't,' he sighed. 'I just couldn't. I knew it wouldn't be the same.'

'Yes,' she replied dryly, 'it'd be hard to recapture bliss like that.'

He shot her a poisonous look. 'You're a cheeky fucker for a goddess, you know that?' he said. 'What are you the patron saint of? Arseholes?'

'Why would a goddess be a patron saint of anything? Saints are Christianity. Last I looked, Danny, goddesses and Christianity didn't exactly see eye to eye.'

Danny waved a hand. 'You know what I mean. It's all ballix anyway.'

'What is?'

'Religion. I don't believe in it.'

She was incredulous at this. 'You're two millennia in the past, standing in a vision granted to you by a Celtic goddess, and you don't believe in religion? This isn't a dream, Danny. Ellie and Luke–'

'Listen,' Danny cut her off with steel in his voice, 'I didn't say that none of this is real. I didn't say you don't exist, or that faeries don't exist, or who-the-fuck-knows-what-else doesn't exist. But I don't have to *believe* in you. Any of you.'

There was silence save for the wind and the sea.

'What are we here for?' Danny said eventually.

She stood behind him. He could feel her breath on his neck.

'Relax,' she said softly. 'Look.'

She moved him, gently, pivoted him as if he were on a turntable. Time seemed to zip forward slightly; the sun moved across the sky, and for what felt like only a second, night fell. Then back came the sun and things were much as before; sun, sea, sand …

… and ships.

They were tall, magnificent. Too much so for this era of human history. Smaller boats, simpler rowboats by the look of them, were disembarking. Some had already landed. Some were coming in. He could see more on the horizon, cutting through the waves with little apparent difficulty. People spilled out of them as they reached the sands; already almost two hundred were gathered, congregating in small groups here and there. He could see a fire sputter into life.

'Vikings?' he vocalised his first thought.

'You can do better than that, Danny,' she admonished him.

He could. These weren't Vikings. If he was standing here a millennia and a half before the town of Ballycastle would be built, and if Ballycastle itself was pretty fuckin' old – he thought that it had been founded in medieval times – that made their current time period … what? Year Dot? Vikings hadn't existed that far back. This was the Roman era. But the ships he was seeing now didn't look like any Roman ships Danny had ever seen in history class.

'They're my people,' she said. 'The Tuatha Dé Danann. This is our landing on Irish soil. As far as such things can be reckoned, the year is 247 BC.'

He squinted to get a better look. Admittedly he was a few hundred feet away and thus he couldn't make out things in any great detail, but as far as he could see, the people he was looking at now were just that – people. They milled and they chatted and they slapped each other on the back. Those who had started the fire were walking over to a more deluxe version of the rowboats that had just successfully beached and helping its crew unload a big cooking pot onto the sand. A huge cheer went up as they manoeuvred it into place above the flaming logs of the fire.

'Yis don't look like elves,' he said doubtfully.

She leaned forward, and placed her chin squarely on his right shoulder while she watched the scene unfold on the beach.

'I wanted to show you this,' she said softly – was that sadness in her voice? – 'to show you that myths are more than just stories.'

'Yeah,' he replied softly, thinking back over the last few days. 'I've sorta gathered that.'

When she talked, her chin moved against his shoulder; it tickled in a maddening way, but he made no attempt to move away from her. 'These were my people, Danny. My family and my friends and my whole world. We didn't see ourselves as gods. We didn't even see magic *as* magic, do you understand? It simply *was*. That was how the world worked. No one thought of it as strange, any more than you think of making a telephone call as strange.'

'Magic …' he said, and despite all that he had witnessed so far, even though he was clearly standing here in pre-Christian Ireland (with all the impossibilities that entailed), the word still evoked memories of crappy TV magicians. Of card tricks and shitty illusions. Paul Daniels. David Copperfield …

Now she did remove her head, and a part of him missed that weight. She looked at him, searchingly. 'Oh, let me guess. You don't believe in magic either?'

'We back to what I believe again?'

'Do you know how electricity works?' she asked him.

'What?' he asked, startled. 'Well … aye, I mean … it's, mmm … it's like a … like a thing that happens when, mmm … two charges build up, like a positive and a negative and,' he searched his memory, trying to recall anything from GCSE science, 'you can do it with lemons and wires.'

'So if I left you here in 247 BC, and visited you ten years from now, you'd have made strides in producing electricity in that time?'

'No,' he admitted. But, feeling very defensive about this line of questioning for some reason, he added, 'this place is too far back, like. There's nothin' to work with, probably. Tools I mean.'

'Oh,' she nodded, 'I understand now. So when, then? 1700s? If I dropped you there, you could change history and become the inventor of the electric light bulb?'

'Maybe …'

'Could you?'

He rolled his eyes and admitted defeat. 'No.'

Having worked him into a corner where he had to supply the

answer she'd wanted the whole time, she nodded, satisfied.

Having this sort of conversation made him suddenly, achingly nostalgic for Ellie.

'But you have electricity all over the place, don't you?' she said. 'You want a light or want a bit of toast or to switch on your PC, what do you do?'

'All right,' he said, 'I see what you're–'

'You flick a switch,' she completed, triumphantly. 'You flick a switch and *boom*, on it comes. You haven't a notion what's going on behind those wires. All you care is that it works. You desire light, you flick a switch, and there is light. You want food heated, you put it inside an empty metal box, press buttons, wait for the beep and the food comes out, piping hot. Now, take my hand–'

He did so and, as soon as his fingers touched hers, he found himself standing amongst the beach people. For a moment he thought he was about to be hit with another head-shattering side-effect of the transportation, but since they'd only moved a few hundred feet all he experienced was a slight dizziness that passed in an instant.

'They can't see or hear us,' she said, answering his unspoken question. He was mostly relieved at this; only *mostly* because he was disappointed that for the first time in his life he was by far the most fashionable person in a large crowd and he was going to be the only person who knew it.

The large cauldron that had caused such a ripple of cheering to pass amongst the settlers was only a few feet away. Ghosts they may have been, or ghosts of a sort anyway, but Danny could feel the heat radiating from it. It was huge, black and well worn, and a man and a woman holding large sharp wooden stakes were stirring its contents intently.

'What's—'

'Watch,' she whispered, cutting him off.

He watched as the crowd gathered at the cauldron, either individually or in pairs or groups. All held empty containers of some sort – some big, some small - which they proceeded to fill from the cauldron. At first he presumed that it contained soup or a stew and it was only when a young woman walked up and received a bowlful of green grapes that he first twigged there was something pretty special about this cauldron. It delivered something different to every person who approached, and in every instance it seemed to be giving the person exactly what they wanted.

The Morrigan was looking at the girl who'd received the rather meagre portion of grapes with a sour expression on her face.

'Ériu,' she said, looking faintly nauseous. Catching Danny's expression, she rolled her eyes and said, in a high, musical and altogether more *girly* voice, 'Oh I don't know how you eat all that red meat! I know you're sort of one of the menfolk, Morrigan, but aren't you even a little worried about your figure?'

She made a face and to Danny's amazement, she spat in the sand at his feet. 'And they end up naming the country after her?' she said in disgust. 'Pah!'

A commotion began just then, silencing any response Danny could have made. Shouts rang out and a group split from the general feasting to jog to a newly-arrived boat. The Morrigan watched all of this in silence and Danny, realising that this was not a good time to ask questions, did the same.

He saw them lift a corpse from the boat. He had no idea how long the Tuatha's ships had been on the water, or where they had come from, but it had been long enough that the body had begun to decompose. A woman wailed in despair. The corpse was a man, and his body was covered as best they could manage. The smell of festering flesh on the boat must have been incredible, and Danny wondered why they hadn't heaved him overboard.

But there was no harshness here. Only calm action. The man's body was heaved onto the shoulders of six men, who carried him aloft like pallbearers without a coffin. Danny moved aside to let them pass, but when he realised where they were taking him, he started forward.

'No!' he said. 'Jesus Christ, they can't put him in there! That's cannibalism!'

The Morrigan clamped her cool hands around his arm and stopped him. 'Watch,' she whispered.

Numb with horror, he made no move as they placed the body in the cauldron. Was this how they paid for its bottomless resources? With the blood of their own? Or worse, were the food offerings actually *recycled* in some sick way from the dead? Was this *Soylent Green*, 247 BC?

The dead man's family had arrived; everyone here spoke a tongue that Danny couldn't begin to decipher, but he didn't need command of words to see grief when he saw it … although for people who'd just seen their dead husband/father dumped into a foodstore, they looked rather matter-of-fact about it.

And then the dead man got up, and roared. And the crowd roared right along with him, including the Morrigan still holding

Danny's arm, a primal holler of joy and defiance of death that made the hairs on his neck stand up.

'The Dagda's Cauldron,' the Morrigan said. 'One of the four Treasures of the Tuatha, brought from Murias, the island of commoners.'

'Where you came from?' Danny asked, just to hear himself say something. He was still reeling.

'Murias is where I was born. This ...' and the Morrigan looked around at the windswept and desolate beach that, despite everything, really was quite beautiful, 'this island – this Ireland – was to become my true home.'

She wasn't looking at Danny, but past him, at the circle of relatives who now took turns embracing the resurrected man. At a little girl no more than seven years old, who took a running jump right into his arms and held him so tightly that the man, laughing as he was spun around by the force of her jump, eventually had to extract her from him limb by limb.

'Okay. I get the electricity thing. I do. Really. But for fuck's sake. You didn't think the dead coming back to life was anything special?' Danny protested.

She shook her head and spoke softly. 'Oh no. I thought it was special.'

'Who is he?' Danny asked, already guessing the identity of the child.

'My thirdfather,' she said, watching the little girl, her expression unreadable. 'Great-grandfather you would call him. Nuada.'

Danny flashed immediately. 'He owns the sword. The silver one that remakes memories.'

'The second of the four treasures,' the Morrigan confirmed. 'Yes.'

'Why are you showing me this?' Danny asked. Being around this much happiness, this much joy, and being as substantial as a phantom amidst it all was beginning to grate on his nerves. 'I just want … *need* to get my little boy back.'

The Morrigan straightened at that, tall and proud and terrible to behold, and for a moment he could see why her aspect had taken the shape of the crow – like her avian counterpart, she was capable of making it seem as if death itself were wrapped around her. 'You wanted to know,' she reminded him, her tone harsh. 'Consider this the first lesson. This – all of this – was how it began. One thousand of us arriving in a new land with hopes of a new life. It reads so easily as the beginning of a myth. I wanted you to see us for yourself. We were *real*. As real as you, and those you care about.'

The little girl and the resurrected man moved away from the main group then, walking down the beach together. After a few steps on the sand the man scooped the little girl up, her almost-black hair whipping in the sea breeze, until she sat squarely on his shoulders, giggling as he ran full tilt to greet the boats yet to beach.

The girl with the grapes watched them go, her face blank.

'Time for the next lesson,' the Morrigan said, and reached out to cup his cheek. Unprepared, he tried to jerk away, but too late; with her touch, the beach and everything around them fell away into nothingness.

*

They won't risk exposure. Not in broad daylight.

This was what Tony Morrigan told himself as he walked out of his front door, whistling a merry tune, with a large rucksack slung over his shoulder. He was taking his life in his hands with every step, and he knew it. His entire gambit depended on the fact that the wolf must have slunk across every shadow to get as far as his back yard. They couldn't bear the sunlight for long, which made walking out a much safer option than staying put.

As for the spider … well, it had no such qualms about the sun, but a wolf sighting could conceivably be put down to someone getting excited seeing a particularly big Irish wolfhound. It would be a bit harder for them to cover up someone spotting a spider the size of a Volkswagen.

He intended to walk to his car, get in and drive off. If he'd stayed inside even for another few moments, he had no doubt the wolf would have broken through the door or the window, and the spider would have squeezed through a gap in the roofspace. He wouldn't have stood a chance. By walking out, he hoped to catch them off-guard, leave them paralysed with indecision long enough for him to get away.

A shadow plummeted from overhead. With far too little noise, barely having to flex its eight legs to absorb the fifty-foot drop, a spider ripped straight from every arachnophobe's worst nightmare landed in his front garden, illuminated by blazing sunlight.

Old Mr Whitaker, in the midst of trimming his verges next door, had time for one strangled exclamation of surprise before it spun to face him. One of the forelegs went through his abdomen and the other through his right knee. A jerk of the carapace and the poor man was ripped in two.

One piece of him went into the spider's maw, the other was tossed to the wolf, who had loped around from the side alley having realised getting in through the back was now pointless. The wolf caught it acrobatically in mid-air and with a crunch Mr Whitaker was gone, as though he had never existed.

The whole thing took less than five seconds.

The only other witness to this horror, a small five-year-old boy out stomping the shit out of some ladybirds, shot like a cannonball back into his granny's house, where he would refuse to come outside again for the next nine months and would wet himself copiously upon sight of an insect for the rest of his natural life.

The car. It was his only hope.

Tony feinted left, pulled an axe from his rucksack where he had left its tip poking out and hurled it end-over-end. The spider avoided it by retracting its legs; the wolf, face caked in blood from its recent feast, had time to try and brush a piece of Mr Whitaker from its muzzle before the axe buried itself to the hilt in its right flank. It went down howling.

Tony didn't stop to look. Arms and legs pumping, he ran for the car, expecting at any moment to have a spider leg crashing down on him, a stinger lancing its way through his back and out his chest.

His hands scrabbled at the door – he'd unlocked the car remotely from inside the house – and he was soon in, slamming the door shut. Only then did he risk a glance around.

The monstrous arachnid had stopped to consume the wolf, to stop its death-howls before the entire street was alerted. They were bold, coming out in daylight, but they weren't yet *that* bold, and the distraction had given him a few precious seconds.

He just wasn't sure it was enough.

As it finished consuming the wolf, the spider turned – its attention now squarely back on Tony. He watched as it began to shrink and change shape, shifting into a woman, a human woman, beautiful and slender.

The car roared into life underneath him.

The woman leapt.

The car's roof buckled as a spider-leg with a human hand at its end and wicked, scimitar-sharp finger claws ripped through, searching for him, trying to slash or throttle him, even as the car jerked forward and he ripped through the gears, zig-zagging frantically from one side of the street to the other to try to throw her off. It worked, a little at least – the leg retracted, but still she clung on.

'We've met!' he had time to shout up at her.

'Yes,' she called back. Her voice was calm, and when a narrowing of the street forced his manoeuvres to wind down, she was able to partially morph herself once more, growing two large spider forelegs to attack at him again. One stabbed him painfully in the bicep, drawing blood. 'Yes, I remember you.'

He searched desperately in the rucksack in the passenger seat, looking for a small bag.

The weight on the roof increased, sagging it further. She was morphing fully into her spider form and if she managed it, he was as good as dead. At the end of the road, he saw a limousine parked incongruously across several lanes of traffic. The doors slid open. Tony wasn't surprised at who stepped out.

'You have nowhere to go,' she spoke again.

Twenty years ago, he would have had some snappy retort to that, but his arm was killing him and he was pissed off. Instead, having found the bag he was looking for, he tore it open with his teeth and threw it straight up through one of the holes in the roof. The bag burst open and scattered the iron filings it contained all over his unwanted passenger.

There was an unearthly scream, a renewed scrabbling, and as Tony threw the car into a one-eighty handbrake turn, the creature fell off his roof and onto the road, eventually coming to a half-human, half-spider heap at the feet of the man standing by the limousine.

Dother.

In his rear-view mirror, Tony had time for one look at his old enemy before he gunned the engine and roared off in the opposite direction. The look on Dother's face was more satisfying than a hundred one-liners could ever have been.

He forced himself to calm down, to breathe, to think. The car, as if on autopilot, was going in the direction of Danny and Ellie's house. His first instinct was to get to his son – he needed to warn him. At a red light, at what he judged to be a safe distance away from any would-be pursuers, he fished out his mobile and placed it into the hands-free cradle, dialling Danny's number.

'Your call cannot be placed as dialled.'

He had time to try again before the lights went green,

checking in his rear-view mirror as he did so. There was no sign of limousines, spiders or wolves. He was dimly aware his hands were shaking. He couldn't get the image of his luckless next door neighbour out of his head. Poor old Jim. Ripped in half before he knew what was happening.

'Your call cannot be placed as dialled. Your call is being diverted. Please hold.'

Tony glanced at the mobile. Was that normal?

'Hello, Tony.'

He had to fight to keep the steering wheel straight upon hearing that voice. 'Dother.'

'One of the perks of owning a monopoly on telecommunications – you should see how quickly I can download porn. Now, let's see if we can save some time here Tony, shall we? I imagine you're heading for Danny. Don't. I imagine you'll want to warn him. Don't. I don't suppose you would believe me if I told you he's in no *immediate* danger, but it's true, so you barging in and filling his head with rubbish really isn't going to help matters, and if you're seen within a hundred feet radius of his house, I'll …' there was a sigh, '… look, can we skip the threatening and the *blah blah blah* because it bores me. I'm sure you know I can make horrible things happen, so stay out of it. Go disappear somewhere for a few days. I hear the Ulster American Folk Park is lovely. All Lircom employees get 25 per cent off at weekends, you know. My idea.'

'We had a deal,' Tony began.

'I know what we had,' Dother replied coolly. 'Nothing lasts forever, Tony. Now, assuming you see sense and scurry away, I promise we'll leave you unmolested, but if you're foolish enough to get involved or to see any old friends, I'm afraid I can make no promises. Sorry about that. As a goodwill gesture, I've had Lircom credit your phone with five pounds top-up. Goodbye.'

Old friends. There was only one man that Dother could be referring to. The danger, though, was that a similar welcome wagon would probably be on its way to him now.

Tony just had to get there first.

COUNTY ANTRIM, 247–109 BC

Time spun past Danny as though he were tethered to causality only by a loose cord that the Morrigan would jerk, dragging him behind her, skipping him through the decades like a stone skimming across the waves.

The Tuatha worked quickly to spread out from their initial beachhead. They had brought the tools of their civilisation with them and they were not shy of a day's work. Woods fell to their axes and villages grew, at first around the North Antrim coast, and then as the years passed, further south.

Danny was able to see it all spread below him, as though he was flying in some ancient airship high above the Antrim plains. And when he wanted to look closer, he found that he could zoom in as much as he desired, until he could have seen the smallest insect on a single blade of grass.

'We had heard tales of them back home,' the Morrigan said, breaking his concentration. He could no longer see her; she was only words on the temporal winds, but when she spoke it seemed to anchor him in the stream and he clung to her voice, fearful of being swept away and lost.

'Them?' he asked, and then saw for himself.

They surrounded the land on which the Tuatha had settled. Thousands of them. Monsters. Some with the heads of goats; some with only one giant eye set in the centre of their foreheads, reminding him of the Greek story of the Cyclops. More yet were misshapen, with only a single arm, or a single leg growing from the middle of their torso and upon which they would balance, like some grotesque unicycle.

'Formorians,' the Morrigan spat.

They closed in a giant ring around the Tuatha's land, and as they did so, the ground shook and rose up toward him until he found himself once more standing on a solid surface. He was in the midst of a great plain, the sea nowhere in sight. A vast ribbon of Formorians lined the horizon to the south; to the north he could see the small buildings of the Tuatha's biggest village. In the middle, where he and the Morrigan stood, a small party from each side approached each other warily.

Danny recognised Nuada immediately, leading his contingent. He also recognised the woman standing to his right. She wasn't a little girl any more, as evidenced by her size, her posture, and the fact that she was carrying a spear so long and solid that he doubted he could have lifted an end of it, let alone made carrying the fuckin' thing look so effortless. It was like a sharpened caber.

'In human terms, I was nineteen years old,' the Morrigan told him, looking at her younger self. 'Full of arrogant swagger and convinced of my own immortality.'

Danny frowned. 'I thought you *were* immortal?'

'Yes,' she admitted, 'but I was *convinced* of it.'

'Is that bunch o' grapes girl beside ye?' Danny said, spying a girl treading lightly beside the young Morrigan. She was everything the Morrigan wasn't; fey, delicate, blonde. He'd seen her type in the city centre all the time checking themselves out in the mirrored windows of every shop they passed.

The Morrigan scowled. 'Ériu. Yes.'

They'd landed in the right spot, Danny realised. He didn't have to move a muscle to watch what unfolded – the Tuatha came to a halt six feet to his left, while the group from the south stopped an equal distance to his right. He found himself wishing he'd paid more attention in Irish classes, though what help it would have been in this situation was probably up for debate.

Jesus, these Formorians were a sight to behold. The guy in front was eight feet tall and one of the goat-headers; he looked like he'd stepped right out of a Marilyn Manson video. His arms and legs were massive; each one looked like one of those sides of beef you'd see hanging from a butcher's hook. He was flanked to his left and right by a Cyclops and a Unicycle. Despite their various handicaps, Danny saw in the way they moved and the way they handled themselves that they were serious bastards.

He needn't have worried about the language barrier. When they began to speak, he could understand them; the Morrigan's doing no doubt. 'Hail Elatha, descendent of Ham, son of Noah of the Flood,' Nuada called out, as the younger Morrigan stood proud beside him and Ériu floated around, flitting between the older man and the six or seven burly looking fellas they'd brought along as a precaution. 'I am Prince Nuada, leader of the Tuatha

Dé Danann. I bring you greetings and tribute for the sharing of your plentiful lands.'

Danny rolled his eyes. 'Did yous all talk like that in them days?' he asked.

The Morrigan looked back at him steadily. 'You have to remember these are primitive times, Danny. It'll be another two thousand years or more before we're as eloquent as you modern people,' and her voice changed to a high-pitched nasal whine that was such an excellent approximation of a young Belfast male voice he almost choked. *'Here big girl, givvus a suck of yer doot will ye, yeoo! What's the craic mucker? Sweet! That's dead on, big lad!'*

There was another contemplative silence. Danny was noticing that these seemed to happen a lot when he and the Morrigan conversed. Either they were the result of a period of shared enlightenment, as mortal man and immortal goddess discovered their own common philosophical ground, or they were because sometimes they *really* pissed one another off.

She was staring at him with a *well?* expression on her face. He wanted to come back with something smart, to defend his own time period, but instead he grinned and inclined his head to accept defeat. To his surprise she returned the gesture with a tiny smile of her own, then she nodded to the scene unfolding and was all business once more.

'I am not Elatha,' Goat Boy was rumbling.

He stepped aside and revealed a fourth member of the Formorian party who had previously been shielded by the formidable bulk of his companion.

Danny gaped. 'Where'd they get *him* from?'

The newcomer was normal in every way – if you expanded your definition of 'normal' to include annoyingly perfect specimens of man. Danny immediately felt himself fidget resentfully in the way men always do when someone with perfect pecs, a lantern jaw and a thousand-watt smile enters the vicinity.

'I am Elatha,' said the beefcake. 'Hail to you Prince Nuada, and to your beautiful daughter.'

Danny glanced sidelong at the Morrigan. 'Fuck. Oul Mitch Buchanan there has an eye for ye. I almost feel like stickin' an oul *Yeoooooo!* in there just for the craic.'

'He's not talking about me.'

She was right. As he looked back, it was Ériu who skipped forward, floating over the grass separating the two parties. Danny turned his attention to the younger Morrigan, who had her gaze fixed on Elatha, then on Ériu and he watched her hands grind and twist around the massive spear as if trying to rip it in two.

'Ah,' he said delicately.

'My lord of the noble Formorians!' Ériu was exclaiming. 'I am Ériu of the line of Nuada of the Tuatha. You grace us with your presence here.'

'It is I who am ennobled by your presence, Ériu,' Elatha returned graciously. 'Tell me, are all the womenfolk of your race so heavenly in countenance?'

Ériu considered this. She cast a glance back at the Morrigan.

'No,' Ériu replied. 'No, my fair Elatha, I fear not all are.'

Elatha laughed. It was a musical laugh, and when Ériu joined in she seemed to match that musical pitch perfectly so that their laughter became a symphony of mirth.

Danny leaned in to his travelling companion. 'Is that the Spear of Destiny you're holding?' he asked. It felt like an age now since he'd heard the new Lircom 'on-hold' narration, but upon seeing that massive spear, his mind had immediately flashed back to the story.

'Yes.'

'The third treasure?'

'Yes.'

'Any chance the fourth treasure is some form of bucket, that I might perchance need to borrow if I listen to much more of this?"

The Morrigan began to laugh. It wasn't as musical a laugh as that of Elatha and Ériu, but it had something theirs lacked; authenticity.

Dammit, Danny thought. Despite his best efforts to the contrary, he was starting to like the goddess.

Negotiations began between the two parties and there was much talk of tribute and land and trade. Danny yawned. It was all a bit *Phantom Menace* for him. He was more interested in the spear-carrying maiden. He compared her to the older version standing beside him and wondered what had happened – the older self possessed all of the confidence and bearing of the younger version, but the younger self seemed to have a spark that his Morrigan did not.

It was familiar. That was what was itching him. That spark versus that lack of spark. He had seen it before.

In Ellie.

Yes. God, he could see it so clearly now. The younger Morrigan, the one staring down the monsters she was forced to negotiate with, the one who kept the retinue of warriors in line with little more than a clipped word here and there … he knew her sort all right.

THE ATTIC BAR & NIGHTCLUB, BELFAST, 2 YEARS AGO

'I said, I know your type all right!' Ellie repeated, having to shout louder over the volume of the music.

Danny put a hand on his chest, aghast. 'How could you?' he said, as the Attic's Saturday night revellers gyrated, gently and not-so-gently bumping him this way and that. 'I've not known you five minutes, I'm offering to get you a drink, and here you are making assumptions about me and my character.'

Ellie put on an equally oh-so-sincere face of contrition at her unforgivable slur. 'Oh, oh my stars,' she said, 'I didn't mean to offend. But you should know, kind sir, that I've had bad experiences in the past with free drink. As a child I was savaged by a Diet Coke and vodka.'

Steve appeared at Danny's elbow, holding two pints and a smaller glass filled with black liquid. He handed a pint to Danny and offered the smaller glass to Ellie who, after the merest pause, accepted it graciously and nodded her head to Danny in gratitude.

Steve sulked at this. 'Aye he bought it but I've just had to queue for the fuckin' thing!' he said indignantly.

Ellie raised her glass in appreciation, as another girl appeared at her elbow. 'Sorry,' she said, 'thank you as well …' and she paused, obviously waiting for someone to supply names.

'J. Forrest Akerman the Third,' Danny said, indicating his wingman.

'Steve,' corrected Steve, catching Danny with a clip to the back of the head just as he was taking a draught of his pint and causing the head to foam in a graceful arc up and over the rim of the glass.

'Shame. The other one sounded so noble.' Ellie said, taking a reserved sip from her glass. They were on the outskirts of the dance floor and had to regularly swing outward and inward like two poles of a magnet to allow others access and exit to the heaving mass of biomatter.

'This here's Maggie,' Ellie introduced her friend.

'All right,' the boys chimed to her in unison. Danny jerked his knee into Steve's thigh fractionally and caught his friend's eye for a microsecond, all the communication that was required to say:

I like the one I was talkin' to. Do you like the other one?

Yep.

So I'll go for my one and see what I can do for you for the other one and you're okay with that?

Yep.

You won't fuck this up?

Try my best lad.

'Are yous at Queen's?' Maggie asked. She was directing the question at Steve, Danny observed. Excellent. The cosmos was falling into place *exactly* as it should.

'Yeah. I'm doin' IT and fuckwit here's doin' English,' Steve said, indicating Danny with a jerk of his head. Danny bowed with a flourish. 'Although he still comes to some of my IT lectures. Follows me round like a bad smell.'

'I go for the educational opportunities, but I stay for the sass and the ready wit,' Danny said.

There was an expectant pause.

'Yeah,' Steve said.

'See?' Danny grinned, delighted.

'My minor is in English Lit. I'm doing Law,' Maggie said.

'Oh? What part?' Danny replied, kicking himself even as he spoke. Steve was supposed to making the small talk with this one.

'I was thinking of specialising in divorce.'

Then I suggest you wear that outfit around married men.

It was right there in front of him. For a moment Danny wished he had the ability to open up Steve's head and pour words into it. He looked at his friend imploringly, but all he was getting in return was, essentially, a smiley face drawn on an otherwise clean whiteboard. The moment passed. Danny sighed.

'D'you know Doc Hammond?' he asked Maggie, starting to wonder if Steve would object to an extra-time switch-up in terms of their intended targets.

Her eyes lit up. 'He's a god!' she exclaimed. 'He helped me *so* much last term!'

Another mark in the positives box. Danny nodded. 'He's a legend. If he didn't look as though he was made out of excess elbow skin, I'd have a crush on him myself.'

Maggie smiled in polite incomprehension, but it was Ellie who burst out laughing at this. Almost without even noticing, Danny's attention swung back to her. She was pretty; no prettier than Maggie, maybe, but definitely lovely to look at. He was vaguely aware through his half-cut fugue that judging two girls based on their respective physical attractiveness wasn't likely to win him Feminist of the Year anytime soon, but frankly, this was a nightclub and he himself had been sucking in whatever small amount of gut he possessed for the last two-and-a-half hours.

'So what do you do?'

'Physics,' Ellie shot back, in a way that said *what of it?*

'Oh yeah? I'm curious,' Danny said, 'what happens when you get up to 88 miles per hour?'

'Then you're gonna see some serious shit.' Ellie said.

Dear God, she's perfect, Danny thought, his nerd senses going a mile a minute. Ellie, meanwhile, had barely paused. She raised an eyebrow as she continued. 'Is that your speciality, then? You build up speed, your flux capacitor fluxes, and you're gone in a flash of light and a trail of fire ...'

'That, and taking my ma to the Prom,' Danny shrugged.

'Oh, I didn't realise you were from Ballymena.'

While this was going on, Steve reclaimed Maggie's attention. 'Don't worry,' he said reassuringly, 'he talks balls all the time. You get used to it.'

'She's the same,' Maggie said.

Embarrassed, Ellie and Danny ceased the reference-off. 'IT huh? So you're the brains of this operation then?' Ellie asked Steve.

'He's everything above the waist, yeah,' Danny interjected. 'Which reminds me, lad,' he said, ostensibly addressing his friend but still talking loudly enough for the two girls to hear, 'I picked up that prescription you were after, but the label was a bit smudged ... I have to ask ye, what the fuck are public lice? Are they the exhibitionist versions or somethin'?'

'What the fuck are you on about?' Steve demanded.

'I think you mean *pubic*,' Ellie suggested.

Danny feigned a penny-dropping expression. 'Ohhhhhh …' he said. 'Well, that'd explain why I saw his Y-fronts makin' a break for freedom out the windowsill the other day, right enough.'

Maggie looked shocked. 'You wear *Y-fronts*?' she asked Steve.

'No!' Steve shouted, now two-nil down and struggling to catch up. 'Just don't listen to this fucker, whatever he says! He has to put that wanky English degree to some fuckin' use!'

Danny laughed. 'Oi,' he said, 'that's below the belt that is.'

'Sure I thought below the belt was your home turf?' Ellie said, only her eyes visible behind the glass she was holding to her face. It should have been ridiculous, using a glass of vodka and coke the way a geisha would have used a fan, but somehow with her it worked.

'Oh, so that one stuck with ye did it?'

'Did all right. Like chewing-gum on my heels, dahling.'

'Oh stop, stop with your sweet nothings,' he protested. 'It's far too early for such poetry. You're comin' on too strong. Don't crowd me.'

'Oh?' she said, and slipped her arm around Maggie's shoulders. 'You heard the man, Margaret. Let us take our fine selves away somewhere else and give the lads their space, eh?'

'All right all right, houl on,' Danny said, holding up his hands in defeat even as Steve's eyes bugged in alarm at the prospect of a buck turning tail and dandering off. 'How about we have a wee dance, see how it goes?' and, as Ellie considered this, he jerked a thumb at Steve. 'It'll save me dancin with that cunt.'

'Why? What's wrong with him?'

'Handsy.'

'Aye? I like handsy,' Ellie replied.

Danny set down his forgotten pint on a nearby surface and extended a hand, which she took. 'In that case, I think I'm in love,' he said with a grin.

They danced off into the crowd, and somewhere in the melee, after much gyrating (and him rotating through the four dance moves he actually knew), as they were pressed together in the crush of bodies, he leaned in and kissed her on the lips with his eyes closed and his mouth slightly open. Her tongue was like a shot of caffeine straight to the heart; with every brush of it upon his own he felt alive.

She tasted of purple.

In the chaos of the dance floor he caught flashes of Steve and Maggie, together, and deep in the depths of his soul, as he danced and kissed this girl with the spark in her eyes he knew one thing with a comforting certainty.

This was a good night.

Tomorrow could wait.

MAG TUIRED, IRELAND, 94 BC

'Uh ...'

Another plain, in what must have been a different part of Ireland – he could tell by the pillars that littered the terrain on which he and the Morrigan now stood.

'What ...'

The pillars were tall, at least fifty or sixty feet. They were arranged in a circular spread outward from a central point, as though someone had been marking out some vast dartboard and hadn't connected the dots yet. He and the Morrigan were standing right where the bullseye would have been. It was impressive on a grand scale; it made Stonehenge look like a garden shed.

'For fuck's …!'

It was high noon. The sun was directly overhead, and it beat down harshly, making him wonder if this really *was* Ireland, but there was that certainty again, the one he'd experienced before, during the first vision she'd taken him to see.

This *was* Ireland.

And the hundreds, no, the *thousands* of heavily-armed blood-crazed bastards rushing from all sides toward where he stood were intent on beating the living piss out of one another.

'Do somethin'!' he implored the Morrigan. She ignored him, standing there stock still, a statue, about to be hit from all sides by the onrushing armies. He felt like shaking her, begging her to get them out of here, but there was no time, there was no time for anything—

He ran.

He ran this way and that, dodging and skidding and ducking and jumping, as the two sides came together, hundred of bodies *thwacking* into one another with no finesse, no fine planning. Carnage ensued immediately. Axes swung. Danny watched a Tuatha warrior take on a Cyclops and with a swing of his sword lop off the Cyclops' left leg with no more apparent effort than someone brushing away a cobweb. For his part, the Cyclops

63

wasn't terribly bothered by this setback, switching instead to the movement style favoured by his brothers the Unicycles, swaying back and forth and whipping his *stupidly* enormous fuckin' axe around in a huge arc.

The Tuatha warrior blocked the first swing, losing his sword in the process,, but could do nothing about the second, which ripped into his torso and all but cut him in two. Danny watched as what seemed like ten miles of intestines spilled out of the fallen warrior and he slumped, blood pouring from his lips, nose and ears. He was still alive, and he was trying to call out for help.

Another swing of the axe, this one down on his head, split his skull and the Formorian had to tug at the axe three times to remove it from the Tuatha's sternum, so deeply was it embedded.

At the third tug, the monster grunted in guttural triumph – and then squealed. Danny watched as a point of steel appeared from the monster's stomach. The Formorian looked down and made a grab for the steel point, but by then it was far too late; the tip of the spear – for such it was – was jerked to the left and right, making a series of ripping and tearing noises as it went.

When it was retracted, the Formorian was a nerveless corpse slumping onto soil already stained red, red as the ground had looked back in the Otherworld under that crimson moon. Danny wondered if he was looking at the origins of that colour scheme unfolding before him.

The spear-carrier, who had just dispatched the Formorian, was now standing before him. It was the younger Morrigan, and for a moment she seemed to be aware of him, standing not ten feet away. She frowned, looking directly into his eyes but then she was gone, leaping across the battlefield in a series of nimble jumps, bringing death to her opponents every time she landed. The spear flashed this way and that. Formorian heads followed suit.

'The battle of Mag Tuired,' the older Morrigan said, now freed of her paralysis and standing beside him. He realised that no matter where he went, he would be left unmolested by the warriors. 'Where we took these lands from the Formorians, despite being outnumbered ten to one.'

Danny watched the Morrigan's younger incarnation hurl the Spear on a horizontal trajectory with such force that, within seconds, there was what appeared to be a Formorian shish kebab impaled on its length. The Spear eventually embedded itself in one of the mighty stone pillars with a thud that echoed around the battlefield. The pillar cracked long and deep with the force of the impact.

Unable to look away, unsure if it was horrified fascination or something deeper and darker that compelled him to watch, he saw the Spear vibrate, faster and faster, shaking the Formorian corpses on it until they fell apart.

The Spear jerked, backward, once ... then twice ... and finally removed itself from the pillar and with a lazy 360-degree turn (that so happened to sweep another twenty or so advancing Formorians from their feet), it returned to the outstretched hand of its mistress, just in time for her to swing it around and behind her and with one forward-backward twitch, poke the head clean off the shoulders of a would-be assailant creeping up behind her.

Ten to one? Jesus pole-vaulting Christ. It could have been a thousand to one and the poor fuckers wouldn't have stood a chance. It was like watching natives with grass skirts go up against Marines, except the chasm between the two sides wasn't in technology but magic.

As if the Morrigan's actions with the Spear weren't enough, her mentor Nuada was despatching hordes of his attackers with ease. In his hand was a sword that made the spear look about as threatening as a toothpick and on seeing it, Danny felt himself tense like a plucked arrow-string; this had to be the Sword with the power to rewrite reality. He knew it was key to everything that was going on; he could feel it.

Danny watched as the Sword grew to thirty feet long and scythed through an entire division. He saw it hover in the air and dart this way and that to intercept arrows, before doing the returning-to-the-hand trick he'd seen the Morrigan's Spear perform. On a few occasions Nuada would stand side-by-side with his star pupil and the two of them would perform deeds that defied description in their cheerful brutality.

The Formorians seemed to catch the scent of defeat on the air. He saw them stop their waves of attacks, turn and order a retreat back to the hills that ringed the east side of the great plain. But the Tuatha were too swift, their numbers too great, even after the battle. They ran the fleeing Formorians down, the Spear's wooden shaft and the Sword's silver blade doing terrible damage.

Awash in a sea of blood, Danny could stand it no longer. 'This is slaughter.'

'Yes,' the Morrigan nodded. 'Glorious, isn't it?'

'No it fuckin' isn't,' he snapped. 'You outmatched them and you must have known it before you came to fight them. You could have shown them they didn't stand a chance and then said, "Right, wise up, lads. Behave your fuckin' selves and we won't have to massacre ye."'

The Morrigan's brow furrowed and expression grew dark. She turned her full fury on him and it was all he could do not to back down in the face of it. *She's a crow. She's a fuckin' crow and she's trapped like that. Remember that.*

'I am the Goddess of War!' she thundered. 'War is what I do! *Look* at me!'

She wasn't talking about the version of herself currently tearing him a new one. Danny looked across the battlefield. Her younger self was walking triumphantly across the battlefield, red from head to toe in Formorian blood, a Formorian head wedged onto her Spear which she held aloft in victory in her right hand. In her left hand she held at least five more Formorian heads, swinging them in an almost jovial way that made it all the more obscene.

Tuatha warriors, big and burly men all, mobbed her and lifted her aloft, shouting and singing in celebration. Blessing her name and bending their knee to give tribute. Even Nuada, similarly feted, bowed his head for a moment when he approached. The entire battlefield, two thousand victorious Tuatha and many more thousands of dead and dying Formorians, rang to the sounds of praise for her prowess.

She was at the peak of her powers.

He remembered that feeling.

*

'You have everything, lad?'

He cast a look around the room that had housed his entire world for the best part of three years; *best part* being definitely the operative phrase. 12 Belgravia Avenue. Three words guaranteed to strike trepidation into the hearts – and possibly the knicker elastics – of girls across the city.

His room had not exactly been a lady trap. During its glory days, it had been a cesspit of beer cans and well-thumbed magazines from the middle-to-top-shelf range. He owned a few mismatched pieces of furniture: a cheap wardrobe from Ikea, a chest of drawers with two handles missing and a rickety desk upon which sat a second-hand PC – which, as Vic and Flan (his other IT-nerd housemates) had theorised, was only working because the multitude of viruses and spyware that he'd downloaded on late-night regret-it-in-the-morning browsing sessions were too busy fighting amongst themselves for supremacy to attack the actual system.

But the bed – ah the bed! – that was his one splash of luxury. For the last three years while his poor deluded housemates had slept, masturbated and had frantic and eye-wateringly noisy sex on mattresses that were about as smooth as Stephen Hendry's face, he had reclined in comfort and style on a posturepedic quadrilateral slice of heaven. More than one member of the opposite sex had commented that it was the most comfortable thing they'd ever sat on, leaving him open to reply *ah, the night is young …*

The bed was gone. His little fridge, his little Pearly Gates, was too. Everything was gone and the room was empty, with only echoes remaining. It had all been lugged downstairs and out into the Sprinter van he'd hired for the day.

'Yeah,' he told Steve, tasting the irony in the words. 'Yeah, I have everything.'

The lads had gathered by the front door to see him off. Not in that obvious deliberate way girls do, with hugs and tears, gifts and promises. That wasn't how fellas worked. It looked for all the world like he'd just happened to catch them while they just happened to be loitering near the door – bit of a coincidence that, but here, since we're all here anyway, may as well do the needful ...

With a terrible jolt, Danny realised that he didn't want to go. He'd sort of known it, of course, but he'd been chasing the same old platitudes round in his head; *Oh, imagine how it's going to feel to have a wee son/daughter, you won't be without them once they're there. You're getting your child-rearing done early – by the time you're forty, you'll be free and easy ...*

Except, it was all complete and utter bullshit. He wasn't sure if he and Ellie would last the week, let alone until she gave birth, to say nothing of the years they'd be expected to be a stable mother and father to a baby. He was risking every single aspect of his comfortable little responsibility-free rut of a twenty-something existence, and for what? The prospect of being suddenly thrust back into the search for fun when he was forty?

Yeah, because when his kid (or Christ, who knew, kids) was in its twenties, it wasn't going to need anything from him – like huge great fuckloads of university money, or to live at home. He didn't want to get his fun years back when he was gonna be too fucking old to enjoy them. They didn't make exceptions on

Club 18–30 holidays for middle-aged dickheads who got their girls up the soap in their twenties. They told them to fuck off. The whole world probably told them to fuck off.

That wasn't fraternal concern in Flan's eyes right now. It was pity, and no small amount of relief that it was happening to someone else, and the knowledge that close as they may have been these last couple of years, there was a very real danger this was going to be more or less the final goodbye.

He remembered one time, about a year ago when he and Flan had been travelling across the city in a black taxi. Unlike black cabs in other parts of the world, Belfast's versions are not private and instead act as little mini-buses, ferrying six hardy souls at a go – five in the back in a 3 vs 2 seating arrangement, while the sixth poor doomed bastard sits up front beside the driver.

On this particular trip, they were sandwiched together on the narrow 3-person rear seat. Flan was pressed so firmly to the window he could have been a tax disc and Danny was squashed between him and the 20-stone munter sitting to his left.

'*Told* you we shoulda got the fuckin' bus,' he hissed.

Moments later, though, with a giggle and an explosion of perfume and tanned flesh, two mini-skirted lovelies flagged down the taxi and took the two fold-down seats opposite. Noting the presence of two lads of around the same age, they immediately pretended not to notice them in the most ostentatious way possible, looking at each other, out the windows, and every three seconds tugging futilely at hemlines so high up on their legs that Danny wasn't sure if he'd get a glimpse of panties or pancreas when they uncrossed their legs.

If they were pretending not to notice Danny and Flan, Flan had no such compunctions in return. He was frantically elbowing Danny in the ribs until Danny was forced to wrench his neck to the right and give his friend a *Yes, I fuckin' see them* look.

Having secured his friend's attention, Flan whipped out his phone, and Danny knew within seconds what he had planned. They were fucked.

He watched as Flan shot through phone menus with Olympic sprinter speed, watched as the camera options screen flashed up and the 'shutter noise' option was turned securely OFF. Watched, as Flan lined up the perfect knicker-shot, all the while giving off waves of 'composing a text'-ness – a performance filled with fake button-presses and casual I'm-not-zooming-in-on-between-your-thighs facial expressions.

As one of the girls adjusted her legs to account for the cramped conditions of the taxi and as Flan moved in for the money-shot, (his finger had already pressed the button) Danny quickly realised that, in his quest for the unnoticed snap, his friend had forgotten one small detail about what happens when a camera takes a photo in a very dark area–

The light of the flash lit up the back of the taxi like the detonation of a small nuclear device rendering everyone in the taxi silent and frozen for a good two to three seconds.

Still, Flan had shaken off the limp eventually.

He smiled at the memory now – Chris 'Flan' Flanagan was an ungainly, lanky streak of piss, and quite clearly a sexual deviant, but Danny loved every sick bone in his body.

'Well, lad,' Flan was saying while Danny worked to suppress a lump in his throat. 'Best of luck, like.'

Vic chimed in his agreement with the banalities. 'King' Vic was tiny and ginger and thus, inevitably and quite rightly, actively despised this world and all who lived within it (there were rumours that he'd once nutted a bouncer one and a half times his height – presumably some sort of stepladder had been involved) but he was fiercely loyal to his friends.

'Am ... how long's she to go?' Vic ventured, seemingly stuck for something to say.

'Three weeks,' Danny said.

They all fell silent at that – three weeks was a crazily short amount of time by anyone's standards. It was also the bare minimum he'd been able to justify to himself before moving out of this house.

Standing on the front doorstep now, catching the eye of the hired driver sitting tapping his fingers on the dashboard of the big white van that now contained his entire life, Danny wanted nothing more than to walk back into the house, sit down on the communal sofa and make ratty comments about the music channel someone had chosen, or complain loudly about someone's tactics on Xbox Live, or just sit and down a few tins and debate the venue of choice for tonight's pints.

A step outside this door and all of that ended. A step back inside the door and he was a cunt. There was no middle ground, no third option, no grey area. He had morals. If he turned his back on this, if he pretended it didn't happen, he knew the lads might have their opinions on it but he also knew they'd deal with it and not mention it.

But just because they wouldn't talk about it wouldn't mean he wouldn't *know*.

He still hated maps. Still couldn't look at one. But Jesus Christ, he couldn't be responsible for a child's misery after what he'd gone through. He couldn't be someone else's biggest letdown. And a step back inside this house and into the carefree life of beer and randoms would leave that fate … mapped out.

The words rose within him, as they always did at the worst possible time.

And I'm glad I did.

'Well, lads,' he said. 'Cheerio. Keep in touch and all that balls.'

Of course we will, they choroused. Flan punched him on the shoulder. Vic shook his hand with a look on his face that said *thank fuck it's you and not me.*

'Lad…' Steve said, when the rest had drifted off. There was something in his best friend's eyes, Danny realised, something that, if it wasn't Steve before him, Danny would have taken for genuine emotion. 'Just wanted to say that I know it seems daunting and all that but … well, there's some out there who might envy ye.'

'You feelin' all right?' Danny replied.

'Ach fuck ye,' Steve replied, and gave him a brief and manly hug, before heading back down the hall.

Danny pulled the door closed behind him and walked to the van, figuring that he might as well get this over with and stop with the long goodbyes and the parting glances. After all, this baby wasn't fuckin' likely to vanish into thin air any time soon, was it?

More's the pity.

*

MAG TUIRED, IRELAND, 94 BC

He should have been dead. Everyone around him was. Thousands of his people, of their finest warriors, slaughtered where they had stood ... and, later, where they ran. He had been one of the runners. What choice did he have? These people – these Tuatha, curse them, curse everything about them – had magics beyond anything he and his kin could hope to match.

He ran and ran. Then with a flash of silver and and burst of incredible pain, he tasted dirt. One of their blades had sliced through his knees, removing both of his legs. The pain was unbearable, and he bit through his own tongue with the agonies of it.

Incapable of anything but moaning, bleeding to death, he had seen them pass above him, jutting their weapons into any of his fallen brothers who yet moved, wiping the injured from existence, completing their victory. He saw their own injured and fallen be thrown into a large cauldron produced from somewhere, and with vision that was growing fainter, he saw them rise again, restored and whole. Not a single Tuatha would die today. The Formorians had been slaughtered for nothing.

The realisation gave him strength from somewhere, and when he detected the movement near him, his fingers curled around his axe. With one last, desperate heave of defiance, he reared up on his leg-stumps, choking blood, and saw the Tuatha before him start in surprise and start to swing his weapon in reprisal, but too late – oh too late! – his axe met flesh and the hateful Tuatha roared in pain.

*

A spearhead emerged from the forehead of the Formorian a moment later, the shaft passing through in its entirety, such was the force of the throw. He was killed instantly, the last of the Formorian warriors at Mag Tuiread that day to know the release of oblivion.

The Morrigan burst onto the scene, eyes wide with grief. 'Nuada,' she choked. 'Nuada, no…!'

Nuada was cradling his right arm. Blood soaked through his clothes at an incredible rate. He stared with shock down at the grass below, where his right hand lay, still curled around the silver sword, struck off by a Formorian too stupid to know when he and his kind were doomed.

The Morrigan carefully lifted the arm and examined it closely. She bellowed for healers, knowing that the Cauldron could not be called upon to heal anything short of a mortal wound, or death. This was neither.

'You will live,' she told her thirdfather.

'Aye I will,' he replied, his voice empty. 'More's the pity.'

Standing nearby, unseen, Danny couldn't help but flinch on hearing these words. The memory he had just relived still burned hot within him but try as he might to stay away from its intensity, he couldn't help but go back to it again and again, a masochistic moth to the flame.

'Consider it granted,' he murmured to himself.

'Did you say something?'

'No,' he said, glancing at the Morrigan, surprised she was paying him any attention given the scene unfolding before them. Her younger self was distraught as Nuada stood on shaky legs and was led away. She tried to go to him, to help him, and was waved away angrily, leaving her to stand and look on.

'What's wrong with your mate?' Danny asked. 'He's still alive isn't he? Could've been worse.'

The Morrigan shook her head. 'No. It couldn't,' and she sighed. 'My people believed in purity. Spiritual, mental ... and physical. We couldn't have a one-handed king.'

'Tsk,' Danny clucked disapprovingly. 'Disability Action would have had a field day with that. So that's oul Nuada out on his ear is it?'

'Yes,' she said, and for a wonder, she had tears in her eyes. That brought him up short. 'This was the beginning of the end for us.'

She reached for his arm but he was ready for it this time; so when the world was sucked through itself and he was pushed through the pinhole opening that remained, he had braced himself. For as disconcerting and debilitating as these bounces through ancient prehistory had been, compared to the trip down Belgravia Avenue he'd just taken, they rather faded in comparison.

Sensing this, the Morrigan felt hope surge within her. Maybe this plan of theirs was going to work after all.

The Washerwoman

'Danny! Danny, hold on! *Danny!*'

Steve shouted and screamed but it was no good. Trying to resist the force pulling his friend into the ground was like jumping into the air and trying to stop yourself coming back down again. He could see Danny's surprise, even as he was pulled inexorably closer to the subterranean event horizon–

He spared a glance for the old woman standing at the far edge of the hole Danny had dug. She was watching Danny's descent with rapt attention. 'Help me!' Steve screamed at her, desperately, even as he lost Danny right up to the waist. 'Help me, you stupid oul fucker! *Help me!*'

She didn't so much as look at him; her gaze never shifted from Danny, though he fancied he could see her lips move. He gave up, dug his heels in and pulled harder, glancing down at his friend's face.

Danny looked calm. 'You have to let me go,' he said.

Steve's fingers slipped then, whether this was because his hands were slick with sweat or because Danny had let go, he couldn't tell. All he knew was that in the space of a heartbeat he went from straining every muscle in his body to stop his friend being sucked inside this impossible vortex in a terraced street, to landing with a wet, muddy *whump* on his hole and then his back, skidding along the length of the garden.

By the time he'd collected his thoughts, scrambled back to the ridge of the hole, he already knew what would await him.

The hole was empty. Danny was nowhere to be seen.

Right. That's fuckin' it. He found the spade his friend had been using and leapt down into the hole. It was less than six foot deep, and its bottom was smooth and unbroken – whatever had consumed Danny had, in the space of the last few seconds, closed over above his head. That was, Steve thought, impossible, but he couldn't deal with that at the moment. His friend was trapped down there, unable to breathe, dying–

With a sense of raw urgency and desperation, he attacked the earth with the spade. *Hold on Danny* he repeated to himself, blocking out the outside world as the soil began to arc in great clods over his shoulders. He worked and worked, dug and dug, until his muscles began to burn and pain began to spread across his lower back.

'Son.'

He wasn't so engrossed that he didn't hear her; the pain had slowed his work already. His arms were on fire now and his hands trembled, but he knew that to stop digging would be to admit that his best mate had disappeared, swallowed by a terraced house's garden, and he just wasn't prepared for that. For fuck's sake, he'd just had a massive fight with Danny – he couldn't be gone.

'Son,' she tried again, speaking gently. 'He's gone. You can stop.'

'You didn't help! You just fuckin' … you just stood there and you just fuckin' watched me! You didn't help and now he's … he's *gone* …!'

He couldn't go on. He was weak, he was unfit and he was a bastard. Defeated, he sagged and sucked in huge whooping breaths and tried not to collapse. The spade slipped from his numb fingers and fell into the pitiful little hole he'd dug.

'Of course he's gone,' she replied evenly. 'What do you think he was digging in this garden for, son? Why'd you think he told ya to let him go? This was what he wanted.'

'What he *wanted*?' he snapped, feeling a sudden, irrational burst of rage at the oul witch now peering down at him from the edge of the hole. 'He *wanted* to commit suicide?'

'He's not dead, son,' she replied. 'Well … not from being dragged underground and buried alive. Beyond that, like …' and she shrugged.

Another face appeared, one Steve didn't recognise at all.

'What was all that shoutin' about? What the fuck is goin' on?' Casey thundered as he looked down in utter disbelief. 'Jesus holy Christ! How deep does fuckin' landscape gardenin' research have to fuckin' be?'

'Landscape *what*?' Steve said, and then dismissed it. 'Mate, ring the fire brigade. There's been an accident!'

'Who the fuck is this? Where's the other one?' Casey demanded.

Steve gestured to the soil underfoot. 'That's what I'm tryin' to tell ye!' he said, gesticulating wildly. 'He was fuckin' sucked underground! There must be …' he floundered, '… subsidence.

Aye, a sinkhole!'

Casey seemed dubious, but *subsidence* and *sinkhole* were things that sounded disconcertingly expensive to fix. He jumped down into the hole Steve was occupying and picked up the spade, looking up at Bea. 'Get inside the house and get the fire brigade rung!' he told her, before (to Steve's eternal relief) putting his considerable bulk to use in the task of digging.

Bea shrugged. 'I'll get another cuppa going while I'm at it,' she said as she walked away.

'Thanks, mate...' Steve said, seeing Casey making short work of deepening the hole he'd already dug. 'There must be like an air pocket or someth–'

Thunk.

Casey brought up the spade. He frowned, and brought it down again. Same result. *Thunk.* Casting a quick look at Steve, he got on his knees and shoved the thin layer of soil away with his hand to reveal a hard surface.

'What is it?' Steve asked, feeling fear grip him. He recalled the stone tablet he'd seen in the hole just before Danny had been pulled downward. The same stone tablet that had vanished completely when Danny had disappeared.

Casey nailed him with a look. 'It's the fuckin' foundations is what it is. This is as deep as the garden goes.'

It was true. This was no tablet. Steve shook his head. 'No,' he said. 'No, mate, it can't be. My ... my friend was fuckin' ... he was just ... he was pulled. Sucked down. He disappeared.'

'Is that right? Through a concrete foundation?'

At this point Steve noticed three very important things. One was Casey's expression and the general size of the man. The second was that the spade he was holding was now no longer pointed groundward. The third, directly related to the first two, was that Steve was trapped in a hole with him.

'What is this?' Casey growled, advancing on Steve. Given the size of the hole, he wasn't able to advance much, but he was managing it brilliantly. 'Fuckin' Rag Week? Eh? Come along to some dopey fucker's garden and spin him some shite about doin' research, wreck his garden, tell him an accident's happened so he gets fuckin' filthy himself,' – and Steve had to admit, thanks to his sterling work digging Casey was absolutely encrusted – 'and then film the silly bastard as the penny drops? Have yis got a wee camera set up or somethin', aye? Where's yer mate? Is he the fuckin' cameraman? Well, let's give him some good footage, eh?'

Faced with the riddle of the disappearing best mate, the mysterious garden hole and the irate burly householder advancing with heavy spade, Steve decided that he had to take decisive action, and taking decisive action was his speciality.

'Please, mate. Jesus Christ I swear I didn't have anything to do with any of this – please don't fuckin' smack me with that big spade. I don't know what's going on any more than you do – I swear, I fuckin' swear – oh holy fuckin' Jesus *please* don't hit me …'

The murderous glint in Casey's eyes died, to be replaced with an expression of disgust. He turned his back on Steve and, with a muscular heave, lifted himself out of the hole.

'Get. The fuck. Outta my garden. Now.'

'Okay, Okay,' Steve nodded, making a half-hearted and

completely unsuccessful attempt to scale the hole. He looked up at Casey. 'Could ya give me a hand up?'

Casey's grip was a little tighter than it needed to be, but given the circumstances, Steve considered himself not too hard done by. He was pulled free of the hole, then shoved towards the gate.

'And tell yer mate if I see him I'm gonna fuckin' murder him!'

Seconds later, an old woman was unceremoniously ejected from the house, again at Casey's hand.

'… last fuckin' cuppa tea you're getting in here you oul fuckwit!'

Slam.

Bea looked down at the half-full cuppa still clutched in her hand. She shrugged, downed it, and posted the cup back through the letterbox. There was the smash of breaking china from the other side and, on hearing this, the old lady turned tail and waddled as fast as her eighty-plus-year-old legs would carry her, catching up with Steve just around the corner.

Not that she had much trouble catching up. Steve was walking the walk of the recently traumatised. She put a comforting hand on his arm and he jerked it away, not entirely to her surprise.

'What's going on?' he said very quietly. 'I just wanna know what's going on.'

'I know, son, I know,' Bea said soothingly, as they stopped outside a house further up the street. She opened the gate. 'Come on in,' she told him. 'If you wanna help your wee mate, son … maybe you can.'

He should have pulled away, should have insisted on going back to make sure the fire brigade arrived – he had a sneaking suspicion Casey was going to cancel the callout – or gone home to Ellie and Aaron.

He did neither, did nothing to stop Bea taking him inside her house and setting him down on her big comfortable leather settee, the kind that old people seemed to love – huge and ornate. It was so well polished that when you sat in it you had to grip the sides to stop yourself sliding off and landing on the carpet tailbone-first.

Of course, there in the corner of the room was the obligatory huge clock, *think-thunking* time away with a shuddering and teeth-jarring finality. He knew for a cold, hard fact that if they turned on the TV, it'd be set to ITV3 and be showing nothing but *Poirot*.

She perched herself on the armchair facing him, head tilted as she examined him with eyes remarkably keen for someone who was clearly about a hundred and twenty. She looked like a wee bird.

'Well I'll get right into it,' she said. 'What Danny told you about himself and you and Ellie and the wee baby is true.'

Danny's garbled nonsense about parallel universes came back to him. He had dismissed it out of hand. But that had been before he'd watched his friend disappear down the proverbial fuckin' rabbit hole. Suddenly it wasn't so easily to dismiss, but that didn't mean he was going to sit here and swallow everything this oul doll threw at him.

'How's that even possible?' he asked. 'Why don't I remember any of it?'

'Are ye *absolutely* sure you don't?' was all she said. 'All of this with the wee one – does it seem right to you? Changin' nappies and gettin' up durin' the night and stayin' indoors all the time? How're ya likin' it all, son?'

He squirmed. 'Part and parcel innit?' he said defensively. 'It's what ya sign up for.'

'But you didn't sign up for it,' she said softly. 'Danny's gone. He was the one they changed the world for, and he's not *in* the world any more. So you just watch it as it changes right back. Think, son. Think. Did ye sign up for it? What about Ellie? How were things with her?'

'Great,' he whoppered.

She smiled thinly. 'Is that right? No fights ner nothin …?'

He flushed hotly, unable to prevent himself from doing so. 'Well I didn't say no fights …' he mumbled, recalling earlier, before Danny and Maggie had arrived for dinner.

'What do you want me to do? I held him and I shushed him and he just kept cryin'. I knew you could quieten him down so I thought it was best to ask you to do it.'

'And that's it? That's the end of it? You just say "fuck it" and throw him to me and come in here and play that fuckin' thing? AGAIN? Oh wow, did ye finish the third level? Clap clap fuckin' clap – can't tell ye how helpful that is. Your son's so proud of his daddy for masterin' that A plus B attack combo. Dinner's on by the way, but if I'm gonna be with Aaron again you can fuckin' well help out with that – unless you think you can't stop the oven from cryin either?'

And he had roared at her and she had roared back at him and an almighty silence had followed before Aaron's crying, renewed at the sound of them two going at it, had broken the peace and sent her off again with one final poisonous look in his direction. So he had sat there, his gamepad in his hand, dry-eyed because, unknown to Ellie, the tears had already come that night, when he had left the baby with her and had stopped by the time she stormed in.

He was *not* a father. He could remember things, events in his recent history. He could remember getting the news he was going to become a da, he could remember the hospital … but they seemed wrong to him and more heartbreakingly, they seemed wrong to the baby he'd tried (and failed) to console so many times.

And with that, something seemed to fall into place – he realised the truth of Bea's claims and the feeling of relief that washed over him was intense because, as incredible as this all was, it meant that he wasn't just a shitty da.

Bea began to tell him the story – told him how things should really be and who should be with whom. And hearing it, to his astonishment – and although none of it brought a second set of memories rushing back to confirm her words – everything she said seemed so right that he found himself unable to dismiss the fantastical story she spun. Slowly, hesitatingly, he told her of his difficulties with little Aaron, and saw her nod in understanding.

'Wee babbies know,' she nodded. 'They're not so easy to fool as us,' and she snorted derisively, '*grown ups* … hah! Heads up our holes if you ask me, son. That wee man only quietened down when his mummy had him, eh?'

He thought about it. The answer to that question ought to have been yes, he knew. 'Um …' he said. 'Well …' and he remembered all the times over the last few days when little Aaron had just screamed and screamed, '… actually, not so much. Ellie's not even been able to calm him down most of the time.'

Bea's expression twisted then, her face draining of all colour.

'What …?' he asked her. For a horrible moment he thought she was having a stroke and he would be responsible for administering mouth-to-mouth.

But no, it wasn't a stroke. She got to her feet and uttered one word – a word that sent this already crazy night down another rabbit hole.

'Changeling.'

FITZWILLIAM STREET, BELFAST, NOW

He had kissed her. She couldn't get over the fuckin' *cheek* of it.

If he wanted to re-establish contact with Steve out of some sense of long-overdue guilt at abandoning his friend at the first whiff of adulthood, well fine. She'd thought that inviting him and that skinny self-satisfied little dingbat of a girlfriend of his to their house would show them that parenthood *didn't* actually equal leprosy.

If he wanted to come to dinner in the middle of some nervous breakdown (and judging from his behaviour the entire night, he'd been going through *some* sort of mental car-crash – maybe he'd finally woken up and realised Maggie wasn't the one for him, maybe he'd realised he was gay, maybe he was thinking of embracing Scientology, whatever) well, that was also fine.

She didn't care.

If Danny Morrigan wanted to flip out and have a meltdown during the dinner she'd fuckin' slaved over for the last three and a half hours and walk out of the house leaving them all paralysed with shock, let him.

She. Didn't. Care.

That he had *kissed* her …

'Prick,' she muttered, scrubbing the last of the dinner plates with unnecessary venom, not even sure which *prick* she was referring to – oh, most likely Danny, obviously, but her own darling Steve was an equally strong candidate. After his oh-so-smart quip when Danny had frigged off to Christ-knew-where, her beloved had spectacularly failed to stand up for her even one iota when Maggie had turned on her …

'What the fuck was that about?' she had demanded of Ellie, the door still ringing from Danny's exit, her eyes wide with rage. She was so ready to jump to conclusions she was practically constructing a conclusion-trampoline.

'I–I don't know!' Ellie spluttered, matching Maggie's movements by rising from her seat.

'Oh *sure* you fuckin' don't!' Maggie howled, throwing her hands up in a *can you believe this?* way. 'How long's it been goin' on?'

'How long's *what* been goin' on?' Ellie had tried again.

'Slut!'

'Steve!'

And he'd looked at her and spoken very quietly. 'Maybe you'd better answer the question.'

'WHAT?' Ellie roared.

'You couldn't handle it, could ye?' Maggie was saying, standing very close to her now. Ellie wondered if her once-best-friend was going to hit her, and wondered what her reaction would be if she did.

'Couldn't handle–?'

'That I got him.'

'That you *got him*? Don't be ridiculous!' Ellie burst out. 'We only dated for a few weeks …!'

'You couldn't handle the fact,' Maggie went on as if she hadn't spoken, 'that you ended up with *this*,' and with one sweeping motion, she indicated the house around her. Which would have been okay … maybe, perhaps … if the sweeping hand hadn't also taken in the sleeping baby lying on the blankets.

That was a mistake.

Ellie hadn't hit anyone since she was seven when she and Lucy Thompson had had a vicious playground fight over which boy band member they were going to marry as big girls. By God, though, she made up for lost time by landing a complete beauty of a right hook on Maggie's pert little chin. Maggie went down like a hooker on a submarine.

Steve was there. Not with Ellie. Not defending her. He was helping Maggie to her feet.

'You … you *bitch*,' Maggie hissed as she stood up, throwing off Steve's assistance and rushing past them both toward the front door.

She had her coat on in a matter of seconds, her pretty little face flushing in humiliation and anger, her lip trembling. Ellie just stood there and watched, a hundred things to say running through her mind, but she rejected each one of them, knowing in her heart that none of them would help in the slightest.

'You're welcome to him,' Maggie said, and was gone a moment later.

You could have heard a pin *deciding* to drop in the room after she left. Ellie turned very slowly to look at Steve who was still standing in the spot where he had helped Maggie to her feet. As she watched, he reached down to the dinner table and popped a piece of chicken into his mouth, chewing on it mechanically.

'Bit dry, this,' he said.

'She called me a slut. She called our lives shit, do you realise that? She was waving at—'

'He kissed ye,' Steve replied immediately. 'On the lips.'

'I don't know *why* though! Jesus Christ! He's clearly a fuckin' lunatic comin' to his best mate's house and … and behavin' like a broody mother! Look at the way he got on when he first saw me earlier!'

'Yeah,' Steve said quietly. 'I noticed.'

'So why did you sit there and say fuck all when that bitch called me a slut? Hey? Thanks very fuckin' much for the back-up, *darling*! Couldn't wait to help *her* back up to her feet though, could ye?'

She tried to bring her breathing under control, tried to make sense of what was happening.

'Why didn't I say anything? Because, Ellie,' he said, saying each word very carefully, 'you kissed him back.'

She couldn't find the voice to reply, to deny. Could only stand there in the dining room, surrounded by the flotsam of the semi-dinner as Steve left the room and the front door opened and clicked softly closed.

Washing the dishes, now, half an hour later, she clattered the last of the plates onto the draining board, fighting a ridiculous urge to pick up the *fuckin'* draining *fuckin'* board and hurl it to the stone kitchen floor, just to hear everything inside smash satisfyingly. It would leave her no closer to solutions, but that half-second of mindless destruction would bring her some modicum of release.

But she didn't. Ellie didn't do things like that. Steady Ellie just kept on keeping on, because that's what sensible girls did, wasn't it?

How she wished she was a flighty airhead like some of the girls she'd known, like, oh just as a completely random example off the top of her head ... Maggie, let's say. That girl was as sharp as a marshmallow. She'd gone through uni with nothing but the next night out on her mind, or the next fella, and – here was the kicker – she'd been no worse off for that attitude.

Girls like Maggie got leeway, got allowances made for them. They could throw tantrums, act like complete arseholes, and people would step back and say – ach that's just her way. She'll come round. Give her time.

Not her. Never her. *Give your mother space*, her father had always said to her. *She's in one of her dark days. You know what she's like.* And he'd ruffle her hair, saying, *but that's not you, is it? My sensible wee girl.*

He'd always praised her for being sensible ... until –

'How could this have happened?' he'd spat at her.

She could have given the obvious comeback, *Well, how do you think, Dad? The usual way.* But she knew her father wasn't asking how procreation worked.

'I ...' she'd looked down at her shoes, 'I had a stomach upset the morning before. Apparently it can ... make the Pill ... not fully effective.'

'And he wasn't wearing ...?'

And then they came, the three words that would destroy her reputation as Steady Ellie in her father's eyes forever.

'We were drunk.'

The memory of her father's expression when she'd told him made her fingers slacken their grip when they should have been tightening it, and as a result the dinner plate she had been drying wormed loose from her grasp, evaded her desperate mid-air interception attempt, and landed on the kitchen floor with a crash.

Surprisingly, the dish's demise wasn't at all as satisfying as she'd anticipated it might be. But then she hadn't *meant* to do it. It had been an accident, a stupid clumsy fumble when she should have been paying attention. Still, that was her speciality, wasn't it?

A plaintive wail began in earnest from the next room, and she sagged further.

'All right, all right, sssh,' she said, having put the dish-drying paraphernalia away and coming through with her best *everything-is-okay-Mummy's-here* expression turned up to full, expecting to see a little red angry bundle kicking furiously at being wakened.

She stopped. Blinked. Aaron was screaming, yes, as she'd anticipated, but he wasn't lying on his back. He was standing up in the middle of the room on his little chubby legs, bouncing up and down in rage as he hollered.

'You're walking!' Ellie squawked, half in delight and half in alarm. 'My little man is walking! Come to Mummy! Come on!'

Aaron's crying subsided as she got down on her knees and held her arms out to him, beckoning him to come to her. He looked at her and took a half-step back to steady himself, but otherwise seemed incredibly rock solid in his balance. She couldn't believe it. He'd been showing no signs of being ready for this – he was only eight months old, after all!

Take *that*, cousin Shelley, walking at ten months. And she's got a massive squint anyway. So that's 2–0 to you, Aaron, she thought with satisfaction, again wishing they made baby scoresheets for competitive mummies instead of those stupid reward charts for the kids. They'd make a fuckin' fortune.

Aaron took a step toward her, and then another.

'That's it!' she squealed excitedly, the emotional turmoil she'd just been going through receding. 'Come to Mummy!'

'Mum-my.'

'Fuck me!' Ellie burst out, and then clapped her hand over her mouth in horror. 'I mean, WOW! Wow, little man, you spoke! You said Mum-my! Clever man.'

That was when things started to get weird.

'Where Dad-dy?'

She retracted her hands instinctively, no longer holding them out to the child, staring at him open-mouthed instead, wondering if she'd gone doo-lally, or if the television had–

'Where's Dad-dy?' he said again, and there was no mistaking it this time; his little lips moved perfectly with the words. He tottered another few steps toward her. 'Want Daddy. Where Daddy go, Mummy?'

He was pale. How had she not noticed how pale he was? He was milk-bottle white. Was he sick? Was he babbling? No, babies didn't babble – well, they did, they were *supposed* to babble … were supposed to do nothing but – but not at eight months. No eight-month-old child walked as confidently as he was walking now. No eight-month-old constructed sentences as effortlessly as he was now.

But that, that meant he …?

Moments later, the front door flew open. It was Steve, panting and puffing from running, red-faced and covered in muck and shite from head to toe, looking like a crazy man.

'Ellie!' he called out, moving into the hallway and checking the dining room only to find it devoid of occupants. 'Ellie, it's Aaron! Ellie, where are you! I have to tell you about Aaron!'

'I already know,' her voice replied from the back room. He ran in there.

She was holding the child, cradling him in her arms, and smiling from ear to ear as she looked at him.

'My wee man's a *genius*,' she said proudly.

BELFAST, NOW

Dermot Scully did not live in a nice place.

Not that Michael Quinn, his hand now pushing the man's gate ajar, particularly cared where he lived. In fact, he didn't much care about anything. He could vaguely remember certain such concepts, but they were blurred and soft, as indistinct as someone shouting underwater. The only clear things in his mind right now were the memory of the goddess back in Mr Black's office, and the mission he had been given to perform.

Kill Dermot. Eviscerate his little brother.

Well. As Michael Quinn always did, he had prepared. He had gone home and he had kissed Christina and made some excuse about the go-live date causing a bottleneck at work and his wife had clucked loudly and flounced off in a stinking sulk. He had accepted this as he'd pulled the largest of the kitchen knives from the drawer and wrapped it in a protective cloth, because after all, that was just her way – give her a day or so and she'd be right as rain again.

He had slipped the knife into his briefcase and driven to this stinking street, ringing ahead several times to warn Dermot of his impending appearance. Dermot hadn't answered the calls, again not to his great surprise – the man made J.D. Salinger look like Jay-Z.

It would probably be weeks, if not longer, before anyone even noticed something was amiss. Presumably, he mused, as he reached the front door, the smell would be the giveaway. He had heard from several sources – okay, television, truth be told – that the odour a cadaver gave off was powerful enough to soak through walls.

It made sense to him; he had always thought most of his fellow human beings were full of shit – small wonder that when they died, their bodies could not contain a lifetime's worth of crap and it spilled out for all the world to smell.

He knocked on the door. And again. And again.

'Dermot,' he called loudly, reflecting that what he was doing now would place him at the scene should he alert any neighbours with his shouts. It should have bothered him, but it didn't. If he was caught – so be it. As long as Dermot Scully was dead in the way that mattered.

Success. Noises from inside. The door opened a crack. 'Michael?' a voice said in disbelief. 'Michael, is that really you?'

'It is.'

'What are you doing here? At this time of night?'

Success was what mattered. Michael would approach this task as he would a business meeting with a recalcitrant prospective partner. After all, he'd eviscerated quite a few men in his time, although strictly in the business sense of the word.

'It's about Mr Black, Dermot. I'm in trouble. Please, let me in.'

'I can't help you,' Dermot replied, his voice growing desperate, grovelling as he tried to make his brother understand. 'Michael, you don't know what it's been like for me. They watch me. They watch me *all the time*. I've had to use ... measures ... to stop them getting into my house. I'm a prisoner in here, Michael. I can't go outside,' the man was almost wailing now. 'They'd get me in a heartbeat. One of them got in a few days ago ...'

'Dermot,' Michael interrupted, his voice icily calm. 'Relax. Inviting me in won't invite anything *else* with me, will it? Now let me inside and we'll talk about this. I'm in trouble, and if you help me, I'll help you. You know I have the resources.'

The door opened another crack.

'You ... you will? You'll help me?'

Michael smiled. 'Of course I will!' he boomed, feeling the comforting weight of the briefcase on the end of his arm, and knowing what it contained. 'You're my brother!'

The door opened, stale air escaping into the night. Michael smiled and walked inside. He would get Dermot to do something – make a cup of tea, reach for a book, whatever – and then he would strike when the man's back was turned. Dermot was not by any means a physically imposing man, but Michael was no warrior and he had no desire to get into a fight. Once incapacitated, he would take out the knife and make a cut across the man's stomach, allowing the organs to spill–

Something hit him, hard, in the back of the head. He went down like a felled tree, unconscious as he hit the floor.

'They've got him,' Dermot Scully said grimly.

'I know,' Tony Morrigan replied, lowering his fist. He was clutching the horseshoe that until recently had hung on Dermot Scully's front door; it was this that had done the damage. He glanced at Dermot in the shadows of the front hall.

'Get him inside,' he said, glancing out at the darkness beyond the property's borders, and knowing full well what lurked out there.

The front door shut behind them.

THE HILL OF TARA, IRELAND, 93 BC

The time had come for a king to be crowned. The king in question was to be Bres, son of Ériu of the Tuatha and Elatha of the beaten Formorians. A proper cock, in Danny's estimation.

'How come they let a half-Formorian wankstain like him be the king?' he asked. 'Seems a bit fuckin' dopey if you ask me. A bit *you've-brought-this-on-yerselves*. Like when you're watchin' a movie and you see anybody played by Ben Kingsley or Christopher Walken be made second in line to the throne. You just sorta lose sympathy for the daft bastards at that point.'

Standing on the hilltop beside him, as the coronation took place below with thousands of assembled Tuatha and a good few hundred Formorians watching, the Morrigan's lip twisted as she replied. 'Seems like a few people agreed with you about the battle of Mag Tuiread,' she said. 'When Nuada stepped down, and details of the battle got out, whispers went around that the battle fury had gone to our heads. That we'd chased down and massacred those who were surrendering or retreating.'

Danny knew better than to comment. 'Ummmmm…'

'I know. We did. We did both of those things …' she sighed. 'I could list a half-dozen examples of similar things going on in modern times for you – from *your* timeline – if you like.'

'I'm sure you could, aye,' Danny replied unfazed. He'd been ready for this particular riposte and, like any fireside working-class lefty from Belfast, he had a few zingers prepared. 'Doesn't mean they should be cheered on. At any time.'

'I can't believe we're related.'

'Ah, I was wonderin' when *that* would come up. So we're …?'

'All in good time,' was all she said. 'Look.'

She pointed to a solitary figure alone on a nearby summit. Bres sat down grandly on the Lia Fáil – the Stone of Destiny, fourth treasure of the Tuatha, and in Danny's humble opinion, the worst fuckin' treasure ever. A resurrection cauldron capable of spewing out pizza and Stella till Kingdom Come? Top drawer. A sword and a spear capable of acting like Obi-Wan Kenobi's guilty wank fantasies? Good stuff.

But a fuckin' *stone*? Whose sole contribution to the mythological spectrum was to cry out 'Hail King!' when the right arsecheeks were placed on it?

'Something to add?' the Morrigan snapped testily, sensing his scepticism.

'So it's a Sorting Hat for king's holes. That it?'

'That,' the Morrigan hissed in fury, 'is the fourth of the greatest treasures the world has ever known!'

'Well I'm just saying, I think the world is safe from *Indiana Jones and the Big Rock of Pre-approved Arses.*'

She'd been about to say something else, but was distracted by the sight of her younger self atop a neighbouring hill, holding the Spear of Destiny.

They watched as Bres sat down.

Nothing. Not a cry, not even the muffled 'get off!' or 'Jesus, when's someone gonna invent the fuckin' bidet?' that Danny had secretly been hoping for.

'So it's official. He's not the rightful king,' Danny said in relief, feeling as though he were back on board with this particular narrative now.

'Watch.'

The crowd were murmuring. A few had started to move toward the false king. As they did so, Bres gripped that immense silver Sword. He held it aloft and a soft, bright curtain of light washed over the watching multitude, all save the two versions of the Morrigan and Danny himself.

Danny understood. 'He rewrote their memories.'

'Yes.'

'Why didn't you go down there?' he asked her. 'Stop him? You knew what had happened.'

'I was tired,' she said. 'I had trained my entire life to be the Goddess of War, Danny. And I had gone out, ridden out on my first assignment, and I had surpassed everyone's expectations, including my own. I killed almost four hundred Formorians that day at Mag Tuiread. But rather than being hailed a hero, we were told we had gone too far, and that we needed to *distance* ourselves from such mindless barbarism.'

The younger Morrigan raised the Spear and with a yell that rang out across the valley, she brought it down upon the earth. It splintered with a crack that drove a fissure deep into the hillside on which she stood, until the entire summit split and one hill became two. Danny watched this mythic occurrence with less surprise than he'd imagined he would; he was more interested in the solitary figure abandoning the fragments of Spear and walking away, alone, into the countryside, away from everything she knew, away from her people.

'In one moment, one act of short-sightedness,' the older goddess beside him said, 'I walked away from the destiny I'd always had laid out for myself. One full of promise and hope and a place among the high ones, and into a future I'd never imagined.'

He licked his lips, even as she touched his arm and he felt the familiar tug of a space-time shift begin to take hold.

'Can't imagine what that was like,' he said.

REGENT STREET, BELFAST, 1 YEAR AGO
Squelch.

That, Danny decided, was never a good noise for a living-room rug to make.

Gingerly, he lifted his foot, sodden sock and all, off the rug. It was dark-coloured and the living room was not brightly lit. The bulb had blown the day before and 'bulb' had been dutifully added to the list of 'things to buy' magnetically affixed to the fridge door.

Danny wondered how many 'o's were in 'noose'.

'Rug's wet,' he called into the kitchen.

'What? Wet? How? How wet?'

His right foot was soaked. Shrugging (in for a penny, in for a pound), he selected the opposite end of the rug and planted his left foot down.

Squelch.

'Very.'

Ellie emerged from the kitchen. Her left hand rested on the crest of her very pregnant, very prominent bulge, as it always seemed to do these days. She was flushed, she was hot, she was irritable, and she'd just come from her second hour of attempting to defrost the freezer with the world's bluntest screwdriver. At the rate of progress she was making, she might as well have been chipping at the ice with playing cards.

'It must be the boiler,' she said eventually.

Danny said nothing. Did nothing.

'You'll have to check,' she added.

'Right.'

She waited another few seconds. 'Well?' she said.

'Well, where *is* the boiler?'

'I don't *know*! Upstairs in that wee hot press cupboard probably. It's my first day in here too Danny! D'you want me to staple a schematic to my forehead?!'

He glanced at the clock. It was 10.42 p.m. By this time, he knew, O'Rourke's would be filling up rightly with the late-night crowd and the short skirt brigade would be out in force. Flan would be making confident predictions of his inevitable success; predictions as delicate and as beautiful as spider silk, composed of purest bullshit.

He'd be cradling a pint and raising it to his lips. Whenever. He. Wanted.

When he opened the hot press door, tepid, grey water escaped in a gush that soaked the landing carpet. He should have jumped back, should have let loose with a flurry of swearwords, but all he could do was stand there and stare into the black innards of the hot press at the leaking boiler within.

If he moved, he knew, he'd hear a squelch again and he knew, he knew right then, that if he heard it even once more, it was over. If his foot came down and a squelch was the result, he wasn't even going to stop, he was going to walk downstairs, put on his coat, take whatever money was in it and walk to O'Rourkes to meet the lads and have a fucking pint and go back home, go back home to Belgravia Avenue and sleep, sleep somewhere, sleep anywhere and not think about anything. That was the sequence of events that was going to happen, right there. Yes sir.

'There's water dripping down the stairs! What the fuck happened up there!'

'Boiler's fucked,' was his detailed reply.

'Phone the landlord! Cheeky cunt'd the brass neck to take a security deposit … oh …'

He heard a sharp intake of breath from downstairs, a deep and shuddering inhalation that contained frustration and pain. He glanced down and saw Ellie at the bottom of the stairs, leaning against the hallway wall for support, clutching her swollen belly, her face red, her knees bending against the strain. Air escaped her lips in a hiss.

She glanced upward and their eyes locked.

He closed the hot press door and went to her, squelching every step of the way.

COUNTY WEXFORD, IRELAND, 43 AD

This place was different. It felt different, but how? He could see the Morrigan beside him, by his shoulder as always, and he knew she would probably have told him if he'd asked, but he wanted to try and figure it out for himself.

They were standing by a well in the middle of a small settlement. The houses were simple wattle-and-daub dwellings arranged in a circle. He could see some sort of rudimentary wooden fence ringing the place, which looked as if it would stop only the least determined of pretty much anything; the villagers would have been more protected by a roll of Sellotape.

But it wasn't the low-budget element of their surroundings that was off-kilter; it wasn't the lack of grandness self-evident in the Tuatha villages he'd glimpsed.

Taste. It was something to do with taste. The air … it tasted …

'Magic,' he said, hesitantly. 'There's no magic here, is there?'

She was impressed, though she tried not to show it. 'This is a human settlement,' she said.

He stopped slightly when she said 'human'. It was easy sometimes to forget that, looking at her, she wasn't really a woman in the *homo sapiens* sense of the word. Clearly she sensed this because she glanced at him with a slight smile.

'Are you wondering who came first?' she said. 'You or us?'

'Kinda.'

'Depends what you want to believe, Danny,' she replied mischievously, and rather than explain any further, she walked a few steps toward a particular clump of huts.

Danny followed, looking around as he did so. The people here worked hard to eke out a living. He saw children carrying water from the well to the houses, women bustling this way and that, fetching and carrying and generally keeping the village intact by undertaking the myriad of daily tasks that made up life here.

They stopped beside a woman who was washing and laying out clothes to dry by a small pond. By the look of the pile beside her, she was doing the laundry for the entire village. She was lean and hungry-looking and so engrossed in her work that even if he and the Morrigan had been visible to her, there was an excellent chance she would not have noti–

'Jesus …' he said softly. 'It's you.'

And so it was. The washerwoman by the pond, laying out strips of fabrics, was indeed the Goddess of War. More weatherworn than he'd seen her when she'd split the hills asunder, with her impressive frame and musculature depleted somewhat. That fabulous raven-black hair that had once been a beautiful maelstrom of curls was tied and wrapped in a simple functional white wrap. Gone were the glorious battledresses and fine garments of the Tuatha; this Morrigan, her hands rubbing two pieces of cloth together, was sporting a simple blue-green woollen wrap.

A smell pervaded the air, and this one had nothing to do with magic. In fact, *magic* was about the last word you'd associate with it.

'What *is* that smell?'

'That,' the Morrigan informed him, gazing down at her washerwoman self, 'is the soap.'

'Christ Almighty. What's it made of?'

She glanced over at him. 'Do you want me to tell you?'

'Will I regret it?'

'Absolutely.'

He nodded. Fair enough. 'Okay, but why? *Why* is that you? What are ye doing here? Is this some sorta ... undercover thing?'

The Morrigan's mouth twitched upward. 'You think I'm on a stakeout?'

'Well why else would a goddess be in a human village washin' clothes in a pond? Was it like Human Experience week in your Goddess exams, or what?'

'After Nuada's abdication and Bres' coronation ... I lost faith in my people. I broke the Spear and I left. I wandered ... wandered for many years. It was different for us, Danny. Time was different. Maybe I can't explain–'

'You live longer, but you live slower,' Danny cut in. 'It takes you longer to mature, longer to grow up. Longer to die.'

Again, he could see she was impressed. 'More or less,' she admitted. 'So while a human might have a long dark night of the soul ... I had the long dark century.'

She looked away from her younger self to some indeterminate point on the horizon, obviously troubled. 'And when I say dark ...'

she said, 'I *mean* dark.'

'You musta been a *right* fuckin' laugh as a teenager. But that still doesn't explain how you ended up here.'

'Just watch.'

Two children ran past them then, towards the young Morrigan sitting by the pond. They were running with the heedless speed of children everywhere, overcome in the excitement of the moment, giving no thought to consequence. They ran full tilt into the pond and sent water flying everywhere – over the clothes the woman was washing and onto the garments already drying on the large plank of wood ten feet or so from the water's edge.

Uh oh. Goddess of War about to get mad …

He was wrong. He was very wrong.

'You little *devils*!' the younger Morrigan screeched, but there was no malice in her voice, only playfulness. 'Just wait 'til I getcha!'

She put down the clothes she'd been scrubbing and waded into the water herself, caring little that her own shawl was getting wet in the process. She lunged for the youngsters and they scattered away from her touch. The oldest, who was around eight, stuck out his tongue as he pirouetted away from her attempt at capture.

The youngest, around four or five, tried to do the same and ended up losing his balance. He flailed his arms desperately to regain his balance but toppled comically into the water. The Morrigan/washerwoman was on him in a heartbeat, dragging him up from beneath the surface as he kicked and spluttered and spat water and the older boy almost died from laughter watching all of this.

'Talk!' the Morrigan demanded of her captive. 'Talk, prisoner!'

'Tell her nothin', Gaim! Nothin'!' the older boy called, moving through the waters with difficulty, closing the distance between himself and the struggling pair.

'I'll never talk!' the little one squeaked in defiance.

At this the Morrigan nodded equitably. 'An honourable choice. I salute your bravery. Right, in you go …'

And good to her word, the Morrigan dunked the little boy's head under the water. From the way the waters bubbled and thrashed Danny guessed he was putting up a tremendous struggle beneath the surface.

'I'll save ye, Gaim!' the older boy declared, and heroically threw himself on the back of the younger boy's assailant. The Morrigan seemed hardly to notice the extra weight on her back.

Gaim emerged from the water, gulping and gasping in air in great breaths.

'You put me under the water!' he squealed in accusation.

'Well, see, it's called torture,' his jailor replied, still radiating glacial levels of coolness. 'Now, are you ready to talk, or are you going to display more bravery?'

'Daddy sent us over! It was Daddy's idea! Daddy did it! Don't duck me again, Mammy. It's cold down there and I near swallowed somethin'. Don't duck me, please! I'm sorry, Mammy!'

Mammy…?

'Did he now?' the Morrigan said grimly, adjusting her grip on her younger son and rotating him around so that he was held under her left arm. She reached around for the other son clinging gamely to her back and, with a manoeuvre Danny couldn't fully follow it was so swift, she had unseated him and tucked him securely under her right arm. Both boys punched and kicked for all they were worth, but they may as well have been punching a mountainside for all the good it did.

'I did so.'

The voice had come from behind Danny. He turned, catching a glimpse of the older Morrigan's expression as he did so. Her eyes were full of tears, but there was more than just sadness on her face. He saw love there too.

The newcomer was a man in his early thirties; not especially handsome or particularly well-built and Danny knew just by looking at him that there was not a drop of magical blood in his body. But he had an open face with blue eyes that for a moment put Danny in mind of his father – a thought he shook off quickly – and in his arms he carried something, a little white bundle. Only when it squeaked and burbled did Danny realise it was a child, wrapped up safely against exposure to the elements.

'I sent warriors Glon and Gaim out on an epic quest to locate the legend of the washerwoman in the stream, the demon who preys on young lads and sends them to a watery grave,' the man intoned, completely deadpan.

'Look! We found the hag, Da!' Glon said triumphantly from under his mother's arm.

His mother turned to look down at him. '*Hag*, is it?'

'I didn't say that, Mammy! *He* said that!' Gaim called from under her other arm. 'I think ye look lovely as a washerwoman demon!'

The Morrigan roared with laughter and bent low, dipping her sons' heads beneath the water again, much to their chagrin. This she kept up for about all of four seconds before she straightened up and carried the two wringing wet little boys to edge of the pond, depositing them on the banks, where they proceeded to pick themselves up and complain bitterly that it wasn't *fair*…

'Away wi' ye O Mighty Warriors – songs *will* be sung of your deeds this day, but for now, the Elders could probably find something for ye to do,' their mother told them, in a voice that brokered no room for negotiation. They duly scampered off, joining up with another pack of children in the village centre.

This fighting force dismissed, she walked to her husband's side and gave him a kiss. 'Thank you,' she said and, as Danny continued to watch, feeling more and more intrusive by the second, she gently took the little white squeaking bundle from his arms and sat down on a nearby tree stump, coo-cooing and gurgling.

Danny moved around a few steps so that he could see the baby's face. It was fat and cute and pink and its owner wavered between utter amazement and occasional flashes of uncertainty as its mother babbled away.

'Good day to you, little Coscar,' she was saying, very formally, as if only to amuse herself. 'And how do you find this world today? Is it to your liking? Should I tear it down and build you a new one instead?' and she laughed as the baby produced a wad of spit and drool, as though passing judgement. 'That bad, is it?' she said, wiping away the gooey mess with the baby's wrappings.

The Morrigan's husband reached out and placed his hand on her shoulder. A look passed between them. It was obvious that not long ago, words had been exchanged and they had not been pleasant.

'I'm sorry,' he said softly. 'I didn't mean to–'

'It's good,' she interrupted. 'Don't–'

'Don't,' he cut off her interruption. 'It's just … difficult to adjust to. I'm a simple man, Regan.'

Regan? Danny mouthed to the Morrigan.

She shrugged. *I needed a name.*

'You're *not* simple … far from it. I think that's what they don't understand about you, or any of you. I know I didn't,' the younger Morrigan said, still staring into her youngest son's face, not sounding particularly proud of what she was saying.

'Why didn't you tell me? I mean … before?' he asked, sitting down beside his wife.

'Because I was afraid,' she said simply.

'But aren't you … I mean, can't you …' the man tried, and then gave up. 'There's so much I don't understand.'

'Ask me.'

'What were you afraid of?'

'That you'd drive me out.'

'Even if I'd wanted to, could I have? Could any of us?'

'I would have gone. If you'd wanted it,' she said quietly.

'I don't. I never will.'

'How can you know that? I scare you. I frighten you.'

'*You* don't frighten me. What you are, where you come from, frightens me. I won't deny it, Regan. The things we've heard … and then that thing last winter – the men …'

Her face hardened. 'That wasn't us. It couldn't have been us. Those hunters didn't do anything wrong. There would have been no reason to do that to them. If they were lost; if they'd trespassed on our lands and had meant no disrespect to us, then we would have simply turned them around and sent them back.'

'Maybe the ways have changed,' he suggested. 'Maybe the …' and he inhaled as if saying the words for the first time, 'Goddess of War isn't there any more to enforce the old customs.'

'She isn't,' the Morrigan pointed out reasonably. She smiled. 'She's right here. With you.'

He looked away. Whatever this was building towards, this was it.

'Slumming it.'

She closed her eyes. Both versions of her did, at the same time, and Danny noticed when she spoke that the older version was moving her lips in time with her younger self's words. If they were truly moving through her memories, did that mean that this particular memory, this specific day, was one she'd relived so many times she knew every nuance of it by heart?

'You think this is all … an *experiment*?'

Human Experience. Danny himself had thought the same thing.

'It had occurred to me. Forgive me, Regan, but our lives together aren't exactly what I imagine the life of a Tuatha Dé Danann to be. Unless the tales of your people have been hugely exaggerated.'

'They haven't been,' she replied curtly. 'We live well. We make merry. We want for little. And I walked away from all that. I wasn't happy so I walked away from it all, the palaces, the feasts, the treasures …'

'Treasures? The Cauldron? It actually exists?'

She nodded. 'Yes.'

He seemed to find this particularly difficult to swallow. 'Six of the village died last winter when the game grew scarce, Regan. Gaim ... gods, little Gaim ... we thought he would–'

'He wouldn't have.'

'You could have–?'

Here came her bombshell. Her big news. The point of no return. He could sense it. 'He's different.'

'Different? Different like you?'

'Yes.'

'How?'

'I don't really know. I never expected to ... I never thought that this – any of this – would happen,' and as she said it the baby started to cry. She brought it up to her shoulder and shushed it gently, rocking it back and forth. 'When we met ... I was expecting to stay a few nights here and move on. I wasn't expecting ... us.'

'A few weeks after *us* and you *were* expecting,' he said, an undercurrent of accusation in his voice.

'And?' she replied, picking up on the undercurrent.

'*And* you know what!' he said, frustrated. 'Gods, Regan, you're a goddess famed for her ability to see the *future*! So what was I? Did I even have a choice in us having sex? Or was it all part of some mystic Tuatha plan? You said Glon was a surprise! *Some* surprise! For all I know his birth's been preordained for centuries!'

Synaesthesia or no synaesthesia, listening to this, Danny's mouth was awash with the tangy taste of irony.

'When I walked away from my people, I gave all of that up. The omens, the portents. Glon wasn't planned,' and the Morrigan gave a short laugh. '*Believe* me he wasn't.'

'But once he was there, what? You thought you'd better hang onto the human in case you didn't know to raise one of our infants?'

'If you don't know the reason why I stayed with you,' the Morrigan replied, with the first hint of steel beneath her words Danny had been able to detect, 'why I've spent the last *ten years* with you, then there's really no point having this conversation at all.'

'Just tell me,' he pleaded, cupping her face in his hands and bringing their heads closely together. 'Please, just tell me. I need to hear it.'

She whispered the reason to him in three words. He whispered the response in four. They kissed.

'I'm sorry, Caderyn,' he heard her say. After that the two of them sat together, the baby's crying dialling down to snuffling which changed to deep, regular breathing.

'Are you okay?'

The Morrigan looked up at Danny, as if she'd forgotten he was there. She jerked away to hide her face in a way that was so reminiscent of his mother hiding her tears that he felt a pang of longing to be home.

'Yes,' she said. 'Keep … keep watching. I'm just going to … to walk for a while, go see Glon and Gaim.'

He frowned. Something in the way she'd said it hinted at an even deeper sadness, but he couldn't find the strength to question her on it, and in a few strides she was gone, leaving just Danny at the poolside with the couple and the sleeping baby.

He sat down on a log about ten feet from them, first checking that he wasn't going to Swayze right through the fuckin' thing and end up on his hole.

'Yous think *yous* have problems,' he said wearily to the unresponsive trio. 'I'm on a fuckin' vision quest or some such shite as a commercial break before I go back into Faerie Central Station and fight some queen for a sword that, even if I get it, I've fuck all clue what I'm supposed to do with it.'

A breeze stirred the air and the pond gurgled and rippled. The sound of Coscar's breathing was a soft white noise. Danny sighed.

'It's weird,' he said, still essentially talking to himself, 'I mean, you seem worried that she's slumming it, mate. But she doesn't look like someone who's unhappy. I mean okay, she fucked off from her ones in the huff, and okay, the first of the wee fellas wasn't planned, but look at yis, ye seem happy. The two big lads … fuck, they're great big fellas. Do yis proud.'

He paused for barely a moment. 'Might wanna watch the oul pond-duckin' stuff but, when social services get invented,' he added.

They made no reply, but he could see they were cuddling closer to one another, finding resolution and solace not from more clumsy words but from touch and physical contact. He remembered similar moments with Ellie – lying beside her, touching her in his sleep even after the most blazing of rows, and finding themselves ensconced in each other's embrace the next morning.

He thought of Glon and Gaim, throwing themselves at their mother in the water. Glon with his warrior's defiance, Gaim with his cuteness and his unashamed folding under pressure.

Would Luke be like that in years to come? Would he get a

chance to find out?

The young Morrigan's head snapped up then. Her eyes widened. He heard it as well as tasted it – a rumble in the woods that surrounded the little village, a thunderous shaking that made the earth vibrate in time as though someone were playing it like an instrument.

'No,' she breathed, standing up and clutching her baby to her chest. 'Oh no. Not *here* …!'

'What is it?' Caderyn asked, even as Danny heard the villagers begin to stir and murmur in apprehension, stopping their daily chores to look nervously at the woods around them. Some of the men hefted axes they'd been using for domestic jobs in a different grip, making themselves ready.

'Formorians. Can't you feel it? Can't you smell it? They're coming,' she answered, pale and drawn and a million miles from the invincible figure he'd seen taking legions of them apart on the battlefield. 'Caderyn, they're coming straight for us …!'

The Temptation

Women had always been something of a puzzler to Steven Anderson. Even as a child he had clashed with his older sister again and again. She was five years older than he was and by the time she hit the big P, she'd come to regard him as a lower form of life than things found clinging to the bottom of things clinging to the bottom of rocks.

But that was then. Now, in his twenties, he and his sister had moved past simple childhood resentment and had evolved into complex, multi-layered adult antipathy.

Still, in all his years he'd never seen any woman act like this.

'Ellie,' he said patiently, seemingly for the umpteenth time. '*Think* about it love. Eight-month-old kids don't walk and talk overnight.'

She was bouncing little Aaron on her knee. As Steve spoke, she clapped her hands over his ears as if to shield him from Daddy's hurtful words. 'Well then my little mansum wansum woo-woo is *special*,' she said.

'He's *somethin*' all right …' Bea said mildly.

Ellie scowled. 'Please, remind me who *you* are again?' she said.

'Bea O'Malley,' said Bea, dunking a biscuit into a cup of tea that Steve could not remember being made. Come to think of it, when had she even appeared? Had she actually been able to follow him as he ran home?

'And what d'you think you're doing coming into *my* house and mouthin' off about my baby boy?' Ellie demanded.

Bea thought about this. 'Trying to break the changeling's enchantment and make you see sense before it turns on you and kills you?' she offered cheerfully, and then swore. 'Left it in too long,' she said by way of explanation, pulling out half a Rich Tea.

Ellie looked at Steve. 'Did you drink and drive and not tell me and she's part of your community service, or what? The Help A Mad Oul Biddy Society?'

'Mad oul biddy!' Aaron echoed, shooting Bea an evil look. 'Mammy! Want hugs!'

'Awwww c'mere my little man for mummy hugs!' Ellie cooed, and embraced him. From behind her back, Aaron looked over to where Bea and Steve were sitting on the big sofa.

Lifting his tiny, stubby little hand, he slowly and deliberately raised his middle finger in their direction.

Bea choked on her biscuit.

Out in the kitchen a few moments later, with sounds of cooing and a disturbingly two-way conversation drifting in from the living room, Steve was practically grabbing Bea's non-existent lapels and shaking her. 'What the *fuck*?' he demanded in a furious whisper. 'What's wrong with–'

'She's still under the influence,' Bea said. 'When Danny left the world–'

'Will you stop *saying* that, for fuck's sake!' Steve exploded. '*Left the world*! You make it sound like he ordered a taxi!'

'When Danny left the world,' Bea said again, acknowledging Steve's interruption in the same way someone might notice a dust mite on their trousers, 'as I told you, the changes started to unravel behind him. So it had to increase its influence over her or she'd know it wasn't her baby. That's why she can't tell anything is wrong.'

'Then how come I can?'

Bea regarded him with far too wise a look for someone he would cheerfully have compartmentalised as a senile oul goat only a few hours ago. 'Maybe because you never fully bought into the *having a child* side of things in the first place?' she said. 'It's focusing all of its energies on Ellie now. Bewitching her. She's the only protection it has now.'

'Did you see him givin' us the finger? The cheeky wee fucker ...'

Bea shrugged. 'I thought all the kids round here could do that at eight months. Anyway,' she went on quickly, seeing Steve's unamused expression at this impromptu piece of social commentary, 'don't worry. There are other options available to us. D'ya think I came round here with two arms the same length?' she tapped the side of her nose conspiratorially. 'I've come prepared, son. Prepared.'

'With what?'

Bea looked him straight in the eye. 'Tea,' she said firmly.

In the living room, with Steve's incredulous stream of curses audible through the adjoining walls, Ellie was playing peek-a-boo. She covered Aaron's eyes. 'Wheresababy?' she said. 'Wheresawiddababy?'

'Still here under your hand,' Aaron replied.

'Wheresababy!'

'Same place as last time.'

'Wheresababy?!'

'Isn't there somethin' on TV …?'

Ellie gave him an admonishing look. 'Now, now. Don't be cheeky.'

He nestled into her immediately. 'Sorry, Mammy,' he said meekly. 'Love you, Mammy.'

She allowed him to burrow into her, feeling a little woozy as he did so. It was odd; she felt as though she'd had a few vodkas … her head felt pleasantly cottony, and that sensation was riding roughshod over an underlying feeling that she was missing something, the sort of feeling she got sometimes when leaving a house or a shop when she'd forgotten to take something with her.

But that sense of loss was being masked by the cottony feeling of contentment, and she would have cared about that, but why should she? Everything was fine, after all.

She kissed the top of Aaron's little semi-bald head and he mewled contentedly and threw his arms around her neck. She was so proud of him for walking and talking like such a big boy already, and Steve … well, he was just jealous because he was out at work all day and he probably knew that the little fella's advancement was down to his mummy.

'Ellie, love?' Steve poked his head around from the kitchen. 'Can you come out? Bring the wee man too, sure.'

Aaron's head was up instantly. 'Don't wanna go,' he said immediately. 'Wanna stay here with you, Mammy.'

'Steve?' Ellie said, suspicion forming despite the fogginess that had descended on her brain. 'What do you want us for?'

'Help with the bottles. The wee man looks starvin'.'

Aaron opened his mouth to protest, and then appeared to think about it – such a little cute face he had when he was mulling things over!

'I could fuckin' *murder* a bottle,' he admitted.

'Come on then,' Ellie huffed, standing up with him still clinging to her like a monkey.

In the kitchen, Steve cast one more doubtful look at his co-conspirator. 'How d'you know all this shite anyway?' he asked her.

'Believe me, I'm an expert,' was all she would say, though he noted that her voice lacked any sense of levity.

Arriving in the kitchen, Ellie made to deposit the baby on the counter-top, but Aaron whimpered and wouldn't let her set him down.

'Aaron,' Ellie said patiently, 'how'm I supposed to make yer wee bottles with you clingin' to me? Don't you want your dinner?'

Absorbing this, the child allowed himself – still a little reluctantly – to be lowered to the counter top. As Ellie moved to the other side of the kitchen and dropped to her hands and knees to fetch the big tub of formula milk from the cupboard there, Steve took the opportunity to return the gesture he'd been offered in the living room with particular gusto.

'Up yours too,' Aaron growled softly. 'Away and get a fuckin' haircut. Hippy.'

'At least I *have* hair,' Steve shot back, just as softly. 'Ya wispy-headed wee ballix.'

'Oh wow, what a comeback,' Aaron rolled his eyes, his little legs kicking as they dangled over the side of the counter. 'Enjoy me pissin' on ye this morning did ye?'

Steve's left eye twitched at the memory. 'You *aimed?*' he choked.

'Aimed?' Aaron chuckled. 'It was such a bullseye I was expectin' Sid Waddell to commentate on it.'

'I'll fuckin' *get* ye,' Steve hissed.

Bea nudged him in the ribs as Ellie, oblivious to the back-and-forth that had just taken place, got to her feet again and shot both participants a beatific smile.

'What?'

'What age *are* you, son?' Bea asked, raising an eyebrow.

Steve scowled and pointed to the eight-month-old. 'He started it.'

Ellie whipped up the bottles with the practised ease of someone who could have done this blindfolded. As she did so, the muscle memories in her arms and hands were nudging other memories as they flared into life, but they were still unfocused and formless and she shrugged them off.

Aaron latched onto the teat and began pulling on the milk in the first bottle as the others cooled in the fridge. He was cradled in her arms, forming a little patch of warmth against her breasts and the crook of her forearms and palm, a fingerprint of heat that felt comforting on one level and yet felt misshapen and wrong on another; as if he were the wrong key for the right lock.

His little cheeks expanded and contracted as he suckled

greedily on the bottle of milk she held, and as ever he stared straight into her eyes as she fed him, his gaze never wavering, as if he were staring into her head and reading her thoughts, reassuring himself that yes she was still here, and yes she loved him, and yes she wasn't going to go anywhere.

And then. He spluttered.

The bottle left his mouth.

She sat him up on his little arse on her knee and rubbed his back, again in a practised do-this-in-my-sleep way (a skill honed at 2 a.m. feeds when she practically was asleep), waiting for a belch that would settle him again. But this was no trapped wind.

'Let me go!' he bit out, suddenly writhing in her grasp, his little hands flailing out towards hers, and she exclaimed in pain – he had sharp little nails, and had just raked them across her forearm, leaving several shallow little scrab marks. Her grip loosened with the shock of the pain.

'Let me go!' he said again, and twisted until he succeeded in wresting himself loose. She squawked in terror and made a grab for him, fearing that he would hurt himself as he tumbled from her knee. With a flexibility that didn't so much as border on unnatural as live deep inside the city limits of plain weird, he launched himself off the sofa, turning in the air until, like the world's tiniest gymnast, he landed perfectly on the balls of his little feet on the living room rug.

He looked up with hatred, not at her, but past her to Steve and Bea who were standing at the doorframe. 'Why?' he asked them. 'Why did you have to spoil *everything*?'

'You're not hers,' Bea answered quietly. She was holding one of the other bottles Ellie had placed in the fridge. Ellie glanced down at its warm cousin, still held in her numb fingers. Oh God ... oh God, what had they done? What had she given her baby?!

'Foxglove,' the old woman said, as if reading her mind. 'Anything brewed with it will send them back to where they came from.'

'How dare you!' Ellie thundered, getting to her feet, her eyes full of maternal fire. 'That is my *baby*! You have no right to come into *my* house and–'

'Ellie,' Steve said, in such an uncharacteristically quiet tone that she had to stop. 'Ellie, *look*.'

She followed his gaze, back to her baby–

Ellie screamed.

Where an eight-month-old baby had stood only moments before, was a hideous little bundle of flesh, all fatness and baldness. It looked half a millennia old; wizened and ancient, with huge tufts of white hair sticking out in random places, and a head that was out of proportion to the rest of its body – far too big, with angular eyes and a ridged nose.

And worst, worst of all, it was still wearing the little blue babygro she'd ... she'd ...

She kept on screaming, one scream following the other as each passing outburst failed to dampen the weight of horror pressing upon her.

The strength went from her legs and she half-fell, half-stumbled, just as Steve surged forward and wrapped his arms around her. He managed to pull her back to her feet, dragging her back a few steps to stand in the doorway while the little homunculus *thing* stood there, its arse jutting out from the size 4 nappy it was wearing. It glowered at them.

Or at least, glowered at Bea and Steve. Ellie saw its gaze shift to her and its expression changed. The last scream choked in her throat and turned into a faint cry, her lip trembling uncomprehendingly at the madness unfolding around her.

'You showed me a rare kindness,' it said. 'I won't soon forget it. Upon my word.'

It turned, and scampered towards the fireplace.

'Wait!' Bea called after it, to Steve's astonishment.

It looked over its shoulder. 'You were the one who banished me,' it reminded her. 'So it's back I shall go.'

'Answer our questions first.'

'Kiss my arse.'

'I think you'd better take another look at who's banishing who,' she said quietly.

The little wizened monstrosity screwed up its eyes and leant forward to look at the three people standing before it. Steve watched as its expression – if anyone could ascertain an expression from something so unaccountably hideous – changed from angry defiance to sheer terror. It took a step backwards, tripped on the hearth, and ended up flat on its backside, where it continued backpedalling until its back was pressed up against the far wall.

'Just as well you're wearing that nappy,' Bea said.

'You had … questions?'

'I trust you'll answer them wisely?' Bea asked.

'I will,' he replied.

'Where is her child?'

Steve felt Ellie stiffen beneath him, felt her stop trembling all at once as the question left Bea's lips, as though some pulse had gone through her body. She removed herself from his position of support, though she glanced at him momentarily with what might have been gratitude, before it was replaced with something infinitely colder.

'Luke,' Ellie said, as a great shudder took her. It looked to Steve as though she were shaking something off; and he wasn't far from the truth. The last of the influence was wearing away. He could feel it too.

'*She* has him, of course,' the thing that had once been Aaron replied. 'He was the ...' and he waved a tiny little hand in the air, searching for the right word, 'the collateral.'

Women were a puzzle to Steve. Take Ellie, for example. One minute she could be collapsing and trembling like a leaf in a storm, pressed so close to him he could feel her heart thudding in her chest ... her chest and, well, other body parts that he wasn't sure whether he should be thinking about or not.

The *next* minute–

He could only watch as she launched herself across the room at the changeling, and scooped it up with a clenched grasp of her fingers, lifting it completely off its little blue-babygro'd feet and slamming it against the far window, the one looking out into their pitiful little backyard. So hard was the final *slam* that cracks spider-webbed across the glass.

The changeling found itself looking into the face of the woman who had been feeding it warm milk less than five minutes previously, the face of a mother. A mother that had promised always to love, never to leave, always to protect.

Not it. Him. Not Aaron. Luke.

'I want my baby.'

If her arm was showing any strain from keeping his not-inconsiderable weight pinned to the window, she was showing no sign of it. She exuded nothing besides cold, hard fury.

'I can't help you–'

She must have increased the pressure on its neck, because it seemed to have difficulty forming words after that. Steve could see the muscles standing out in her arm like rope, but still her hold held.

'I. Want. My. Son!' she screamed.

'You don't understand ...' it wheezed, staring wide-eyed over her shoulder. 'I'd tell you if I could ... please, believe me. This is so much bigger than any of you ... than me. When the network comes ... none of it is going to matter anyway.'

'Network?' Steve said. Beside him he saw Bea rear backwards, her eyes wide.

'Get away from the window!'

Too late.

The window Ellie was holding the changeling against shattered inwards, and *something* came through from the back yard outside. Throwing his hands up to protect himself from the flying shards of glass, and only partially succeeding, Steve's brain ceased to function in normal time and instead began to send him snapshots to process.

Teeth. Claws. A wolf. Too large. Far too large. Something else. Something worse–

Ellie, screamed. Hit the floor. The changeling, freed from her grasp.

The beast was in the room – watching Ellie. Teeth showing. Gathering itself for a spring.

Bea, screamed. Ellie, sprawled, bleeding. Helpless.

The wolf in the air.

'No!' a cry came. Not from his mouth.

Massive jaws closed with a wet *crunch*. A sound of something mortally wounded.

Ellie. Ellie, alive. Ellie, unbitten.

The monster backed off a few paces until its massive bulk was against the wall, and shook its great head so that the thing between its jaws fell to the floor. Blood ... Jesus God, blood *everywhere*...

But not Ellie's blood.

'Mammy,' the changeling wheezed with destroyed lungs, looking one last time at Ellie before lying still. The not-wolf, confused at this turn of events, came around from its momentary stupor and sank to springing position once more ...

Something exploded against its jaws. Something that sent white liquid in all directions, a few droplets landed on Steve's lips.

'Eat *that*, ya fucker!' came Bea's triumphant shout.

Instinctively, his tongue reached out to taste the droplet. It was milk.

The wolf howled long and loud, a howl of outrage and betrayal, thrashing around wildly, overcome by pain and incomprehension. The howl was at such a volume that all three present were forced to clap their hands over their ears; the pitch seemed to scrape directly across the mind, jagging its edges. Steve sank to his knees, closing his eyes to block them from this sonic assault lest they exploded in their sockets.

Seconds, maybe minutes, passed before he realised the sound was gone, that he was still alive. He opened his eyes, steeling himself for whatever horrors might greet him.

Broken glass. Blood. Bea was slowly getting to her feet. Ellie was weeping, her knees drawn up to her head, her body slowly rocking back and forth. The changeling's body, already looking as if it had been dead a hundred years, was no more than stringy strands of flesh stretched over a bleached skeleton.

The creature was gone.

Bea saw his look. She pointed at the now broken bottle of milk she'd hurled. 'My backup plan in case the first 'un didn't work,' she croaked, her voice weak and shaking. 'Twenty times the amount of foxglove than in the other one. Sent the bastard packin'.'

Steve knelt down beside Ellie. She emerged from her cocoon, and he flinched to see how haggard she looked, how suddenly exhausted. He saw her stare at the body of the changeling.

'It saved me,' she said, in a small voice. A child's voice.

'Yes,' he said, not knowing what else to say.

She got up and opened the back door in the kitchen. For a moment he feared she was just going to walk out, but she sat, alone, on the back doorstep, chin on her legs, staring into space. He saw her shake her head violently, clearing it. He saw tears come. Once or twice, she dry-heaved as it became too much for her to process.

He wanted to go to her, but was stopped gently but firmly by Bea.

'She needs me.'

'What she needs is a moment by herself. And *who* she needs ...'

Bea looked at him, 'isn't you.'

He couldn't deny the truth of that, so he sat back down amidst the chaos and glass and waited, as his own head sorted the Tetris blocks of memories – *real* memories – into rows as best it could.

She was back, standing in the doorway. She looked pale, and tired, but there was an edge to her. 'I don't understand what's happening. I just want my son back. I just want ...' she paused, tasting the air, tasting reality. 'I want ... I think ... it's strange–'

'Danny,' he finished for her.

Her confusion cleared a little at the word. 'Yes ...' she said, sounding a little taken aback, and then looked at him in despair. 'Steve, I don't know what's real and what's not real any more.'

'You will,' Bea said. 'But we need to go.'

'Go?' Ellie said faintly.

'Back to the garden thing? To where Danny went?' Steve guessed.

'Danny went? Danny went *where?*'

Bea shook her head, ignoring Ellie's question. 'No. That closed altogether when he went through. If ... *when,*' she amended, 'when he comes back, he'll have to come out somewhere else.'

'Back? Back from where?' Ellie demanded. 'Where has he fuckin' gone? So help me, one of ye better answer me!'

Bea looked to Steve. *You tell her.* 'Where those things come from,' was all he could think of to say, mostly because it was all he knew himself. He looked to Bea for approval of this explanation, as did Ellie. Bea nodded.

'You're sayin' he *knew* about this? He knew about Aar– ... about ...' and she faltered, had to suck in a steadying breath, unable to look directly at the hideous corpse in the middle of the room, but unable to quite look away from it either, 'about … *that?*'

'No,' Bea said firmly. 'No, he didn't know. He wouldn't have left ye if he did, love. He's daft as a fuckin' brush, but he loves ye. He does, aye.'

Ellie frowned in incomprehension at Bea. 'Who *are* you?' she said. 'Why are you talkin' like you *know* us?'

Bea looked back at the young woman. 'I know this is … well, I know how it is,' she said. 'And I might have some answers for ye, but likely as not I won't for most of it. But one thing I know for sure,' and she looked then at the body lying between them, 'is that we can't stay here all night and chat. Unless ye fancy it …?'

'No,' they chimed in unison, memories of teeth and claws flashing through their minds.

'Network …' Steve said, the changeling's words returning to him. 'Did it mean the Lircom thing?'

'Lircom thing?' Bea asked.

He shook his head. 'Dunno exactly. Some sort of massive internet upgrade all across the country. Faster connections, and it's cheap as fuck. Everyone's getting it. It's going live tomorrow. Danny mentioned it to me …'

'What would these … these fuckin' *things* … have to do with that?' Ellie asked. 'What has any of it got to do with taking my son away from me?'

Her mobile rang, sending a startled jolt through all three of them. She grabbed it from the fireplace and stabbed the answer button immediately.

As she talked, low and urgently at a volume the others couldn't make out, even at this close proximity, Steve gave up trying to eavesdrop and sank to his haunches. The body of the thing that had pissed in his face less than twelve hours ago in the guise of his pretend son, was undergoing the most rapid loss of form he'd ever seen; it was like watching the footage from a motion time-lapse camera that had been trained on a bowl of fruit for six months, compressed into the space of five minutes.

The flesh was dissolving, revealing the bones, which themselves seemed to be losing some of their own integrity. He watched the edge of one bone turn to powder. At this rate, there would be nothing left in a few hours; the remains of that strange little being would have returned to the ether.

And as the body wilted and warped, so too did the memories of the last year or so of Steve's life, eroded by waves of a parallel life. Recollections of attending Aaron's birth now stood alongside memories of receiving a text message from someone ... from *Danny*, yes, from Danny ... a text message that had listed all of the important facts about the birth. Of Danny's child's birth.

The real one.

Two feet away from him, his fake child was becoming dust, and taking his fake fatherhood with it. All of the panic and the giddy sense of vertigo he'd felt over the last few days had almost broken him. He'd had a small child and a partner who depended on him, but he had behaved like a spoiled kid himself.

He had an explanation for that now, of course. He had never been a father. This had been some sort of bizarre, skewed, tangential version of his recent past, in which he, and not Danny, had been the one to sleep with Ellie, he'd been the one to get her pregnant. And they – these monsters, these faeries or whatever they fuckin' called themselves – they had been so clever, creating an entire set of fake memories.

It had only been in the last two days that he'd found he wasn't coping; the confusion and the panic he'd experienced had not just been at the bind he suddenly found himself in, it had been at his own rush of cold feet after a year or so of making a pretty decent fist of fatherhood.

Except he hadn't. It had all been made up.

The moment it had *ceased* to be made up – in the last two days, where there was no new set of memories, just these ones, no parallel train track of existence – he had started to fuck things up.

Despite having the knowledge of how to make bottles dropped into his head, like a *Supernanny* version of *The Matrix*, he'd ballsed up making them time and again. Not because he didn't know how. Because he didn't *want to do it*.

What had he said to Danny, before the ground had opened up and claimed him?

She was mine and the wee man was mine and even though you had this amazin' job and a big house an' all, I thought – well, there we go, finally I've beaten him to the mark on somethin'. I thought – when it's time for him to have a wee one, he'll be the one comin' to me for advice.

Memories continued to unfurl inside his mind, and he was astonished at how many of them he wasn't welcoming back. There was one in particular he would have done anything to continue to forget.

*

BELFAST, 1 YEAR AGO

'How did this happen?'

She kissed him somewhere between *this* and *happen*, mashing his words into unintelligible mumbles, but he didn't mind one bit. He was kissing her back, and they were rolling on the bed, back and forth, like a horny pendulum. If someone had stopped time and asked Steve what day it was, what month, or any question that required an iota of thought, he'd have made the duelling banjo rednecks from *Deliverance* look like the next stage of human evolution.

Afterwards, when they were lying there panting and exhausted, with the worries of the world leaving his body in a hot-air balloon of contentment, he reassembled his pre-sex train of thought one carriage at a time and asked the question again of the girl lying beside him.

'Maggie?'

'Hmm?'

'*How* did this happen?'

Her head was resting on his chest. 'Because Danny and Ellie asked you to check in on me, make sure I was all right? If I was coping with the trauma of being single again …'

He laughed. 'That was four months ago.'

'Well?' she shot back, tugging on one of his chest hairs until he yelped in alarm and slapped her hand away, at least until he could muster a more manly pain noise. 'You're just being *really* thorough.'

'I …' he said, and his mouth was suddenly dry as he realised this was it, 'I love you.'

She held her breath for a few seconds – he could feel it when the up-and-down movement of her chest on his stopped – and when it resumed it was quicker and shallower than before. He fancied he could feel her heart thudding against his skin.

He'd considered possible replies. Obviously he was hoping for one in particular, but he'd come up with a list of others that covered the whole spectrum. On the positive side were alternatives like 'I adore you', or the admittedly nauseating, 'You complete me', or something like that. Then there were more neutral replies that wouldn't cause him to lose hope completely – something like 'I'm falling for you too', perhaps.

Of course, she could always give him the dreaded 'Thank you' and they could lie there in embarrassed silence until he worked up the courage to do the decent thing – get up and chuck himself off the nearest high ledge.

The response he got was one he hadn't expected.

'I'm pregnant,' she said.

FITZWILLIAM STREET, BELFAST, NOW

Ellie had finished her phonecall. Steve brought himself back to the present as he registered her expression. 'What is it?'

'Mum. My da's missing. He said he was going to work tonight but she can't get him on the mobile, and when she phoned work they'd no idea what she was on about.'

'Work? At this time of the night?' Steve said, trying to force some politeness into his voice. He had a whole set of fake memories of her ones being dickheads, and the funny thing was, they were bumping against a whole set of *real* memories of her ones being dickheads.'And she believed him?'

Ellie's voice was brittle. 'He's working with Lircom.'

Steve's apathy died on his lips. 'Oh,' was all he said.

'We have to find him. If one of those things, those wolf things ... we have to find him. He's my da and we have to find him,' she said, beginning to pace back and forth.

'Love, I don't mind where you two go,' Bea said, yawning. 'I'm an oul doll and I've had enough excitement. I'm goin' home. You can drop me off on the way.'

'It's not safe–'

'It's safe,' Bea said quietly. 'Trust me.'

'On the way to where?' Steve said, changing tack. 'Where exactly are we even goin'?'

Ellie stopped pacing, suddenly struck by an idea. 'All this shite ... faeries and changelings ... fuckin' hell!' she raged at herself. 'Why didn't I *think*? He'll know what's goin' on! He'll know something!'

'Who?'

'My uncle Dermot,' she said. 'That's where we'll go. He'll help us find my da. Plus, like I say, he's an expert on all this ... we'll be safe there.'

BELFAST, NOW

'This is a serious criminal offence. You do realise that. And I fully intend to prosecute you both to the maximum extent of the law. You'll do time for this, Dermot, and with your health ...'

Tony Morrigan rolled his eyes as he watched Dermot Scully

poring over extremely old documents at the ancient writing desk in the corner of his living room. 'Does he ever fuckin' shut up?' he asked, shooting a hostile look at the man currently fastened to the swivel chair. The room was dark, the only light coming from a few strategically placed candles, and the flames gave Michael Quinn's eyes an otherworldly glint that Tony didn't care for.

'Oh, so you *can* hear me,' Michael said. He struggled against the industrial duct tape that had been looped around his wrists and ankles, but he had been bound so tightly that he could do little but vibrate with intent. 'Let me out of here!'

'So you can kill me?' Dermot Scully said mildly, without even looking up from his reading.

'*What?*' Michael Quinn looked shocked beyond measure. 'Have you gone completely round the fuckin' bend, Dermot? You're my brother. Why in God's name would I do a thing like that to my own flesh and blood?'

'You tell us,' Tony replied.

'I'm not talking to you,' Michael snapped. 'I can't think of a single reason to waste my time on someone like you.'

In response Tony picked up a small bundle from the desk where Dermot was working, unwrapped Michael's kitchen knife and held it in front of the captive man.

'Ah,' he said.

'Always carry one of these in yer briefcase do ye?' Tony asked him, allowing the cloth wrapping to fall and the knife's blade to catch the meagre candlelight.

'Self-defence,' Michael sneered. His lip curled as he looked at Tony. 'I'm only amazed to see you sober, Tony. Feel free to fuck off with your tail between your legs if things get too much for you.'

Tony sighed, and set the knife back down on the desk where Dermot, looking small and old and frail, was still tracing lines of text with his finger. 'Any closer to finding anything?' he said.

Dermot shook his head and sank into his chair. 'There are a multitude of incantations in here, any one of which could be exactly what we're looking for ... or the worst thing we could do. You have to remember that the protections I've put on this house are finely balanced as is. If anything went wrong in whatever we try for him,' he nodded at Michael who was absorbing all of this silently, 'and it might all come crashing down.'

Tony pinched the bridge of his nose with his fingers – something Danny also did in times of extreme stress, though whether father or son would have been aware of the other's usage was doubtful – and, after a few seconds, had an idea.

He snatched an object from the desk, palming it too quickly for anyone else to identify what he had taken, and pulled a chair to sit alongside Michael Quinn, whose reacted in alarm, not only at the gesture but at Tony's expression.

'Right,' said Tony. 'Fuck this spellbook shite. Let's try somethin' more real-world, eh?'

'What are you talking about?' Michael demanded.

'You made a deal with Dother.'

There was a pause as Michael Quinn tried, unsuccessfully, to conceal his surprise.

'Dother? Who's that?' he said weakly.

'Do *not* waste my fuckin' time,' Tony said softly. 'Every single person in this room is immune to the Sword. Dermot, because of the things he knows. You, because you probably made the fuckin' request to Dother in the first place, and if you weren't aware that anything had changed how would you pay your debt to him? And me … you *know* why I'm not affected.'

Michael said nothing, but sweat started to form on his brow.

'*You* did this. You started all of this. You invited them in. You got your own grandson taken below, and now my son has gone below too. What was he, Michael, you fuckin' bastard? Was Luke the price for what you wanted?'

Tony saw it then. A flicker, a flash, something moving behind the man's eyes. 'Get out!' he shouted, raising his fist and pressing the horseshoe he'd been concealing into the forehead of the captured man before him. When the metal met flesh, there was a noise like meat sizzling on the grill pan and Michael Quinn *hissed* in pain, writhing like an animal. There was a ripping sound and Tony realised Michael had worked his left leg free, but that only caused him to press harder, to grit his teeth and bring his entire weight to bear to keep the man down–

With a final convulsive jerk, the fight went out of his opponent.

Black liquid poured from Michael Quinn's mouth, from his nostrils, ears and nose. Black tears seeped down his face and within an instant of them appearing, Michael howled – a rising wail of pain and agony.

'Wipe it off! Get it off him! Quickly!' Dermot exclaimed, almost tripping over himself in his urgency. He grabbed an old cloth and wiped Michael's face. The black liquid was viscous, reeking of raw sewage. The cloth began to smoulder and smoke. Quickly Dermot deposited it into a metal coal bucket.

'What *was* that?' asked Tony.

'Spider venom,' Dermot replied, coming around to examine his brother. The shock of the fluid's expulsion from his system had thrown Michael into a stupor. 'I think he's coming round ...'

'Michael?' Tony tried. 'Michael?'

With great effort, Michael managed to focus on the two men in front of him. Gone was the confrontational air from a few minutes ago – although his eyes still bugged to see Tony Morrigan standing before him – but when he caught sight of Dermot ...

'Dermot!' he sagged in relief. 'Oh God! Oh God, they asked me to–! Jesus Christ they wanted me to ... to ...' and he gagged, the bile rising in his stomach. Tony tried to locate a suitable receptacle for any puke the man might produce, but could see only the coal bucket and decided against using it – for all he knew a mixture of faerie venom and boke might produce something he didn't even want to think about.

Michael had managed to bring himself back under control. He had also noticed his current tied-up status. 'How did you know I was ...?'

'I didn't,' Dermot admitted, nodding to Tony. '*He* did.'

'Family talent,' Tony said, sitting back down in the chair beside Michael. 'Now start fuckin' talkin. We don't have much time, am I right?'

Michael paled. 'You don't know the half of it,' he said.

*

Outside Dermot's house, just beyond the radius of an invisible barrier that had no effect on humans but was impenetrable to his kind, Mr Black alighted from his limousine. The house was perhaps thirty feet away. Maddeningly close. Any humans walking past would notice nothing amiss, would not see the shimmering sphere formed by the protective spells cast from within, but he could not set foot on the property. Which was why he had tried to use Michael Quinn, powerful arsehole that he was, as a walking weapon.

'What can you see?' he asked the massive spider looming beside him. In her human guise, Sarah had taken up hardly any of the interior of the limo. Once outside, she had unfolded herself to her full and glorious extent. It was a transformation he never tired of watching.

Her many eyes were as mirrors. Everything that crawled, everything that scuttled on more than four legs inside that house was hers to command; every set of compound eyes was a window she could look through.

'They have him tied up,' she said. 'It's as you thought. The older Morrigan is there too.'

Mr Black spat out a curse. Even as a bewitched weapon, Quinn was worse than useless. He took a step forward, and hit the barrier almost immediately. It wasn't a physical thing; not a brick wall, more like a persuasion, a command that even he could not disobey. His legs refused to go any further.

'If he somehow opens a gateway to the Otherworld ...'

'Is he capable of that?'

'I don't know,' Mr Black admitted. 'The man vanished for a decade, remember, and did a good job of it too. Who knows what he studied in that time?'

'Do you want me to try from above?' she asked, and at his nod, she reared up, front legs straight up in the air, scrabbling for purchase on the perimeter of the barrier. He watched with pride as she heaved her resplendent obsidian body onto the barrier itself, seemingly floating in mid-air. He watched her as she moved on a curved gradient to the apex of the sphere, thirty feet directly above the house.

'What da fuck?' came a voice to his right.

Mr Black glanced over. There was a young lad standing beside him. He was holding a joint the size of a small dog and it was drooping alarmingly. Mr Black thought, as he met the boy's eyes, that he hadn't seen pupils that big since the last series of *Fat Academy*.

'Here cunty,' said the youth, 'is that a big fuckin' spider hoverin' in midair over that gaff or what, fuck's sake?'

Mr Black spared a moment to sigh even as Sarah's body tensed and her stinger emerged from her carapace. Down it came on the barrier. There was a shimmer in the air that was visible for a brief second and, pressing forward, Mr Black felt the barrier give minutely before returning to its previous strength.

His new friend, meanwhile, had tired of waiting for him to answer. Walking forward – frustratingly, maddeningly, walking *right through* the barrier that was causing him so much chagrin – he vaulted the wall of Dermot Scully's garden until he was standing more or less underneath Sarah's massive bulk, thirty feet above.

'Here!' he shouted upward. Sarah's stinger paused. 'Are you a fuckin' big spider, are ya, aye? Fuck me!'

Mr Black recalled Sarah with the merest of gestures. She scuttled back to him with a speed that was completely at odds with her size, legs flowing in a rhythm that only arachnids could master. The youth was staggering back toward them.

'This boy has absolutely no sense of self-preservation,' said Mr Black.

'Are you a big–'

'Yes,' said the massive spider right in front of him, 'I am a big spider.'

'What da fuck is that about, like?' the soon-to-be-dead stoner asked. Despite the disappointments of the last ten minutes, Mr Black smiled.

HILL OF TARA, IRELAND, 26 MAY 1798 AD

As bullets pockmarked the trench in front of her, Molly Weston reflected that this was a strange way for a young lady to spend her Saturday night. No matter, though; despite being holed up in close quarters with several dashing young gents, she had her four brothers right with her, and woe betide the Rebel, be he a United Irishman of any rank, who fancied his chances with Molly Weston in the company of her four human chastity belts.

Besides, she thought with a grim smile as she reloaded her twin pistols, she wouldn't want to be anywhere else right now.

They were swarming up the hill, the English, hundreds of the bastards with their shiny uniforms and their bayonets, screaming in rage and defiance – a party of their fellows in the Reay Fencibles had been put to the sword by a Rebel force shortly before. She had been part of that force, had fired a shot that had seemed to take an age to travel the distance between her and the Englishman whose head it had caved in. She had watched him fall to the soil, surprise written all over his face.

Women were fighting. *Women* were killing. Recruited not long ago – though it seemed a lifetime – she had been drawn in, not so much by the fine speeches about a free land, but by the simple amazing fact that the recruiters had not patronised her, had not suggested she could contribute to the cause by sewing uniforms or providing 'home comforts' for the fighting men. They had asked her to familiarise herself with a weapon, not realising she'd been shooting since she was six years old. She was a better shot than two of her brothers and the equal of a third.

Shouts and chaos all around her. She looked to her right, at the body of her white horse, Dagda, cut down from under her by a long-range lucky punt of an Englishman who, at the hands of her comrades, had lost his life moments later. How she wished she could have done the deed herself. Tears stung her eyes, but she pushed them back: she wasn't going to succumb to the clichéd weaknesses of womanhood now, not when she'd been granted this opportunity to prove herself.

Bedecked in green and gold from her belt buckles to her hat, she knew how she looked. She knew at some level that she was being used by the local leadership as a sort of rallying call, as bait for the local lads to sign themselves up. She didn't care. She wanted to be bait, but not for the men. If just one little girl had seen her dressed in this finery – with her sword on her belt and her pistols holstered at her sides, riding through the towns of Meath on Dagda – and thought of a life beyond that of husband, work and children, then she would go to whatever lay beyond this life content.

The English battle cries grew louder. Her hands tightened on the pistols. She wouldn't be leaving this life just yet.

She let out a shout and burst upward from the ditch in which she had been sheltered. The rest of the men, her brothers among them, followed suit, their guns primed. They let off a volley of shots and more than a few of the advancing English went down, screaming as an arm or a leg was hit. Some did not have the opportunity to scream at all, before a Rebel bullet found its target.

But the English were good, professional, while the Rebels were little more than a ragtag bunch of volunteers from local villages. Too many of their shots went wide of the mark, too many of the men felt adrenalin surge through them and forgot to exhale as they fired, forgot to aim in the right places.

Reloading took time, too much time, and there was too little cover. They were almost at the summit of the hill of Tara, a place she'd roamed all over as a little girl, somewhere she knew as well as anywhere. That the English were now making it their own burned at her, and she was satisfied to see that one of her shots – that from her left hand, which had always been her strongest – had brought down its target. He went down without a sound, the ball scything clean through his throat and out the other side, covering the two men running close behind him in blood and fragments of bone.

Pistols were discarded in favour of swords, and the English

bayonet charge met Rebel steel with a flurry of metal-on-metal. Molly pulled out her own sword, knowing she was much better with a pistol than she would ever be with a blade, knowing that whomever she faced would have been trained in the arts of the bayonet and would know how to counter her moves, would have male strength to draw upon.

A gurgling cry reached her ears amidst the melee, and Molly knew before even turning her head in the direction of the source of that terrible sound, that one of her brothers had died.

It was Pat. Pat who had been the worst shot. The second eldest and slow since birth, he had joined up because his three brothers had. He had just been run through from stem to sternum by a bayonet blade from one of the swifter English runners. He jerked on the metal for a few seconds and she watched, *watched* as the Englishman put his foot on Pat's chest and tugged at the bayonet until it came loose, taking some of Pat with it as it came.

Something descended on Molly Weston at that moment; a rage so complete that it took her past anger and into a place of calm, where she ceased to value her own life and, instead, existed for the sole purpose of killing.

Her distinctive uniform drew the English to her like moths to a flame; upon recognising her gender, however, some hesitated for a vital second, perhaps out of a long-learnt sense of chivalry, perhaps out of surprise, perhaps in amusement. Whatever the reason, for three Englishmen it was the final, most fatal mistake of their lives.

She slit the throat of one with a clumsy rush manoeuvre that should never have worked, barrelling into him and slashing wildly, feeling warm blood spatter her face and sensing him go limp and crumple before her. She had to wipe her face with her green jacket to see properly and when her vision cleared, she realised that another opponent had just paused mid-swing in a stroke that would have cleaved her head from her shoulders. She was able to duck under the swing and stick her sword right into his chest, lancing his heart and killing him instantly.

'Whore,' a voice sounded from behind her, too close, far too close–

Time began to skip, to come in fractured bursts. She saw her brother, little Fergus, the youngest … saw his face as he killed the man about to run her through. Saw him smile at her, just as the tip of another soldier's bayonet emerged from his forehead and became lodged in his skull.

She watched the Englishman trying desperately to get his bayonet free of her dead brother's head, wrenching his weapon this way and that and causing Fergus' corpse to jerk and twitch crazily in some grotesque parody of life.

Molly Weston died truly in that moment, not eight minutes later when her body stopped breathing. She took her sword and chopped the Englishman's legs from under him. She was not strong enough, and her blade was not sharp enough to cut through them completely, but her cuts went deep and he screamed as he tumbled, knowing from the amount of blood he was losing that he was as good as gone.

She stood over him, as the battle raged around her and the Rebels fell in their scores, panicking, abandoning the ancient defences of the Hill of Tara, built in a different age for a different world. He pleaded in words that didn't even seem to be English any more. He babbled and choked as she drove the point of her sword right into his mouth, so hard that it went through his head and into the soil, pinning him in place like a butterfly in a glass case. His body went into spasms and he kicked and tried to break loose.

She found herself moving through the carnage even as it raged. Something about her step made the combatants ignore her, and she was able to walk through several duels unhindered. The English were largely ignoring her now, and despite having been outnumbered ten-to-one at the start of the battle, their superior skills and training meant they were, in the main, winning their duels with ease.

She stepped over the body of her oldest brother Finn at one point. It took her ten paces more before she stepped over his head.

Her once resplendent green uniform was now scarlet, soaked in blood. Molly Weston did not resemble a rallying call to womankind any longer. Walking slowly and deliberately through the savage ferocity of a slaughter in progress, she looked like something from another time, another world.

The stone was cool and solid to her touch. She had sat with her back to it on many a Sunday evening, regaled by her brothers and cousins, and on special occasions her uncle Lorcan, with tall tales of heroes and demons, of faeries and monsters. This sacred stone had been the centre of it all – the Lia Fáil, the Stone of Destiny, the throne of the High King of Ireland.

She leant against it and screamed as though she could undo all of the horrors with a single showing of despair. Her scream was long and loud and rose above the clashing and thudding and hollering of the deathscape around her. Then she sank to her knees and let out a shuddering breath.

The metal, when it slid into her, felt cold, incredibly cold. She was shocked at how much pain her body could feel – the bumps and scrapes she'd experienced as a child were nothing compared to this, the feeling of a foot-and-a-half of metal being pushed through her spine and into her stomach.

After a moment, the coldness vanished, the metal with it, and was replaced with warmth as her blood seeped from the gaping hole in her body. She was able to turn, and saw with faint disappointment that her killer had not stayed to ensure his job was complete – he had moved on, confident that she was beyond help. How professional.

You had to admire that … in a way …

Slowly, with care, she settled herself against the Lia Fáil, refusing to look down at the sea of blood now pooling around her. Instead she tried to remember those gentle evenings with her family beside her, death nothing but a far-off impossibility.

As she died, Molly Weston's blood seeped into the soil of the hill of Tara, along with the blood of more than four thousand of her fellows, cut down with such brutal ferocity that the collective violence of their deaths sent a shockwave through those forces normally undetected by humanity.

With that blood, a barrier was weakened. A door was opened.

Not completely. Not for long. But wide enough. For long enough.

*

Three days passed, and in that time the bodies of the fallen (United Irishmen and English soldiers alike) had begun to decompose. The hillside was a stinking fetid sea of corpses, covered in mayflies and maggots, all in the early and most vigorous stages of decomposition.

All save one.

A hand, its fingers long and tapered and immaculate, reached out and gently touched Molly Weston, turned her lifeless face this way and that. She was propped still against the Stone of Destiny, all but drained of blood. And yet not one maggot crawled in her wounds. Not a single fly feasted on her. She was untouched, preserved.

'We have you to thank,' the man cupping her face whispered to her. He was on his haunches before her, and closer examination of him would have challenged that definition of him as a *man*. His face was angular, his smile needle-sharp and hiding a tongue too darting, his limbs overly long and unnaturally flexible.

Sensing something in the air, the pale man whipped his head up and held out his hand, palm flat, as if warding something off.

'Not her!' he ordered. '*Not* this one! Go! Find one of the fallen.'

There was silence across the hilltop. Until, twenty feet or so away, one of the decomposing English corpses began to twitch. It was only a finger at first, and only the slightest of movements. A few seconds later, however, the torso jerked, as if some kindly and hopelessly optimistic time-travelling doctor had decided to try to revive the dead man with a set of defibrillators.

The pale man looked over at the act of resurrection happening not a stone's throw from him. The only emotion on his thin face was that of impatience.

'Are you planning on taking all day, Dian?'

With horrendous clumsiness, the corpse got up. It took several attempts. In the three days it had lain on the grass, worms, insects and moisture had already set to work with terrible efficiency. It lurched to the side, barely able to stand.

'Dooooother,' it croaked, through a throat torn to shreds from bullets and beetles. 'We muuuust go…'

'Patience, brother Dian,' Dother replied, holding up a hand. 'Credit where it's due. Mother has sent us ahead to prepare this world for her arrival. This one and her kind have made this possible, ending our exile through their sacrifice. You, go. Find a more hospitable host for yourself than that pathetic vessel.'

Dian, looking out at him through the one remaining eye the English solider possessed, said nothing. He shambled off, jerking like a puppet, but making remarkable speed across the fields. Dother remained there until he sensed Dian was at a sufficient distance. He brought his face close to that of Molly Weston, almost brushing her unblemished lips with his own.

'How to reward you …?' he mused.

And then he saw it.

Alone of all the life on the hilltop, a single creature had made a home on her corpse. He saw it flit across the top of her breasts and, with a speed and dextrousness a human could never hope to match, he captured it in his fist, which he now uncurled, even as he commanded the creature not to escape. It obeyed, though not really understanding why it did, and he smiled at it.

'Yes,' he said with quiet satisfaction, 'you shall be mine.'

Slowly, reverentially, he placed the spider inside Molly Weston's mouth.

'Your world,' he said, indicating the hillside carnage, 'does not want you. Your country is overrun, your family gone. A woman fighting in a man's war. There is no place for you here. Join me. I can give you a home. With me, you will belong.'

It was as though he were asking the spider to memorise the speech. Pausing only a heartbeat more, he issued a command to the tiny creature inside Molly Weston's mouth and watched as it duly scuttled down her dead throat. From here he took over, knowing the spider had only moments of life left to it in the oxygen-starved environment of her interior.

He took the tiny spark of life that flickered inside the spider, feeling the little thing die as he did so, and he brought it to the dried-up well of life that had once housed Molly Weston's soul.

With a cry that had not been heard in this realm for many centuries, he smashed the spark into the wellspring.

Molly's eyes jerked open instantly. He hopped to his feet lightly, acrobatically, bounding backwards to be sufficiently out of range of her wildly thrashing body, though not beyond the range of her squeals and cries and shrieks of outrage and fear and pain as the remaking fit overtook her, and the spider's lifespark, fused with her human soul, began to have the effect he'd known it would.

She grew. Her skin darkened and hardened. Her mouth closed up and then was reopened as a huge and hungry maw ringed with teeth, her human DNA overwriting the spider's influence. Hard bristles formed all over her new skin. Her legs melded together and fused, rippling around and above her distending head and torso to become a monstrous carapace. And the legs – oh! The glorious legs, four pairs of them, erupted, each pair causing her to emit a roar that shook the ground on which he stood.

When completed, feral and confused, she launched herself at him and he dodged her attacks effortlessly time and again, spinning and ducking under her legs as she crashed to a thrashing heap, her human instincts colliding with her new spider-form.

Until eventually, as he'd known it would, the hunger overtook her and she stood before him, defeated in her attempts to attack him. She still possessed all of the fight and the spirit she had possessed as a human. He had chosen well.

'If you're hungry, you're knee-deep in the dead,' he pointed out, his first words to his greatest servant, whom he would one day call Sarah.

She refused. For the longest time, she refused, but was too terrified to move from that hilltop, retreating into a deep dark hole, wallowing in bewilderment and horror at the thing she had become, slowly starving to death.

He waited outside her parlour, the fly to her spider, and he told her the legends anew. The destiny of the faerie race. The gift he had bestowed upon her. Immortality. He would teach her, he promised, to project a glamour so that she could walk amongst her former kind, if she so wished.

There had been no afterlife upon her death, no Christian heaven, no Abrahamic God to salve her eternal soul. She had killed. She was a murderer. He represented her only hope, not for salvation, but for something more glorious.

He watched her emerge from that hole into the fields of the dead.

He watched as she feasted.

*

BELFAST, NOW

More of his wolf-shapes were joining him, at either end of the street. They had the place surrounded by now, Dother knew, but that barrier seemed as resolute as ever. He had to hand it to Dermot, and by that, of course, he meant he was aching to kill the little prick.

One of the wolf-shapes misjudged the radius of the barrier and was pushed backward onto the road. An oncoming car filled with fat useless stinking fetid humans blared its horn and swerved around, almost careening into the fence of one of the houses further down the street–

Yes. Yes, he *had* it.

He glanced at Sarah. 'Don't play with your food so,' he told the spider, as her mouth closed over the luckless boy's torso. He tossed the discarded right leg to a grateful wolf behind him. 'We have work to do.'

COUNTY WEXFORD, IRELAND, 43 AD

It was the Battle of Mag Tuiread all over again.

The little settlement had been forged in a clearing in the woods, built around the river, its circumference slowly widening as new homes were built and sons and daughters grew up to occupy them.

The Formorians had burst in from all sides, with a synchronicity that would have been impressive had the consequences been less horrific.

The people here may have known of the beings that walked the land. Hunting parties may have glimpsed them in the distance, moving through the trees. Whispers from travellers beyond their small borders spoke of secret doors in the plains, of fires seen on distant hilltops and the sound of song and savage laughter carrying across the night air. There may have been talk, and whispers, but none of that could have prepared them for the slaughter to come.

Danny witnessed a huge, one-eyed Formorian warrior cleave a man's head in two with one blow of a warhammer the size of a twelve-year-old. The man's wife, whom he had been shielding, screamed like nothing he'd ever heard before and he realised dimly that he was hearing an entire person's life spill out from their mouth as they made the last sound they knew they were ever likely to make; it was a scream that raged of loss and injustice and fear.

The warhammer curved in the air. The scream ended in a bloody gurgle.

This was no fairytale.

It was the same story wherever he looked. The village had a population of maybe two hundred, judging by the houses and by the numbers of people he could see fleeing, running from their homes or into their homes, depending on where the Formorians currently were – and they were everywhere, it seemed. On horseback, on foot, they rode or stomped on thunderous legs through everything these people had built, weapons swinging, the end of every swing seeming to find soft human flesh.

A few of the men tried to fight back. He ached to see it; their bravery, as they stood up to these great impossibilities on their own all-too-mortal legs, swinging makeshift swords or farming implements with whatever measure of skill they possessed. What strikes did get through the Formorians' casual defensive measures simply rebounded off the creatures' hides as though the men were battling beings made of rubber. He saw the knowledge of their own doom appear in their eyes before that doom was meted out at the end of a spear, an axe, a sword, a hammer.

Blood ran until the soil was red.

Staggering on nerveless legs towards the central well where he'd first materialised, he was almost face to face with a Formorian before he knew what was happening. It was monstrous, nine feet tall, and with a great horn protruding from the centre of its forehead like a rhino. Whatever it was, it seemed to have the mental capabilities of a beast, too; it swung that great lumbering head, nostrils flaring as it scented the air. Two tiny eyes, almost completely blue, were set deep a few inches below that horn and they searched the massacre for a new victim amongst the scattering villagers.

It spotted two little boys, huddled together on the grass between two dead warriors. They clung to each other, not crying, not screaming, but so pale they looked like ghosts in the sunshine.

Two boys he recognised.

Glon. Gaim.

'No,' Danny breathed.

The rhino smiled, exposing two rows of teeth in both its upper and lower jaws; the foremost teeth were needle-sharp for tearing, whilst those at the back were thick and blunt for grinding. Hefting the axe he carried in both arms, he took a long step toward the boys.

Danny remembered the Morrigan's tears as she watched her younger self play with her two oldest sons in the pond; her insistence that she leave Danny and go to watch over them. He'd assumed it was so he could witness that little tête-à-tête between the younger Morrigan and Caderyn that had given him such pause for thought. But perhaps it had been to be with her boys, to see them in the last few moments of their innocent lives, before … before this.

He had a feeling that this was a memory she visited often, condemned to wander through it as impotent and ineffectual as a ghost. He could not see her younger self now, or any version of her, but he assumed the younger version was somewhere apart from this horrific event, perhaps protecting her husband and youngest child.

He did not want to be immaterial. He did not want to be powerless to stop this from happening; to have to stand by and witness horrors like these.

Standing there, in the midst of that chaos and slaughter, screams ringing in his ears, the smell of blood and death flooding his nostrils, fear and terror in the air so thick he could taste them and sights assaulting his eyes that he had never imagined to see, all of it seemed to coalesce somewhere deep inside; he felt his synaesthesia bleed sights into sounds into smells into tastes …

… and the Formorian, about to step through him, stopped in his tracks.

Blinked.

Took a step back.

Danny cocked his head. The Formorian did the same, that

massive horn tilting, the sun glinting off the axe's bloody blade.

'Oh …' Danny said as the penny dropped, '*fuck.*'

With a roar that seemed to shake the world, the Formorian swung his axe. Danny saw it coming, and knew as soon as the movement began that he would never be able to get out of the way of that swing; the Formorian was as strong as he was ugly, and that blade would soon bite into his midriff and carry on until it exited him somewhere around the right shoulder, slicing him neatly–

– or it would, except he wasn't standing.

He was ducking. He'd *already* ducked.

The axe whooshed as it cut through the air directly above his head, passing harmlessly over him. He straightened up and realised the Formorian, expecting his weapon to meet some resistance (in this case Danny's internal organs) was now slightly off-balance. Of course, he wouldn't remain this way for long; he'd soon step into the swing, regain his footing, and bring the axe around for another–

– except he couldn't.

He couldn't because, with a snarl, Danny had leaped onto the giant's back.

It was as if, a part of him mused, some portion of his consciousness was existing a few seconds ahead of time and had the ability to review courses of action that would or wouldn't work and pass them back to his past self.

The Formorian yelled in outrage, and Danny's world tilted crazily as he began to ride the world's ugliest mount. For a split second, as the Formorian danced a jig of fury designed to unseat his rider, Danny had the attention of the two astonished little boys witnessing this performance; unknown to them, two more Formorians were approaching them from the rear, weapons raised.

Rhino *should* have dropped the axe to the ground, freed his hands and reached around to pluck off his passenger. Failing that, he *should* have simply flopped backwards full-length onto the soil and squashed Danny into a thin paste.

Mighty warriors, the Formorians. But not too bright.

Instead what Rhino did was swing his axe up above his head to try and bring it down on Danny, intending to split this annoyance's head open like a log on a chopping block. It was a massively difficult stroke and one that Danny had no difficulty whatsoever in avoiding.

Unfortunately for Rhino, he had somewhat more difficulty in avoiding it.

Danny dismounted the beast as it thumped into the ground. He planted a foot on its chest and with a heave that set his arms afire with strain, removed the axe from where it was embedded in skull and brainmatter. By the time he had lifted it (*How? How am I doing this? How am I strong enough?*), the approaching Formorians' footfalls had alerted Glon and Gaim, and they had scampered towards Danny, sheltering behind him and peering out.

He faced the beasts down, their rampaging approach slowing to something considerably more careful as they caught sight of their fallen brother, lying in a pool of his own head-guts.

It was only then that Danny realised the sounds of battle – one-sided battle though it may have been – had ceased. He risked a quick glance around him. The Formorians had stopped; they were holding the humans they had been herding for slaughter in position to prevent them from escaping, but for the moment, the killing had ceased. About a hundred pairs of terrified human eyes were fixed directly on him.

'Are you a god?' one of the two facing him now, a cyclops, rumbled at him.

This was it. That crazy reflex-stuff switched itself off for a moment and he felt back in control.

Roll with it. Tell them you're a god. Tell them to fuck off. Most importantly, for the love of Christ, at all costs avoid having a fight with these fuckers, because, first of all, there's no guarantee that that stuff with horn-boy wasn't one incredible run of good luck and, second, just holding this axe is miracle enough. If you actually have to swing it, it's going to take you a fortnight to complete a stroke.

'Not *just* a god!' he proclaimed, loud enough for all the Formorians to hear. *Where's the fuckin' Morrigan? Either one of her? Where is she?*

There was a silence.

'Yes …?' Cyclops prompted.

'I'm a hero! The biggest fuckin' hero you bunch o' cunts will ever see! And this village is under my protection, so you'd all better hit the fuckin' beach. Now!'

Danny paused.

'Who are you?' one of the Formorians asked. He was huge, and shaggy, and about the size of a small cottage. He wore a skull ring on one of his fingers. The skull was human.

He couldn't say 'Danny', could he? What, then? Setanta? Was he even about yet? And if he called himself that, would he be doomed to an inglorious collapse? John McClane? He could look good in a progressively-dirtier white vest, no problem. *Now I have a big fuckin' axe. Ho. Ho. Ho.*

'I am the Morrigan!'

He heard the words, heard them come from somewhere right where he was standing, but he had no memory of speaking them.

What was more – he glanced downward – he seemed to have grown breasts. Rather nice ones, in point of fact.

'Okay, ride's over. Time to come out of there,' a voice from beside him said.

He glanced over. It was the Morrigan – the older version, his travelling companion. She reached over with a muscular arm and, with an extremely strange sensation that felt like someone had just plunged his head into liquid ice and then slapped him, hard, she pulled him free from inside the body of her younger counterpart.

'What …?' he said, dazed, things belatedly falling into place; the way the boys had run to him, had sheltered behind him. His instant command of reflexes and fighting moves well beyond his ability. Okay, so he knew *what*. But he didn't know how–

She shushed him with a gesture and pointed back at the warrior maiden, currently clothed in the modest garb of a peasant woman, standing over the body of an extremely dead Formorian with both hands on a *ridiculously* large axe, an entire horde of beasts facing her down.

Skull Ring came forward. From his bearing and his stride, and the way his fellows scattered from about him, Danny instantly surmised he was the leader of this particular band of merry murderers. He sized up the woman before him, approximately one-fifth his size and probably one-tenth his body weight. A massive grin cragged across his enormous face, as if the San Andreas Fault had just fissured his jaw.

'You?' he said. '*You* are the Goddess of War? Living here amongst these … rats?'

Danny could see the Morrigan's eyes flash. 'They are *not* rats,' she said softly.

'They die as easily as rats,' Skull Ring pointed out.

All things considered, this was not a wise thing to say.

The Morrigan spat. The glob of spittle landed square on the disembodied head of the fallen Formorian. Every single person, captor or captive, was silent as she did it. She eyed Skull Ring.

'Some rats are bigger than others,' she said.

Over the Morrigan's shoulder, Danny's chest tightened as he saw three newcomers on the scene – Caderyn, with little Coscar still a bundle in his arms and a large Formorian who stood guard over them, prodding them along with a vicious-looking pike. Caderyn's eyes bugged as he took in the scene; his wife facing down the Formorian leader, in front of the entire surviving village. If the Morrigan saw, or sensed, his arrival, she made no gesture to indicate it.

Skull Ring reached around his back and brought out a spear so huge that a human-sized equivalent would have seemed a matchstick in comparison. He let it lie across his hands, rolling it in his grip. He got no outward reaction from his opponent, but Danny noticed that, without quite making it obvious, she was retreating inch by inch, pushing Glon and Gaim further and further back, giving herself more room to manoeuvre when the need arose.

'What happens,' he rumbled, 'if I kill the Goddess of War in battle?'

The Morrigan smiled. Skull Ring was getting ready to strike, but the Morrigan was coolness personified. 'Come and find out.'

By the time the words left her mouth he was already charging in fury, his roar ringing through the ears of the throng. Danny despaired; such was the bastard's size and power that it would take nothing short of a nuclear warhead to have stopped his charge, and he doubted the Morrigan had anything like that in her arsenal.

She didn't. But it didn't matter.

Rather than try to stop him, she let go of the axe-handle for long enough to shove her sons away from her in either direction, sending them safely out of the sphere of the battle. This done, and with only a second or so left before he crashed into her, she allowed herself to drop to the earth below. Skull Ring's charge steamrolled over her a moment later.

When he came to a halt and turned, the Morrigan was nowhere to be seen; only the blade of Rhino's enormous axe was visible, glinting in the light, the rest of it having been forced into the ground. Skull Ring actually lifted one of his massive feet, then the other, to see if her flattened body was pressed to their soles, as if she were a leaf he'd stepped on. Seeing nothing, he blinked, confused, and then began to laugh. The Formorians scattered around the village joined in.

That was when the axe began to rise.

She *had* been stepped on. But she had not been flattened; this was not hard concrete, it was soft and yielding soil. Even so,

Danny could only guess at how much it must have hurt to have been pressed so far into the earth as to actually sink beneath the surface – the bones in a human body would not have been able to cope.

One thing was perfectly clear, though, as she rose from the muck, covered from head to toe in its debris. The Morrigan was *not* human.

With no apparent effort, she hefted the axe. Skull Ring made a noise of outrage and fury that might have been words but they were too swallowed in anger to be comprehensible. He brought the spear he carried around, ready to hold it before him – so angry had he been by her initial taunt that he had all but forgotten his weapon in the charge. Not this time. This time he would drive it through this impudent wretch.

He managed one step forward.

This was because the Morrigan had pirouetted, moving like a hammer thrower at the Olympics, flinging the axe thirty feet through the air; a flash of metal and wood that whipped around end-over-end too fast for the eye to follow. Too fast, that is, until it entered Skull Ring's chest. The axe buried itself so deep that it disappeared from sight. Danny expected to see it rip free from his back, having passed clean through. It did not.

Everyone's gaze shifted from the filthy, earth-encrusted Morrigan, her chest heaving and her eyes white and wide, to the Formorian chief, stock still, mouth gaping in surprise. A dribble of red blood appeared on his lips.

In that moment Danny had absolutely no trouble whatsoever in believing the woman before him was more than human, a goddess made flesh.

Danny felt the impact as the Formorian's massive body toppled to the earth. Looking around, he felt as though he were in one of those sixties TV shows where they ran the end credits over a frozen shot of the cast. No one within a half-mile radius of that woman, that incredible goddess, was moving so much as a hair.

It was a coin toss to say who looked the most stunned, although the onlookers fell into three distinct groups on that score: the Formorians, who looked stunned and nervous; the villagers, who were stunned and terrified; or Glon and Gaim, who looked at their mother with amazement and hero worship in equal measure.

Only Caderyn fell outside the group entirely; his eyes were just as fixed on her as everyone else's, but his expression was unreadable.

'Go,' the Morrigan said, turning slowly in a complete circle as she spoke, pointing a finger at a Formorian here and there to make it clear whom she was addressing. 'Leave this village now. It is under *my* protection. Return here and I will hunt down *every single* member of your race. Do you understand?'

The cyclops who had been one of the original two Formorians to approach her before the ill-fated intervention of Skull Ring was the one to respond. He seemed to stop just short of falling to his knees and grovelling. 'Goddess, we did not *know* that you–' he gabbled desperately.

'Is that an excuse for this massacre?'

His single eye blinked furiously in a gesture Danny translated as the creature's feverish attempts to explain. He waved his arms in the air. He even took the extremely brave step of moving a pace closer to her. 'You do not understand. We were *order*–'

Thunnnng.

The eye blinked, more slowly this time. The cyclops swayed on his feet and then pitched forward, dead before he hit the ground. An arrow protruded from his back.

Another wave of noise, much like the din that had signalled the arrival of the Formorians, began to rumble from all sides of the village. Both the remaining villagers and their Formorian captors reacted to the rumbling nervously. Danny saw Caderyn motion furiously to the surviving men to tell everyone to gather in the centre of the village, near the young Morrigan.

The Formorians were much too thrown by recent events, and now this new development, to resist when their hostages began stealing away. In only a few minutes what was left of the human village was gathered in a tightly-packed circle around the Morrigan. No. Danny looked closer; by all rights the circle *should* have been around her, but a detailed inspection revealed that the only people standing truly close to her were Glon and Gaim, with Caderyn and Coscar beside them. The rest of the village huddled around one another, sending fearful glances in the Morrigan's direction.

A horn blast sounded. A cry went up.

For the second time, the woods around the village disgorged a party of invaders. Not Formorians this time – these newcomers were human in appearance, albeit taller, grander, stronger than humans had any right to be, all of them riding white horses that were likewise perfect specimens. He recognised them immediately as Tuatha: their appearance had not changed one iota since that landing on the beach he had witnessed a few hours and a few centuries previous.

Formorian shouts rang out. Danny thought he heard a few voices, raised not in battle cries, but in attempts at dialogue. No weapons were raised. The Formorians clearly did not want a fight with these Tuatha. In that respect, they got their wish; this was no fight.

It was another massacre.

In less than sixty seconds, it was all over. The final Formorian body lay twitching on the soil. Riders dismounted their white horses, slapping glistening flanks while the horses whinnied and stamped their hooves, steam rising from their bodies in the frigid air.

One Tuatha, magnificent in gold armour and wearing a gold helmet, was the last to dismount. He left his horse, the biggest on show, with his fellow warriors and walked with a swagger over to the assembled humans and their special guests. Even before he reached up to unclasp that golden helmet Danny had identified him, not only from the regal silver sword that hung from his belt, but from the swagger with which he walked. Only life's true pricks had a dander like that.

'Bres,' said the Morrigan.

The Duty

'OhmyGod! Howisshe? How'sthechile? Jesus!'

Danny removed his mother's hooked claws from his upper arms. The woman was vibrating like a hummingbird on crack, hovering a quarter-inch above the hospital floor, giving off waves of terrified pleasure and ecstatic worry. He gestured down the maternity ward corridor and made to open his mouth to tell his ma where to go to get to Ellie's bed, but it was too late. With another outburst that was half-orgasm, half-stroke, his ma was away.

Like a granny homing missile she turned correctly to the left and there was a wet, delighted shriek.

'He's fine,' he said weakly, knowing at this precise moment his exhausted girlfriend would be too tired to argue at the sudden appearance of the maternity ward's newest grandmother, and that a very tiny, very pink bundle would have been unceremoniously plucked from his incubator.

'All right, son?' came a voice from behind him.

Danny turned. His da was there. He'd obviously been outpaced in the Tour De Grandson – though knowing Linda Morrigan,

Superman could have taken so many performance-enhancing drugs that Ben Jonson would have staged an intervention on his behalf and he still wouldn't have beaten her down that hospital corridor.

'All right,' he returned.

'Congratulations,' Tony said, offering his hand. Danny shook it. He could see the intention to hug flash in his father's eyes, so he rocked back on his heels, only very slightly, but enough to make it clear that the attempt would not be welcomed. The moment passed, about as swiftly as moments usually did between the two men these days.

'Everything okay with the wee one?' Tony half-spoke, half-coughed. He started moving down the corridor toward Ellie's room. Danny fell into step beside him robotically.

'Aye, seems grand.'

'It's some experience, eh.'

'Yeah,' he said hollowly. *Wasn't wonderful enough to persuade you to stick about Da.*

'I remember ...' Tony began, moving to let a nurse pass between them. But as he did, he must have sensed the unspoken words hanging in the air between them, and when the nurse had passed, the thought remained unfinished and the words unsaid.

'Do you want ...' Tony said instead, his throat dry. 'Do you want something from the machine? I might grab your ma a wee tea or something.'

'Now?' Danny said. 'Right now?' *With the grandson you've never seen fifteen feet away, you're concerned your wife might be gasping for a cuppa? Really, Da?*

'Yeah. So can I get you something …?'

Danny looked at his da and made zero attempt to hide what was dancing behind his eyes as he did so. 'No, Da,' he said with finality. 'No, I don't want anything off ye. Thanks.'

With that, he turned the corner and left him behind.

THE MOURNE MOUNTAINS, IRELAND, 1968 AD

'C'mon you, big lad!' James Morrigan called affably behind him, as he swung his legs over the fence gate and landed softly in the field beyond. 'Not tired already are ye?'

The fourteen-year-old hard on his heels shook his head in response, too breathless to compose a reply verbally. James watched as his son clambered over the metal rungs of the rusted gate and felt once again a surge of pride. Still a boy perhaps, and a little skinny, but what wee Tony Morrigan lacked in muscle he made up for in sheer bloody-minded determination.

Tony looked into the eyes of his father now and, as if reading his mind and proving his point, adjusted the weight of the pack he carried, a smaller version of the pack James himself had around his shoulders, and pressed on. Any hint of a drivable road had ended miles ago; they'd had to abandon the trusty Triumph Herald, a big red monster of a car, to make the rest of the journey on foot.

Five miles over countryside on foot carrying a heavy bag and, but for a hint of ruddiness in his cheeks and a deeper rhythm to his breathing, you'd scarcely have noticed James was bothered.

'Not tired yet, Da. Gonna tell me a few more stories before we get there?'

James clapped his son on the back, partially in amusement, but mostly so that he could push the boy ahead a few paces so he couldn't see the trepidation written on his face.

'I think you know them better'n me now, son,' James said as they began to walk briskly across the field, the rolling greenery around them thinning out as the landscape tilted upward and the hills started to become the Mournes. Hard to believe Warrenpoint and Rostrevor weren't all that far away; the only hint of human civilisation as far as the eye could see was a solitary farmhouse, and even that would soon be swallowed by the horizon as they continued to climb.

'Tell me about Carman and the Morrigan's final battle,' Tony begged him.

'Ach son, I must have told you that one about ten times ...'

'I know, but it's my *favourite*,' the boy replied. 'I love all that final battle stuff. Isn't there like a prophecy–'

'*No*,' James snapped, a mite more sharply than he meant to. He saw the boy recoil slightly as if stung, and regretted it instantly, but the more his son talked about this, the more he realised that, as intently as Tony had taken everything in, he hadn't really *heard* what his father'd said. 'This isn't Tolkien. I wish you'd never read those daft books ...'

Tony was walking faster now, outstripping his father's walking pace, obviously hoping that he could outrun the lecture. James disappointed him in this by stretching out a hand and placing it on his shoulder firmly enough to get him to stop. Tony halted, looking up at his father in the way children did, recalcitrance mixed with resentment at being rebuked in the first place.

'Son, you're a Morrigan,' he said, realising even as he said the words that this was almost the exact same speech his father had given him, though he'd been three years older and a foot taller than Tony when he'd received it. 'My only son, just as I was my father's only son, just as he was his father's. For centuries, our family has continued in a line of single sons born. Why?'

'Because–'

He raised a finger, and Tony fell silent. 'Because,' he said, 'we're charged with defending this country from *them*. From the Low Folk.'

'Like Mr McStravick.'

James sighed. 'Anthony Morrigan! For the hundredth millionth time, Mr McStravick has a harelip, God love him. That does *not* make him an agent of the powers of darkness.'

'Ach, Da!' Tony burst out incredulously. 'It's not just the lip! Wee Seamy McGlinch from Nansen Street kicked his ball into his back garden and nobody seen him for a fortnight after he tried to go and get it!'

'A fortnight?'

Tony fidgeted. 'Well,' he allowed, 'it was ages, like. Definitely the next day.'

'Same wee Seamy McGlinch that broke our back fuckin' window last summer playin' hurley?' James said hotly, scowling at the memory. 'He probably got a toe up the hole and spent the night cryin' into his soup over it, wee ballix. Must get oul McStravick a pint when we get back to Belfast ... but anyway, stop interruptin'!' he said, his voice rising in annoyance at himself as much as at his son. Somehow this wasn't proving to be the big inspirational speech he'd hoped it to be.

He glanced around. The farmhouse hadn't quite disappeared, but it was at least three miles away and looked deserted; given the time it seemed likely that the farmer was off tending to one of his fields or at market. Yes. This was safe enough.

'This place,' he said, gesturing around him even as he unshouldered his bag. 'This place, son, goes way back. Some places, cities especially, they've been too modern too long. Magic slides off them like oil tryin' to mix with water. But places like this … old places … they've still got the ley lines.'

His son perked up at this. This was new. 'Ley lines?' he echoed.

'That's the word for them now,' James said, as he set the backpack down on the grass, grateful to be rid of its weight but unable to stop his stomach from churning at what was going to come next. He kept talking. It kept him occupied. 'Words change, son, as time passes. What used to just be called *magic* – well, that changes most of all. They call it all sorts of things now. They call it intuition. Psychic ability. Precognition. Telekinesis. It's all that new thing, that whaddaya call it? Sci somethin'?'

'Sci-fi,' his son supplied instantly. Too instantly for James' liking.

James rolled his eyes. 'Sci-fi,' he repeated mockingly. 'Never catch on, you wait and see. It's like that *Lord of the Rings* shite – it's good for a laugh, and that's about the height of it.'

'*Right*, Da,' his son nodded, and James failed to detect the faint note of impatience in his voice, which was probably just as well. 'So, um. You were sayin', about ley lines …?'

'Know them big electricity pylons up around the city?'

Tony frowned. 'Yeah …?'

'Imagine an ancient, invisible version of them. Strung up all over the country – and I mean *all over* son; not a corner left out, not a patch of land that's not on one or near one – except it's not electricity they carry.'

'It's … magic?'

James was crouching now, his fingers fumbling at the zip of the backpack. He looked at the boy. 'Why d'you say it like that?' he asked.

'Like what?' the boy replied, feigning innocence, before crumbling in the face of his da's expression. He started scuffing the ground with his feet, finding things to do so that he wouldn't have to look at his father. 'Ach, Da …' he said. 'I mean, this was a laugh when I was younger, but I thought it was sorta like Santa, y'know. When I got big enough you'd have a wee word with me. I'm *fourteen* now, like. I'm gettin' a wee bit old for the …' he faltered, 'for the stories. I still love them, like, and you tell them *amazing* but, well, you get on like I'm s'posed to think it's all *true* …'

James unzipped the bag.

'About fuckin' time!' a voice called from within.

The older man tried not to take too much satisfaction when he saw the colour drain from his son's face. Or when Tony took a few steps backwards, away from the occupant of the bag now clambering free from inside. Only eighteen inches high he was, an incredibly wizened little old man, wearing a tiny little grey-green suit buckled with big black round buttons and capped off with smart little black shoes. He rubbed at his back and cast a filthy look in James' direction.

'You coulda strapped the fuckin' bag down! Six fuckin' hours in that boot bein' thrown from one end to the bastard other!' he said indignantly. His voice wasn't high-pitched in the slightest; it was amazingly deep for someone of his tiny stature.

'Buh ...' Tony gibbered, losing his footing as he tried to take another long step backward, shooting terrified looks at the newcomer and accusatory ones at his father. He landed on his arse on the grass and scrambled backwards on his hands and knees as though he thought the little creature was going to launch itself at him.

'What's up with *him*?'

'Brian, this is my son Tony. Tony, this is Brian.'

Incredulity penetrated the fog of amazement and fear that had descended on the teenager. 'Brian?' he said. 'As in *King*–'

James waved a hand desperately to try and stop him, but it was too late.

'That's right! That's right! *King* Brian's the name!' exclaimed the little man, doing a happy jig of joy and doffing his little cloth cap in respect to Tony, who by now had recovered sufficiently to get to his feet again. He sidled around in a long circular motion to stand once more beside his father, giving Brian a wide berth.

'*King* my arse,' James scoffed. 'He only took that name on after watching that stupid film.'

'But he *is* a lepre–'

'Yes I am! Fifteen centuries born and bred. Begorrah!'

'Leave out that *begorrah* shite will ye? Does he *look* like an

American? He's not a leprechaun. He's one of the Low Folk.'

Brian scowled at James. It was amazing how quickly darkness could descend on a face that only moments before had been full of twinkle and mischief. 'Low Folk indeed!' he muttered, adding a few other choice comments under his breath – Tony couldn't catch the words, but the tone definitely wasn't complimentary.

'I don't believe it,' he said faintly. 'I don't ... I mean, he's a ... but that means ...'

'Yep,' his father said, clapping him on the back. 'So' – and he was really twisting the knife now – 'what were you sayin' before? Sorry, I musta tuned out for a bit there ...'

His son flushed scarlet. 'Nothin,' he said.

'Attaboy,' James grinned at him, and then his voice lowered. 'Look ... I don't blame ye, son. I had my doubts too and when I was a boy we grew up with all this stuff; everyone did. The world seems to be movin' on ... its hard to believe in magic when there's a box in everyone's house that can show them anything imaginable. God only knows what *your* son will make of it when you have to tell him one day.'

Brian muttered something. James whirled on his heels so suddenly that the little creature almost died of fright. '*What* did you say?' he hissed.

'N-n-nothin ... save that, God willin', his son will be big and strong,' Brian protested, face contorted in contrition. Tony knew that Brian was lying. He'd stared directly into those tiny little eyes and for a split-second could see something buried there – he'd glimpsed resentment, and more besides – before it was gone again and Brian was all smiles and beams. He reminded Tony of the informants the police used in the gangster movies – shifty, untrustworthy, but *just* useful enough to merit their survival.

James too knew that Brian couldn't be fully trusted, but today they needed him. He was to be their guide. Besides, for one whole day and night, Brian was bound by the same incantation that James had used to summon him and he was duty-bound to obey their commands.

So Brian scouted ahead – he had caught the scent of what they were after (something that James had still not revealed to Tony). The farmhouse had long since vanished and they were now deep in the Mournes. On another day, in another state of mind, Tony might have wished for a few moments to linger and appreciate the breathtaking vista laid out below them, the blue ribbon of the sea along one horizon, the landscape of County Down on the other.

He remembered the stories his father had told him – could visualise the battles and chases and legends springing up fully-formed from the soil, but with the revelation that at least part of that was *real*, he found the images even more vivid.

Every so often Brian would reappear and give them new directions. Occasionally he would mutter to himself and give only the most cryptic of statements about how close they were to whatever it was they pursued. He knew his father wouldn't have appreciated the comparison, but there was something distinctly Gollum-like about Brian now, and chills went down Tony's spine: after all, Gollum had led Frodo and Sam into a trap …

'Oh, don't worry about him,' his father said softly, when Tony finally found the courage to voice his concerns. 'His masters know the help he's given me in the past, you see, and they aren't the forgiving sort. They won't care if he was under an influence or not: for helping a Morrigan, he's as good as dead if they get him. That's why he comes so quickly when I call him, you know,' and he smiled grimly. 'It's not just because of the comehither I have on him; it's because he daren't stray too far from me.'

'Even in the city?'

James glanced at him. 'You think they don't come to the cities, too?' he said, and shook his head. 'Son, some of them can make themselves seem as human as you or me. Some of them …' and Tony shivered on seeing the fear on his father's face as he spoke, 'some of them, you'd never know a thing until it's too late, and they'd get you. Then if you're lucky, all they'd do is eat you.'

Tony's head spun – he had learned so much already that he felt as though his head weighed twice as much with the increase in knowledge. Until today the biggest concern he'd had was catching Pauline Scullion's eye next time the disco was on down at St Bridget's Hall, and now his father was telling him anyone, Pauline included, could be a monster painted with a human sheen, slavering over the prospect of sinking fangs into his soft flesh. Although ironically, in a way, that *would* make what he'd read about Pauline in the boys' toilets at St Bridget's accurate (after all, that was what had piqued his interest in her in the first place).

The more he heard about this, the more he was beginning to wish it *had* been filed under 'Santa'. He learned from his father that in their true form, faeries could be as tiny as Brian, or smaller, but they could also be twelve foot tall. They could change form. They could command creatures similar to themselves: a faerie with wolf aspects could command dogs, while a spider faerie – Jesus Christ, he wasn't going to sleep for a month imagining one of *those* – had complete control over every creepy-crawly that scuttled within a half-mile radius.

Their only weakness, the only thing that stopped them completely in their tracks was iron – good solid iron. Apparently that was where the myth about horseshoes bringing good luck came from; some sort of buried racial memory.

This was terrifying. But it was also *class*. This was beyond his wildest dreams. His mind raced with the possibilities. If all this was true, then surely he and his da had to have some sort of–

He asked the question breathlessly. The response was not what he expected.

'Nothing? What'd you mean, nothing?'

James laughed. He seemed to find his son's consternation hilarious. '*Powers*? Why, what were you expectin'? Did you think I only bought the car for show and I really flapped my arms and flew to work?'

'Ah, but come on, Da!' Tony wailed. 'These things have claws and fangs and can do all sorts of fancy magic tricks and we're the only ones that can stop them, and we've got *no* powers at all? I thought we were descended from the Morrigan! Wasn't she some goddess or what? She coulda give us *something*!'

'She did,' his father replied. 'She gave us a role in the world, son. She gave us a purpose. There's precious few people out there can say similar. And,' he added, as if making a concession, 'if it's any consolation, we've got … well, you'll know it when it happens … we have a knack. An instinct. I wouldn't call it a power, but it sets us apart. Makes us able to see them. Sense them. As for powers though, no, I think you're gonna be disappointed. Unless you're the one in the prophecy,' and he laughed again.

Tony stopped. They were almost at the top of one of the peaks, and he could see a flicker of movement ahead that was probably Brian returning with fresh directions. His legs ached, his lungs burned, and his mind was reeling from what he was hearing. He wasn't about to let *that* one pass without comment.

'Prophecy?' he said. '*Prophecy?* I thought this wasn't Tolkien, Da?'

'Don't be cheeky, son.'

'But …' Tony protested. 'But you said …' and then he gave up, because this was the sort of argument fathers always won by virtue of being fathers. 'So what does it say?' he said, changing tack, his mind already buzzing with the possibilities.

James smiled for only a moment. 'I had the same look in my eye when I heard about it,' he said. 'Suppose we all did. Doesn't do any harm to hope I suppose.'

'Da …'

'Okay,' his father held up a hand. He stepped closer to Tony and his voice dropped to a conspiratorial level – whether for dramatic effect or because he, too, had spotted Brian's imminent arrival Tony wasn't sure. When he spoke, it wasn't in his father's own speaking voice, not really; he had the oddest sense that he was hearing the combined voices of his male ancestors down the generations, reciting words they had all been taught.

'They say that one of us, one Morrigan … one of us will be chosen to represent her in the final battle against Carman.'

Tony frowned, trying to sort through the names and the stories.

'Carman,' he echoed. 'She's the one came over from somewhere with someone and done something.'

'You're a born storyteller, son.'

The name finally clicked. 'She's the witch with the demons for sons. The one that made all the fruit die and who tried to take over Ireland.'

'She's the enemy,' James said quietly, avoiding his son's gaze and looking out instead at the beautiful landscape around them.

'So she's our Sauron?'

A breath escaped his father's lips with a resigned *whee*. 'If you want. Anyway, when we face her, the Morrigan who is chosen will endure more than the rest of us put together, but he'll have been granted the power of the Tuatha Dé Danann – a god's power to remake the world with a thought.'

Every hair on Tony's head was tingling as though electricity was passing through his scalp. *It's me. It's bound to be me. I'll be the one that has to battle her and end it all, and when I do I'll be fuckin' unstoppable. I'll be like Superman and Cú Chulainn rolled into one. Fuck Pauline Scullion – I'll have Raquel Welch!*

His father chuckled on seeing the look that passed across Tony's face. 'Sorry, son,' he said ruefully. 'I know what you're thinking, believe me I do, but I already know it's not gonna be you. And I hope to God it's not going to be your wee fella either, whenever he comes along.'

'Why?'

James shushed him. 'Well?' he said instead, turning to Brian.

Brian pointed. 'It's two hundred feet up that slope. A few trees. You can't miss it.'

James gave him a hard look. 'You're leaving?'

'Yes, I'm fucking leaving.'

'I could make you stay,' James said mildly.

'For the good of our friendship, I wouldn't advise it,' Brian said, in exactly the same tone. The man and the sort-of leprechaun stared at each other. Finally, James nodded.

'I'll be off then. Not that your company isn't as delightful as ever. Good to meet you, Tony,' Brian said, turning to him and ignoring James. He smiled a smile that did not reach his eyes. 'The family line's in good hands, if I'm any judge. Be seeing you. Be seeing you soon.'

He doffed his cap again, and seemed to dissolve into the air and the soil. Tony started backwards with an exclamation of surprise, all of the fears that had been running through his mind shortly before, coming back to him with a vengeance. How were you supposed to fight things that could do something like that?

'Come on, son,' his father said. There was a rough edge to his voice now, fraught with apprehension. 'We're almost there.'

They walked on in silence for a few minutes. When the trees were almost upon them, James reached across and put his arm across Tony's chest, stopping him.

'You don't have to go in there with me if you don't want to,' he said.

Tony swallowed through a dry throat. Nothing could be seen through the canopy. The branches rustled and blew, but nothing supernatural seemed to be occurring. 'What's in there?' he asked.

'They're long gone,' his father replied. 'We're too late. So there's no danger, but … it might not be something you want to see, son.

If you want to stay outside until I return, I understand. You'll be safe. I promise.'

He looked again. No danger, his father had said. And much as the 'not something you want to see' was giving him the willies, the idea of staying here alone and waiting for his da to come back was less attractive. He had visions of night descending upon him, his wait stretching into hours ... Who knew what horrors lurked up here?

'I'll come with you,' he said. And so in they went.

The smell was the first tipoff. The flies were the second.

The bodies were arranged in an unbroken circle. He counted eight of them. Feet met head met feet. They were naked. They were dead.

They were human.

In the centre of the circle, an altar of sorts had been constructed; a cairn of stones with ashes atop the pile, remnants of a fire that had burned until recently.

Eyes. Dead bodies should have closed eyes. *Eyes closed.* That was how it was in the cowboys, in the gangster movies. Closed eyes. If you got shot it always went the same way: a bit of a clutch at the stomach and a stagger about the place, maybe a collapse and a few minutes to say your last words. Then one final twist ... and you died, *with your eyes closed.*

Three of the bodies were women. He could see their breasts. The first pairs of naked breasts he had ever seen. Mickey McTiernan, his best mate, had talked long into the night some nights about how great it was going to be when they first set eyes – *dead* his mind broke in with a scream, *dead eyes, dead and open and staring and empty eyes* – on a real pair of tits and not a crumpled page of some dodgy French magazine that had seen so many circuits of the playground and so many previous owners you felt like handling it with tongs.

Here they were. Pale, white and covered in flies …

He threw up. He threw up so many times it felt like he would never stop throwing up, as if he would grow old and die and still be dry-retching, hunched over on this little patch of Ireland covered in his puke, his father standing over him saying nothing.

Strength came back to him only slowly, his body afraid to embrace movement too quickly. He got to his feet on unsteady legs, his father supporting him, and still he couldn't break his gaze from a pair of dead eyes. This pair belonged to a young fella – no older looking than his cousin Tommy. They looked into him accusingly.

His mind, unable to cope, saw the bodies unfolding from their perfect circle and rising jerkily to life, arms outstretched, the flies teeming off them in a great cloud, coming for him–

He wrenched himself free of his father and he fled, back through the brief canopy of trees that ringed that terrible awful place of death and back out into the Mournes where his childhood, though unknown to him at the time, had just ended.

The sunny afternoon was gone – he had indeed lost some hours to his nausea in the clearing – darkness was falling, and falling fast. Panic was biting him over and over again now, sinking its fangs so deep inside him that all he could do was run, run, run; he was capable of nothing more cerebral than that.

He had to run. He *knew* that if he stopped, they would get him, they would find him, they would descend upon him in an action as inevitable as the sun sinking into the horizon. They would turn him into one of those lifeless husks they had left in that place.

So he ran. Bounding over depressions and leaping over streams, it was a run without dignity or form, motivated purely by terror. He arrowed down the slope with a clear and pressing need to put a lifetime's worth of distance between him and that little clearing within the trees. Where Tommy's dead doppelganger lay, furious at him for being alive.

Something grabbed his legs. At this speed, he couldn't compensate for it. He screamed as the world tilted horizontal, the scream interrupted as the ground knocked the wind from his lungs. He kicked out, legs flailing again and again. They had run him down and they had caught him – any minute now he would feel–

'Tony!'

It was his father's voice. His legs weren't listening, and they connected anyway. He heard an 'oooofff', and then his name, repeated again and again. With a force of will, he looked up to see his father standing above him, chest heaving with the effort of chasing him down, trying to fend off his son's attacks.

'Daddy,' was all he could say, and he was up and into his father's arms as if he were a baby again, hugging himself into his father's chest and sobbing.

'It's okay. Tony, it's okay. I'm so sorry...'

They stayed this way for some time until Tony grew self-conscious and separated himself from his father once more. He was still breathing heavily, from the shock and from the race down the mountainside. His father gave him a rueful look.

'You'll make the running team in your school yet,' he said.

Tony tried to smile at the weak joke, but couldn't. He had to ask. 'Why, Da?'

'That place was a rath,' James said, glancing back up the slope. Darkness had almost completely fallen and the trees were inky silhouettes against the dusk skies above. 'One of their places, son. Remember the ley lines I told ye about? Well, a rath occurs where a lot of them crisscross one other. By making these sacrifices, they keep the power flowin'. But ...' he sucked in a breath, and Tony could see for the first time that his father was also deeply affected by what they'd stumbled across up there. 'Jesus Christ, I've *never* seen eight before. I've never seen them arranged in a circle like that before.'

Tony ached for home. Ached to be sat at their wee wooden dinner table in their wee kitchen, smelling his ma's stew and complaining loudly about what a lot of oul shite *Gunsmoke* was. Rather than be stuck here on a hillside halfway up fuck-knows-where talking about what eight dead people meant. He knew what it meant. It meant the world was fucked up beyond anything he'd ever suspected. But he asked anyway.

'What does it mean?'

'They're planning something, is what it means,' his father replied grimly. He nodded to Tony. 'Trying to start something. Something really fuckin' *big*. Come on, we have to go, son. Time to go home.'

'What ... what about ... what about the ...' he heard himself ask, much to his own surprise, because he could have sworn that any suggestion to go back to that blessedly familiar little Triumph would have had him a faint dust trail on the horizon.

'I'll make a call when we get back.'

They walked in silence. Shadows moved in the dark, but in every case it proved to be only a rabbit or a mouse out foraging. The downward slope slowly levelled out and, after scaling the metal gate he dimly remembered from a lifetime ago, grass gave way to asphalt once more.

As the Triumph wound its way through the country lanes, Belfast coming closer with every bend and with it the sights and smells of home, he watched the countryside blur past outside the wondow and knew the world would never be the same again.

'You don't have to follow me, son.'

The words were spoken softly. He'd thought his father considered him asleep; apparently not. He turned to look at him and James Morrigan spared his son a quick glance before turning his attention back to the winding country lanes. 'It's a lot to take in: a lot to deal with. Maybe too much. You're only fourteen for fuck's sake. You've got your whole life ahead of you ...'

Dead eyes. Dead eyes staring. Why am I dead? And he realised, they weren't angry at him for being alive; they were angry at him for not stopping their deaths in the first place.

'I'm with you,' he said. 'We have to stop them, Da. It's like you said. We have a purpose. That's more than can be said for a lot of people.'

James smiled and nodded, and Tony imagined for a moment he could see ...

No. His da had only ever cried once, and that had been at

Granda Joe's funeral when he'd been only little.

Granda Joe. Had he been a Morrigan too? He supposed so. Had he taken James as a boy out somewhere and broken him into this world as he'd just been? Had he told him the story of the prophecy?

The prophecy …

'Dad … why did you say that about being sure the prophecy didn't apply to me? And hoping it wasn't my son?' he asked.

James shifted in his seat. 'You don't forget much, do ye?' he said. 'Because, son, the part of the prophecy that says he'd have to endure more than any of us includes losing their da. Not seeing him for ten years. And believe me, son, that's just for starters. Whoever it is, he'll have to go through hell … and I'm not talkin' figure of speech here. I'm talking about things that would make what we saw back there on the mountain look tame.'

Tony found that he couldn't think of a single thing to say to that. He only knew that he would try help his da stop whatever it was *they* were planning. Perhaps it was the arrogance of youth, but even after the shock of seeing those corpses, he permitted himself a moment of confidence.

After all, this wasn't ancient times. This was 1968.

What could they possibly do that would be so terrible?

COUNTY WEXFORD, IRELAND, 43 AD

'Bres.'

Bres stepped forward, threw open his arms and let loose with a fulsome and hearty laugh. He was a handsome fucker, Danny had to concede that much. If he'd been about in modern times he wouldn't have looked out of place coming out of a pool shaded in blue and advertising aftershave.

On behalf of all men who'd never once been given the once-over by a lust-struck female (however drunk), Danny had no hesitation in taking an immense dislike to this dickhead.

'The Morrigan!' Bres boomed. 'Upon my life! This is a blessed day indeed that I should uncover the greatest of our wandering number through sheer good fortune!'

Standing there, still covered in dirt and grime and spattered Formorian blood, the contrast between the Morrigan and her Tuatha brethren couldn't have possibly been starker. She looked much more like the filthy, shell-shocked humans in whose company she stood. The villagers themselves remained huddled together.

None of them looked on the Tuatha with the sort of regard you'd associate with rescued people appreciating their new saviours. The children shivered violently against the parents and adults that had survived the Formorian ambush. The adults watched the Tuatha warily, their eyes flicking between Bres and the Morrigan.

Could they even understand what Bres was saying? After all, it was only thanks to the older Morrigan's presence that *he* had a clue what was going on in the exchanges thus far.

'Fortune, Bres?' the Morrigan replied, forming her words slowly and deliberately. 'Was that how you found me?'

Bres looked so astonished you'd have thought he'd just been told antlers had sprouted from his testicles. 'Of course!' he said.

'We had heard rumours of a rogue band of Formorians roaming the coast, descending upon human settlements and butchering them. As King of the Tuatha *and* as Regent of the Formorians, I could not permit this to continue.'

The bastard was lying through his teeth. Danny's fists itched and he found himself wishing very much he could materialise right here and now and plant a big one right in the spoofing bastard's mouth.

Bres frowned. So did the younger Morrigan. Their heads turned toward where Danny stood–

– and the older Morrigan's hand settled softly on his shoulder, as gently as an autumn leaf fluttering to the ground.

The moment passed. Bres and the Morrigan went back to staring at each other.

'Don't,' the older Morrigan whispered in his ear. She was close again, closer than she'd been since that initial vision of the beach landings, and again he felt a tickle of pleasure wind through his nervous system.

'I thought this was just a vision ...'

'It needs to *stay* that way,' was all she said in response.

'But–'

'Sssh ...'

He obeyed, wondering as he did so how much of a say he actually had in complying with her command.

'Regent of the Formorians?' the younger Morrigan was saying.

'Much has changed since you have been gone.'

'And much,' she replied acidly, 'has stayed the same.'

'But not you,' he countered. 'You have changed, Morrigan ...'

and he gestured to the two children she still shielded behind her. Children who, unlike the remainder of the villagers, did not seem to be regarding the Tuatha with fear on their faces, but with awe. 'You have changed. Goddess of War! Harbinger of Death! Living Weapon! Wielder of the Spear of Destiny!'

He paused. His words echoed off the mud huts of the humble village in which they stood, and Danny got the impression that even if the humans couldn't understand what he was saying, they were getting the gist of it – particularly after witnessing her distinctly inhuman performance against Skull Ring.

'Now, look at you,' he said. 'Washerwoman? Wife? *Mother?* Tell me, Morrigan, Eternal Harbinger of Doom, Triple Warrior Goddess … do you make a good vegetable broth?'

The rest of the Tuatha dissolved into laughter at this.

Danny exhaled. *'Please* let me smack that bastard,' he said softly.

'Very bad idea,' she whispered back, though he could detect an undercurrent of amusement and, unless he was reading too much into it, a certain level of gratitude.

'I have accepted this life,' her younger counterpart clipped. Danny could tell she had burned at the laughter directed at her from warriors who once would have counted her their unquestioned superior, their idol.

'Have you?' Bres shot back. 'You seem to have retained your Tuatha abilities, for all your acceptance of humanity, Morrigan! Or does *every* human woman possess the power to kill a Formorian warlord?'

'You might be surprised.' Her eyes were blazing with fury now and Danny thought she was about to leap, to strike at Bres. He wondered how the other Tuatha would react if that happened, and saw the younger Morrigan assess the warrior party herself. She was wondering the same thing. Her attention turned to the terrified huddle of humans. If the warriors didn't react well, what for them? They wouldn't stand a chance.

'Indeed,' Bres returned, looking at the ragtag bunch of humans with undisguised contempt.

'What,' she said, each word a conscious effort, 'do you want, Bres?'

'Want?' he frowned. 'Morrigan, I want nothing. I have found you by happy chance, and I would not presume to give you an order, though I may be your king ...'

'No,' she said quietly, 'you are not my king.'

Bres stiffened. His warriors did the same. Danny felt his pulse quicken. The atmosphere had darkened, thickened; he saw the warriors shift their stance from fairly relaxed and at ease to one of battle readiness. Hands went to sword hilts, tightened around spears. Shields were lifted.

Amongst the humans, women held children tightly and the men on the outside of the rough circle pressed further inward, drawing the circle closer together. The Morrigan didn't miss any of this of course, but neither did she react.

'You are correct,' Bres said, to Danny's surprise. 'Since you chose to leave us, I cannot claim to be. That is a shame, Morrigan. I will not deny that I want you to return to us. We face trials ahead; the soothsayers are certain of it. You are the mightiest of us.'

'I will not return.'

'Then you will have to give up your powers. That is our law.

You know it must be done.'

Her shoulders slumped at this, but her defiance remained. 'I will,' she replied firmly. 'I will renounce them. I will live as a human. I have a life here.'

'A happy one?'

'Yes,' she shot back. 'Yes, a happy one. I wash clothes and I make soup and I do not rush off to war and kill thirty men with one stroke. I do not lie with our generals on the eve of battle to ensure our victories. I lie with my husband for no other reason than because I want him. I am content. I never knew that as a goddess.'

'Humans have no magic.'

'Yes they do,' she said softly. 'Oh yes, they do.'

Danny found to his utter amazement that at some point during the last few minutes, without fuss or drama, he had started crying. Hot tears rolled unbidden down his face and he was perversely glad to be immaterial and ghostlike: he had never cried in public before, but by God he was doing so now.

The longing for his little boy, his Luke, and his Ellie, which had seemed pressing before, was now so raw, so primal that he couldn't stop the tears from coming.

The woman before him, covered in detritus, had given up the sort of destiny most people couldn't imagine. She had stumbled into a life that she hadn't foreseen and she had discovered, probably to her own amazement, a side of herself she didn't even realise had existed.

He was an idiot. A complete and total dickhead. He had been so obsessed with wondering about what *might* have been that he had almost – no, fuck *almost*, he *had* – completely failed to see what actually had been.

Did it matter if plans didn't pan out, if the end result was a day-to-day existence that meant something?

Not just to him, but to people who mattered. He had a little boy who *adored* him – a baby son who needed him to wipe his ass and try (mostly in vain) to pilot lumps of baby-mush into the reluctant aircraft hangar of his mouth.

Easy things. Mundane things. But the time would come when that same little boy would come to need him for vastly more important and more complex things than that. Would need his father to guide him into becoming an honest-to-God person in his own right.

He looked again at Glon and Gaim, peering out from behind their mother. Their magnificent mother. He felt like embracing her, but in his current less-than-real state, he wondered if that would end up with him somehow steering her body again. That, or it would count as cheating on Ellie...

'And this,' the older Morrigan's voice said sadly, 'is where it all starts to go wrong.'

It took three words.

'Humans,' said Bres, 'are mortal.'

The younger Morrigan flinched. Danny saw Bres light up at this. He pressed the line of attack. 'You are prepared to live as a human? To die as one?'

'Yes,' she said, but her hands gripped her children tightly, and Danny knew.

'And your children?' Bres said softly. 'They will be human too.

Subject to the ravages of winters. Of time. Of disease. Hunger. Thirst.'

He dropped to one knee and smiled such a warm and winning smile that it was hard to reconcile it with the words he'd just spoken. He beckoned, and before the Morrigan could stop them, Glon and Gaim freed themselves from her grasp and padded over to this shining stranger, this broad-shouldered crowned warrior who smiled at them and spoke to them in words they didn't understand – not *fully*, but they could almost make some of it out – and he patted their heads and nodded approvingly while they preened with pride to be given such attention by this god.

Watching them, watching all of this, the younger Morrigan seemed to be visibly shrinking in size. She closed her eyes and when they opened, Danny could see the spark of defiance that had shone within them had dimmed markedly.

A few shouts came from the group of humans. Seeing his older sons with the leader of this fresh band of strangers, Caderyn, little Coscar in his arms, had abandoned his former post of marshalling the villagers. He walked to his wife and seeing her expression, he extended his free arm and put it around her waist, drawing her to him. She didn't resist, and they embraced.

'Da!' Gaim shouted. 'Da, did you see our ma fightin'?'

'Come here to me,' Caderyn said, breaking off from the embrace. 'Both of you. Now.'

Bres winked at the boys and, to Danny's displeasure, very slightly inclined his head toward their father – who did the bastard think he was, to give permission? Glon and Gaim duly trotted back to their parents' side, fairly bouncing with excitement still.

'I will do my best to protect this settlement,' Bres said graciously. 'But if the trials ahead are as challenging as our soothsayers fear, we may not have the warriors to spare. Who will protect you then, from rogue Formorians, or from worse? Who will protect those you love?'

'What's he saying to you?' Caderyn asked his wife.

'He wants me to go back to them.'

'To your people?'

'Yes.'

'And become the Morrigan again?'

'Yes,' she sighed.

Glon and Gaim squealed with joy, their reactions overlapping with one another but in a very similar vein. 'Do it Ma! Do it! Let's all go! Go live with them! Go be warriors! Kill *real* monsters! Just like we always played, but for real, Ma! Please, Da, can we?'

'No.'

Caderyn looked at his wife as she spoke. Danny felt a surge of respect for this man. Fuck knew what year this was, but whether he'd ever had anything that could in modern times be described as an education, Caderyn was clearly nobody's fool.

'Because of me,' Caderyn guessed.

'Yes.'

The excitement of the children was snuffed out instantly. 'Why, Ma? Why?' Glon asked.

It was Caderyn who answered. 'Because I'm just a man, son. You're like your mother. Or enough like her and her people anyway. They wouldn't have me where they live.'

'You wouldn't survive there,' the Morrigan said. She couldn't meet her husband's eyes. The baby began to fuss, so she took little Coscar from his arms and shushed him, and for a few seconds no one moved or spoke until the baby was silent again.

'What do you want?' he asked her. 'Who do you want to be?'

She looked at him and she smiled. 'I'm Regan,' she said. 'You are my husband and I am your wife. Now and for always.'

With that, she kissed him and passed him little Coscar. This done, she patted her two boys on the head and looked at them with what seemed to be an apology on her face, before she turned to Bres.

'I've made my choice,' she said. 'Now go.'

Danny half expected the Tuatha king to throw a tantrum or order his warriors to attack. He was steeling himself for the massacre that would ensue if he did so, and preparing himself to try and wish himself into existence here. Much as she was reluctant for him to meddle with events here, he wasn't going to stand by and witness another bloodbath without doing *something*, even if all he managed was one solid hit on that smug bastard's nose … Bres only nodded.

'Your heritage will take nine days to fade,' he said shortly, beckoning for his horse and hopping lightly onto its broad back with an athleticism a human could never have hoped to match. 'You have that amount of time to come to your senses.'

'I already have.'

'We shall see,' he said. 'You would have been welcome back in my halls, Morrigan. I can only hope there is still a welcome for you here … among your *chosen* people.'

At a signal and with a cry, he and the rest of the Tuatha rode off, hooves thundering into the distance. It took several minutes before they passed into the shade of the surrounding trees, and the village – or what remained of it – was again free from outsiders.

All save one, it seemed.

Already Danny could see the looks. As the survivors scattered, some to weep over fallen relatives and friends, some simply to retreat to their homes and shiver, no one came within twenty feet of the Morrigan and her family, and those who came closest outside of that radius looked at her with such suspicion and fear, bordering on hostility, that Bres' words made sharp and cruel sense.

All alone in the crowd, the Morrigan and her family walked home.

Danny looked at his companion with a heavy heart. 'It's not as simple as that, is it,' he asked. 'Not as simple as making the good choice and living happily ever after with it.'

She shook her head, looking at her younger self.

'It never is,' she said.

The Road of Trials

The bar was full of smoke. A jukebox in the corner blasted out Mott the Hoople's 'All The Young Dudes' and dancing before it, mouthing along to the words, were three young ladies wearing a third of a skirt each. Tony Morrigan watched every bump and grind, the pint glass held in his hand unconsciously mimicking their motions.

'You're gonna get eye strain. Ya dirty fucker.'

He sipped his pint and grinned. 'My vision's 20–20 Johnny, believe you me.'

'I wasn't talkin' about *those* eyes,' Johnny retorted, poking his fingers at his friend's face. Tony laughed and blocked the attack, turning back to the bar and away from the show, albeit reluctantly. 'You're like a man just outta Long Kesh. Anybody'd think you hadn't seen a flash of gee in years.'

'Aye, well,' Tony replied, swirling the beer thoughtfully in the glass as he spoke, 'work keeps me busy Johnny, ya know? I'm out on the road for a fair few weeks at a go, like. Feels good to come home and let off a little …' he paused, and winked exaggeratedly for comedic effect, 'steam.'

'Aye. Steam. Sure.'

Tony caught the barman's attention. 'What'r the ladies drinkin', mucker?'

'Vodkas. And see the wee blondie in the middle?'

'Yeah?'

The barman raised his eyebrow with the conspiratorial air of someone passing on a hot tip for the 3.30 at Chepstow. 'Doubles.'

Johnny patted his shoulder. 'I take it you've chosen your victim then, man?'

'Watch me go,' Tony grinned. He signalled to the barman who dutifully began pouring three vodkas, one a double measure, and prepared himself for the task at hand. He'd saunter over with the drinks held casually – Johnny in tail – and open with a nice wee line; *Jesus that dancin' must be makin' yis all thirsty. And after watchin' yis I know my tongue's hangin' out …*

Cheesy, but it'd do. He'd never had much trouble with the oul gift of the gab. It was what happened after the first few liaisons that gave him the headaches: they'd inevitably start asking questions about what he did, where he worked, making noises about meeting his family … how was he meant to respond?

He smiled humourlessly to himself as the first two vodkas were placed on the bar in front of him. In these crazy times, in this bloody city, a guy could make some serious headway with a girl by claiming to be with one paramilitary group or another, by flashing a wee pistol stashed away in his jacket.

'Fighting for the cause', so far as he could see, was less about political idealism or nationalistic fervour and more about having something exotic about you that would make the wee dames drop their knickers at the first flash of a gun barrel, imagining they were jumping into the sack with Michael Collins or Gusty Spence, depending on what bar it was you happened to be drinking in.

Imagine if he tried telling the truth as a chat-up line.

'Hey, how's it goin'? What's this in my jacket? Ach it's only my iron knuckle-dusters. Did you know they can cave a faerie's head in if you hit it in the right place hard enough? Course they're not as good as foxglove tea – I have a few home-made hand-grenades filled with that back in the house, if you're interested. Why the fuck would I have these, you ask? Well it's to defend the country from being overrun by magical creatures from the Otherworld trying to tear down the dimensional barrier between their world and ours ... wait, where are you goin'? Who's these cunts with the white jackets ...?'

What would the army make of his armoury if they ever decided to raid his house? He might end up the only person in history interred for possession of herbs and spices.

Seven years. Seven fucking years, since that day on the Mournes. Up and down and across this miserable wee island, chasing shadows and shades and worse things besides. He'd fought changelings in castle ruins, battled faerie soldiers in back alleys while the British fought the IRA mere streets away. He'd even caught a glimpse once or twice of the upper ranks of their forces. Only the speed of his car had allowed him to escape from one such near-encounter; it had taken him three bone-chilling hours the next day to remove the webbing from its rear bumper.

Webbing. His body convulsed involuntarily as this memory resurfaced. Forcing the thought away, he handed a twenty pound note to the barman, who muttered to himself as he went to the till – giving Tony change out of that would probably use up most of his float.

Of course this life did have *some* advantages Thanks to Brian and his continued assistance, he hadn't wanted for anything financially for some years now. Creepy little faerie he may be, but he had a knack for casting a luck charm so potent that it made picking winners at Aintree a simple matter of closing your eyes and jabbing a pen at the right page in the newspaper.

The money that little skill generated from betting shops across the province allowed him to maintain the façade that he had some high-paid job or other. He told people he worked in consultancy, a job that sounded so dull no further questions were forthcoming. But the stark facts were that Tony Morrigan was twenty-one years of age and, for him, nights like this – where he was not concerned with humanity's safety, but was *deeply* concerned with the safety of wee blondie's hemline – were so rare as to be practically extinct.

He grabbed the vodkas, gave the nod to Johnny, and turned ready to seize the night–

'Ach for fuck's sake…' he said.

'Sorry, son,' James Morrigan said. He nodded to Johnny then returned his attention to Tony. 'We need to go. Now.'

'No, we don't,' Tony replied. He tried to move away from his father and bring the drinks to their intended audience.

James, however, blocked him easily – there was some sympathy on his face, but it was draining away rapidly. 'Son,' he said again, his tone harder, 'you know I wouldn't come here unless it was urgent. We need to *go*.'

So go Tony did, handing the drinks to a confused Johnny and walking with his father to the front door of the bar. As his father walked into the cold December night and the blast of frigid air rushed in, fresh and crisp, Tony wanted nothing more than to stay where he was, in the sweaty warm mass of bodies of young people out for a good time together, and the sniff of a possible fuck in the air from the girls in the corner. He even caught blondie's eye for a moment and saw her pause in her dancing, before she turned away from him. Well, why wouldn't she? He was leaving after all.

The car journey was far from silent, but the vast majority of the talking was being done by the driver and not his moody passenger, who stared at the lights of Belfast as they began to recede into the distance.

'… listening to a word I'm saying?'

He sighed. 'Yes, Da. Sword of Nuada. Unstoppable magic weapon. Have to stop them getting it. Orders received and understood.'

Tony could sense the irritation coming from his father. 'You gonna get on like a spoiled fuckin' brat because I ruined your night out? Is that what this is?'

'Yeah,' Tony shrugged. 'Yeah that about sums it up Da, yeah.'

'Listen to yourself. Jesus Christ Tony, this is *important*–'

'Why us?' Tony cut him off, now glaring directly over at the older man. 'Why us, Da, runnin' about like two fuckin' lunatics all over the country? Ya know what Johnny Dougan – that was him in the bar, by the way, last seen makin' his way to the three dames in the corner – ya know what he did with himself last month? Joined a fuckin' five-a-side team. Woo. Big fuckin' excitement, eh? Except guess what? He *loves* it. He was tellin' me all about it. That's why I don't see much of him any more, even when we *are* back in Belfast, because he's out drinkin' with them after the matches. I'm losin' them, Da. I don't see wee Seamy McGlinch or Mickey any more either. Why? Because I'm too busy savin' the fuckin' country from supernatural apocalypse!'

They drove on in silence for a few miles after that outburst. As usual, Tony began to feel that hot pressure in his gut, that little ball of shame that only formed when he knew he was in the wrong. He suppressed it. He pushed it down as best he could, because he was *determined* not to give in on this one.

'I told ye on the mountain, that first day,' his father said, in a voice almost swallowed by the rattle of the Triumph (a car whose name was becoming increasingly sardonic with each fresh year of wear and tear that settled upon it), 'that you didn't have to follow me into this life.'

'Yeah, ye did,' Tony replied. 'And you lied, didn't ye.'

There it was. He'd said it. Long years he'd been waiting to get that off his chest, and finally there it was, out there, and contrary to his expectations and hopes he didn't suddenly feel a great release of pressure at its passing. He felt suffocated and wretched. His father had flinched at the words, physically recoiled, and the car had weaved for an instant on the road before he'd brought it back to an even keel.

'Yes,' James Morrigan said. 'Yes, I lied.'

'Why?'

'Because you deserved to think this life was a choice.'

'But it isn't. It's either us or nobody. And if it's nobody, then they win.'

'Yes.'

'You're expectin' me to put my son through all this?'

No reply was forthcoming, and that was answer enough. Tony said nothing further.

The miles wore on. How many days and nights had they spent like this, driving from one end of Ireland to the other? How many hills and ruins and standing stones had he seen? By now he knew the Hill of Tara better than he knew some of the adjoining streets where he'd grown up.

'We're getting close,' his father remarked, as they passed some nondescript landmark or other. Judging from the road signs they'd passed – those he'd been able to read with the meagre headlights this oul death-trap possessed, at any rate – they were somewhere in Armagh. Great. Two fellas in a car filled with melee weapons in the middle of Armagh in the dead of night; *that* didn't look suspicious at all now did it? If the faeries didn't get them, the army probably would.

'Close indeed ye are,' came a familiar voice from the back seat.

The car swerved before returning to its proper path.

Tony waited for his heart to resume normal operations again as he turned to berate their uninvited guest who was now grinning innocently. Brian accepted the tirade of abuse with nothing but a placid expression on his face. When Tony paused for breath, he shrugged.

'Finished?' he said. 'Good so. It's about another mile down this road. Not much time left by the way, boys. Ritual's near complete.'

Tony's blood ran cold. Rituals had many different forms, but their one universal currency was always the same. Blood.

'How many?' he asked tersely.

'Two,' Brian replied, all businesslike. 'But don't let that fool ye. This one's a powerful one. Not seen its like in many a year. And to be bein' done where it's bein' done, with the energies and all,' he whistled softly, 'plenty dangerous as well as powerful.'

The car lurched forward with as much speed as it could muster, which wasn't all that much. Tony tried to hold on as best he could as he was pogoed around in the passenger's seat.

'Powerful enough for them to get the *Claíomh Solais*?' Tony asked.

Brian shrugged. 'Who knows?' he replied lightly. 'Personally I think that oul thing's a myth. But hey,' he indicated himself knowingly, 'look who's talking, lads, eh?'

'They won't be able to raise it,' James said, with such confidence that both human and faerie passengers within the car reacted with surprise.

'They won't?' Tony said.

'Not a chance. Trust me. Stupid faerie fuckers don't realise the Morrigan anticipated how dangerous the sword would be if it was ever brought out of the Otherworld. She's protected it so that it can't happen.'

'Then forgive me for bein Mr Obvious here, Da, but what the *fuck* are we doing gallivantin' round the bastardin' countryside?' *And ruining my chances of a quick fumble, or even a fuckin' long and quite complicated fumble, in the process?* Tony added internally.

'Because them even *tryin*' somethin' like this is bad news,' his father replied grimly. 'Tryin' to get one of the *Treasures?* That's cocky, even by their standards.'

With an effort of will, Tony forced down his frustration at this line of reasoning and changed the subject. 'So Brian. Haven't seen you around for a good wee while. What have you been up to?'

'Me?' Brian touched his hand to his chest as if offended by the intrusion into his personal life. 'Bit o' this, bit o' that. Ya have to admit the North is an interesting place these days. Almost reminds me of the old days. Hard to believe it all started in a wee clearing on the Mournes those years ago.'

'You expect us to believe that shite caused this sorry fuckin' mess goin' on now?' Tony scoffed, hoping he sounded more dismissive of the notion than he actually felt. More than one evening he'd lain awake listening to the sounds of chaos outside wondering that exact same thing.

Brian's eyes twinkled with mischief. It wasn't hard to see how his race had earned the mistaken reputation as harmless tricksters. 'I'll grant ye, there's plenty of human places in the world as bad if not worse than here that my kind haven't a hand in. To *my* humble knowledge, anyway. So maybe you're right. But I remember you, Tony … just a wee boy back then, following his da about with a song in his heart and all the joys of spring. How things change, eh?'

'How long have you been back there?' Tony demanded.

Brian looked confused and hurt, as innocent as a week-old puppy. 'Sure whatever do you mean?' he asked, before smiling a thin quicksilver smile. 'This'll just about do yis at the end of the lane here.'

'What are we up against?' asked James, keeper of the big picture as ever.

Brian's smile disappeared. 'I'm not fuckin' invisible to *them* am I?' he grumbled. 'What did you expect me to do, have a dander round? Be your scout? All I know is there's more'n a few. Rumours of a bigwig too,' he jabbed a finger, 'that's *your* department, Mister Morrigan. I'm outta here.'

'Cheers, Huggy,' Tony said as the faerie faded from sight.

The car crunched to a halt on the gravel track. James looked across at his son.

'*Huggy?*'

Tony sighed. 'Don't you *ever* watch TV, Da?'

They left the car, and went to retrieve their weapons. This bit, he had to admit, had a certain appeal. The boot of the Triumph was filled with all sorts of strange objects, enough of which were recognisably pointy that it would certainly get them arrested if stopped for a checkpoint. That would be an interesting interrogation, that was for sure. Thankfully they hadn't been stopped yet; Tony wondered if this was another facet of Brian's skill with the luck charms.

Tony hefted an iron short sword and a silver shield. Both had had enchantments woven into their design to make them additionally deadly to beings of faerie origin. Theirs was a familiar weight; how many twenty-one year old Belfast natives could claim *that* in 1975, he wondered?

His da carried his customary pair of silver daggers; only five inch blades on each, but wickedly, lethally sharp. During one long car journey to Cork to deal with a changeling outbreak, Tony had repeatedly pressed his da into naming his weapons, citing the coolness factor of doing so (based mainly on Westerns he'd seen). He didn't *quite* get the results he'd hoped for.

'Pinky and Perky ready to strike fear into the hearts of evildoers?' Tony asked sarcastically.

James Morrigan spun the daggers in his hands, the blades glinting in the twilight. He smiled. 'Fear's not all I'll be strikin',' he said. He looked at his son with a smile playing across his lips. 'And how's, er …?'

'Moonblood,' Tony said, trying to sound heroic and not, for talk's sake, more than a little embarrassed. That long weapon-naming trip to Cork had included a few stopovers in pubs, which he was beginning to regret.

'Oh aye. Moonblood, aye. Sorry, I keep forgettin' that …'

'It's a good name for a sword, all right?'

'Oh it's the best name for a sword ever, son. Period.'

'I've told ye before that's *not* what Moonblood means, Da!' Tony exploded. 'If I wanted a name that was gonna strike fear and the promise of death into my foes I wouldn't name it after a woman's monthlies!'

James blew out a breath. 'Wait til you're married, son. You'll think different.'

The fire on the summit of the nearby hillside was hard to miss. Father and son exchanged a glance and a nod and began moving towards it, keeping low to the ground, avoiding the direct glare of the moonlight. Voices were travelling in the night air; low and reverent and rhythmical. Chants. Ritual chants. Whatever was happening was happening now, and there were two terrified people on that hilltop who probably didn't have very much time left to them–

There were shapes slinking in the shadows. Wolf-faeries. The soldiers. Sheltering behind a few rocks, Tony made out two, three, Jesus Christ, *four* of the things within view. Brian hadn't been messin' around with his predictions of a heavy presence here tonight. If you had four solider faeries patrolling the lower slopes of the hill, what the fuck was gonna be the cherry on the cake?

Tony let his mind slip into the headspace he'd come to occupy when in a situation like this, feeling only a fleeting twinge of annoyance that situations like this were becoming all too prevalent. Then the irritation was gone, and his mind was clear apart from two driving motives: first, he had to get to the top of that hill in as quick a time as possible.

Second, he had to stay alive.

A nod was all it took. He and his da edged out from behind the rocks, fanning out to use whatever other cover the hillside could provide. The high ground was a powerful tactical advantage to have, but thankfully the wolf-faeries weren't too bright and didn't possess the best eyesight. Their hearing was good, but both Morrigans had long experience in making as little noise as possible and, on grass, it wasn't hard to pad undetected so long as someone wasn't looking in your direction when you moved. Smell was the big worry. Tonight, mercifully, the wind was still – unusual for December. Tony hoped it was a sign that someone out there was helping them.

His father talked sometimes of the Morrigan, the original, the goddess. Undoubtedly real though all of this mythological stuff was Tony still wasn't sure what to think of this War Goddess. Little had been passed down about her beyond that she was the origin of their bloodline and had passed the torch of responsibility down through the generations to them. They were to defend the above-ground world, the human world, from Carman and her ilk.

If that were so, why didn't she help with that task herself? Why wasn't she kicking Carman's hole down in the Otherworld and preventing these repeated attempts to thin the dimensional walls and escape? During long nights in dark places, Tony had thought of this deity, his supposed superior, and his thoughts had not exactly been complimentary.

One wolf-faerie only eight feet or so further up the slope was moving in a rough patrolling line, and as Tony crouched half-hidden behind a rock he watched it pause, turn and sniff the air. The fucking thing was *huge*. He'd encountered a few of these bastards in his time, and had taken down a few, but none had been the equal of this specimen; it was as if they'd been throwing the rookies at him until now and here they'd reserved space for the real deal.

He reached into his inside pocket and took out the thin tube within. An observer might have wondered why he was carrying a peashooter, but his ammo wasn't vegetables. He affixed a tiny silver dart into the end of the tube. Each dart was handmade to a very specific set of instructions and blessed at a certain spot in Fermanagh.

Last year they'd encouraged Satanists to set up camp around the sacred wellspring. That had been hilarious. Presumably through whatever arcane methods they'd used to bring them there, they'd been imagining the Satanists to be the real deal, and not, say, a few spectacularly nervous-bladdered teenagers messing around with a crudely modified Scrabble board in hopes of impressing some dim-witted local. His da was darkly predicting that next year they'd get serious about it and try to arrange a Bay City Rollers concert to take place there.

A quick glance to his right – James was in position, as he'd known he would be: he could just about make out his father's silhouette about thirty feet to his right. At a hand signal from his da, Tony pivoted, the blowgun at his lips, aiming even as he started counting down from five ... *four, three, two, one.*

The silver dart left the gun and pierced the wolf-faerie's hindquarters, immediately loosing its toxic venom: a cocktail of fairly mundane ingredients that were harmless to humans and which constituted the 'special tea' his da had insisted on drinking. It had the most loathsome aroma he'd ever come across. He'd always suspected brewing it was his Da's way of getting him out of the house so he could have sex (and in this, quite unknowingly, he was half right).

Tony's mother, Marie, had passed away three years before. Heart disease. His father had been inconsolable for months thereafter and Tony suspected the man would never really recover from it. He was beginning to understand why: it wasn't simply that he'd loved her – although he had, in an obvious way quite uncharacteristic for most fellas of his generation – it was that he'd been forced to keep so much from her.

Marie had gone to her grave thinking her husband was a fairly run-of-the-mill sort, a labourer-for-hire who was good enough at his line of work to be in demand all over Ireland and who, because of this, would have to spend quite a bit of time away from her. James had been adamant that Tony must never even think of telling his mother anything about the real line of work they were both involved in.

'She wouldn't understand, son. And I wouldn't *want* her to. Take the day at the Mournes. Eight people, dead, and feeling them with me the whole drive home. But I was able to come in the door and spin her a yarn about some miserable oul farmer not paying me the bonus I was due for finishing a day early and to cheer me up she made me a big dinner and brought me a pint. That's the sort of her, son. She's apart from all of this and I want her to stay that way, you understand me?'

The wolf-faerie fell to the ground. Thirty feet to his right, his father's target did the same – but this one, even bigger and with more spirit than the one Tony had gone after, had managed a howl of pain before it collapsed.

Answering howls went up immediately from the remaining two guards. The element of surprise was gone. Tony caught sight of one of them loping down the slope toward his position, covering the distance in big awkward bounds that were as speedy as they were ungainly, its mouth opening in anticipation for the battle ahead.

He stood, and drew the short sword, catching a glimpse of his father doing something similar as the fourth wolf-faerie found him. There wasn't time for Tony to see anything else before his aggressor was upon him, leaping and snarling.

He dodged the initial lunge, barely, his shield flashing as

it swung and connected with the beasts' left hind leg. Where it touched flesh it burned and the wolf-faerie howled long and loud.

'Hoooooooounnnnddd!' it snarled. 'Fffffiilllllllltttttttthyyyyyyy dooooggggggg!'

Eastwood would have had an instant riposte – *every dog has its day*, maybe – before he pulled the trigger on his Magnum and blew the fucker's brains all over the grass.

Unfortunately, Tony Morrigan was no Clint. For one thing, he was terrified out of his fuckin' wits. Still, something – the code of the action hero, perhaps – compelled him to reply to this. So, too terrified to think of anything particularly clever he settled for snarling back the first angry words that entered his mind.

'I could be gettin' a blowjob off some fuckin' bimbo by now, ya hairy cunt!' he screamed with heartfelt passion, and he charged.

Short sword met flesh. It wasn't textbook; he'd had some training, obviously, with his father over the last seven years, but the main thing has father had taught him was to stay within killing distance whilst staying out of 'getting killed' distance. Most of the things he'd fought had possessed no weapons save their own teeth and claws, and his short sword tended to have a longer reach than those if used carefully.

He lunged, jumped back, lunged again. The shield saved his life more than once, blocking the creature's attacks and returning them with interest, since every time the wolf's flesh came into contact with the shield's surface it was wounded further and its mobility reduced another notch.

But this wasn't some piss-ant little bog-faerie or a pathetic little post-discovery changeling. It was a soldier. The fucker was big, it was strong, and it wasn't giving up despite the burns the shield was inflicting. His arms were tired from swinging the sword and his reaction times slowed, and still it advanced. Its initial bloodlust had faded, and instead of mindless attack, it probed at his flanks and forced him back, staring at him with calculating eyes that seemed to say *I've got the measure of you. I'm better than you. And you know it.*

On the hilltop, he could hear screaming. Something was in pain up there, and standing in his way was a thing from an ancient world that didn't care what year it was, or how ludicrous it would be for Tony to die on a twilit backwater of Armagh and be found in medieval garb. If he was ever found.

He saw its muscles tense, those massive shoulders ripple. It was going to spring and, even if he blocked it with the shield, the weight of it would send him sprawling, make him lose the grip on the sword, and it would ignore whatever wounds he could inflict on it and rake those needle-pointed claws across his stomach, and his intestines would spill out like a reel of film from a movie projector. The two opponents stared at each other, predator regarding prey, and he had the horrible feeling they were looking at each other for the final time.

It was an accurate feeling, as it turned out.

James Morrigan, coming in unnoticed from behind, hopped on the creature's back and, before it could do more than wriggle in surprise at this development, he had driven Pinky and Perky up to their hilts into each side of that massive skull. The wolf had time to blink, to twitch, and for its tongue to flit in and out of its mouth before it fell lifeless to the turf.

'Come on,' James said, retrieving the daggers with one, two, sharp tugs that Tony knew required a lot more strength than they seemed to, 'I don't think there's much time.'

Tony ran. He was faster than his father but he kept pace with him as they raced up the slope. They passed the corpse of the fourth wolf as they did so. James had had time to despatch his opponent, every bit as big and bad as the one Tony faced, and to save his son. Not for the first time, either. He was good at what he did. Of course he was. He'd had decades of practice at doing it. Decades that had taken him from his wife and his son. Never once had Tony heard his father's resolve weaken. Even when his mother had passed away, his father had withdrawn a little further into himself, but the work had gone on.

He *believed* in this, in all of this, with all his heart. Tony only wished he could say the same for himself. He hadn't the stomach for this. Never had. Any romantic notions he'd had about this great familial dynasty he'd been born into had died in a terraced house in Belfast five years ago, on the night of his first mission …

The night his father had–

No. He pushed the memory away with an effort, came back to the present.

There were no surprises at the summit. Seven standing stones, in a circle. A fire set in the middle. Four figures, all outwardly human-looking, stood at the four compass points around the blaze, chanting something or other in ancient Gaelic that he couldn't even begin to translate; the complexities of the language had been something he'd given up understanding a long time ago.

They'd seen them, of course. But the cocky bastards didn't even pause in the incantation as he and his father charged toward them. Tony raised the short sword and yelled his best blood-curdling challenge. He tried once more to enter the eternal contradiction that was the peaceful calm of battle-mode, but wasn't able to do so - there were things tugging, pulling at him for attention and, as he passed within the circle of the standing stones, he realised what they were.

Where were the sacrifices?

Why weren't the four showing any signs of fear?

Where were the fucking sacrifices?

As the two Morrigan men advanced, blades aloft, one of the four around the fire stopped chanting and looked directly at Tony with an expression he would never forget.

'Welcome,' the figure said. And then, '*Now*.'

The short sword was yanked from his grip, and as he tried to readjust to being disarmed, perhaps to bring the shield around and use that instead, his legs were taken from under him and he fell forward, tasting dirt. A split second later he heard the thump that signified that, a few feet away, his father was suffering a similar fate.

He held onto the shield with all his strength but, as with the sword, an unknown force simply plucked it from his fingers, almost tearing them off in the process. He yelped in pain and, anticipating killing strokes about to rain down on him in his prone position, he rolled from his stomach onto his back so that he could see what had–

He screamed.

There were nights he'd woken in a cold sweat wondering what

would have happened if, on that mission years ago, the Triumph's engine hadn't caught when it had, if he'd had more than webbing to wipe off the back bumper. It looked like the day had come when he would find out.

A massive, monstrous spider hung over him, over the entire standing stone circle; a huge black mass against the night sky, one leg perfectly balanced on the summit of each stone with one leg left spare.

His sword, his shield, and one of his father's daggers hung from lines of webbing; lines that jerked and bobbed until, with a flick, the weapons were thrown high to fall a long way from the hilltop.

Fear flooded his body, froze his limbs and overwrote all of his training until all he could do was lie there and scream, waiting for that monstrous shape to descend on his helpless body to finish the job, to *feed*.

'Restrain them,' came the voice that had spoken before – he was obviously the boss here. More webbing arced downward. His arms and legs were held fast within it in a matter of seconds.

Terror confused his perception of the events that followed. When his panic level dropped, when his body simply couldn't process any more dread, he found himself suspended between two of the standing stones, bound in webbing from his shoulders down to his ankles, Directly opposite, like an aged mirror image, his father had been subjected to the same treatment.

It seemed laughable to call the gigantic beast a spider, just as it seemed laughable to call the beasts on the hilltop wolves. Spiders were scabby if hateful little beasts that strayed into the wrong bed or crawled out of the wrong plughole, and this … this was a million miles from that. But a spider it was, at least until it descended from the stones and, before his eyes, shimmered and flowed *into* itself, shrinking and reforming until it was human. A woman. A *girl*.

The leader – he of the coldly satisfied look that had first informed Tony something was seriously fucked with this whole plan – affectionately stroked the girl's cheek. His three companions – and Tony, now able to see them properly, blinked in amazement – all dressed in actual honest-to-fuck *business suits*, stood with heads bowed and said nothing.

'Thank you, Sarah. I believe our guests have left four of our number dead on the hillside. Remove them.'

Sarah bowed her head in acceptance of the order and walked out of the standing circle of stones into the night. She passed within eight feet of Tony as she did so and, pausing, she turned her head, her human head, and she looked at him with a face that was centuries old and had seen more horrors than even he could begin to fathom.

It was not the face of a monster.

'Why?' he asked her.

'Someday perhaps you will know how it feels to play the villain,' was her reply, before she was swallowed by the night.

If the ringleader had heard the exchange, he did not comment. Instead he spread his hands wide and beamed broadly, turning from Tony to James and back again as he spoke.

'Morrigans!' he said delightedly. 'Splendid sport we've had these past few hundred years, don't you agree? James, isn't it? Knew your father well. Met him twice. Killed him once. Lovely man.'

Tony's mouth dropped open. His father said nothing.

'You know who I am, I assume?' their captor continued, seeming as if he'd be hugely offended if the answer was in the negative.

'Dother,' James said.

Dother hopped in excitement and nodded. It was such an absurdly childish thing to do that it should have been laughable, but given their current circumstances Tony didn't find it remotely amusing. Dother had a way of staring – a shine in his eyes that communicated intelligence, madness and a complete lack of mercy in equal measure – that made the wolf-faeries look about as threatening as doilies.

'Yes!' he crowed. 'Yes, James! And this *must* be Tony ...' he seemed to glide towards the younger man now, moving this way and that like a snake, coming almost close enough to touch, that infuriating *I've-got-you* smile never leaving his lips. 'Ohhh he's promising, James. Very promising. I can see big things ahead for you, my boy.'

Again, the Eastwood urge surfaced. This time, however, he wasn't even able to muster a clumsy Belfast substitute for a classic comeback. Right then and there, Tony Morrigan's full attention was on the sickle in Dother's right hand: he really didn't want to die tonight, didn't want to feel that blade slice through the webbing and him at the same time.

'What are you going to do with us?'

'For a fair few years now we've been playing around with this and that,' Dother said, not answering his query, walking back into the centre of the circle instead. Picking up a stick, he stoked the fire set there. 'You remember your trip to the Mournes with

Daddy, Tony? The male bonding? The inspirational coming-of-age? The clouds of flies settling on rotting flesh … the smell of the corpses … the way you ran and ran? And hasn't it been a fun time on this island ever since? But it's time for the next stage, as we might say in the corporate world. I'm becoming quite the fan of this human concept of *business*, it's so deliciously cut-throat I'm quite ashamed we didn't invent it.'

'Can you get to the fuckin' point, dickhead?' James interrupted. 'If I'd wanted to take my son somewhere and have him bored shitless by a ranting lunatic I'd have taken him to St Bridget's tomorrow for the Mass.'

Dother didn't hesitate. He strode over to James. The sickle flashed and there was a roar of agony and a spurt of blood.

'No!' Tony cried out, throwing himself against the webbing, straining every muscle and sinew in his body.

'Now,' Dother said, holding up the severed ear to James' face as if for emphasis and jerking it around like a puppet on a string, 'shut up and listen, okay? And here – can't have you bleeding out or passing out, can we?'

He passed a hand over the wound and James, still hollering and roaring with the pain, seemed to relax. A shiver passed through his body. The wound had cauterised instantly as Dother's hand had passed over it, the blood loss stopped.

Dother talked directly into the ear as though it were the receiver on a telephone. 'Hello?' he said. 'Come in, James? Can you hear me, James?'

'You bastard you *bastard* you fuckin' bastard if you touch him I swear to fuck I'll fuckin' *kill* you you *bastard*!' Tony was saying, his mouth running on auto as he struggled once again to stay above the rising waters of panic.

The webbing wasn't budging. His father, groggy and heavy-eyed, blinked and came back from the brink of the agonies he'd experienced. Without the ear his head looked unbalanced, unfinished – a child's clay model. He focused on Dother with some effort.

'Fuck you,' he said softly, in a voice only just loud enough for Tony to make out. 'All these fuckin' years you and your wee fucked-up family have been bangin' on the door, screamin' and cryin' because you couldn't come in. We've moved on. The whole fuckin' *world* has moved on. No matter what you do to us, what you try to do tonight … it won't work. You've been left behind, Dother.'

Dother smiled, not a madman's smile, more the smile of a man who was utterly confident in his own abilities. It was not reassuring.

'Stirring. Your illustrious ancestor herself would have been proud. Oh you're wrong, of course, but still – bravo. Humankind hasn't changed *one bit* in the last two thousand years. You've advanced technologically beyond all recognition, but in terms of morals? Of ethics?' he laughed. 'The only thing holding you back is that now your world is suddenly much more connected. Massacres are global news. Serial killers are renowned worldwide. You feel under scrutiny and so you rein in your instinct, which I'm delighted to say remains as constant as ever – if it moves, fuck it, possess it, or kill it. You're animals, to be used as livestock. As sport. And after tonight, the glorious destiny that awaits your kind will move one step closer.'

'After tonight,' James replied, voice calm and steady, 'that *hoor* of a mother of yours will be down to two sons.'

'Da, shut the fuck up!' Tony pleaded. Fuck bravado, that was his da over there, with a stump where his right ear should be. He had no desire to see any more of him mutilated as punishment.

'You should listen to your son,' Dother said softly, rolling the sickle he'd used to cut off James' ear between his fingers. The blade moved so fast it was hard to see; the faerie possessed an incredible degree of dexterity.

'Stay outta this Tony,' James told him. To Dother he said, 'He helped you, didn't he?'

Dother grinned. 'Of course he did.'

'I fuckin' knew it,' James bit out, then barked out three words in Gaelic that Tony couldn't translate.

Brian popped into existence, as if the universe had belched him into being, sitting on the grass midway between James Morrigan and Dother. His eyes bulged in surprise at the suddenness of the summoning, before his head turned to take in his surroundings and absorb its implications.

'Ah,' he said.

'You sold us out,' James spat. 'You ungrateful wee cunt. The number of times I've protected you–'

Brian, by now recovered from the shock of materialising in the thick of things, responded by flicking James the middle finger. 'You did me no favours, Morrigan. You used me for nineteen years to kill my own kind. Did you think I was going to turn down Prince Dother's generous offer?' and as he said it, he turned and made a simpering bow to Dother, who was impassivity itself at this display.

'Offer. Let me guess. Help lure us here and it's safe passage back to the Otherworld, all sins forgiven?'

Brian nodded and shrugged in a *so what* gesture. 'Yeah, that's about the size of it.'

'You stupid wee bastard,' James said. 'In all the centuries you spent with this fucker and his family, did you ever see them forgive anyone?'

Dother smiled at this. Brian did not.

'Yeah, but ...' he said, and then turned to look at his Prince. Tony was sure that, had there been a bit more light, he would have seen the colour drain out of the little faerie. Dother took a long step toward Brian, and another.

'The deal was real, r-right?' Brian stammered. No reply was forthcoming, and in another two steps Dother had closed the distance between the two very different castes of faerie. The sickle still in his grasp shone in the moonlight. This did not escape Brian's notice.

'Cast the luck charm!' James said urgently. 'Cast it *now*!'

'That,' Dother said, 'would be unwise.'

Brian's lips twitched and hope surged within Tony, but died again almost instantly. The little faerie said not a word and merely dropped to his knees before his Prince, bowing his head, ready to accept whatever fate was to befall him.

'Well done, my child,' Dother murmured. 'You shall be rewarded. Please, stay for the ceremony. I promise you won't be disappointed by the entertainment.'

He walked away, leaving Brian unharmed. The chanting resumed a moment later, with Dother leading the incantations, his voice rising higher and higher as the Gaelic was spoken faster and faster.

The air seemed to thicken, laden with some indefinable quality that Tony had never experienced before, and he wondered through his despair if this was what raw magic felt like. Was this what the ancient world had felt like? Was this what Ireland would feel like if they succeeded in breaking down the barrier and unleashing the full force of the Otherworld?

Maybe. But it looked like he wouldn't be around to see it.

The wind had picked up now. Where there had once been an eerie stillness there was now a raging torrent of air whipping around in a tight circle – and as severe as the wind was inside the standing stones, judging from the sensations on his back Tony got the impression it was five, ten times worse immediately outside. A twister was forming with the fire on the hilltop as its eye while further toward the centre, barely a hair moved on Dother's head as his voice rose in pitch and speed and intensity–

Tony recognised only one word – *iobairt*. The Gaelic for 'sacrifice'.

One of Dother's lieutenants knelt to the soil and picked up a *gae bolg*, a belly spear, four feet of wood which ended in a wickedly sharp barb. He began to walk toward Tony, spear in hand.

So this was it. This was how he died, barely into his twenties: as part of an archaic ritual to bring a mythical superweapon into existence. Well. It was more interesting than cancer, at any rate. The wind shrieked, making even thinking impossible, but there wasn't much going through Tony's mind anyway apart from the very clear thought that his father would have to watch his son die. He didn't want that, and not just for the very obvious reason, but also because of what losing his mother had done to James. Seeing his son murdered before his eyes …

At least he won't have long to mourn.

The black thought didn't make him smile, but he was feeling fatalistic enough that, even in the face of impending death, he chose not to struggle against the bonds of webbing that held him. He knew they'd hold fast.

Dother paused in his chanting to bark out two words. Tony didn't catch them or their meaning, but it was enough to stop the lieutenant in his approach.

And to make him turn away from Tony, toward his father.

Tony screamed and wrenched, all of the strength and determination that had deserted him only moments before now returning, with interest. He shouted obscenities, strings of nonsensical threats and sobbing promises of revenge, and he tore and pulled and tried to *will* himself out of the constricting bind of the webbing and across the standing stone circle in time to intercept that bastard with the spear before he got to his father, because he was so close, *oh God so close—*

His father wasn't looking at his approaching executioner, or at the tip of the barb that would shortly enter his body. He was looking directly at Tony, waiting for his desperate thrashing to cease so he would be still enough to be able to understand him when he spoke, and when he did, despite the freight-train hurricane that raged around them, somehow the words carried clear across the circle to his son's ears.

'Keep our line going,' his father told him. 'Pass on who we are.'

The lieutenant drew back the *gae bolg*, gathering momentum for the killing thrust. Dother ceased his fevered chanting. Tony howled in grief.

Prematurely, as it turned out.

His father's second dagger ripped through the webbing holding him in place from the inside. Somehow he had concealed it from the spider, prevented its confiscation. The hole it cut through the webbing gave him enough freedom of movement to twist his body to the side to step half-out of the cocoon that had held him and escape the lethal thrust of the belly spear.

Though elation was surging through his veins, for some reason Tony found himself watching Dother, to gauge his reaction to his father's escape. What he saw choked that elation stillborn.

The Prince wasn't furious. He didn't even seem surprised. And still that smile was there.

Seizing the spear from his opponent, James Morrigan threw the attacker off-balance by jerking it forward. Stumbling, Dother's lieutenant walked right into a beautiful right cross that sent him sprawling. His father spared another precious second with his dagger blade to sever the remaining webbing holding him in place. Now free to move, he tossed the dagger to his stronger right hand and, with a small, economical movement, brought it down blade-first into the exposed back of the faerie who'd attempted to run him through.

Dother moved, but not toward James.

Tony gasped as a cool blade was pressed against his throat. He had barely seen the faerie prince cover the distance between the fire and himself.

'You don't disappoint, James!'

His remaining lieutenants stood between James and his son. Brian, shaking like a leaf, had retreated to the most easterly standing stone and cowered with his back to the rock, covering his eyes. The spider was beyond the circle somewhere in the darkness. Tony fervently hoped she stayed out there; hoped that the winds encircling them would be sufficiently strong to prevent her return.

'Let him go.'

The lieutenants moved to flank him. Holding the gae bolg in his left hand and the remaining silver dagger in his right, James watched them intently, waiting for an attempted attack. Every chance he dared he turned his attention back to Dother and Tony. The knife's blade pressed harder and Tony felt a warm trickle begin to well against it as it broke his skin.

His blood spattered the grass below.

The fire, until that moment a rather modestly sized blaze, abruptly let loose a jet of orange flame that shot straight up into the clouds. The heat blast from the explosion was unbearable; Tony shut his eyes lest they boil away in their sockets, and felt his skin' wilt under the intensity of the flare. He expected to feel Dother's blade sink into his flesh – surely the demon would choose this moment to strike?

Nothing happened.

He opened his eyes, and as they adjusted and the searing-blue afterimages faded, the scene before him reassembled itself. The grass was browned by the heat; the fire was back to its former intensity and Dother was now nowhere to be seen. Judging by the chunks of steaming flesh, the smell of charred meat, and the leg still in a business suit that was smouldering not five feet away, Tony figured that at least one of his lieutenants had not fared well.

His father ... where was–

There.

There he was, groggily picking himself up from where the explosion had tossed him like a ragdoll. Battered, bruised. *Still alive.*

Behind him, unseen, Dother's last remaining underling was bearing down on him.

More out of reflex than anything else, Tony wrenched once more at his bonds even as he shouted a warning. With a rip and a jerk and an indescribable smell, his cocoon split: it had absorbed so much of the heat from the explosion that its tensile strength had been fatally compromised. He hit the ground, free and, apart from burning flash-damaged eyes and ringing ears, fairly unharmed.

His father had heeded the warning. As the faerie, business suit still smoking from the blast, tried to leap on his quarry, his father, silver dagger in his hand, leant into the lunge and added his own boost to his opponent's momentum, accelerating him through the air.

Knowing what was about to happen, Tony sprinted towards his father, arms and legs pumping. He had to get there in time, before–

The faerie screeched pitifully as it landed directly on the flames.

Tony barrelled into his father, knocking them both to the ground as the fire exploded a second time. A wall of flame rolled over their bodies, washing out in all directions, sending another spout vertically up into the night sky.

The heat was incredible. Even as they lay flat and felt themselves cook, Tony knew that he shouldn't even be alive; to be so close to two such blasts and to emerge with only singes to show for it was impossible … unless the flames weren't entirely physical.

As if to prove his theory, the wall of fire stopped dead in its expansion, as if some cosmic force had pressed 'pause', and then promptly began to rewind in on itself, reversing with the whoosh of a thousand aircraft taking off simultaneously, back to its humble source in the centre of the standing stones. Once there, it extinguished itself. The winds stopped. Dead. Silence fell, almost absurd in its completeness.

Something landed on the soil in front of Tony and his father. Something long, and sharp. Something silver.

'The Sword,' Tony breathed, getting up, sucking in steadying breaths, his heart beating a tattoo in his chest. He nudged his father. 'Da … the Sword. Nuada's Sword. Should I take it?'

The silver light the Sword was throwing off illuminated the scene around them. It was beautiful, ethereal, otherworldly, for want of a less-obvious phrase. Tony wanted very much to hold it. It looked like the sort of weapon that should be held; the silvery light that suffused everything around him and his father in a regal glow seemed to beckon to him …

'Da?'

It was now that he saw what else the silver glow had revealed: a the patch of darkening grass under his father's body.

'Da!'

He rolled his father over, the sword forgotten. The strength left his legs and he crashed rubber-ankled to the ground, unable to stand.

Stuck in James Morrigan's chest, buried to the hilt, was his own silver dagger.

Tony's brain throbbed as he tried to process this fresh horror. He became hyper-aware of every passing instant – the feel of the air, the deathly quiet, every contour and curve of his father's body, every angle and line of that dagger protruding obscenely from his chest, and the ragged, weak rising and falling of his father's chest as he struggled to breathe. No.

No. No. No. No. No. Impossible. Impossible. *Impossible!* His father hadn't had that dagger when he had run toward him, when he had tackled him to the ground to save him ...

He had the silver dagger in hand. When I knocked him to the ground. Silver dagger in hand. Knocked him over. Me. Knocked him over. Silver dagger. Hit the ground hard. Had to run as fast as I could. Course I did. Cos he was dead otherwise. Had to get to him in time. Knocked him over. Dagger in hand. He fell when I knocked into him. I had to. I did this. I did this. I ...

A weak cough. Blood. Tony knelt beside his father and cradled his head, wiping away the blood.

'Son?'

'Da ...'

'Don't,' he said, his throat making bubbling noises, his chest heaving. He tried to focus on Tony's face. There was a light in his eyes, borne of determination to speak. 'Don't ...'

It was a sentiment James Morrigan never got to finish.

Tony held his father's head against his chest and rocked back and forth, squeezing his eyes shut and sobbing for what felt like an age.

Eventually the world began to move again. Shadows fell over him – one human-sized, one much larger. The sword was retrieved from where it lay on the grass. Dother turned it over and over in his hands admiringly. Beside him, Sarah, in her full-spider form, waited for the order to strike at the pathetic figure before them.

'You've done me a favour, Tony,' Dother said. 'I owe you this sword' and he knelt, addressing the sobbing youth, the glowing weapon laid across his palms. 'You see that little heroic show back there? All a bit of a glamour, I'm afraid. The Morrigan – the *real* deal – she placed a charm on this magnificent specimen. Only one Morrigan killing another could summon it. I just had to conjure up a situation where your own over-eagerness and crippling ineptitude would bring that about. So, just like your father, you didn't disappoint me.'

Tony's sobbing had ceased. He raised his head to look at Dother feeling nothing but hatred and heartbreak in equal measure. 'I'm going to be the one who kills you.'

Dother's smile was so ever-present it may as well have been painted on. 'No,' he stated. 'Not as simple as that. You see, your little … mistake … will have consequences for you, Tony my boy. You'll find out what those are, in time, and when you do …' he lifted the sword, as if about to strike, 'you'll come to me to ask for my help.'

With a barely-human bellow, the paralysis of grief left the young man and he launched forward, intent on getting his hands around Dother's neck and squeezing until the life left his body.

Idly, Sarah flicked out a leg, catching him full force. Tony was unconscious before his body hit the ground.

Dother ran his fingers lovingly over the sword's blade.

'Your mother will be pleased,' Sarah remarked.

At that, Dother's smile finally vanished. 'Yes,' he replied, in a strange tone. 'Yes, of course she will. Come, Sarah. We have much to accomplish, and you must be at my side.'

'Of course. I remain your sentinel.'

He tilted his head. 'Hmm. Yes, sentinel. Partly that I suppose.'

'*Partly* that?' she echoed, puzzled.

'Tell me, how are your typing skills …?'

COUNTY WEXFORD, IRELAND, 43 AD

Time had moved on by several days; Danny knew it without having the Morrigan tell him. The bodies of those killed by the Formorian raid on the village had been removed. He didn't know where they'd been taken – what did the people of this time do? Bury immediately? Put them in a burial chamber? He couldn't even remember that much, couldn't recall what any history book or teacher had said about this time period.

They remained in the centre of the village during the slight time shift, as if anchored there. As the world swung into regular motion again, he saw that it wasn't only the bodies that had vanished. Gone was the hubbub of the place. This little collection of huts and hovels may have seemed to be worlds away from life on Regent Street but when he'd first come here, he'd been struck by how many things were familiar – the occasional streaking past of a few kids as they played together; the cursory nods exchanged between neighbours; that sense of community. Property and living conditions may change over centuries ... humans, it seemed, not so much.

But the mood of the place was very different now.

The streets ... or rather, *street* – this place was like a one-horse town that had eaten its horse – was markedly less crowded. Understandable perhaps given that almost half of the population had perished in that terrible afternoon. But those that were visible were all male – there were no women and children in sight – and these men had changed. Each one carried a weapon of some sort about his person. The nods were still there, but there was a jumpy quality to them.

This was a place still raw with shock and terrible grief.

He was about to ask the Morrigan where the women and children were – in their homes, presumably – when he saw examples of both, walking out of their home and toward the central well. It was the younger Morrigan with Glon and Gaim, and all three carried empty buckets.

Silence descended so quickly it took his breath away. The men who had been going about their daily errands stopped what they were doing to exchange looks.

The younger Morrigan, of course, was neither blind nor stupid. Outwardly, however, she gave no indication that she had noticed the ripple of paralysis that she and her sons had caused. Glon and Gaim, younger and more naïve, tugged at their mother's tunic for attention, obviously wanting to ask questions. Danny saw Glon start to wave at one man only for his mother to slap down his wrist before the gesture was complete. She spoke, quickly and sternly, and the three of them hurried toward the well and began to fill their buckets.

Like a noose tightening, the men standing around began to walk, slowly, deliberately, toward the three figures.

One man was moving faster than the others. His trajectory took him past the pair of ghostly observers, and as he passed within only a few feet of Danny a truly *incredible* smell wafted from the man, almost enough to make Danny gag.

'What the fuck was that?' he hissed.

The older Morrigan's face was a study in concealed agony. 'See any pubs around here?' she asked pointedly. 'It's what passes for Carlsberg in 43 AD.'

Pissed. That explained the man's crab-walk; Danny had thought he'd been trying to sneak up on the trio at the well, but in actuality the man was smashed off his face and it was all he could do to stay even roughly on course.

The effect might even have been comic, if not for the short, rusted and altogether diseased-looking blade he clutched in his right hand.

As if sensing his approach, the Morrigan's hands slipped around her sons' shoulders. They had filled the buckets, but the noose of men had tightened to a degree that there was no way back to where they'd come from without passing at least five of them.

Danny heard the murmur of voices and, looking around, he saw that, as if by magic, doorways that had been empty only minutes before were now populated – by women with grey, hard faces, the children they shielded, silent. Unnaturally silent.

The Morrigan stood with her two children, her back now to the well, facing them all. She did not look afraid. The same could not be said of Glon and Gaim, who were shrinking further and further behind their mother, their little mouths moving with silent and increasingly alarmed questions. Where was Caderyn, Danny wondered. Home with Coscar?

Still the men came closer, closing the gaps between one another, until it was impossible to imagine even dodging between their reaches. Only the drunken man was not included in this rough formation: he was a few steps further ahead, his eyes wet with tears.

Danny's heart was pounding. In a way this was worse than the Formorian assault. That had been brutal and horrific, but it had been done by *monsters* out of … well, out of fairytales. You don't expect much from fuckers the size of houses with too many limbs, or too few. This was altogether different. The faces around him, not a smile between them, were all too human.

Speak, he silently implored the younger Morrigan. *Speak, or run, or fight. Do something!*

'I am not one of them,' she spoke up, as if she had heard him.

'You are not,' the drunkard said, words surprisingly clear despite his condition, 'one of us.'

'I have *chosen* to become like you,' she said. 'Me and my children, we will give up our heritage and live amongst you. That is all I want. Everything I want. Please, allow me.'

'Give up?' the drunkard scoffed. 'What have you given up?

What have you sacrificed?'

With a start, Danny placed the man's face. Saw him during the massacre, pleading with a Formorian looming large over him. Not for his own life, but for that of his family.

'My wife. My little daughters. My babies,' and he sobbed openly now, almost stumbling to his knees before recovering his balance. The faces of the villagers watching were ashen. 'Murdered. By *your* kind. Why? Why did they come here? *Why did they come here?*'

'You have been on the hunting parties!' she replied desperately. 'You know they have struck at other villages, other settlements!'

He lost it at this. 'They were looking for *you!*' he screamed at her.

The words, and the accusation behind them, echoed. So loud had he shouted that a few birds took off from a nearby roof.

'Do you deny it?' he whispered into the silence that followed.

'Please,' she said again, her voice pleading this time.

Danny moved towards her before he quite knew what was happening. He had made himself a promise during the Tuatha standoff not to stand by and watch any more horror unfold, no matter how ineffective he might be in his ethereal state. Every instinct he had was screaming at him that something terrible was about to happen here.

'If we let her stay here, how long before those things return? To finish the job? And if she truly *is* becoming one of us, then who shall protect us?'

Murmurs of agreement. Nods. A rising current of electricity was passing between the men, a precursor to action. The men did not look excited at the prospect of what they were about to do;

most looked grim, and a few looked nauseated. But none stepped back. None dropped weapons from readiness. None broke ranks.

'Stop this!' Danny demanded, *willing* himself into existence, drawing up all of that strange wellspring of power deep within himself he had tentatively begun to explore.

Nothing. No one turned in his direction.

He walked to the drunkard, just as the man lifted his weapon to point at the woman and children before him. Shouted in his face. Did a dance. The man's gaze never wavered. He took a step forward and Danny lunged for him and with a strange feeling akin to being plunged into an ice bath, he was out and through the other side of the man, who was now behind him. The drunkard didn't notice a damn thing.

Fifteen feet away, his guide stood like a statue. He cried out to her for help, begged her to make him corporeal. He may as well have been invisible to her too given the complete lack of response he received.

And Glon. Little Glon, seeing the net closing in and feeling his mother's grip slacken for just a moment, decided to make a break for it.

'No!' his mother and his unseen would-be protector screamed in unison.

'Daddy!' Glon screamed, sprinting for home and calling for his father, while the circular formation of men made their move. Danny, redoubling his efforts, threw himself into a last-ditch dive at the drunkard. He felt the ice again, and then soil.

A little cry reached his ears. Not a dramatic scream, only a little 'ompf' that sounded more surprised than anything else.

Getting to his feet, he saw what he'd prayed he would not.

Glon swayed, his eyes wide, his skin pale. His mouth was open in a little round 'O'. The man standing over him looked only slightly less sick, and when he saw the blood on the end of his spear, he reacted violently, as if stung. The spear fell to the ground.

'Mammy?' Glon gasped at the Morrigan, who was standing in frozen mid-tussle with the drunkard, little Gaim cowering in terror at her feet. 'Mammy … I'm hurt …'

Behind him, attracted by the screams and the commotion, Caderyn stood at the door of their home. He had seen it all.

Down Glon went, in a tangle of arms and legs. A little puppet with its strings cut.

Time seemed to stretch. In the quarter-second or so it took Glon's body to crumple to the ground, the Morrigan freed herself from her opponent. The bright afternoon day darkened to blood red as though someone had blown out the sun. The air went from crisp and clear to heavy, pregnant with magic, and all of it swirling around the figure of the woman once clad in the humble rags of a peasant.

But no longer: the rags became armour, golden and resplendent. A fearsome headdress moulded itself from nothingness around her features, obscuring everything save her eyes and mouth. Her right arm reached toward the crimson-soaked skies above and with a crack of thunder, a twelve-foot spear dropped from the heavens to land perfectly in her outstretched hand.

She bared her teeth in an animal snarl and the War Goddess roared, so loudly that the villagers were knocked from their feet, the huts shook, and Danny was forced backwards several paces as through trying to fight against hurricane-force winds.

The Morrigan of Mag Tuiread had returned.

Danny broke his promise. He stood by and he watched, moving not a muscle to stop it.

He did nothing as she scythed through the village's men: first, the luckless man whose spear had caused Glon's death, the drunkard second. She did things to them both that made what the Formorians had done to the villagers seem like an episode of *Teletubbies* by comparison. His fellow warriors were next, impaled two and three at a time, cut down and sliced in half as they tried to flee.

Blood had been spilled, revenge had been taken for the unimaginable crime perpetrated. There she could have stopped.

She didn't.

When the last of the would-be attackers had perished, she paused, the mammoth spear in her hand encrusted with blood, her long tresses of jet-black hair flying as sparks leapt from her skin and earthed themselves around her.

She drew breath, and turned slowly, meeting the gaze of every woman and child huddled terrified in their doorways. They were all shaking, pleading for mercy.

None was shown.

She looked more than human now; had cast away the limitations of a body and become a swiftly moving wave of death, a black cloud that went from house to house. When she entered each dwelling, shrill screams were heard from the inside. Screams that were quickly cut off. When she exited, there was only silence.

Finally, in the whole of the village there was only one man

left. He faced her without fear as she threw herself toward him, staring unflinchingly at this terrible avenging angel as her spear bore down–

–and stopped.

'Caderyn …' she said.

Her husband held little Coscar in his arms and stood amidst the dead and dismembered bodies of his former neighbours, toe to toe with the War Goddess that was his wife.

'Strike,' he said softly. 'Please.'

'How can you ask me that?' she returned, her voice shaking.

'How can I? How can *you*? How can you do this?'

'Look what they did! Look what they did to our *son*, Caderyn!' she screamed in fury, pointing at Glon where he lay. Realisation dawned on her then and she ran to the body and scooped it up, throwing it easily over one shoulder as though he weighed nothing. 'I must go,' she told Caderyn, 'I must place him in the Cauldron.'

'He'll be like you?'

'He'll be *alive*!' she roared back. 'I want him to *live*! Not to die like some *human*!'

Caderyn gestured to the massacred villagers. 'Yes,' he said hollowly. 'Yes, we seem to die easily enough.'

'Gaim, come to me,' she instructed, and the smaller boy obediently scampered to his mother and was duly scooped up also. One of her sons over each shoulder, one living, one dead, she looked at her husband, at his eyes and what they said.

'I can't go with you,' he said.

'No,' she replied. 'But even if you could–'

'I wouldn't.'

239

'I can't come back to you,' she said.

'No,' he replied, staring her down. 'You don't want to come back.'

There was the smallest of pauses. 'No.'

At this he nodded, taking one more look around at the massacre the woman he loved had wrought. 'Glon will make a fine warrior,' he said weakly, 'and Gaim will need him. He's always needed him.' He paused and looked down at the baby sleeping in his arms, 'but you will not take Coscar. Coscar stays with me.'

'I won't condemn my son to a mortal life–'

'Condemn?' he choked. '*Condemn?* To be spared the fate of becoming one of you? Capable of *this?*'

She did not reply.

'Daddy?' Gaim said uncertainly. The Morrigan set him down and the little boy looked tearfully from his mother to his father. 'Daddy, what's happening? What happened to Glon? Is he … is he alive?'

Caderyn dropped to one knee, rebalancing baby Coscar as he did so. He beckoned the boy to him and embraced him. 'Yes,' he said, hugging him fiercely, though Gaim was too stunned to return the gesture. 'Yes, Gaim. Your mammy is … is magic, you see. And she's going to take him to a special place that'll make him well. And you get to go too and this is the best bit – all three of you are going to be *real* warriors! No more pretending for you, oh no! You're the real thing! Isn't that great?'

Tears dropped from Gaim's face. 'I-I-I just want Glon,' he said, his lip curling as his face crumpled. 'I want Glon and I want Mammy and you and Coscar and I wanna go home.'

'I know,' Caderyn whispered. 'I know you do, son.'

'Daddy ... why is everyone dead? What did Mammy do in those houses? I want that to go away, Daddy. Can Mammy magic that? Can you Mammy?'

'Yes,' Caderyn said firmly, turning the boy around. 'Yes she can. So you go and make sure your brother gets well and while you're away, everyone will come back to life, and you'll be back here before you know it. And I-I'll,' and his voice wavered, 'I'll be waiting.'

Gaim wasn't fooled one bit. He was about to start another round of questions when a light touch from his mother made his eyes roll white in his head. She scooped him up over her shoulder again.

'I'll always love you,' she told him.

'If you ever see Regan,' he replied, 'tell her the same thing.'

She leant down to touch and kiss Coscar on the cheek. Caderyn took a step back, drawing the child tighter into his embrace. The heavens rumbled overhead, the red skies darkened as though the wound she'd ripped in reality had started bleeding anew.

'Time's up.'

Danny blinked. It hadn't been the Morrigan's younger self who had spoken.

The wretched little village, scene of two massacres, dissolved to nothing and Danny braced himself for the next vignette, preparing to reacclimatise to wherever she chose to deposit him.

This time the space in-between seemed longer than normal. Transitioning from vision to vision before had been quick, like stepping through paper walls. This time it was as though he were passing through a sort of nexus, a busy crossroads in reality – shapes and colours, smells and sounds passed before him as though on a conveyor belt in a game show, but he couldn't get a fix on any of it, on anything … save her voice.

'You've seen things no one else has,' it came to him, from such close range that it felt like she was whispering directly to his mind. 'You wanted to know who I was. What this was all about. Consider that your introduction.'

He tried to reply and found that he could, so long as he didn't care that he had no clue where his mouth currently resided, or even if he still possessed one in this between-place.

'*Introduction? You mean there's more?*'

He sensed dark amusement in her voice. 'Yes, Danny. Time has run short. We are too close to her now.'

The between-space began to solidify around them. He felt his arms and limbs come back online, one after the other. He was coming back, from the visions she had sent him, back to another nightmare.

'Coscar,' he said, knowing the crow was nearby even if he could not yet bring his eyes back into working order to see it. 'He's my ancestor, isn't he. The one we're all descended from.'

'Coscar is …' and the Morrigan's voice paused, 'where you came from, yes.'

'What happened to him? To all of you? How did you go from that goddess to the crow?'

'You'll learn, Danny. Soon enough, you'll know. But what's important is that you embrace the gifts you've been given.'

The Otherworld solidified around him. Sensations of cold,

and something moving below him in great bounds – something big and alive and moving fast across the grass, with him on its back. And beside him, the crow, still perched where it had brushed its wing against his face to trigger the most incredible experience of his life.

'My synaesthesia. It's more than a condition. It's … it's connected to what you can do, what the Tuatha can do. The magic.'

'That's not the gift I was talking about,' the crow said, and before he could reply or protest, it fluttered free of their shared mount with a chaotic flapping of wings and was gone into the Otherworld skies.

On they went, bounding toward a hilltop no more than a half-mile distant, on which sat the biggest circle of standing stones that Danny had ever seen. Each slab had to be forty feet high and twenty feet thick at least. Crowning it, resplendent in its impossibility, was a hovering circlet of stone that had decided not to bother with the inconveniences of gravity. Four huge and hungry bonfires bordered the structure to the north, south, east and west.

Impressive as this was in terms of scale, Danny was rather more immediately concerned with the other feature of their destination. Namely, that the whole thing was absolutely *heaving* with every conceivable type of horrendous creature imaginable. Hundreds of them, circling the blazes at each of the compass-points, with another multitude within the central summit's stone circle perimeter.

He caught the smell of magic, immediately familiar from the visions. But magic was far from the only aroma permeating this place. Somewhere, meat was cooking. A lot of meat. Somewhere else, meat was rotting. The twin smells, one alluring, the other overpoweringly nauseating, hit him simultaneously.

'Wwwwwe haaaaaaveeeeee arrrrrrriveeeeeed,' Wily the wolf-faerie informed him. 'Caaaaaaarrrrmannnn awwwwwwaitsssssss youuuuuuuuuu.'

'Oh ...'

A thousand possible ways to end that thought sprung into Danny's head, some of them involving long and spectacular strings of swearwords; others resulting in an exit so swift and cowardly he'd make Scooby Doo look like William Wallace.

Instead, he closed his eyes and recalled every single memory he had of Ellie, of Luke, of every time in his life when he'd felt calm and happy and at peace, and all of the sensory inputs that had come with them.

When he opened his eyes again, the faerie fortress was still before him, but he felt better, despite the seemingly endless hordes undulating and chanting, already noticing his arrival. Teeth glinted. Claws shone and they all began to draw closer to him. Wily was leading him into the thick of the crowds. There was no possibility of escape. The crow was gone. He was alone against them.

'Take me to her,' he told Wily, readying himself for a speech of manly defiance that would show these fuckers he meant business. 'And what the fuck are you bunch o' ugly cunts looking–'

'*Everybody, yeah ...*' trilled a familiar voice.

He trailed off. The crowd of faeries that were gathering around Wily as he padded forward all turned their attention towards the pocket of Danny's jeans.

'Rock your body, yeah …'

'– looking at,' Danny finished, but by that stage the wind had rather left his sails.

'Yoooooouuuuurrrrrrrr arrrrrsssseeee isssss sinnnnnginggggg,' Wily observed.

'Aye … I noticed,' he said, fighting down the urge to blush. He hadn't thought for one second that his phone would get signal here, yet here it was ringing merrily away in an all-too-familiar ringtone. Fishing the phone from his jeans pocket, he saw that it was indeed Ellie calling.

'I ammmmmm taaaaaakinnggggggggg himmmmmmmm tooooo seeeeeeee ouuuuurrrr Quueeeennnn,' Wily rumbled to the assembled crowd. One got too close and reached towards Danny with its claw. Wily's head snapped around, his jaws clamped together, there was a shriek of pain, and the claw was gone. Forever. The crowd shrank back.

'You will die, human,' one of the horde surrounding them slavered. It looked like a giant upright wasp; a segmented body, filament-thin wings, red and white hoops rather than yellow. A curved stinger protruded from the crown of its head.

'Our Queen will tear you apart,' said another, a creature that seemed to have no solidity to it whatsoever; it oozed along like a great slug, but at speed that had enabled it to push to the front of the crowd. He could see no mouth and for a moment wondered where it had spoken from … no, wait … there it was – vertical and four feet long and running half the length of its mass, revealing pulsing innards. He thought he caught a glimpse of something moving inside; something alive, perhaps still being digested …

'Our day of victory is at hand!' squealed a two-foot tall gnarled little thing, jumping up and down with barely repressed excitement. He was as bald as a cue ball and as wrinkled as a thousand-year-old paper bag.

Don't show fear. If you act like it's not your inevitable right to be brought before Carman every single one of them will fall on you right now and rip you to shreds. You're the first human most of them have ever seen. They have no idea what you're capable of and they are scared out of their wits.

He glanced around for the crow. It was nowhere to be seen, but clearly the lines of communication had not been closed; surely that had been the Morrigan's voice sounding in his head. *They were scared of* him? *Could that be possible?*

'*Gonna bring the flava, show you how …*'

Possible or not, it was his only chance. Danny slumped his shoulders and adopted a look of pained impatience. 'Lads,' he said, in as exasperated a tone as he could muster, 'will you shut the fuck up? For two minutes?'

'You do not command us, human!' drooled Wasp Thing. A huge drop of what could only be poison welled at the tip of that head-stinger. The wings began to thrum as if it were preparing to launch an attack.

'Get him! Get him! Get him!' squeaked Pint Size. 'Kill the filthy … aaaaarrrrghhh!'

Danny waited until Wily's head had stopped moving and the great wolf's jaws had stopped crunching. In the sudden hush that had fallen, the crack of bones was very loud indeed.

'*Backstreet's Back – All right!*'

'Prrrrooooceeeeeed, Dannnnnyyyy Morrrrrrriggggggannnn.'

I have got to change that fuckin' ringtone, he thought.

Baulking slightly at the ease with which his mount had brutally despatched and devoured his miniscule agitator, Danny answered the call. 'Ellie?'

'Danny …'

He frowned. That wasn't Ellie's voice.

'*Da?*' he said.

'Yes, Danny, I–'

'Da, I–' he began.

'Danny listen to me. We're in trouble. Ellie's–'

'Ellie's with you? What's going on?'

'You've gotta get back up here as quick as you can. Get the Sword. Get *something*. There's too many of them out there, son.'

The Sword? His da talking about the Sword? How was that possible? His da knew about the Sword of Nuada? Danny's legs dug into Wily's sides to stop himself toppling off. His head was spinning. If his da knew about the sword … what did that mean? Too many of *what*?

It was his father's voice, he was sure of it. But there had been something new there too, an edge. In the years since Tony Morrigan had re-entered his son's life he had seemed like a man going through the motions. Danny had chalked his da's lifelessness up to disappointment. No doubt his decade-long adventure with his new life and whatever old slut he'd shacked up with had finally come to an end – maybe she'd kicked him out, sending him crawling to the one woman stupid enough to take him back.

Disappointment that he was back with the family, back with the son he'd deemed not good enough.

None of that dead quality had existed in his father's voice just now. He had sounded firm, in control …

Alive.

Danny had so many questions, but got to ask none of them. There was a strangled cry from the other side, and a single click. Not even a disconnect tone – the call had simply ended, and his mobile had returned to its menu screen as if nothing were amiss.

'Da!'

He redialled. Nothing. No connection. Tried again. Same thing. On his main menu screen, the signal strength dropped from four bars to three, to two, to one, to lost. Seemingly the Otherworld had finally decided to stop switchboarding his calls.

Not the Otherworld. Her.

It was the Morrigan's voice in his head. Danny glanced back up to that imposing, primitive fortress at the summit of the hill – more a mountain, in actuality – on whose slopes they now stood.

Hurry. It seems you've caught her attention. She fears what you may know.

And if she discovers what I know? Danny thought back at her. Or more to the point, what he *didn't* know. He had a power, of some sort; but it had failed him in the lead up to the Morrigan's massacre of the villagers, though whether that was due to her own intervention he didn't know. From what he'd gleaned thus far, Carman was undisputed ruler of this entire domain. That included the thousand or more hellish creatures into whose midst he was now going. What chance did he realistically have of coming out of *any* sort of confrontation with her?

Her answer was immediate. *Does it matter?*

And she was right, it didn't matter. He had to see his little boy again. Had to do whatever it took to make that happen. If that meant walking into the gingerbread house and prostrating himself at the feet of the woman licking her lips and pointing toward the oven ... well, so be it.

And then there was the desperate cry he'd heard before the call had died. It hadn't come from his father, which left only one possibility: Ellie.

Ellie was in trouble and Luke was gone. In terms of motivation, he wasn't immediately lacking.

'What are we waiting for?' he whispered to himself. Patting Wily's massive back, he pointed to his destination with as much heroic intent as he could muster. 'Let's go.'

The crowds parted to let them pass.

The Hard Choices

High-pitched squeals rang throughout the house. Those emitting them rocked back and forth, fingers scrabbling, only to emit fresh shrieks seconds later. It was enough to reduce anyone to tears.

'*Look* at him!' Linda Morrigan roared, her sides shaking with laughter as she pointed down at the photograph in question. The big brown album was balanced, left leaf on her right knee, right leaf on the left knee of Shelley Brogan, little sister and co-squealer.

Tony Morrigan glared up at them from the page below, wearing his groom's suit and waistcoat, looking like he'd rather have hot needles rammed through soft areas of his body than be standing there getting his photograph taken. The photographer must have been urging him to *smile, smile* – and smile he had, in a fashion; if smiles had musical accompaniments, this one would have been the theme from *Jaws*.

'Ach dear love him,' Shelley sympathised, rubbing tears from her eyes. She reached for her cup of tea and took a sip, still chuckling, even as her sister turned a few more pages. 'That's a lovely one.'

'That's me and him the day we moved in here. Four years ago

now – can you believe it?'

'Four years!' Shelley spluttered. 'You're jokin'!'

Linda shook her head and exhaled. The smile she'd been wearing since they began this little nostalgia-fest wilted a little for the first time. 'I remember looking round this place,' she said, glancing at the living room in which they sat, 'and thinking how big it seemed and how empty and …'

Shelley, freshly arrived on a fortnight-long holiday – 'vacation' – from America, where she'd emigrated three years ago, diplomatically held her tongue about the scale of the house. In Colorado a place like this would have been seen as cramped. But she knew that wasn't really what was bothering her sister anyway.

'Are yous still …?'

Linda nodded.

'Is he still away a fair bit?'

Linda nodded again. Shelley licked her lips. This was going to be a riskier question, but she couldn't count herself a sister and shirk away from it.

'You don't think he's–'

'No.' The answer was immediate; clearly Linda had been expecting the question.

'It's just that he's away so much and–'

'No,' Linda said, in a door-slamming tone. She sucked in a breath and looked over at her sister in a way that contained enough apology to assure her that she knew the reasons for asking. 'Shelley, he's not like that. And I love ye, I really do, but ye haven't been here. If ye had been you'd see he's wantin' this for us as much as I am. Sometimes more, I think. Since I've known him all he's talked about is havin' a wee son.'

Not knowing what to say, Shelley accepted this and for a moment they sat in silence, the big old album still sitting on their laps. Linda flicked the pages back to the wedding photographs and to the double-page spread of bride and groom, of her and Tony, staring at the camera. The huge levels of discomfort Tony had felt being photographed solo seemed conspicuously absent when Linda stood beside him.

'He said to me,' she said quietly, 'when we got married, he said ... he wished his da had been there to see it. He'd have been proud, he said.'

'It was terrible what happened to him,' Shelley murmured. She couldn't suppress a shiver. 'I always felt so sorry for Tony.'

Linda nodded. 'I could never really get him to talk about it. But when he did ... I swear, it was almost like he thought it was his fault or somethin'. He was an only child, y'see. Him and his da were so close. I think that's what he wants with our son. If,' she smiled ruefully and cradled her stomach unconsciously, 'he ever decides to put in an appearance, that is.'

'What if it's a daughter?' Shelley asked, with a wicked gleam in her eye.

Linda didn't smile. She shrugged. 'It's weird,' she said, 'every time I ask him that, he just smiles and says, "It'll be a boy. Trust me."'

Shelley snorted. 'Fellas. What do they know?'

At this re-emergence of feminine togetherness, Linda couldn't help but regain some of her former cheer. She lifted the big album off her knee and placed it reverentially in the stereo storage unit where it sat, its last half unfilled.

'C'mon,' she said, 'he'll not be back till tonight. Another meetin'. Will we hit the shops?'

'*Now* you're talkin'…'

THE ROYAL VICTORIA HOSPITAL, BELFAST, 22 YEARS AGO

'You're sure?'

The doctor didn't look away, didn't flinch from the question. There was sympathy in his eyes, Tony gave him that much. 'Few things are certain in this field of medicine, Mr Morrigan,' he said, obviously getting out his rose-tinted paint and applying it liberally to the news he'd just broken. 'But it's fair to say, that from the results of the tests, the chances of you being able to conceive a child with your wife are extremely limited.'

Tony sat in the uncomfortable chair in the too-bright, sterile little room in the Royal and absorbed the most devastating news of his life. 'Limited …' he said slowly. 'Can you … could you … I mean, is there like a number? I mean, if the bookies were coverin' it, what odds would they give?'

He wasn't making this easy on Dr Sinnet and Tony saw the sympathy on the man's face change into a frown of outright concern. 'Tony, I'm not a betting man.'

'But if you *were*,' Tony replied, a mite sharper than he'd intended to. He bit his tongue almost immediately, but too late.

'I wouldn't put my house on it. You're looking at hundreds to one, Tony. Maybe thousands. These things are difficult to gauge accurately.'

'So you might be wrong.'

'I might be, yes,' Dr Sinnet admitted readily, 'but given that you've told me that you and your wife have been trying regularly for – what? Coming up on four years is it now? – without success, I'm inclined to believe what the tests are indicating.'

He was right. Of course he was right. Tony felt his hands bunch into fists; he'd never felt as helpless … as impotent … in his entire fucking life as right now. Coming here and having these tests had been difficult, a blow to his pride, so difficult that Linda thought he was away working now. Ironic to have covered up one lie with another – her idea of what he did for a living was, of course, rather different from the truth.

Keep our line going.

He could almost see his father in front of him. His face contorted in pain but staying strong. He had died that night because of Tony, because of Tony's stupidity and incompetence, and now he was going to go one huge step beyond that fuck-up; he was going to be responsible for ending the entire family line. There would be no new generation of Morrigan to take on the mantle. No one to train.

It was more than that, of course. He didn't ache for a protégé, for a student. He had idolised his father, even before that afternoon in the Mournes when he had learned the full extent of the family secrets. Afterward, seeing his da in action, that hero worship had deepened. Only at the end, when he'd become too fucking selfish, too wrapped up in his own desires, had he turned from him, and look how that had ended.

Having a son of his own was about more than just continuing

the family line. More than just making up for his own mistakes, or living up to his own father's legacy. It involved all those things. It would also mean the world to Linda. He knew his wife, saw her spoil her nieces and nephews to ever-increasing lengths with every Christmas that passed. Mystical destinies be damned – they were steady, they were in love. Ready for a child.

A child that would never come.

'There are options,' Dr. Sinnet said. 'Fertilisation methods. A few have achieved results, good results.'

Tony frowned. 'You don't seem too excited about them,' he observed.

'I just don't want to get your hopes up, Tony. There's a long waiting list. The rates of success aren't great. And frankly, given your test results, even with the assisted fertilisation methods ...'

He couldn't take it any longer. 'What *about* these fuckin' results?' he said, irritated and ashamed in equal measure. 'What was so fuckin' horrific about them anyway? What's wrong with me? Are they lazy bastards down there, is that it? What's my sperm count? Six? *What?*'

Dr Sinnet spread his hands helplessly. 'It's ... it's got me a bit puzzled, Tony, to be honest. You'll recall that when the first set of results came back I asked you about your job and then had you retake the test?'

Tony stiffened. 'Yes,' he said. 'Yes, you did.'

'Well, I was trying to ascertain whether you'd ever worked in hazardous environments, been exposed to toxic substances, worked with pesticides or,' Dr Sinnet gave a humourless laugh, 'radioactive materials, although I doubt there's much chance of that ...'

Trailing off, he felt his concern go up another notch. Tony Morrigan had gone deathly pale. The man was definitely a candidate for counselling over this, although the chances of getting a man to talk about his feelings at being diagnosed as sterile in this day and age were ... well, about the same as his patient fathering octuplets in the next year.

'Is that what the results showed? Exposure to ... something?'

'They were consistent with it, yes, but we've established you've never come into contact with any such materials. The truth is, Tony, that the cause of some infertility is never properly determined,' and Dr Sinnet, who was a kind man and a good doctor, smiled sadly at his patient and reached out to place a hand on his shoulder. 'Tony, I really am sorry. I wish I had better news for you, I really do. Who knows, if there's someone up there, watching,' and he felt Tony twitch when he said this, 'maybe they'll see fit to intervene.'

'Yeah,' Tony said, staring at the floor. 'Maybe they will.'

Your little ... mistake ... will have consequences for you, Tony my boy. You'll find out what those are, in time...

The words Dother had spoken. The night he ...

The night his father died.

He stood up and shook Dr Sinnet's hand, thanked him, promised to contact him if he decided to proceed with the fertilisation options, and took a leaflet for a counselling service. He binned the leaflet on his way to the car.

The man sitting in the passenger seat lifted his head from the newspaper he had been reading.

'Well? What's the plan, chief?' Dermot Scully said cheerfully.

'Linda's expecting you back for this big dinner with her Yankee sis, remember?'

Tony gunned the engine and the car jerked forward, so forcefully Dermot had to brace himself to prevent mild whiplash. 'Jesus!' he said, reaching for the seatbelt. 'What's going on? I take it we're not going to dinner?'

'No,' Tony replied, his mouth set in a thin line. 'No we're not. I've got someone to see.'

'Oh? Who's that?'

'Dother.'

He could practically *hear* Dermot's mouth drop open.

'Aye *right* ...' the younger man said, laughing nervously. 'I'm sure. What's the plan? Drive up to his building, walk in the front door and ask for a meeting?'

'Pretty fuckin' much, yeah.'

As he moved the car into Belfast traffic and headed for the city centre, there was a strangled choking noise from his passenger. 'Are you out of your mind?' Dermot demanded. 'You know what sort of security he's got in that place. We tried hittin' it last year and look what happened. Lucky the Provos got the blame. What's gonna be different now?'

Tony's mouth curled. 'This time,' he said, 'the bastard's *expecting* me.'

LIRCOM TOWER, BELFAST, 22 YEARS AGO

The tallest building in Belfast by some distance, Lircom Tower loomed large over the Lagan, dominating the city skyline – Belfast

City Hall, well under a quarter of Lircom's height, seemed modest by comparison. Construction on the twenty-four-storey concrete and glass monolith had finished the previous year.

In a country where large-scale building projects were subject to inevitable delays – due to bomb alerts, both hoax and genuine – Lircom Tower had been constructed three months ahead of schedule and more than a million pounds under budget.

In a city where the army had already commandeered the rooftops of much smaller buildings to build observation posts – and in locations that offered much more limited views of the surrounding areas – Lircom Tower's roof was entirely untouched.

The telecommunications spire at its summit thrust high into the Belfast skies, a jagged finger stabbing accusingly at the heavens above.

Standing in his office on the top floor, overlooking the city, the CEO of the company stared at the copper dome of City Hall. From this height it looked no more than a stone's throw away. Quite an apt unit of measurement for this particular era, he thought to himself, a smile tugging his lips upward.

A lot of attention had been directed at this particular part of the world over the last two decades; horror and revulsion at the barbaric acts that were being committed. The idiots had no idea. Not the first clue what the world had once been like.

They lived in a time so gentle that even the minor skirmishes that had erupted in this small corner of the world sent shockwaves through them. Nothing he had seen in the last few centuries had come close to recapturing the flawless brutality, the majesty of the epoch he termed home.

Since the Industrial Revolution, it was an inescapable truth that the way humans thought had changed. Take their so-called 'World Wars'... what was glorious about taking something as inherently poetic as death, and applying production-line efficiency to it?

His desk phone chirruped for attention and he lifted the receiver. After a pause, he smiled. 'Send them up.'

He sat on his comfortable black leather chair and steepled his fingers as he waited.

The doors were flung open. The man responsible for the dramatic entrance strode toward the desk, his chest rising and falling in shallow bursts, his clothes damp with perspiration.

'Tony,' said Dother.

Tony Morrigan made no reply, merely leaned on the desk and studied Dother, unconcealed hatred written all over his face. Dother, for his part, ignored this scrutiny in favour of greeting the second arrival to his office. 'And you've brought a friend, I see,' he observed. 'Dermot Scully, I believe? Nice to meet you, Dermot. You know, you remind me of someone ...'

Blinking furiously in the harsh artificial light of the office, gawping at the almost three-sixty degree view of the Belfast cityscape afforded by the enormous windows, Dermot Scully looked as though, given the opportunity, he would rather be abseiling into the mouth of an active volcano wearing a tweed mankini than be here now. His hands twitched at Dother's words and his casual identification.

For a second his mouth moved as if he were about to reply to Dother's greeting, but a quick glance at Tony seemed to stiffen his resolve. He said nothing, but did not fail to notice the two very large security guards that had drifted into the office to stand by the doors. If you looked at them in a certain light, on a certain night, both of the guards may have struck an onlooker as being ever-so-slightly lupine in their movements.

The guards looked at Dother, awaiting instructions, but he shook his head a fraction and they stayed put – for now.

'Where's the bug?' asked Tony.

Dother frowned. 'The *bug*?' he echoed with distaste. 'You're referring to Sarah?'

'You're *naming* them now?'

'Just her,' Dother replied calmly. 'If you must know, she's otherwise detained this afternoon. But I have every confidence in her replacements …' he continued, gesturing towards the two sentinels. The day he needed wolf-faeries, or Sarah come to that, to bail him out of a fight with a human would be a sad day indeed. But he kept his temper and his smile.

This day was crucial. Everything he had done on this miserable plane had been building to this. He had to play it just right.

'What did you do to me?'

Dother pondered the question. 'I'm afraid you'll have to be a little more specific than that, Tony. I've *done* many things to you over the years.'

Tony vaulted onto the desk, drawing the silver dagger in one smooth motion. He dived for Dother.

The guards moved, but by the time they'd covered the first few steps – on all fours, their glamours slipping – Tony had already reached Dother and was holding the dagger's silver blade to his throat.

'Don't fuckin' *move*,' he hissed.

The only person in the room to disobey this command was Dermot, whose legs gave way from under him. White as a sheet and shaking, he pulled himself up from the floor and sat himself in one of the guest chairs, moving as far away from the two guards as possible.

'Recognise the blade?' Tony asked the demon.

Dother looked down as much as he could without risking his tongue becoming a necktie. 'One of James' heirlooms?'

'I buried the other one.'

'Ah,' Dother nodded. Again the gesture was minute, but the intention carried. 'That would be the one you killed him with?'

The blade broke flesh. Blood welled up. The guards took a long step forward.

'What are you *doing?*' Dermot squawked in alarm, getting to his feet and retreating further into the room until he was standing alongside Tony and his hostage.

'What,' Tony said again, his voice rising another notch at each word, 'did you do to me? You killed my granda. You killed my da. And now you've taken my *son* from me? I told you that I'd be the one to kill you. That day is today.'

Dother sighed. 'As you wish.'

He moved with such speed Tony was only able to piece the sequence together later. Dother's right hand snapped upward and grabbed the wrist holding the knife, there was a squeeze and a thankfully brief sensation of incredible agony and the blade clattered from Tony's grip. Then he stepped forward out of Tony's reach and casually, slowly, he raised a leg and almost lazily extended it, directly into Tony's stomach.

Tony could only process what was happening to him in flashes as Dother's kick sent him arcing through the air. Very tall building. Floor-to-ceiling windows. Fast moving body. *Impact.*

The glass spiderwebbed to such a degree that Sarah, had she been there, would have found the effect quite beautiful.

But the window held.

Slumped against it, pain radiating from his stomach and from his head where Dother's foot and the thick glass window had both made their respective marks, Tony felt a rippling of nausea through his innards and he threw up, tears flooding his eyes.

Dother was standing over him. 'I told you there'd be consequences for what you did that day. The charm cast by *your* glorious ancestor wasn't designed to be broken lightly, Tony. If one Morrigan ever killed another, well then, it would be reasonable to assume that Morrigan wouldn't be a particularly good tutor for the next generation, would it?'

The demon pulled him to his feet. He didn't resist – if Dother had wanted him dead, he would have kicked just that little bit harder and Tony would be a human skidmark on the pavement by now.

Through his returning vision he could see the two guards were flanking Dermot but they weren't touching him. Not yet.

'I also told you when you realised what the consequences of your actions were, that you would come to me for help. To borrow your own phrase … today is that day, Tony.'

'Help me? Why would *you* help me?'

At this, Tony saw Dother lick his lips. It was a small movement, involuntary, over in a heartbeat, but seeing it, he had the sudden chilling insight that Dother, too, was wearing a glamour – one much more sophisticated than those that cloaked his wolf-faeries and his spider-general, and one that hid something infinitely more monstrous.

'You're familiar with the prophecy regarding the line of Morrigans?'

The day in the Mournes. His excitement at thinking it might be him, quickly dashed by his father's words. 'Yes.'

'I know you think of us as enemies, Tony,' Dother said, his voice low and urgent, as if he knew he had only a limited time to say what needed to be said, 'but in reality we're two sides of a very ancient arrangement. It is our role to try to reclaim what was once ours. It is yours to try to prevent it. We accept this. We honour it. You are held in high esteem among us.'

'High esteem!' Tony choked. 'You've killed, destroyed my family!'

'We've met your line in battle and won some victories. Your ancestors won some too over the last few hundred years, believe me. But we've done so according to the laws. Do you really think,' Dother said, his voice now like silk, 'for one moment, that we didn't know *where* your father lived? Your mother, Marie – a lovely woman,' he said, ignoring Tony's look of horror, 'do you *seriously* believe if I had given the order, a legion of my warriors couldn't have torn her apart while her husband battled at the other end of the country?'

Tony found himself unable to reply. Memories of his mother

and her death flashed back. It had been cancer that had taken her. Nothing unnatural.

'Do you think,' Dother went on, as if discussing pleasantries over a pint, 'that I don't know where to find Linda? Her sister Shelley's home from America, yes? How is she? Still have that laugh that sounds like a donkey being castrated?'

'You fuckin' *touch* her–'

Dother waved a hand impatiently. 'You're not *listening*, Tony. I have no intention of harming Linda. My point is that although you Morrigans and my people are enemies, we do *not* extend that war to the innocent. Your father and grandfather were actively engaged in war against us. Forgive us for wishing to defend ourselves. So when I tell you that you are held in high esteem amongst us, believe me on that.'

'Okay,' Tony said, curiosity temporarily winning out over the other emotions raging within him, 'so what the fuck's this got to do with helping me? With the prophecy? Shouldn't you be delighted if the Morrigan line dies with me?'

Dother shook his head. 'The Morrigan the prophecy spoke of is the one to be present during the final days, when this intolerable stalemate we've descended into is finally capable of being broken. His role is to stop our victory, and destroy us all … or,' and Tony could see that animal hunger descend over him again, 'or to *cause* it, to release our forces trapped in the Otherworld. To usher in a new age of magic. But without him, without the possibility of him existing, *neither* can ever occur.'

Dermot spoke up then, to Tony's surprise. 'Then it's vital you *don't* have a son. He said it himself – if that Morrigan never exists, they can never win.'

'Neither can we be destroyed,' Dother shot back, shooting Dermot a poisonous look that caused the smaller man to blanch. 'And those of us, like me, like my prodigal brother and our creations, who remain in your world ... we will remain here. Forever. Able to spawn more of our number. Look at what I have constructed in the years since we last met. *Imagine* what I could do in another century. If the Morrigan the prophecy speaks of never comes to pass, you lose the opportunity to banish us forever.'

'All of this is fuckin' pointless,' Tony said, anger bubbling within him again. 'Even if I believed anything you're tellin' me, if some curse is stopping me from having a son, what am I meant to do about it?'

Dother smiled. He moved to stand beside an innocuous-looking part of the office wall and pressed a hidden switch set into the pattern.

Seconds later, silver light bathed the office.

'I assume you remember this,' he said, retrieving the Sword and waving it through the air with a few easy thrusts. It looked sharp enough to cut the oxygen from the very air around it.

'This sword,' Dother said, 'can be used to remake reality. Bend it to the wishes of the one who wields it. There *are* limits to its power, of course; were there not, I'd have simply raised the remainder of my people from the Otherworld and we wouldn't be having this conversation. But,' and he smiled, 'I *can* use it to help you. To give you a son.'

'How?'

Dother smiled. 'In good time. I have explained what I have to offer. Now I need to know if you are prepared to accept your end of the bargain.'

'Tony, don't do this,' Dermot warned and one of the guards moved as if intending to strike. Dother raised his hand and the guard stood down, although the low growl that escaped his lips betrayed his frustration at having his strike rescinded. 'You can't trust him. Everything he's saying is a lie. That's what they do. That's *all* they do.'

Dother shrugged. 'I suppose that's possible,' he admitted. 'But ask yourself – why would I bother with all of this? I have you both here. I could kill you without effort, ending the Morrigan threat to my kind. I'm freely admitting that I only want to help you to try and align circumstances so that one day my people can have our final victory and overrun your world in an orgy of blood and death. But, in doing so, I will also give you a chance – your *only* chance – to rid us from your world. I hide nothing. I only ask, are you prepared for what you must do?'

'And that is?'

'Tony, *no*!'

'He's right,' Tony shrugged, trying to ignore the look of betrayal on Dermot's face. 'He's *not* hiding anything. And he could have killed Linda at any time, and more than likely me along with her. He hasn't.'

'But he's a cunt!'

Dother actually gasped. 'Dermot,' he said, rebuking. 'Keep it classy, will you? Any more of that and I'll have to ask you to leave the office. Via the window. You people are *entirely* too fond of that word these days.'

Tony turned away from Dermot, his attention now fully on Dother. 'So?' he said. 'What is my end of the bargain? What would I need to do?'

Dother planted the tip of the sword into the floor and leant forward to rest his chin on the hilt. With his face bathed in the silver light, he looked even less human than before.

'I'm not just giving you a son,' he said softly. 'Not just a Morrigan. Your son *must* be the one prophesied. *You* must see to it that he is. If you fail, if you move away from the demands of the prophecy, I swear, we will break all bonds of behaviour. We will massacre you, your wife, your son. *Everyone* that you care about. Do you accept?'

Keep our line going. His father had told him that the night he died. The only way to do that was to place his trust in a being saturated in lies. To make a deal with the demon that had plagued his forefathers for generations.

It was more than that. He remembered the full extent of the prophecy his father had told him that day in the Triumph only too well. What happened to the Morrigan it spoke of. What he would have to do when the time came.

Another not altogether welcome thought presented itself. As Dother had pointed out, he was deep in the lion's den, helpless and weak from the single kick he'd received and the impact on the glass that had almost meant his end.

If he said no, if he refused this offer, what exactly was there to stop Dother from killing him?

He would have a son. A little boy. He pictured the look on his wife's face.

'I accept,' he said.

Seeing the look of triumph Dother was unable to disguise at his decision, Tony swore to himself in that moment that somehow, he would find a way to make it work.

GRIFFIN STREET, BELFAST, 22 YEARS AGO

'What is it, love?' he said.

Standing at the doorway, unwilling to let her husband get any further into the house, Linda Morrigan rubbed away the tears from her eyes and tried to stop trembling. Three days he'd been out of touch in some godforsaken place deep down South, three days of jumping up every time she heard a car pull up outside. If those 'mobile' fuckin' phones the Flash Harrys on the TV were carrying about didn't cost an arm and a leg, she'd have bought him one ages ago. But it didn't matter now. Nothing mattered, because–

'I'm pregnant,' she said, and promptly dissolved into a torrent of tears. He picked her up and spun her around then hugged her fiercely to him ... and then he froze, his grip loosening as he lowered her gently to the ground.

'I didn't mean to squeeze ye, love. Oh God, you don't think I ...?'

She laughed. 'Jesus God, would you listen to yourself! Ten seconds you know and already you're frettin'! I'm fine, the baby's gonna be fine, and you're gonna make a *fantastic* daddy. I just *know* it.'

Kissing him then, she felt the tension of the last few years, the disappointment and the waiting, melt away. She was going to have a baby with the man she loved and right now the world was perfect.

'Aye,' he smiled back. 'Aye, I hope so.'

'Right,' she inhaled sharply and patted him on the cheek, 'now that that's finally done, I'm away to use the phone. I'll be back in about four days.'

'You're ... you're going to tell everyone? Now?' Tony frowned. 'Already?'

'Are you jokin'?' she returned. 'If you'd been away much longer it was to hell with ya and I was gonna take out ads in the national dailies. You have any *idea* how long I've been waitin' for this, love?'

'But don't ... I mean, don't people usually wait until the baby ... until you're about twelve weeks gone?'

Linda just shrugged happily. 'That's the thing,' she said, 'the doctor said I was already fourteen weeks gone. Which sounds crazy because I haven't missed my time of the month until a week ago. I asked the doctor about it – he says it's rare, but it can happen all right. Just one of life's wee surprises I suppose!'

With that, and a final feather-light kiss on his cheek, she skipped into the living room, hell-bent on grabbing the phone, her little floral patterned book of numbers, and enough hankies to make a small quilt.

He watched her go.

GRIFFIN STREET, BELFAST, 12 YEARS AGO

Up, down. Dip. Up, down, up, down. Dip. The fuckin' paint fumes were stinging his eyes, causing them to water, so he wiped his face with his sleeve and continued right on lying to himself.

'Da?'

The voice startled him, and as he turned, the brush spattered a few drops of white paint on the landing carpet. Tony swore, replaced the brush in the pot and scrabbled for a cloth and some white spirit. If Linda saw the mess he'd made she'd squeal the place down; he was already fast approaching doghouse status for taking too long with this.

'Son, fer Jesus' sake ...' he muttered to Danny, who was standing in his school uniform looking up at his father from halfway up the stairs. The paint was shifting. That was something at least. 'Don't creep up on me like that, will ye? What is it anyway?'

Danny looked as if trying to work out whether to say what he wanted to say or whether to just go back down the stairs. Finally the urge to speak won out.

'I thought you were gonna pick me up. From school.'

Tony closed his still-streaming eyes, his back to his nine-year-old son. *Fuckin'* paint fumes. 'I had to get the house done, son,' he said. 'Sorry. It's a big job, you know, and with me bein' away it doesn't get done and then yer ma, she ... well, you know how women are,' and he turned and gave a half-shrug heavy with male solidarity which caused his son's mouth to curl upward as he'd hoped it would.

'It's okay, Da,' Danny said.

No. No it *wasn't* okay. Tony's fingers curled around the brush handle and he resumed painting. It wasn't one bit okay. It was another lie. But what was another one to add to the list? What was another made-up story about having to survey some arse end of nowhere, as a way to cover for his *real* activities there, his actual work?

Work. That was a fucking laugh. At least when his father had fought, it had *been* a fight, a genuine battle. He knew that the occasional soldier-faerie or banshee spirit he was called out to combat wasn't the real problem.

The real problem lay in the centre of the city, in what had started out once upon a time as a small company with a big-for-its-boots headquarters, a situation now turned on its head entirely. These days Lircom was a continental leader, a company that, despite its standing across Europe, had shown admirable loyalty to Belfast by remaining in the city.

Tony was being thrown scraps from the table, leftovers to keep him occupied while the real work went on. For a few years he hadn't cared much. He had gloried in having a son, particularly one as wonderful as the one that stood behind him now. Danny was everything he'd ever wanted – intelligent, questioning, shrewd, kind, decent. He reminded Tony of his own father in a way that just about broke his heart.

But time had ticked on. Relentlessly. Inevitably.

Danny's tenth birthday was six days away.

'Can I … can I help ye out, Da? I'm pretty good with the oul brush, like …'

'No, you can't!' Tony said, keeping his back to the boy, forcing harshness into his tone. The tears were running freely down his face now and he knew he'd be unable to hide them from his son, who would ask why. Danny couldn't know why. Couldn't know anything. 'You'll only get in the way. Now go on, go and call for

Steve or somethin'! Be back for dinner!'

'Da … ?'

There was a hint of shock in his son's voice. At that moment Tony wanted nothing more than to turn and take him in his arms, to tell him he was sorry for snapping and that he loved him. To tell him everything; to tell him what he had to do, and why he had to do it.

'Go!' was all he said.

Only when the front door slammed shut did he allow himself the luxury of breaking down.

*

'You'll be back for my birthday, won't ye?'

'Course I will, big lad.'

Linda escorted him out. She was still making a face. 'I can't believe this,' she hissed when they got to the front door. 'I've never heard of an urgent surveying job in my life. And away down there in the backside of nowhere an all. You *sure* this is gonna be finished in time?'

'I'm sure.'

'Right,' she nodded, convinced. She kissed him, on the lips. She tasted of home. He left that moisture on his own lips, wondered how long it would take for it to disappear.

Tony left the house and got into the car idling outside, Dermot Quinn at the wheel. Linda stood at the front door to see him off, but he couldn't look at her. Or at the small figure standing beside her, waving.

Waving goodbye.

'Go,' he croaked.

'You're sure?'

'*Please.*'

Dermot nodded and the car glided away. For the next several hundred miles, as they drove down motorways and winding roads, through county after county, he didn't speak. He just waited as Tony broke down – the sobs came and they kept coming until all that seemed to be left was the husk of a human being.

They came eventually to a squat, modest little whitewashed cottage with a thatched roof, perched on a hillside deep in Wexford – the house that Tony Morrigan was now to call home. Not a single other human dwelling existed from horizon to horizon.

'What will you do?' Dermot asked as they pulled up outside.

'I don't know,' Tony replied getting out of the car. 'What about you?'

'Me?' Dermot shrugged. 'I can't face them alone, Tony. Call me a coward if you want, but it's true. You were always the fighter. I think I'll just keep my head down, get into the lecturing circuit full-time. Not too many of us out there can translate ancient Gaelic. Suppose I could tell a few of the tall tales to kids, try to keep the word alive. My wee niece seems to like them.'

'Be careful.'

'You too, mate. And if you need anything …' Dermot trailed off, unable to complete the sentiment, knowing it would sound hollow given the circumstances. He changed tack. 'Look, 'the prophecy doesn't say you're separated from him forever. It says you have no contact for ten years. You can come back …'

'In ten years time? When he's twenty? And say what? That

I was kidnapped by aliens?' Tony snorted. 'He'll not want me anywhere *near* him, Dermot. And he'll be right.'

'At least you got ten years, Tony,' Dermot said and his face darkened. 'My da left me and my brother when we were younger than Danny is now. And I don't think he did it because of some mystic prophecy, either. I think he just couldn't be fucked. You've had ten years to turn Danny into a big, strapping lad. You should be proud of him.'

'Proud doesn't cover it. He's my whole world, Dermot. He's the best thing I'll ever do on this planet. I love him. And after today, he's going to hate me for the rest of his life. That's what they wanted. That was their price. Give me the son I always wanted, and then make him hate me. God forgive me.'

He shut the car door without another word and made his way into the cottage. Dermot sat where he was a few minutes more, hoping in vain that Tony would come rushing back to the car and they'd set off on a desperate gambit to take down Dother and to fuck with the risks, like the day in the hospital car park when this whole fuckin' mess had begun.

Nothing happened.

He set off down the winding dirt road, beginning the long lonely drive back to Belfast.

BELFAST, NOW

It was difficult to know what to say, really, Steve thought as they drove to Dermot Quinn's house. The fake memories of his not-life still floated in his mind, bobbing alongside parallel memories of being Danny's friend, of Ellie being Danny's girl, of Maggie ...

Actually, upon reflection, maybe silence was *just fine.*

Clearly Ellie hadn't gotten the memo.

'Look, um...' she began. 'Can we just talk a wee bit, about the last few days?'

Eyes on the road. Eyes on the road. Mind on the road. Mind on the fucking road. La la la. Hum de dum. Wow look at that wee sporty number. Nice. And yer woman over there with the nice legs ...

Last night you fucked your best friend's girlfriend.

Balls. Big, hairy, balls. Well, fuck it. Time to go for broke. What the hell. 'I don't think we did anything wrong.'

'Agreed,' Ellie said instantly.

You fucked your best friend's girlfriend!

'We were ...' he almost hiccupped over the words, felt them catch in his throat and threaten to make him gag they sounded so ludicrous. 'We were ...' he coughed a half-laugh at the absurdity of even having to find a word to say it. 'We were ...what did the oul doll say? How did she put it? What was the exact word she used? It was a good word.'

'Bewitched?' Ellie said numbly.

'Right?'

'Yep. Hundred per cent. Absolutely.'

You fucked ...

'There's no way I would *ever* ... if I'd *known* it would have been ... I mean it goes without–'

'–without saying! Yes, same here! I mean,' she laughed weakly, 'we don't even probably need to *say* that do we. It goes without saying. Like you said.'

... your best friend's ...

'Yeah. Yeah, this is it. This is it.'

... girlfriend.

Silence fell once more with an almost audible thud. He wished his mind was as quiet.

Not just his girlfriend. The mother of his child.

Just how bewitched were you anyway, Stevie boy, eh? You had your suspicions didn't you, eh? Not suspicious enough to stop you clambering on board for a quick fumble after Match of the Day *was over, was it?*

He gritted his teeth, realising that his go-for-broke, we-done-nothing-wrong line of reasoning wasn't meeting any resistance. He had been almost hoping for a yes-we-did-we-should-be-ashamed rebuttal. That he hadn't received this had somehow made things worse.

'This is *crazy*,' he said, ostensibly to her but really as a proclamation to the universe at large.

'I know,' she sighed.

He shot a glance at her as he pulled to a stop at a set of lights. 'Can I be honest?'

'That'd make a change from the last few minutes, wouldn't it,' she said, the palms of her hands pressed into her eyes as if she were trying to force everything they'd seen through the back of her head and out of her memory.

'I didn't even really *like* you.'

She grunted with amusement, not moving her palms away. 'No, *really*? You don't say.'

'You're dour. You're needy. You're about as much fun as a kick in the ballix. That's what I thought about you. Bein' honest, I thought Danny coulda done better. I thought he felt obliged to step up cos you two got caught with ... with Luke,' he said, his resolve wavering at having to say the name, considering the child's unknown whereabouts. A bout of fresh guilt washed through him.

'Well,' she said, lifting her head from her hands and looking at him with one of those unreadable female expressions that seemed to convey about fourteen emotions simultaneously, 'I must say, when you wanna be honest, you really don't fuck about, do you?'

To his own amazement, he barked out a laugh at that. 'And then,' he went on, 'then this fuckin' craziness and, well, now I see what he sees in ye. I mean there we were with fuckin' Cousin It in the cot and you still ... I mean, ach, fuck's sake,' he shook his head in frustration at his own ramblings. 'Look, what I'm trying to say is I know now how tough it is and, despite what I just said before, I am tearing myself apart with guilt over what we did, so if we manage to sort all this out I'll accept whatever you want to tell Danny.'

What the hell. Say it. Throw it out there. This is your one chance.

'*If* you want to tell him anything, that is.'

'So if I tell him that I knew something was wrong and didn't want to, but that you pushed me into it, you'll back me up?'

His hands tightened around the wheel. 'Yep,' he said, and meant it.

He shot a quick sidelong glance at her and was surprised to see that, amongst those female emotions raging across her face, there was something that looked suspiciously, amazingly, like admiration.

'All right,' she said amenably, 'you've been honest with me, so I'll be honest with you. I didn't like you either. You undermined me every chance you got. You hadn't the first fuckin' clue what me and Danny were like when the front door hit ye on the hole but you didn't seem to give a shit – you were like his mistress, only without the sex; reminding him every chance you got what a wonderful time he was missing out on because of the fuckin' shrew he was stuck with. And that pissed me off, Steve. That pissed me off somethin' fuckin' royal, let me tell ya.'

'That's not–' he began in protest.

'Let me finish,' she stopped him, holding up a hand. 'I thought that was it, that was your game, because I thought you hadn't a mature fuckin' bone in your entire body. I thought you were a man-child and I thought you needed to grow up; there was Danny trying to cope with all this responsibility and doin' pretty well, all things considered, and then there was you, capering around him like the fuckin' court jester.'

He absorbed this. 'So glad I let you finish.'

'You haven't yet. I know this was all some fantasy world we've been livin' in these last few days or so – you and me with a baby between us – but I saw you with ... with Aaron. He may have been a ... I don't know *what* the fuck he was,' she said with a heartfelt shiver, 'but we didn't know that until tonight.'

'You *saw* me with him?' Steve echoed incredulously. 'I was a fuck up from start to finish. Don't patronise me by tellin' me otherwise.'

'I wasn't gonna.'

'Oh. Well,' he said, licking his lips, forcing a cough. 'Good.'

The GPS said there was less than a mile to go. If only there was a fantasy world they could create for him where he owned a rocket car. *Anything* to make this journey end.

'You were a complete fuckup,' she went on. 'But it *bothered* you to be, Steve. You saw you weren't cuttin' it and it got to you. You *tried*. And if you'd asked me once upon a time what you'd have done faced with responsibility I'd have said you'd have run a mile and not thought twice about doin' so. I was wrong. So maybe all that act around Danny wasn't you playin' the serpent. Maybe there was a bit of jealousy in there.'

They stopped at another set of lights. He put the handbrake on with unnecessary force, something that wasn't lost on Ellie. She looked at him quizzically and out it came.

'Maggie was pregnant.'

Ellie's mouth fell open. She started to say something and then stopped. The traffic at the lights began to move. They were close to Dermot's now. Only a few streets left. Absurdly, where a few minutes ago he'd have cheerfully donated a big toe to the Get Me Out Of This Conversation telethon, now he found a small part of himself wishing he could have more time. He'd never spoken of this to anyone, not even Danny.

'She ... lost it?'

'No,' he said. 'No, she didn't lose it. She just didn't keep it.'

'I'm sorry,' Ellie said softly.

'So was I,' he replied evenly, angry at himself for feeling a prickling pressure behind his eyes.

'Oh Steve,' Ellie said, and he didn't dare look at her now,

because there was a tremor in her voice as she spoke. If he saw her cry, he knew he would follow suit and there just wasn't time. Things were far too fucked up right now to begin dealing with all of that mess.

'Look,' he said harshly, 'what does it fuckin' *matter* anyway? This is all so fuckin' *impossible*. I'm still expectin' to wake up in my bed any minute now. I dropped a bit of acid in my Queen's days and never had a trip this fucked up. Hope springs eternal though, eh?'

'Steve ...'

'Ellie, forget it,' he said as firmly as he dared, slamming the door firmly shut on the conversation. 'Are we there yet?'

She pointed ahead. 'Yeah, this is the street. It's up here. Last house on the right ... wait what's goin' on ... is there a party or somethin'?'

The house was surrounded by people. Actually, *shapes* would have been more accurate. They stood three deep on the lawn. As Steve craned to look, he swore some were on the *roof*? He and Ellie exchanged a glance as their car continued up the street, now only a few doors away.

'Do I stop? Do we drive on? What?'

'Drive on,' she said urgently. 'We'll try the back ... *look out!*'

He slammed the brakes, but too late. The car whirled, thrown into a desperate spin and something whipped across his vision, something huge and dark...

Glass shattered. The car flipped. Sparks flew.

The world went away.

*

'Rumours?' Mr Black frowned. He shrugged. 'I'm sure I don't know what you mean, Michael.'

Michael Quinn glared at him across the elaborate, obviously expensive desk. He was a rich man himself, but he'd never seen an office like this – never seen a *building* like this, come to that. Lircom Tower stood out in the Belfast skyline like some glorious mistake, a piece of a jigsaw plopped into the wrong box.

'No one plays the market like you do,' Michael returned. 'We all have our little hunches and feelings. We all make deals. But in, what, almost twenty years of trading, you've *never once* put a foot wrong. Never seen a company go belly up. Never had your investors lose confidence. Never failed to back a piece of tech that goes stellar.'

Mr Black shrugged. 'I wasn't aware that sound business sense equalled witchcraft, Michael.'

'What are you still *doing* here?' Michael shot back. 'Where'd you come in the rich list last year? Sixth?'

'Fifth,' the correction was immediate.

'And here you are, balls-deep in Ireland and hardly a toe anywhere else on the planet.'

'Ireland is my home.'

'That's not the way a tycoon thinks.'

'Clearly, it's the way *this* one does. Now,' Mr Black went on, neatly cutting off Michael's next query with a hand gesture and a look, 'I granted you this meeting despite having several pressing engagements, Michael. Is there something I can do for you?'

Michael, his mouth dry but his hands steady, saw his chance.

'I know everything.'

Mr Black's eyes widened. 'Really.'

'Yes.'

'Your fiscal performance last quarter would seem to suggest otherwise. FormorTech is down 28 per cent, if I'm not mistaken? Hardly indicative of an omniscient hand at its tiller,' Mr Black checked his watch and rose from his chair. 'Now if you'll excuse me ...'

'Dother.'

The air temperature in the room seemed to drop by about ten degrees. Mr Black froze, his eyes settling on Michael. The only sound in the penthouse office was the soft hum of electronics. Michael swallowed through a throat that seemed moisture-resistant.

Mr Black sat down.

'Michael,' he said, with a look of concern, 'what makes you say a thing like that?'

Michael Quinn shivered to hear the undercurrent of regret that shaded his words, but carried on regardless. 'It's your name, isn't it?'

Dother's eyes flashed then. Michael actually saw them flash with an inner light.

Christ in heaven, he thought with sudden, terrifying clarity. *He really isn't human. What am I playing with?*

'Naming is power, Mr Quinn,' Dother said softly. 'My people have a fractious relationship with those who bandy our names about without due consideration for what it might entail. Be cautious. Now I'm going to ask you some questions, and when you answer you're going to be more honest with me than you have ever been with your wife, your doctor, and your accountant combined. Do we understand one another?'

Ten minutes ago Michael had been dizzied by the scale of this office, filled with envy at its size and luxury. Now, he felt claustrophobic; he was trapped in this room with a being that radiated power and menace in equal measure.

'Are we clear on that, Michael?'

'Yes,' he said.

'How?' Dother asked. He didn't need to specify what he meant, and Michael knew it would be extremely unwise to play dumb at this moment.

'Dermot Scully is my brother.'

'Let's be kind to that precious ego of yours and pretend that I wasn't already aware of that, shall we?' the man formerly known only as Mr Black said, drumming his fingers on the desk. 'Hmmm, I thought Dermot was keeping his head down, hence my allowing him to live. Generous of me I thought. Are you going to give me cause to regret it?'

'Keeping his head down? You mean drinking himself out of a job?'

'Drinking?'

'And running up debts. With the wrong people.'

'How foolish,' Dother said, his patience beginning to fade. His fingers thumped hard on the desk, beating a tattoo that Michael felt through the chair.

'He came to me. Begged me for help. I said no, of course.'

Dother's mouth twisted at that. 'Oh, of course,' he echoed, and

Michael missed entirely the mocking undercurrent in his words.

'He was drunk. And that's when he told me about him.'

'The Morrigan?'

Michael frowned. 'Danny? Why would he talk about Danny?'

Dother seemed surprised by this, but hid his reaction quickly. 'Who, then?'

'Dermot had this plan, to entice him, to bring him forth, and to capture him … he explained the rewards for doing so. What he could do.'

Leaning forward, Dother's eyes blazed. '*Who?*' he asked.

Michael Quinn lifted the bag resting by his feet onto the magnificent desk. It was a large kit bag, and he had found it almost impossible to disguise its weight bringing it into the office.

He pulled the zipper across and the reason for much of the weight spilled out. Horseshoes tumbled onto the desk, a clanging metal cascade.

Dother leapt back as if stung. A ripple passed over his features and the face of the reserved businessman became bestial, fearsome to behold. He pointed a finger that now more resembled a talon at Michael. 'How *dare* you bring those in here?'

At some unseen signal from the man before him, Michael felt a rush of air at his back as the door to the office opened. Now standing himself, he shook from head to toe in terror, but it was too late now to back down, too late to do anything but press on and hope that he lived through this and that that crazy bastard of a brother of his had been right.

'He captured him!' he gibbered. '*He* captured him and now *I'm* returning him to you! Please!'

He could sense something behind him moving toward him and much as he wanted to look to see what it was, a deeper, more primitive part of his mind kept him rooted to the spot and told him in no uncertain terms that *it was better if he didn't see.*

With commendable timing, that was when Brian decided to get out of the bag.

'Ohhhhh sweet Jesus,' he said, staggering, 'my fuckin' head.'

Seeing this, Dother's white-hot rage cooled. He gestured to whatever it was behind Michael to stop.

A hand appeared on Michael's shoulder.

'Hello,' said Sarah.

'Hi,' he returned, nonplussed. No one else was behind her. From Dother's body language he'd been expecting a squad of goons to have been charging for him, not a slip of a girl.

'Brian?' Dother said, his attention on the tiny little man still regaining his bearings, 'Brian, is what he says true? Did Scully capture you?'

Brian kicked away the horseshoes with a shudder. Michael noted how Dother seemed almost to flow out of their way as they rained onto the deep-pile carpeted surface. He reached into the bag and fished out his hat; a little black bowler, to go with his tiny little charcoal suit and pinstripe braces.

God she smells good, Michael thought, desire managing to dull the otherwise all-encompassing fog of terror that had settled on him.

'That bastard Scully,' Brian growled. 'True all right m'lord. Gave me the comehither and trapped me like a fly in amber. Wanted me to get him out of his money troubles.'

'Shall I ...?' Sarah said.

Dother held up a hand to stay her inquiries. 'And this man freed you?'

Brian squinted at Michael, took off his miniature round glasses, polished them on his sleeve, and put them back on before peering intently at him again.

'Aye,' he said eventually, 'aye, that's him. Although he stuck me in that thing with naught but iron for company for the last day and night ...'

'I was trying to decide what to do!' Michael replied, feeling Sarah's grip intensify slightly and wondering why this worried him so, 'I didn't want to just let him go and have myself blamed in some way!'

Head cocked to one side, Dother regarded the human before him as a scientist would have inspected a baboon in a cage who'd just explained Pythagoras' Theorem. 'It seems,' he said, drawing out each word as he spoke, 'that we owe you a debt of gratitude, Mr Quinn.'

'I know what you owe me,' Michael replied.

Sarah applied pressure, and a moment later he was sitting down in the chair again without quite understanding how it happened. Dother vaulted over the massive desk as though it were the easiest thing in the world to do, and landed softly on Michael's left side. He crouched down on his haunches, his legs bending in ways that human legs shouldn't be able to, or at least not with that easy grace.

'And what is that?' he asked.

'A wish.'

Dother smiled. 'A *wish?*' he echoed, making the word seem so ridiculous that Michael cringed. 'I think you've been watching a little too much Disney, Mr Quinn.'

'Scully explained it all to me,' Michael said, keeping his voice level. 'You trap a faerie, it has to buy its freedom with a wish. He said it was something to do with probability – reckoned your kind can manipulate the world on a quantum level to affect odds. Win bets.'

'Quantum,' Mr Black returned mockingly. 'What nonsense words you invent for something that's as old as time. And that's what you want us to do for you? Win bets? Reverse the fortunes of FormorTech, perhaps?'

'No.'

'Then what, Michael?' Dother's voice was almost a purr now, and Michael's eyelids were, remarkably given the circumstances, actually getting heavy.

'You're … you're the prince. He told me … he told me everything: about you, about the Sword – it makes sense. That's how you're so successful. I want you … want you to change things.'

'And what do you want changed? By most measures, you're a successful man. Rich. Powerful. What in your life displeases you, Michael?'

Stay strong. The figures above him swam now, as though he were in the dentist's chair and being sedated; the silhouette of Dother moved fluidly in front of him, then suddenly there was a silver light. And to his right … no. No that couldn't be the girl … much too large to be the girl … looked more like a giant … a giant … stay awake … *stay awake* …

'Not in my life,' he said, with an effort. 'In my daughter's. Things weren't meant to go this way for her … she's with the wrong man.'

The silver light … was everywhere, then he slipped into darkness.

But the light continued to pulse, moving outward with the guiding force of Dother's will behind it. Invisible to mortals, it passed through them and through their realm: the power to change the human world, to bend reality to the will of he who wielded it.

At that exact moment, three floors below, Danny Morrigan's mobile phone erupted into static, cutting off his call to Ellie.

Dother lowered the sword. He stepped over the prone body of Michael Quinn now sprawled on the floor and placed the sword back in its cubby in his wall.

'This. *This* is how it begins?'

He turned and smiled at Sarah, who had spoken. 'Yes. Yes indeed. Wonderfully unexpected, but beautifully elegant, wouldn't you say?'

Sarah merely shrugged. It was one of the gestures her human form allowed that her true form did not. She directed her attention down at the unconscious form on the office floor.

'What of him?' she said. 'Should I consume him?'

'Him?' Dother laughed derisively. 'This pathetic, selfish fool? He is of no consequence. Wake him up and send him on his way. And don't look so disappointed,' he added, seeing her annoyance at being denied this feast, 'he'd get stuck in your teeth …'

*

'I didn't *know*!' he said again.

'What fuckin' difference does *that* make?' Tony Morrigan said, disgust plain in his voice. 'You went to Dother and you *wished a baby* out of existence!' And, finding that he couldn't quite put into words his feelings about that, he simply decked Michael Quinn, a real beauty of a punch that impacted squarely on the man's right cheek and sent him sprawling across the room.

'He was my *grandson*!' Tony bellowed, as Dermot threw his arms around him to stop him following up on the initial assault. 'He was *your* grandson! You selfish *bastard*!'

Picking himself up, Michael wiped away a trail of blood from under his nose. There was no anger on his face, only misery. 'I thought Danny wasn't good enough,' he said. 'I looked at him and I could see he was shit scared of having found himself in this situation and I knew … I knew one day, he'd wake up and he'd think, fuck this, and he'd leave her. And that would have broken her. She's my little girl and I didn't want her to end up a single mother.'

'Balls,' it was Dermot who spoke up, to Tony's surprise. His voice was heavy and he spoke with conviction. 'This isn't about Danny, Michael, and you fuckin' know it.'

'What are you talking–'

'This is about him, isn't it? About Da.'

Tony looked from one man to the other. 'Somebody wanna let me know what I'm missing?'

'I told you before, Tony, a long time ago,' Dermot said. 'Our da walked out on us. Decided he couldn't handle it and left our ma to raise us both. I was only five when he went. Michael was eight. Our ma tried her best, she really ...' his voice wavered, '... she really did. But it was too much for her. The strain.'

'His fault,' Michael whispered. 'His fault she died.'

'I'm not *debating* that,' Dermot shot back. 'But just because our da wasn't up to the challenge doesn't give you the right to make judgment calls about someone else's.'

'She is my wee girl!' Michael roared back with a ferocity that stunned everyone in the room, including himself. 'I would have done anything to spare her that, do you understand?'

'You sacrificed your grandchild's life just in case your daughter ever wound up raising him by herself?' Tony asked. His surprise over Michael's passion had subsided somewhat to be replaced with the comforting veil of fury once more.

'I didn't *know*! I thought all I was doing was changing *who* she ended up with. I thought things would shift – that she'd have a crack at a good career and that she'd be with someone else, someone settled, and that they'd have kids together and that she'd be happier. I would *never* sacrifice my grandson, I loved him!' he threw up his hands. 'I thought I could make a deal with Dother. It was stupid, I was wrong, I fucked up – what do you want me to say?'

Dermot laid a hand on Tony's arm, gently. 'It'd be a bit rich of you to take exception to someone making deals with Dother now, wouldn't it?' he said softly, too softly for Michael to overhear.

There was some truth to that Tony had to admit. He allowed his rage to cool, but only by a few degrees.

'So the price for all of this,' Dermot spoke up, obviously

wanting to move the conversation on from the blame game, 'was that you had to sell your company to him?'

Michael nodded miserably. 'He didn't tell me there *was* a price, at first. But he called, he called the day after he ... did it. Wanted FormorTech's expertise on distribution for the upgraded network. Threatened to ... oh God, you don't even want to *know* what he threatened to do. You don't know how he *looks* at you.'

Dermot sat down heavily on the nearest chair. 'Don't you see what he's *doing*? What this network is? The last almost thirty years he's been building up this telecommunications business of his. Super advanced. Top secret. *Only* within Ireland. Nowhere else. Why?'

'He said it was his home,' Michael offered, trying to feel useful.

'Yeah,' Dermot shot back darkly, 'not just *his* home. The whole rest of his sick and twisted fuckin' family's home too. How long before the network goes live?'

'Tomorrow,' Michael replied.

Dermot swore, head in hands.

'And so what?' Tony said, still struggling to comprehend the significance of all this. 'He'll be able to send porn to Cork twice as fast as he can now?'

'This isn't about the Internet!' Dermot said, slamming his fist down on the table. 'Think, Tony. Think about what those cables mean. *Communication amplification*! Hundreds of thousands of thoughts – *human* thoughts – travelling across *lines* ... Jesus Christ, the power he'll able to draw from that, if he's laid those cables in the right places.'

He looked up, shaking his head.

'We have to get out of here,' he said, standing up and starting to pace, running his hands through his hair. 'We can't stay in here. We have to get out.'

Tony went to the curtains, twitched them aside, gestured. 'There were at least twenty of them out there last I looked. They'd tear us apart and you know it. Want to check again? I'm takin' bets it's upwards of thirty by now.'

Michael paled at this new information. 'Th–*thirty* of them?' he choked. 'But what's to stop them just coming in?'

'Same thing that made them try to use *you* as an assassin – enchanted circle around the place. They can't cross it,' Tony smiled with some satisfaction, 'I'd like to see the bastards even try–'

It was then that the car, spinning end over end, crashed through the front window.

Instant by instant the terrible scene unfolded, as though God had the DVD remote and was repeatedly stabbing the pause button on reality.

The window imploded at the impact, each shard of glass a dagger searing across the room; Tony dimly felt a few lines of fire streak into his arm and hip.

The chassis of the car smashed through the wood and plaster of the house, pulverising it as it flipped, utterly destroying the television and turning the furniture to splinters. The large settee was propelled backward and it was that which saved their lives, impacting all three of them squarely and pushing them out of range.

The car slammed to a final halt, tilted up on its right side, wheels spinning, engine running, horn blaring, and, over the roaring and the horror, the three men tried to come to terms with what had just happened.

'Ellie! Oh Jesus God, Ellie! Ellie *no!*' Michael Quinn was screaming.

His daughter was slumped limply in the passenger's seat, hair matted with blood.

He surged forward and scrambled onto the car before the other two men could react, yanking the passenger door open with the superhuman strength of a desperate parent, almost taking it off completely. He released Ellie's seatbelt and lifted her into his arms, pulling her clear from the wreckage.

The driver, somehow, was still conscious, though he was clearly in shock. He mumbled incoherencies as Tony and Dermot, unable to open the driver's door, climbed up onto the bonnet and, ignoring the broken glass that was everywhere, pulled him through the broken windscreen and free of the wreckage. Smoke had started to curl from the engine, thickening the air. The car was hot, and it was getting hotter.

'Steve,' Tony said, as he identified the boy he was rescuing. 'Steve, you're gonna be okay.'

'Had to come ...' Steve was mumbling, his head lolling. Blood was seeping from his ears, from his nose, through his clothes.

'Ellie. Oh Jesus, oh God ... what have they done to you?' Michael Quinn was crouched at the far end of the room cradling his daughter's head in his lap, tears falling off the end of his nose and onto her head like rain. One look at him and Tony knew the man would need no further lectures. His loyalty had been bought.

He was holding the true price for his wish.

As he and Dermot carried Steve clear, Tony kept his back to the entry wound the car had left on the house, his back stiffening as he sensed their enemies approach.

Dermot was first to glance back, what little remained of his hope draining away. 'The protective circles. They're gone.'

'Danny ...' Steve was mumbling. 'Danny ... gone below ... swallowed up ... have to help him ...'

The car would provide a momentary blockade, but no more than that. Tony eased Steve down, resting him against the far wall and reached for his weapon. His father's silver dagger. Closing his fingers around its hilt had never failed to ease some of the despair he'd felt down the years.

He heard the sound of breaking glass from the back. They were trying to get through the kitchen windows and into the house. Tony had reinforced these only a few hours ago, in case they managed to get through the mystical protection. That foresight was saving their lives now; had bought them time.

'Get them to the basement,' he told Dermot, indicating Steve and Ellie. 'Lock yourselves in. Michael, *move!*'

Through his grief Michael complied, carrying Ellie as though she weighed nothing. As she was lifted up, her mobile fell from her pocket and tumbled as it impacted onto the floor.

'Go! Go!' Tony urged picking it up as he covered their retreat. The car in front of him rocked as those *things* hit it from the other side, trying to topple it.

Then they were through.

He heard the basement door slam shut and the bolts, big,

solid iron bolts being thrown back. He was alone; the last line of defence.

He made the call to his son, not expecting for a second that it would work.

'Ellie?'

'Danny ...'

'*Da?*'

'Yes, Danny, I–'

'Da, I–' his son began.

'Danny listen to me. We're in trouble. Ellie's–'

'Ellie's with you? What's going on?'

What to tell him? The truth? Now wasn't the time.

'You've gotta get back up here as quick as you can,' he said instead. 'Get the Sword. Get *something*. There's too many of them out there, son.'

They weren't *out there* any more, though, that was the trouble. The car crashed onto its roof, forcing him to leap backward out of the room entirely or be crushed underneath it. He jumped straight into two of them; not the wolf-faeries (they probably wouldn't fit inside this modest place as well as some of the others), no. These were humanoid, if you could look beyond the needle-sharp teeth, the purple eyes, the pointed heads, the spindly bodies, the pale yellow complexion. There were three of them, all armed with claws and teeth and they skittered from the kitchen toward him, emitting an unearthly *tik-tik-tik* noise as they did so.

He whirled. The dagger tasted blood and the nearest *tik-tik* burst into a shower of its own guts with a high-pitched squeal of agony. The phone was knocked from his grasp and he went down under the other two, hoping, even as he felt claws tear and teeth bite, that his son had heard enough.

Hoping for forgiveness.

The Apotheosis

Passing through the circle of the standing stones – if standing stones could be used to describe them any more than 'a few bits of steel' could have been used to describe the Empire State Building – Danny knew that his journey in this place was drawing towards its end.

The interior of the circle was immense. Far too big. Even though this was quite a big hill they had ascended, he knew instinctively that the space he'd just entered was significantly larger: it defied the laws of physics. If such a trivial thing as physics meant anything in a place like this.

The more time he spent here, the more visions the Morrigan had shown him, the more he felt as though he was working this place out. Science and logic were secondary here. Twenty-odd years of living in a human world where cause preceded effect and you couldn't make things happen by *willing* them so had almost robbed him of the necessary perspective required to make sense of this dreamscape.

He was dealing with it, though. The key was the synaesthesia – his ability to take one sensory input and effortlessly transform it into another was similar enough to how this place worked that his mind could deal with the adjusted rules.

He wondered if this was the difference between him and any other humans who'd been here before – both Bea and the Morrigan had alluded that he was the first mortal in centuries to survive a visit here.

The legions of faeries who'd growled threats at him had, largely, been left behind on the slopes of the hill. A few lurked in this interior space within the monoliths, and those made his blood chill. Clearly only the crème de la crème of faeriedom got past those standing stones, because the things stalking around in here were nothing short of living nightmares – like their brethren on the slopes, they were a hideous mixture of animal and man, but exponentially larger and nastier.

In the centre of the massive interior was a raised stone platform: a circular slab with nine steps leading up to it on all sides. On the platform were two thrones, ornate beyond comprehension. The larger throne, golden, was occupied by the largest and most intimidating example of manhood Danny had ever seen. Although he was currently seated, Danny knew that if he stood he'd be well over ten feet tall. He was clad in a king's robes, long and flowing and deepest green. He wore a modest circlet of thin gold around his head. Fingers the size of pint glasses drummed on the throne's armrests. His eyes seemed to bore into Danny's skull.

And yet for all this, Danny barely spared him a glance.

Because to his left, seated on a smaller, more modest throne comprised of a jet-black substance that seemed to suck light into itself, sat Carman.

Carman the witch. Carman the queen, mother to all of the faeries around him. He knew without question that it was her.

He'd had an image of her in his head of course – had pictured her from the moment he'd first encountered her name. He had imagined a tall and statuesque woman, strikingly beautiful and fearsome beyond measure – somewhat similar to the Morrigan herself, truth be told, He'd wondered if he'd get within thirty feet of her and she would just snap her fingers and cause him to fly apart.

She was none of those things.

She was all of those things.

Her features did not settle. They *flowed*. Her body was not one shape. It was many, forming and reforming itself, her queenly attire impossible to make out as it pulsed between every dimension and format possible and cycled through every colour known and a few that seemed new and disturbing in equal measure.

As Wily approached the bottom of the stone steps Danny tried to focus on her, tried to get a bead on what she looked like. He could not. He found himself thinking of the boundary between sea and land, constantly in flux as the waves wash up onshore, forever changing.

Looking at her, his mind began to water, his sanity to crumble. This was her strength, he realised, her first line of defence: she existed on a different plane. He thought about the tales of Medusa or the Basilisk, mythological creatures able to petrify or to kill with a single glance. Carman, it seemed, was in the same league.

As with her appearance, her voice when she spoke was neither low and booming nor high and shrill, but both and all things between, and he felt himself further thrown, dizzied by it.

'Destroyer of our rath,' she said/shouted/spat/hissed. 'Why have you come here?'

His skin itched as though ants were crawling beneath it. He felt wetness on his face and touched his fingers to his nose. It took him four tries to find it, and when he did, his fingers came away crimson with the blood now dripping steadily from his nostrils. He felt wetness from his ears, pressure building up in his eyes and he realised that blood was welling up behind them too.

He was, quite literally, falling apart under her gaze.

Wily shifted under him, breaking his stupor, bringing him around a little. Danny dismounted like an infirm octogenarian, managing to reach out with a trembling hand and pat the wolf-faerie on the flank, glancing into its long lupine face. Wily seemed surprised at this gesture, and stared back at him until it seemed that Danny was glimpsing past the creature's appearance and into its essence.

His synaesthesia flared, but differently – before it had thrown smells and tastes, pictures and memories of seemingly random places or events at him. He knew now that was only because he had not learned to adapt that skill. The core of the ability was to take something and *make* it something else, to change it, and in changing it learn something about what made it work.

Danny saw it then. The wolf-faerie's mind was mapped out before him, its memories like paper files in a cabinet that he could skim through as effortlessly as he might run a hand through his hair. Files that he could take things from, if he so chose.

Files that he could add to …

'Thank you,' he told Wily and he performed his first real act of magic on the creature.

He turned from Wily to address Carman, his senses burning as he tried to focus on her fluid countenance once more. She was confusing his sight, she was muddling his hearing; it was what she did to throw her opponents off-balance.

The answer came to him then – it was so simple – the answer was to *hear* her appearance. *See* her words.

The pressure faded behind his eyes. It was as if someone had been crushing his mind under their boot and he had just wriggled free. Feeling that weight lift off his thoughts was wonderful. He inhaled sharply, strength flooding back into his limbs.

'This one shows promise,' the king said. His voice was discernible, even if it was so powerful that it seemed to shake the soil as he spoke. Aftershocks rocked the surface as the echoes of his words faded.

Carman had not come into focus. Not yet. She was leaning forward in her throne now though, and for Danny even to be able to recognise that was a measure of his progress.

Danny spoke the words written in twenty-foot high flaming letters all the way from his skin to his soul: words that had taken him through the looking-glass and into this realm of madness.

'I want my son.'

'He is ours,' Carman replied. Her voice fluctuated, but not to the same degree it had, and this time he did not feel the wave of paralysing nausea that had almost been the end of him mere moments ago. 'He is ours by right.'

'Where is he? Where is my son?'

At some invisible signal from their queen, the faeries that had stood within the standing stones took a long step toward him, surrounding him. He sized up his chances against these things, and with difficulty forced down his anger. This wasn't how these fuckers worked, they were products of a different age. To get out of this alive, to get out of here with Luke in his arms, he needed to play by whatever rules necessary. Nothing else mattered.

'Tell me what I have to do,' he said.

The king clapped his hands. Each time they came together it was like a sonic blast. Danny staggered back a few paces, *seeing* the sound waves as they rippled toward him and, with a flicker of effort, he *reached* out and *changed* them, tweaking their flight path so that they curved around him.

The sound died in his ears, leaving a faint taste of Wednesdays in December behind.

'I *like* this one!' the king rumbled. He seemed oblivious to the power of his approving applause. 'Live thee, or deal? Speak! Answer!'

Danny blinked. *Live thee, or deal?* Was that some sort of faerie riddle? What would the penalty be for a wrong answer? Obviously *live* seemed the right response; but since he wanted something from them – the return of Luke – he felt sure they would demand some price in return. Whether he could afford, or even survive that price was in question, but with his abilities – embryonic through they undoubtedly were – surely he had at the very least a chance?

'Deal,' he said.

'Yes?' the king inclined his head. 'You agree?'

'Yes,' Danny confirmed.

The king roared his approval. Danny was forced to remould the sound into the smell of strawberries to avoid his eardrums perishing forever. He barely had to think about it this time; the groove the ability wore within his mind was deepening, becoming quicker and easier to access each time he went back to it.

'He has chosen! Hail the courage of he who will live the Ordeal!' the king was roaring.

An answering roar of appreciation rang back from the faerie hordes who, Danny dimly perceived through each gap between the monoliths, were now a hundred-deep. They crowded around the outside of the standing-stone circle to observe its interior. He dimly perceived this because he was a bit preoccupied by what the king had just said.

'Live the Ordeal?' Danny choked. '*Live thee, or deal? Live the Ordeal?* Wait!'

And as the king threw up his hands and led his race in their rhapsodic agreement with Danny's choice, the sound of Carman's laughter rang in his ears. The circle expanded, the monoliths faded,,the horizon rushed toward him ... and there was a smell of rotting fruit.

He'd heard that laugh before.

That was his last thought before hands as big as serving platters wrapped themselves around his arms, his legs. They felt warm. Blood roared in his ears.

Wait, he wanted to say. *I didn't know.* But there was no time. Somewhere, surprise registered inside him. He'd known it was unlikely he would prevail in this place, but for it to come to this ...

They ripped him apart. Tore him limb from limb.

As the dancing and the revelling reached fever pitch, as the king screamed his approval, as the blood loss and the trauma reached Danny's brain and shut it down, five unimaginable creatures, who each held a piece of what was formerly Danny Morrigan, moved to stand before their king and queen.

'Throw him in,' Carman commanded and with a wave of her hand, a cauldron appeared in front of the thrones. The dismembered parts of Danny were tossed inside where they lay haphazardly on top of one another. Firewood appeared without having to be gathered. Fire was produced without a spark or fuel. This was not a realm of physics. There was no need for cause and effect.

The pieces of Danny Morrigan's body began to blister and burn.

Watching this impassively, Carman unwrapped something that had been lying in her lap. On her knee, the infant – around four years old, in human terms – looked up at her with massive eyes. Remarkably, given what he was looking at, he was calm, composed. There was not a hint of fear.

She smiled.

Soon. Very soon now…

BELFAST, NOW

Surprised to still be alive, Tony Morrigan stared into the face of the man he was fairly sure was about to correct this anomaly.

'Tony,' said Dother pleasantly, standing in the ruins of Dermot

Scully's front room. The car that had reduced half the room to rubble was ablaze now. Dother gave a casual wave in the direction of the vehicle. The flames died instantly.

This done, he glanced down at the bodies of his fallen foot soldiers and frowned at the man being held securely before him in an admonishing way.

'Was all of this *really* necessary?'

'I'll show you *necessary*, you fucker …' Tony retorted, struggling to get loose, more, in truth, for the sake of appearances. Even if the two faeries currently holding him in place were to slacken their vice-like grip, he wasn't sure he had the strength left to stay upright, let alone launch into another round of resistance.

Dother shrugged. 'You *will* insist on these silly circles. What choice did we have?'

'It doesn't matter,' Tony shot back. 'Danny's down there. He's–'

'Can we skip the part where you tell me how your son's going to kill this and end that and bring about an end to the evil empire of the other?' Dother asked, his face pinched in what seemed to be more impatience than anger. 'We don't have much time …'

He trailed off, stopped. Sniffed the night air. The faeries holding Tony did the same. Sarah came to stand beside Dother then and Tony couldn't help but jerk in fear at the sight of her. She hadn't aged a day since the night his father had died.

'The Ordeal?' she asked, a touch incredulously. 'I sensed …'

'Yes,' Dother nodded. 'Remarkable of him to have made it that far.'

'Danny?' Tony guessed. He struggled despite himself. 'What Ordeal? What are you *doing* to him down there …?'

Dother pointed to the basement door, nodded to Sarah. 'Break it down,' he ordered her. 'Bring the others. Alive, if possible. Time is short.'

Sarah melted into her true form, or at least as much of it as the restricted space left inside the house would allow her. Tony's feet scrabbled desperately on the ground as all earlier notions of exhaustion fled his body and he tried with every ounce of strength he had left to break free of his captors. Not to assist those in the basement, but simply to put more distance between himself and the monstrous shape unfurling in front of him.

Terror choked him, made him incoherent; he babbled inanities, cursed any who came near him, begged Dother for mercy.

On hearing this plea, Dother merely smiled. 'Someday, I must introduce you to my mother,' he said softly.

THE OTHERWORLD, NOW

Carman turned her attention to the wolf-faerie who stood in the inner circle, far beyond where his kind were usually permitted to travel.

'You carried him to us.'

'Yes.'

'Why?'

Wily pondered this. 'It seemed correct,' was all he could offer. Only later would he note his speech pattern had changed: his difficulties forming words receded.

'He named you.'

'Yes.'

'Why?'

'I don't know, my queen,' the hulking wolf-faerie responded.

'Get out. Get back to your kin,' the king boomed. 'This place is not for you. You do not require a name. Tell your fellow warriors. Tell them everything.'

Wily cast a look at the Cauldron where the remains of Danny Morrigan had been tossed. His massive head swung back to take in his king and queen.

'As you wish,' he rumbled, and padded from the circle. Carman's eyes were upon him all the way.

BELFAST, NOW

The basement door shuddered, resounding under blows of immense power coming from the other side.

Ellie was still unconscious. Steve, barely upright. He perceived little of what was going on beyond that Ellie was hurt and that somehow, he felt this was his fault. He tried to prop her up, make her comfortable.

'Danny's okay,' he told her. 'Danny's okay, Ellie. Danny's okay, you'll see. He's … he's different now. Danny's okay.'

The dim light of the basement made it difficult to see exactly what was going on around them, but he was aware of Dermot frantically shuffling around on his hands and knees beside them, though he couldn't really make out what the man was doing.

There was an almighty crash and the basement door came clean off its hinges, slammed against the opposing wall, and tumbled down the staircase.

Ellie opened her eyes.

'Car,' she said weakly. There was blood in her mouth.

Steve nodded. 'We crashed. Your ... your da pulled you from the wreckage.'

'Daddy?'

He looked around for Michael Quinn and stopped, thinking for a second that the first signs of his inevitable concussion were beginning to materialise. For surely, surely that man standing in front of them wielding a weapon in each hand, facing the staircase and looking like he'd just stepped from the set of some Bruce Willis movie, surely that wasn't Michael Quinn.

'Come on you bastards!' Willis/Quinn hollered and Steve could see the flecks of spittle fly from his mouth. 'What are you fucking waiting for, eh? Come and get it!'

'Quinn!' Dermot shouted over the other man's battle roar. 'Get inside the fucking circle!'

'Keep her safe!' Michael cried out, glancing over his shoulder, not budging an inch from where he stood. 'Do whatever you have to!'

Michael was, Steve realised dimly, holding two golf clubs. He had successfully raided a decades-old golf bag stashed in a dusty corner of the basement.

'Daddy?' Ellie said again, more coherently this time. She tried to sit up and groaned with pain at the movement in a way that Steve didn't like at all. 'Daddy, what are you ...'

'I'm–' he began.

He got no further, for that was when it appeared, blocking out the light filtering down the staircase from the house above. At first it was merely one massive leg, thick and hairy, and then another followed, and two more, until four of the legs were visible on the staircase.

There was a clang as one of Michael's golf clubs fell to the floor, presumably dropped from numb fingers.

Behind those first four exploratory legs came the creature itself.

Ellie's scream lit up the basement with noise, rebounded from the walls and resounded in their ears, reflecting their own silent screams.

As the remainder of those horrifying legs skittered down the staircase, as the spider stood fully inside the basement and successfully gained its bearings, it swayed once, from side to side, as if gauging its tactics for the short battle ahead. This done, one single leg flicked out, casually, with enough power to pulverise brick, right through the space where Quinn–

–had been.

Quinn had ducked under the strike, under and forward, and was running while he screamed, a sound of challenge and terror perfectly mixed. He held his one remaining golf club high above his head, securely gripped in both hands and charged. The spider's legs spasmed in surprise at this prey's entirely unexpected decision to fight back.

It had legs to spare, any one of which could have sliced a man in two on impact. Steve watched them twitch and begin to move–

Beside him, wearing a grim smile of satisfaction, Dermot barked out a single word in Gaelic, and flicked the lightswitch.

New lights came on all over the basement, and Steve realised that while he had been tending to Ellie, Dermot had been making himself *very* busy.

Chalk circles covered the basement, peppered here and there, on the floors, on the walls. The circumference of each one glowed fiercely for a second as if, like the hitherto unused lights, they too had just been switched on.

The enormous spider suddenly found six of its legs, those which had skittered inside one of the chalk circles, completely immobilised. Just as a small but *massively* pissed off human with murder in his eyes bore down upon it.

'Die!' came the cry, and the golf club smashed right into that nightmarish visage of compound eyes, and again, into that mouth full of impossible teeth.

Blue blood spurted out in great glooping rivulets, splashing across the basement, sizzling like bacon on the griddle when it touched the enchanted circles and then evaporating into nothingness. The pieces of the spider's body caught within the circles were decomposing at an accelerated rate.

An unearthly scream of pain erupted from the creature. That massive body seemed to ripple, to try to change, and Steve fancied for a moment that it almost – *almost* – made it to human, a change that would perhaps would have shaken it loose from the trap that had been sprung upon it.

But Michael Quinn – who knew deep down that his beloved daughter, currently lying there bleeding and injured because of these *fuckers*, was a much better human being than he would ever be – had a handicap of five, and a *mean* backswing.

Again and again the club came down, until the twitching of

the spider's leg changed from desperate attempts to shake itself loose to something else entirely – to the spasmodic shaking of a creature whose body is sprinting to catch up to the fact that it's already doomed.

Only then did Michael pause for breath, and only then did the creature utter anything other than shrieks of agony. It spoke, and when it did so, it spoke in the voice of an idealistic girl from another time, caught up in the heady romance of rebellion, cursed to be a monster.

'Kill me,' the long-forgotten voice of Molly Weston whispered. 'Save me.'

Her wish was granted. The golf club came down one final time with every ounce of strength the man grasping it possessed, pulverising the remains of the brain below.

With one last horrendous screech, that nightmarish body shuddered and lay still. The trapped legs dissolved, and now the spider's form *did* change; it shrank, collapsed, imploded back to human.

'Jesus ...' Michael gasped in shock at the human corpse laid out at his feet.

Beside Steve, Ellie had managed to grit her teeth against the pain of her injuries and sit up. Tears of disbelief ran down her face as she processed what she had just seen.

'Daddy?' she said again.

Michael turned, gasping for breath, no doubt trying to process his own actions and coming up as short as his daughter was. He smiled at seeing his daughter sitting upright, looking at him the way she was.

'Ellie,' he said, and took a deep breath, 'I'm sor–'

The sword burst through his chest at heart level. It was glowing silver, and covered in blood. Michael Quinn's blood. Then it vanished, pulled back through his body with as seemingly little effort as it had taken to insert it.

For a moment, Michael stood there, his mouth open in surprise. Dumbstruck with horror and grief, Steve, Dermot and Ellie could only watch.

Without another word, he collapsed, dead before he hit the ground.

'I'm just speculating, but I think he was about to say sorry,' Dother said. Bloody silver sword in hand, he paused to kneel and wipe it clean on the front of Michael Quinn's suit. 'Rest assured, he wasn't as sorry as the rest of you are about to be.'

With a muttering of ancient words and a few gestures, each of the circles chalked into the stone, including the one all three were currently huddled within, glowed once more and then faded, the white outlines disappearing as if pulled down into the bowels of the earth.

As Ellie's screams began to fill the air, all three were taken, bound and bundled into a large limosine waiting outside the house. At some stage the trauma must have become too much for Ellie and she passed out. That or she was knocked out by a faerie unable to stomach any more of her screaming. As he was pushed into the car, Steve caught sight of Tony Morrigan, still alive but bound, just as trapped as they were.

Danny, wherever he was, was their last hope. Steve had to believe that his friend was alive and could do something about all of this madness, and he tried to hold on to that thought as he felt the car move away from the pavement.

They hadn't gone too far when he felt hands upon him, with a grip like steel.

'We don't need this one,' came Dother's voice and there was scorn in his tone. 'He's of no value.'

He felt a sudden draught of air beside him, shockingly cold and fast, as someone opened the car door beside him while the limo was still moving. Why would anyone do that? He wasn't of any value? What did that mean? What were they going to do with–

He knew the answers to all of those questions.

The sensation of being thrown while bound was not a pleasant one; the world spun crazily as he fell and the cold night air pierced through him. He thought he heard a muffled scream, and realised belatedly it was coming from his own throat.

Impact was going to be bad, he knew. Already injured from the car crash, bleeding from cuts and covered in bruises, the bonds around his arms and legs meant he had no way to brace himself.

How can I have the time to think all of this? he wondered. Normally Steven Anderson was not someone exactly renowned for his quicksilver speed of thought. In this, too, he already knew the answer. *I have time because this is it. This is all the time I have left to me. When I hit, I'm not going to survive.*

His second to last thought, before the impact, was of Maggie, and of one day and one fatal outburst in particular.

His last thought was *I wonder if this is going to hurt.*

*

He looked down at the tickets he held in his hand. Two tickets. Return. To Liverpool. Steve was a lifelong Red. He'd been to Anfield seven times and had been salivating at the prospect of an eighth journey whenever he could justify the expense. He'd been handed a free trip. He should have felt like he'd died and gone to heaven.

'I don't think I can,' he said.

'Why?' Maggie, provider of the tickets, asked him. 'The procedure should only take an hour or so and then we would have the rest of the weekend. We could go to a game.'

'Go to a game,' he said. He didn't know why he repeated her words. It felt good just to be saying something. Right now he would have recited the alphabet just for the comfort of hearing something come out of his mouth. 'You hate football.'

'I'm sure I can make that sacrifice.'

He flinched as if struck and almost stumbled, almost fell onto the kitchen chair where he sat, dumbstruck, looking down at the tickets in his hand.

'We've never talked,' he said.

'About what?'

'About. Options.'

She tapped the tickets. 'You're holding them. Come with me. Or don't come with me.'

The enormity of what he was trying to discuss yawned before him, a crack in the world so big that he felt its gravity pulling him in. Every time he worked out what he wanted to say, the weight of the future would warp it and destroy it and prevent it from actually escaping his lips. Someone was tightening the screws. In a few minutes the lid would be firmly affixed and it would never, never come off and he was standing by and watching the whole process.

'It's ...' he gulped for air. 'It's not ... I mean, well, it's not ... it's ...'

'It's ...?' Maggie asked. She had turned away from him and was looking out the kitchen window. The sun was shining in through the vertical blinds and silhouetted against its light she made the loveliest hourglass shape he had ever seen. She was beautiful. She was his.

'It's not ... it's not the *baby's* fault that we don't want it. That we think we're not ready,' he said.

'Well, are *you* ready?' she asked him. 'Because *I'm* not.'

'No,' he answered. 'Jesus, God, Christ, fuck no, I'm not ready. But is that the point?'

'I think it's *exactly* the fuckin' point, yeah, actually!' and she stabbed a finger accusingly at him. 'Don't dance around it, Steve. Don't sit there with the big eyes and the noble look. Come out with what you want to say. Hit me with it. Come on. Do you think I'm totally fuckin' stupid? Do you?'

'What?' he asked, mystified.

'Ellie and Danny,' she said with twisted triumph. 'You're sitting there and you're thinking, *they're* managing it. *They're* dealing with it. This is another one of your wee pissin' contests with your mate, eh? Can't have him gettin' one over?'

He looked at her, outraged. 'You think,' he said, keeping his voice steady with some difficulty, 'you think I'm talking about other options because I don't want Danny to have *one up on me?'*

She shrugged. 'Aren't you?' she asked, and then seemed to dismiss it with an impatient wave of a hand. 'You know what? I don't care. Do you seriously think I'm going to let one bit of stupidity ruin the rest of my life? I have plans, Steve. I have things I wanna do. I was there the day Danny found out. I saw the look on his face. The *oh fuck* look. Ellie might not have had the strength to deal with it the way she should, but not me. That'll not be me, I'm tellin' you that right fuckin' now.'

'You were there? What do you mean, you were *there?'*

'We were still together when he found out. Why do you think he went back to her?' Maggie said, bitterness evident in her tone.

'Jesus Christ,' Steve said, putting his head in his hands. The tickets fell to the floor, unnoticed. He couldn't have cared less about them. He squeezed his palms into the sides of his head until it was painful, hoping to crush his brain; this was too much to take. Couldn't she *see?*

'I thought you knew,' she said. 'I'm sorry.'

'*Sorry?'* he snarled back, standing up, all traces of restraint now gone. '*Sorry?* You're apologising to *me?'*

'Who else should I be apologising to? To him? To Ellie?'

'How about apologising to the baby you're aborting for the sole fucking reason that it reminds you of the reason you got fucking dumped, you stupid, selfish *bitch!'* he screamed at her.

The words reverberated through the kitchen, through the house, through their entire relationship. He knew as soon as they had spewed from his mouth that once they were said, it was over and finished. Not just for him and Maggie.

In saying those words, in losing his temper, he'd lost any chance he ever had of changing Maggie's mind.

'Get out,' she told him.

He left without another word, stepping on the tickets as he did so, and went back to the once-glorious squalor of Belgravia Avenue and straight up to his tiny little room, ignoring the greetings of his housemates on the way. He stood for a few minutes with his back to the door, staring at the Liverpool posters that were plastered all over the walls, and then began to tear down every single one of them, ripping them up into the smallest pieces he could manage.

NOWHERE

Being dead hurts.

Wait. I just thought a thought. Dead people don't think thoughts. Unless all that crap about the afterlife was true.

In the void of nothingness, whatever portion of it made up the consciousness of Danny Morrigan pondered that. *Okay, considering all that has happened over the last few days, maybe some of it isn't as far-fetched as I imagined. So ... am I alone here? Hello? I can't see anything. Well, of course I can't see anything. My eyes are probably fifteen feet from the rest of my body.*

Wait. If I can't see anything because I don't have eyes, then how come it hurts? How can I feel pain if I don't have a body any more to send, what is it, electrical impulses or something along the nerve cells, isn't that how it works, to my brain?

Try to move. Try to move in the black. There's got to be something more to this than just blackness. Time. Is time passing? How long did it take me to think that? How long since I got here? Okay, it takes a second to say one Mississippi. Okay. One Mississippi.

Was that a second?

How come this hurts so fucking much? Oops. Better not curse.even years in Purgatory for every swearword, that's what Miss Denham told us all back in P2, the evil oul witch. Is that where this is? Purgatory?

I can't believe they just killed me like that. I mean, I thought I was getting all these powers for a reason. I thought I went on that fucking vision quest thing for a purpose: that it was going to unlock some abilities or something. Maybe I've been playing too many computer games. Oh well. Least that's not gonna be a problem any more.

I'll never see them again. Ellie. Luke. I fucked up everything.

That's why it hurts. It's not my body. It's my … me. I'm hurting. I'm alone in the black and all I have for company is myself and the knowledge that everyone I love is probably going to die because I got myself torn to shreds without so much as a whimper.

Time is passing here. Time's going to pass here, because how else would I measure the hurt?

I can swear all I want.

This isn't Purgatory and this certainly isn't heaven.

This is the other place.

Time passed. After some of it – hours, days, weeks, the disembodied entity that had once been Danny Morrigan could no longer tell – he came to the realisation that nothing was ever going to change.

This is what hell is, he thought, for the hundredth time, for the thousandth. It didn't matter. The repetition was comforting somehow. *It's ourselves. Being locked away inside your own mind with*

318

only your own thoughts for company, and knowing there's no escape.

And then it dawned on him: here, where nothing was everything, thoughts were the only form of matter that existed and after so long here, they could almost feel like physical entities.

Something *was* changing.

This place isn't staying the same. It's the hurt. The hurt is getting worse. Every time I go round the loop – every time I cycle from desperation to grief to screaming myself stupid trying to find something, someone, anything else inside this place, and back again – the hurt gets a little bigger, a little more unbearable.

I'm losing it.

He giggled a little at that. The giggles seemed to pop in the emptiness, little stepping-stones of black on a sea of deeper blackness.

Going out of my mind inside my mind. Like stepping outside the universe. Stop the cosmos, I want a wee-wee. That's a good thing, right? Maybe that's my out. Going completely bug-fuck crazy until this place seems normal and boom, there's my doorway of light and I can step through. Extra life. Continue. Back to level 1, with cheat codes.

But he was lying to himself. Crazy wasn't the way to go.

I'm all that's left. Literally, all that's left. If I lose that, there's nothing left to lose and out I go like a fucking light. Some part of me is still around.

The Ordeal. That's what they called it. Death is the Ordeal?

This was different. This wasn't part of his usual cycle of thought. He clung to it like a drowning man to a rubber ring, exploring the thought from all sides. Here, that seemed easier than normal to do, as if it really were a three-dimensional object that he could turn over, examine.

No. How can Death be a test? Unless they were simply fucking with me and were always going to kill me. No. No, that's not cruel enough for them. If they were going to do that, they wouldn't have let the things that tore me apart do it so quickly.

Think.

If Death isn't the ordeal, then I'm not dead. Or maybe not permanently. So that means there's a way out of this. I don't have a body. This place goes on forever. So how to get out? It's like a prison and I'm locked inside. What's the key?

Fuck the key. Where's the door?

No. Focus. Some prisons maybe don't need doors. Just keys. I'm just thoughts, so thinking has to be the key. The right thought. It can't be as simple as 'get me the fuck out of here' or 'I'm sorry' or any kind of regrets about Ellie, about Luke, because Christ, I've done all of those a million times. If they'd been the key, I'd have been out long ago.

I am this universe. I'm all that exists within it.

So … I control it?

What can I create?

If it were possible, self-conscious embarrassment radiated out from the centre of the Morriganverse as he gathered himself and thought the words:

LET THERE BE LIGHT.

And lo, there was fuck all.

Bollocks, Danny sulked. *I bet God never had this trouble. Mind you, he was the real deal and I'm just some dead twat going round the bend and imagining I have god-like powers.*

Wait a minute. 'Imagining' I have powers? I do have powers. Even back in the … in the real world, I was able to see through the illusions.

The synaesthesia. Take it down to the Otherworld, their world, and it's indistinguishable from magic. You take one thing, and you turn it into another.

But here … here that won't work. There are no sights, no sounds, no smells, no tastes. Nothing but me and my thoughts. And it's not like I can turn thoughts into …

Into reality…

I'm doing it wrong. I thought 'Let there be light', but all I really thought were the four words. I didn't actually believe that, just by thinking about bringing light to this place, I could light it up, as if I could–

And lo. There was light.

Bright, shining light that seared through the nowherescape he inhabited. Radiance that burst forth and turned the black to white. If he currently owned eyes, it would have seemed like every nuclear warhead on Earth had detonated. A bring your own supernova party.

Time passed. He dealt with the shock of the transition, and then a thought emerged from the snide little side of his brain.

Brilliant. You made a big black nothing into a big white nothing. Whoopee-fuckin-doo.

He bristled, if that were possible without skin. He was so sick of that snide little internal monologue. If only it were a separate entity that he could–

'Oh. Oh great, thanks. *Now* look what you've done.'

Huh?

'You've made me a separate entity, you idiot. Wonderful. All the things you could be doing with your time, and so far you've whitewashed the cosmos and made your self-doubt corporeal. Oh *superb*, Danny. Bravo. If I had hands, I'd be clapping.'

Don't you ever shut the fuck up?

'I would if you gave me cause to! But you keep fucking things up on such a regular basis that I have endless material to work from!'

Oh piss off. I'm young, Irish, and I'm the centre of the universe. And I'm done talking to you. Come back inside and shut up.

He tried. To his surprise, he couldn't recall the voice, much to the voice's evident pleasure.

'Looks like I'm sticking around for a wee while yet,' Doubt said smugly.

Right, fine. Now … I've had enough of this disembodied shite …

His body popped into existence, arms and legs and head – oh thank Christ for the wondrousness of heads – and immediately began plummeting downward (upward? sideward?) through endless white space.

'Ohhhhhhh *fuuuuuuuuuckkkkkkk!*'

There was something extremely disconcerting about this. How was he supposed to function like this?

I need something solid under my feet. Nothing fancy. A field'll do–

He hit the turf of a thin space-time slice of Wembley Stadium at what seemed to be the speed of light.

There was a sound like a splat, but with a faint hint of splintering thrown in.

Dying hurt just as much the second time, it turned out.

Bollocks.

'Doing well so far,' Doubt chortled. 'God had the world knocked out in six days. At this rate you'll be lucky to produce Ballymena by the end of the millennium.'

With another pop, a replacement body appeared. He patted himself down. He was clothed in his normal kind of outfit; jeans, casual shirt, trainers.

'See,' Doubt said, conversationally, 'your problem was that, as soon as you had a body in this place, you imagined gravity applied. And then when you imagined the field beneath your feet, you imagined that you were travelling really fast and that there'd be an impact and, well...'

Danny glanced around the Wembley turf, bordered on all four sides by the endless white. His first incarnation had made quite the splashdown.

'If I'm gonna have to listen to you, *you* can stop being disembodied an all,' he said, and brought the voice of Doubt into the physical universe.

To his complete lack of surprise, it looked like–

'Ohhhh,' the body of Tony Morrigan said, a slow smile spreading across his face as he patted himself down, just as Danny had done a few seconds earlier. 'You imagine a physical form for the nagging little voice that keeps telling you that you're not good enough, and *this* is the one you pick? Hmm ...' and the voice grew singsong and playful as his father's head bobbed from side to side like a bird, 'does someone have daddy issues?'

'Fuck you,' Danny replied evenly. 'I don't have *time* for this, anyway. I have to figure out how to...how to get *out* of this... wherever *this* is,' he waved a hand airily to indicate the alabaster cosmos.

'Fine,' Doubt shrugged. 'I understand. You've had, what, a decade, decade and a half, to build up some serious psychological

baggage over you and dear old dad. Trying to deal with that ...
sheesh,' he sucked in a breath, 'that *would* be a bit of a *tribulation* ...
you know, a stern *test*, a bit of a *hardship* ...'

Danny got it. Doubt rolled his eyes with relief at seeing
realisation dawn across his face.

'Oh *good*,' he said, 'for a minute there I was afraid I was going
to have to hit you over the head with a big fucking sign saying
That's the ordeal, dickhead.'

'So I'm supposed to sort out my ...' Danny paused. He hated
the word; it was so American, '... my *issues* with who? With you?
You're not even my dad. You're just every annoying part of me,
distilled.'

'Oh not *every* annoying part. Believe me you'd be here for hours
imagining different bodies for *all* the annoying parts of you.'

'You gonna answer my question?'

'*You gonna answer my question?*' Doubt mocked, puppeting its
hand as it spoke. 'Listen to yourself! You're asking a part of yourself
to answer a question that you already know the answer to!'

Doubt was right. Somehow it had been easier to think when
he lacked physical form. Or, of course, maybe it had taken him
centuries to get this far. Still, he *did* know the answer to this. There
had to be some effective way of getting the questions, the tears,
he'd always had over his dad's decision to vanish from his life.

If only he could go back and ...

As Wembley began to dissolve around them and an entirely
different landscape to form in its place, Doubt smiled, so faintly
and so subtly that even the Cheshire Cat wouldn't have caught it.

*

'Ach, in the name of ...' Tony Morrigan sighed, as the picture before him dissolved. The cottage's miniscule little television had the world's shittest indoor aerial perched on top of it. He used an outdoor one whenever possible, but with the cottage a good few miles from any kind of shelter, come winter the winds hit the place hard and any aerial, no matter how strapped down, inevitably broke its moorings and was scattered across the fields.

'ffffsshhshshshhhhhhh ... am I this time, Al?' Dr Sam Beckett was saying on the screen, when he wasn't endlessly whirling from the top of the television to the bottom, as if on some invisible Catherine wheel.

'fffshhhhshshshshhhhhssh ... teen sixty-eight. Your name is .... ffshshshshss ... Ziggy thinks you're here to—'

Al from *Quantum Leap* was cut off aruptly as a particularly fierce gust howled outside and the meagre signal the indoor aerial was able to receive was lost in the fury of the elements.

'Fuck it anyway,' Tony said, switching off the set and wondering whether to really push the boat out excitement-wise by going to the kitchenette and whipping up a cuppa. It'd only been his fortieth or so of the day, after all.

That was when the knock came at the door.

Tony moved with muscles that hadn't been used regularly enough recently. The silver-tipped dagger was in his hand in just a few seconds. He moved toward the cottage's front door, balancing on the balls of his feet, ready to spring back or roll out of the way if required, cursing the fact that he still hadn't installed a peephole in the door. A glance from the side window revealed nothing –

whoever it was must be standing in the eaves under the overhang.

The knock came again.

'Who is it?' he called.

'It's me, Da,' came Danny's voice.

His legs turned to jelly. He grabbed the nearest corner of the table for support, mind racing, heart pounding. Danny? Here? Now? *How*? Scully? Dother? *Why*?

This will ruin everything, was the first thought. *Your son is out there*, was the second.

'Danny?' he croaked.

'Aye, Da,' the voice came again. 'Are you gonna let me come in? It's windy as fuck out here ...'

Tendrils of doubt crept into Tony's mind. The voice didn't sound right. It sounded deeper, older. The cadence was off. And his ten-year-old son had just casually dropped the word 'fuck'.

His hand tightened around the silver dagger. So. They'd found him, detected the safeguards he'd put around the place. Everyone knew you could put all the mystical defences in the world down and they didn't count for jack shit if you were stupid enough to invite the fuckers inside.

'We had a deal!' he shouted, over the howl of the winds, moving from one window to another, trying to see where they were lurking. There'd be more than the one at the door, he knew. They'd be in the grass, low against the earth, biding their time. When the deception worked and the one at the door got in, presumably his mission was to bring down the warding charms from the remainder of the house and allow the rest to storm in.

There was a sigh from outside. An honest-to-God sigh.

'Dother and I had a deal!' Tony shouted.

Silence from outside. It stretched on for seconds, then minutes, until he began to think that the invocation of their boss's name had been enough to scare the bastards away. His grip on the dagger loosened – not by much, but a little.

And then ... then, someone who looked an awful lot like an aged version of his ten-year-old son walked through the front door. Literally, *through* the front door.

The winds died outside. The television flickered into life, now with a perfect picture, just in time for Al to step through his shimmering white square of light and out of Sam's world.

'Huh,' the ghost of his son grunted, eyes on the TV, 'if only it was *that* fuckin' easy.'

Tony gaped. He backed up, felt the kitchen table behind him, and manoeuvred himself around it so that the comforting slab of wood was between him and this invading apparition. The back door was only a few feet more away. It was bolted, of course, but a few well-timed arm movements and he could be through and away from this nightmare.

'Oh would you *stop* with that look, Da? I feel like you're about to tell me there's more of gravy than of grave about me or something. Jesus.'

What are you? How did you step through the wood? How did you get around the defences? Three very coherent and reasonable questions that Tony Morrigan framed in his head but by the time they reached his mouth, they had somewhat lost their coherency. 'Buh?'

'It's me. It's Danny. I know this is nuts, but I'm real. Well, I think so. I'm reasonably sure. I'm as sure I'm real as I'm sure *you're* real, put it like that.'

Something about this rambling nonsense actually made Tony pause in his determined crabwalk toward the back door. Nothing evil was ever *that* incoherent.

'Who are you?' he managed. 'You're not Danny. You can't be. My son is–'

'Ten years old and, what, two or three hundred miles northeast of here. Yeah I know. And he is. But I'm ...' the image of Danny shrugged, 'I'm here too.'

'From the future,' Tony said numbly.

Danny had the decency to look embarrassed. 'Er, I know how it sounds.' After a slight pause he added, 'If it makes you feel any better, this is my first time too.'

'How did you get here?'

'I ... I kind of ... I had to come,' Danny finished.

'But that doesn't tell me how.'

'Well it's all I've got, Da, to be honest.'

Tony sat down on one of the kitchen chairs, his legs like rubber. He kicked one of the other chairs out and Danny slowly, gingerly, lowered his transparent form.

'Hey,' Danny said brightly, 'my arse didn't go through. Class.'

'Yeah,' Tony replied, his voice seeming faraway. 'Cos the time travel and the walking through walls ... workaday stuff.'

'Beats being dead.'

A deep chill shot straight through the older man's heart at hearing his son say those words. 'Dead?' he said hoarsely.

Danny held up a hand. 'Relax,' he said. 'I think it's temporary.'

'Temporary,' he echoed.

'Yeah.'

'Temporarily dead.'

'I think so. I think the Cauldron has something to do with it. The Morrigan showed me it being used ... before, I mean, in ancient times and ... and I'm really not helping here, am I?'

'Well I'm pretty sure I'm dreaming,' Tony said, with remarkable cheerfulness. 'Or I've taken drugs. I'd remember taking drugs. Or maybe not.'

Danny shrugged. 'Okay. Dreaming. Fine.'

'So what happens now?'

'Ummm ... what do you mean?'

'Well ... do we, I dunno, do we suddenly find ourselves performing a one-man-show in Vegas; do we open a whelk farm; or I dunno, start fighting off cheese toasties with fangs, or what? How's it work?'

Danny regarded him. 'It works like this,' he said. 'I ask you some questions, and you answer them. And you answer them truthfully.'

'And then you'll go away?' Tony said.

'Aye,' Danny said, his anger rising. 'I go away. Because God knows at this point in time you wouldn't want to spend any time with your son, now would you?'

Tony laughed. He didn't seem to notice (or care if he did) the expression on Danny's face as he did so.

'You think this is a big joke? You've a wee son at the other end of the country waking up every morning expecting, hoping, to see his da. Every time the fuckin' doorbell rings he thinks it's you, that you've lost your keys while you were kidnapped by pirates or stuck down a lost diamond mine or rescuing some abandoned kids. Not sitting here in a hovel in the middle of nowhere trying to get a picture on a shitty TV.'

Tony looked at him, or to be more accurate, through him. When he spoke, Danny got the impression he wasn't really talking to him any more, that he'd dismissed the idea that his son was really here and was talking to himself.

'So that's what this is,' he mused. 'I'm torturing myself in my sleep now too. Of course – that explains your age. Twenty or so?'

'More or less,' Danny replied, thinking of the untold eons he had spent as a free-floating consciousness. Now didn't seem the right time to mention that.

'Right. And your attitude.'

'My *attitude*?'

'I was gone from your life for, what, ten years?'

'To the day.'

Tony smiled at that. Danny felt his hands clench into fists. 'To the day,' he said. 'I went back as soon as I could, yeah. But never said why.'

'You never had to. See, right about now's when I get the letter.'

'Letter?'

'Yeah. The one you send explaining everything. Suppose you meant for my ma to get it and ordinarily she would have, but she was knackered that day and I was off school: stomachache. My balls. I was just sick of the looks I was getting. And the letterbox went and there it was. I wouldn't have even known it was from you but, considerate fucker that you are, you drew a wee shamrock up in the corner, like you used to doodle all the time, so I knew. And I ripped the fucker open thinking this was it, that something had pulled you away and this had been the first chance you'd had to let us know what it was.'

Danny took a steadying breath. Sitting across from him, his father didn't say a word. Outside, the shadows lengthened as the day waned. 'I read it so many times. I had it memorised by the end of the week. My ma thought she'd thrown it out but I went to the bin and I got it back and I kept it, I kept it in my room and I'd take it out every so often and read it again, in case it said something different or in case it was written in code, like if I took the first letters of all the first lines it'd spell out something like "Ignore this letter, I'm being held hostage".'

He stopped again. This was painful, physically painful. The ache he'd felt in limbo had just been a prelude to this, it seemed.

'Dear Linda,' he said softly. 'I know by now you must be going out of your mind. I can't imagine what you must think of me. I should have had the courage to tell you all of this before I walked out of the door, but I couldn't. So instead, I'm writing to you to offer you some sort of explanation as best I can.'

Another breath. This one caught slightly. Danny blinked through wet eyes.

'Please understand that I didn't want this. If it were in my power, I would be back with you and with Danny now. But I can't do that. And the reason why ...'

Again, he had to stop. Only for a heartbeat, before he could go on.

'...the reason why is that I simply can't do it. I can't go on pretending to be happy with the life that has become mine. For years we thought that having a son would make our lives complete. I thought that I could be an amazing father. But the truth is, I'm a fraud. All I do is pretend; pretend that everything is fine, pretend that this life makes me content, pretend that I'm thrilled to be coming home when I have spent time away from you both.'

The tears fell freely now, spilling down his cheeks. All the while he continued to talk.

'It's not you. It's not Danny. It's me. I'm not good enough for either of you, and so I think it's best for all of us if we all try to move on with our lives. I know you'll be a wonderful mother. I know Danny will grow up into a person, a man, to make you proud. And I know how it sounds, but please believe me when I say that I love you both, so much. I'm telling you all of this because I wanted you to have an explanation, to stop thinking that it might be somehow your fault. It isn't. It never was. Having a family is just … it's too much for me. I had to escape.'

As they always were, the last five words were the hardest to force out. The five words that had popped up like a cartoon thought-bubble throughout his life for over a decade. Five words his inner voice had supplied again and again throughout the unfolding relationship with Ellie, and then when little Luke had come along.

'And I'm glad I did.'

It was dark outside. Night fell with finality in rural Wexford. The cottage was chilly, draughty. Danny drew in breaths, angry at himself, wondering how in the world he could walk through walls and not stop his nose from running like a fucking tap when he cried. He waited for his father to speak.

'And reading that … you felt …?'

'How do you *think* I fucking felt?' Danny spat back. 'I cried myself to sleep for a fortnight. And then one night, when my ma had fallen asleep, I got it from the floorboard where I kept it and unfolded it, and instead of reading it like I thought I was gonna, I ripped the fucker up. I ripped it up so small until I couldn't rip it up any smaller and believe me, I tried to, and I went to sleep hating you that night, and every night after.'

'You moved on.'

Danny's mouth fell open. 'I …' he began, and then tried again. 'Moving on? Moving *on*? You call white-hot, to-the-bones anger *moving on*?'

'It is. Denial to anger: the first stage of grief moving to the second stage. Trust me, I should know. I went through the same thing when your granda was killed. Only in my case it took me a lot longer …'

Danny interrupted him then. 'Was *killed*?' he said. 'Granda Morrigan died of a heart attack.'

His father laughed hollowly. 'Of course,' he said, with a mock flourish, 'The years of lies. How could I forget?'

'Lies? What are you talking about?'

And with those words as a prompt, the story began to spill from his father's lips.

*

For hours – who knew how many – his father talked, outlining a family history he had known nothing of and casually rewriting *everything* Danny had ever thought he'd known about his life.

At some point in the proceedings his father, talking all the while, had made them a cup of coffee. Danny hadn't touched his, but his father was knocking back the dregs of his cup now, his hands shaking wildly as his story drew to an end.

When he'd finished, for a long time all Danny could do was sit there, dumbfounded.

What to say? Where to begin? To hear his father talk about the Morrigan lineage and the traditions was crazy. He told Danny the story of that first day in the Mournes with his own father, the circle of dead bodies, discovering his place in the world.

He told him how his granda died and Danny had ached with sympathy for his father. All of the agonising he'd done over his own worth … he couldn't begin to imagine how it would feel to be, however accidentally, the cause of your own father's death.

Tony was sitting now, staring into nothing. Still convinced, no doubt, that this was all some dream he was having. He looked lost, haunted, and every time his eyes focused somewhat and he saw Danny sitting before him, a look of pain ghosted across his face.

He hadn't abandoned Danny by choice.

Except … he had, in a way. He'd chosen to reverse the curse and accepted the price for it, knowing full well it would drive a wedge between father and son, destroy any semblance of relationship he'd built over the first ten years of Danny's life.

Danny had known little Luke for less than a year, and having him taken from him had been the event that had sent him down this rabbit hole. He wanted his little boy back so badly it amazed him.

What would it be like to be with your son for *ten years*, and then to have to walk away from him? More than that, to have to walk away and *pretend* that it was something that you wanted to do?

'Talk to him.'

He started. The voice that had just spoken was not his father's.

'Hello again,' said Doubt, perched vulture-like on the end of the kitchen table. 'Miss me?'

'You've–'

'Changed. Yes, I know. Well I thought two of *him* might get confusing. Doesn't he look so sad? I think you should talk to him, Danny. That's why you're here, isn't it?'

'Why are you shaped like *him*?'

Tony glanced around. 'Who are you talking to?' he asked.

Doubt, now in the person of Thomas Doonan, Lircom employee and Danny's boss/underling, depending on which parallel universe you subscribed to, tilted his head to the side to regard father and son. Together with the birdlike stance he'd adopted on the table, the overall effect was disconcerting to say the least.

'It's … nothing. Just daydreaming,' Danny told his father.

'My imaginary grown-up son … is having a daydream … inside my dream?'

'Yes.'

'I need a drink,' Tony said with some certainty, standing up and walking in a rather wobbly line to one of his cupboards.

'Thomas' tutted disapprovingly. 'This is probably how it starts,' he said ruefully. 'Wee drink here, wee drink there … and then when he eventually does come back, they're not so wee any more, are they?'

Danny turned his attention to the apparition. 'What do you want?' he hissed. 'I thought I left you behind.'

Thomas giggled. 'Left me *behind?*' he said. 'Jesus Christ, it's a wonder I can squeeze myself into only *one* body, Danny, the amount of issues you've got wandering about upstairs,' and he tapped his head.

'I'm past that. He's explained–'

'Yeah. Daddy's in the clear. Hooray. It's what every abandoned child wants to hear, isn't it – it was all a big mix-up! Daddy had a gun held to his head! He didn't *want* to leave me!'

'Fuck off,' Danny snarled.

His father started as he set two shot glasses down on the table along with a bottle of whiskey. 'All right,' he said equitably, 'I wasn't sure if I *should* be encouraging my son to drink–'

'Not you. Him.'

His father looked in the direction Danny had gestured. Thomas danced a merry little jig.

'Who?' he said.

'He's … he's … ach it's complicated. He's my nasty wee inner voice. I accidentally brought him to life when I was creating the universe.'

A shot glass full of whiskey slid to a halt in front of him a few seconds later.

'Drink,' Tony said firmly.

'You think it'll help me?' Danny said as he lifted the shot glass to his lips.

'It'll help *me*.'

Knocking it back, he felt the whiskey enter his system. It was beyond strange – slightly out of phase as he was, he could feel the liquor go places it wasn't supposed to go. He shivered and then felt a warmth spreading from his gut.

'Another?' Tony asked

'Another.'

The second was even better than the first. When he'd finished draining the glass, he risked a glance over to where Thomas had been perched, hoping that he'd be gone by now. He was disappointed to see that, not only was he still there, he actually seemed to have grown a little.

'The one thing you always had,' Thomas was chortling, 'the one crumb of comfort you clung to when you were miserable, was that, hey, no matter how unhappy you got, as long as you stuck it out, saw it through, you'd be better than that bastard of a father of yours.'

Danny shut his eyes and found, to his horror, that even this didn't completely banish the vision from sight. His eyelids were transparent.

'What's wrong?' Tony asked.

'That was what made you stick around,' Thomas continued. 'It wasn't love. It wasn't even a sense of obligation. It was a way to stick two fingers up to your da. To say, *I'm better than you*. And now … now you've found out the old wanker didn't walk out on you. He was torn away and it almost killed him.'

'Danny, what's wrong?' Tony tried again.

'He … he won't shut up,' Danny whispered.

'He made a deal with the devil just to get you *born*, knowing that the price would be to sacrifice his relationship with you. Meanwhile you, Danny Morrigan – carefree student, professional loser – you stick your cock in some random girl while drunk one night, you get her pregnant and what do you think? You think *oh no, why me? Why'd it have to happen to me? How'd I get so unlucky?'* and by now Thomas was rocking with laughter. 'Who's the better man now, Danny?'

Tears stung Danny's eyes, but even as they did so, he felt for the first time that something was wrong. Self-doubt he could accept; but this was more than that. This was self-loathing, and much as he may have second-guessed himself over the years, much as he may have felt deep down that he wasn't as good a person, a partner, a father as he could be, he had never had the sense that he hated himself.

But if this thing in front of him wasn't speaking in his own inner voice ... Two things happened the moment he had that realisation. The first was that Thomas abruptly stopped laughing, as suddenly as if someone had just flicked a switch.

The second was that Tony Morrigan stood up with a yell and a string of swearwords, almost knocking over his chair as he did so.

'Who the fuck are *you?'* he demanded, pointing right at Thomas.

'You ... you can see him?' Danny asked his father.

Tony didn't reply. Instead the colour drained from his face and, as Danny brought his attention back to where his father was pointing, he could understand why.

He hadn't been imagining things before when he'd thought the Thomas-shape had grown. Now fully nine feet tall, and broad as a tree trunk, the former Lircom team leader was looking less and less human with each passing moment and more and more like one of the monstrosities Danny had walked amongst in the

Otherworld. This one was bearlike in its bulk, but with four-inch claws sprouting from its hands and feet, and teeth like a shark.

'The circles ...' his father croaked.

'Circles don't work if I'm brought in,' the thing slobbered, and it smiled hideously at Danny. 'Right, Danny?'

'You never were a part of me.'

'*Part* of you? I *am* you!' the bear-thing howled, and then it attacked. Danny had started steeling himself for this once he saw the thing transform; was thinking back to the things he'd learned during his time in the Otherworld, trying to line up the knowledge in his mind. Making himself ready for the thing when it came for him.

Problem was, it didn't come for him at all.

Tony had time for one shout of alarm before the thing barrelled into him full-tilt, sending him sprawling through the cottage. Furniture splintered as it captured Tony in its grasp and shook him violently like a ragdoll, before tossing him to the floor, looming over him.

'Da!' Danny shouted. Before he had time to plan, he had thrown himself onto its massive back and wrapped his arms around its neck. The *smell* was overpowering; his mind reeled from the sensory overload even as it tried to bring its massive arms around to tear him off.

When this failed, it adopted a different tack and slammed its entire bulk backwards, crushing itself against the nearest wall, or more accurately crushing Danny's body. Except Danny's body wasn't solid enough to be crushed by the impact.

He phased partially *through* the wall. The world spun crazily as his opponent threw itself this way and that in a desperate bid to shake its passenger loose, while Danny tried with everything he had to squeeze his arms more tightly around its neck and ignore the stench coming off the fucker.

Tony was up and charging, something in his hand. Too slow. A massive hand swung out–

'NO!' Danny shouted, and in that moment the thing finally managed to get him loose. He crashed through two of the legs of the table and phased through the remaining two, half of his left leg passing through the floor, though he was able to pull it back up before the urge to solidify got too much.

His father was down, and bleeding. Out of the fight. Danny picked himself up and circled around until he was between the thing and his father's prone body. Around him, the cottage's interior was in ruins.

Just like that, the bear-thing was no longer. It shrank, condensed, and now–

'All right, lad?' said Steve.

'Never better,' Danny said grimly, never taking his eyes off the shape in front of him, watching for a flicker of movement, anything that would signal the next attack.

'Enjoying all this aren't ye?'

'Yep. Laugh a fuckin' minute.'

'Come off it. You, the centre of some mystic prophecy? You, the last hope for Ireland against the powers of darkness? Right up your alley this is. Always so pleased with your own cleverness. Loved putting one over on dopey Steve. Funny how I ended up with the life *you* envied, isn't it.'

'You're not Steve.'

'You always were an egotistical cunt,' the Steve-thing carried on as if he hadn't spoken. 'That's why family life wasn't floatin' yer boat, right or wrong?'

Danny didn't reply. He was trying to stay calm. Everything he'd learned, all of the synaesthesia tricks he could employ to fight these fuckers, they depended on him staying calm. If this thing got him angry, he was dead.

'If all this hadn't happened, how long do you think it would have been? Before you fucked off and left them, I mean. Oh maybe not the way your da did it, admittedly – the total walkout, the complete vanish – no. You'd have done it the standard way. Probably had a wee affair with some random buck from work and then gave the speech,' and his voice changed to Danny's. '*It's not working out, love. It's not what I'm after. I'll see yis right though, never you worry – and I wanna see wee Luke every weekend … every other weekend … every month … every few months … on special occasions … definitely next birthday, sorry about that last one there, I'd a lot on …*'

'No.'

'You'd have left them and gone back to the life you thought you were robbed of,' and the Steve-copy smiled, 'and you'd have been glad you did.'

'You don't know that.'

'So I'm wrong?'

Danny didn't answer.

Steve was gone a moment later, replaced by another phantom facsimile.

'Why? Why wasn't I good enough for you?' Ellie asked him.

'I'm not playing this game,' Danny replied, his voice betraying him and quivering as he spoke. 'You're not Ellie. You're not Steve. You're not *anyone*. You know fuck all about me.'

'I don't know you?' Ellie laughed mirthlessly. She took a step toward him. Danny had to stop himself from matching the gesture. She looked, sounded, smelled so perfect ...

'I know you all right. Do you think when I found out I was pregnant, when I rang you, I did it because I wanted to *trap* you? I thought you had a right to know. That was all. I didn't ask you to leave Maggie. Didn't ask you to come back to me. So when you did those things I thought – I *hoped* – it was because you loved me, not because you thought you had to. Did you really think I didn't know, Danny?'

'It's not true–'

'So I'm wrong?'

His head was spinning. Any hope of remaining calm had long since been pissed away. He was barely keeping upright, let alone staying calm. The cottage around him was swirling.

He half-expected the attack to come then, with him so off-balance.

He was right. Just not in the way he'd expected.

'Hey, Da,' said Luke.

Not Luke the baby. Not Luke who he'd held in his arms, listening to his full-stomach breathing until he himself had drifted to sleep.

This was a grown-up Luke – he looked around Danny's own age. It wasn't just the *Hey, Da* that immediately made it obvious who he was; everything about the boy – no, the *man* – before him said to him, plain and simple, *this is your son*. He was tall, he was broad-shouldered, he looked a little like Danny but more like his mother truth be told. But he had Danny's eyes, just like his baby self.

As a baby those eyes had twinkled with mischief and merriment, and now ... now they were dead.

No hate, no anger. Nothing.

'Luke?' Danny croaked. 'Luke, I ...'

'How's things?' Luke said, glancing down at his watch. He was smartly dressed, in tailored trousers and a fitted white shirt and tie. He looked good, like a successful young man.

He also looked as if he was impatient for this meeting to be over.

'I tried ...' Danny sobbed, staggering forward, the cottage long forgotten. 'Luke, I tried ... I tried to get you back.'

Luke held up his hands as if to ward him off and the smile he gave Danny reminded of him of the looks he'd get from Ellie's father – it was an expression that seemed to ooze disgust, disdain.

'That's grand, Da,' Luke said. Another check of the watch. 'Look I ... I don't mean to be rude, but I've got so much on at the moment and ...' and he sighed heavily. 'Look let's not kid ourselves, right? Every few months we do this lunchtime thing and we talk about football and the price of mortgages and whatever shite we can think of to get the time in. Why not just call it quits, eh?'

'No ...' Danny breathed, aghast. 'No, please, Luke. I'm sorry ... I-I don't know what I can do to make it up to you–'

Luke shrugged expansively. 'Forget about it. You said it

yourself, the fatherhood thing came too soon for you. You weren't ready. Hey, at least you gave it nearly a year, eh? I turned out fine, and things turned out ...' he paused and there was that fleeting expression of disgust again, '... all right for you too. So where's the harm?'

No. No, I didn't want this. You're my little boy. My baby boy. You looked up to me and I was your whole world and I can't lose that.

Luke spread his arms. His eyes glittered with an inhuman light that Danny was too far gone in grief to notice. 'C'mon, then. One last hug,' he said, and beckoned.

Danny staggered toward him without hesitation, spreading his own arms wide, ready to throw himself into his son's embrace ... and was pulled back.

'Stay away from him,' said Tony Morrigan, covered in blood and looking like shit, but very much up and awake.

Luke's expression darkened instantly. 'Let him go,' he hissed through teeth no longer square and human, but pointed and predatory.

'He's my son ...' Danny said weakly, trying to struggle free of his father's grip.

'No he isn't. But you're *my* son.'

Luke launched himself forward. Tony shoved Danny to the floor and brought something around from behind his back, swinging it in a wide arc.

There was a wet noise from somewhere above Danny's head. As he heard it, he felt the fogginess that had descended upon him begin to clear almost immediately. The thing that had taken the shape of his son coalesced into a being designed to terrify. It had too many arms (legs?) and a head that began somewhere on its chest. To call it monstrous would have been to undersell its alienness. It was unrecognisable even as something humanoid, let alone human.

Danny did, however, recognise the outline of a sword as it impaled the thing right through its chest.

After what seemed an eternity, the creature pitched forward and slammed face-first into the floor, unmoving.

'Your son, eh? Hope that comes from the ma's side of the family,' his father grunted.

He extended a hand to Danny and pulled him to his feet.

'Thanks ...' Danny wheezed.

'This isn't a dream,' Tony Morrigan said. It was not question.

'No.'

Tony absorbed this revelation and all of its frankly staggering implications for the timeline.

'Shame,' he said.

'Nice sword.'

'This,' his father said with satisfaction, putting one foot on the corpse and yanking the sword free with not inconsiderable effort, 'is Moonblood.'

'*Class* name,' Danny said approvingly.

His father smiled so broadly at this that if his lips had been sharper the top half of his head would have rolled off. 'See,' he said, 'I *knew* it was.'

It was then that the corpse decided it wasn't a corpse after all.

Catapulting itself upward, it struck out, sending first Danny and then the shortsword flying from Tony's grasp, leaving the older man defenceless.

Danny rolled and got to his feet, reminding himself as he did so that no matter how convincing the illusion or strong the enchantment, what he was seeing *wasn't* Luke …

His caution was unnecessary, as it turned out. The figure before him, the thing that had his father by the throat, lifting him clean off the ground and throttling the life from his lungs, was not Luke.

'Kill me once, shame on you,' James Morrigan growled, looking into the wide and terrified eyes of his son. 'Kill me twice …'

'Daddy?' Tony choked. He made no move to fight back, or even to struggle, as the air was cut off from his lungs.

'You *caused* all of this,' James said, even as his grip intensified and black spots peppered Tony's vision. 'Your incompetence. You doomed us all, you miserable, worthless excuse for a son!'

'*Akkk*,' was all Tony could manage, the only sound his collapsing windpipe could form as the life was squeezed from him. He was about to die, and the last thing he would see was his father's angry face. Just as he'd always known it would be.

Moonblood's blade erupted from James' throat.

Tony was released and the blade was retracted. James turned, and even as he did those features began to ripple again, to change as it probed the mind of its attacker searching for a new form to exploit, to cause weakness–

Not this time.

With a roar that shook the cottage, Danny swung the sword and took the monster's head clean off its shoulders.

The head fell one way, the body another. The two men waited, watching for another resurrection, until both pieces of the thing began to steam and then dissolve, leaving behind only a foul-smelling gunk. It was only then that they allowed themselves to relax, finding a place to sit amongst the wreckage.

For a while, neither of them spoke. Danny had endured many awkward silences with his father since he had reappeared in his life. This was somehow different; for one, they were both fucked from the craziness that had just ensued with the shape-shifting monstrosity and the manipulation of their thoughts ... but there was something else. Or maybe, on Danny's part, it was for the first time in twelve years a *lack* of something else.

'You know ...' Tony was the first to speak, although with the damage he had taken to his throat he could scarcely manage more than a fierce whisper, 'it's not easy having kids. You doubt yourself. You have bad days, and if, from time to time, you tell yourself that the only reason you're not leaving for something easier is because of some sense of duty, well, that's not cowardice. That's having balls enough to see a responsibility through even in your long dark nights. Then before you know it, you're through it, and you realise you were just over-thinking it.'

'And what if I'm not?' Danny said. 'Over-thinking it. What if I'm not?'

'D'you love her?'

'How do I know?'

'Does she make you happy?'

Danny paused. It was such a juvenile question. Love couldn't be defined that easily, could it? Was that how two-dimensional love was? Wasn't it more of a question of having a deeper, more primal, spiritual–

'*Ow!* What the *fuck?*' Danny said indignantly, because his father had just clouted him very rigidly across the back of his head.

'It's not a fuckin' quadratic equation, son! You're *thinking* again aren't ye?'

'Of course I'm—'

'Jesus. You must have gone to university or something, am I right? Too fuckin' clever for your own good. Stop *thinking* about it, just answer. Does she. Make you. *Happy?*'

'Yes.'

'Now. Again, no thinking or I'll clout ye again. Does making *her* happy make *you* happy?'

'Yes,' the answer was out almost before he'd realised he'd spoken. The suddenness of his reply amazed him.

'Then I'd say one, you love her, and two, for the love of *fuck* stop over-thinking it.'

'How do I stop over-thinking it?'

'How about this,' Tony grunted, trying to stop from grinning and not quite succeeding. 'If you find yourself thinking about over-thinking it, you're over-thinking it. Take a kick in the balls and see me in the morning.'

Danny couldn't help but laugh at that. 'I just …' he started, and then stopped. 'I just … when you walked out on me, and on my ma, you didn't seem unhappy. And I always thought, is that how it happens? Do you not even realise and then one day you just up and walk away?'

'I'm sorry,' Tony said, very quietly.

'Don't be. You did what you had to do and you couldn't have done anything different. In fact,' Danny exhaled and said something he never thought he'd say aloud, 'the whole reason it *hurt* so fuckin' much when you left was because you'd been a great da.'

He could see those words settling on his father like snow. Tony didn't meet his son's gaze at first but when he did, it was with gratitude and tears in his eyes.

'Thank you. But you're wrong, you know. There's some things I could have done differently. Done better.'

'His death wasn't your fault. It was an accident.'

'Do you think he knew that?'

Danny smiled. 'Given the stories you're after tellin' me about you and him, against the worst Carman had to throw at ye? *Now* who's over-thinking it?'

Tony's mouth opened to respond … and stayed open. Danny thought at first his father was reacting to something he'd seen behind him, so he whirled around, expecting to see the wet mess of the shape-shifter reforming itself, like Dracula in a Hammer Horror movie or the T1000. Nothing was there.

'Dad?' he said, now concerned. He waved a hand in front of his father's face. Tony didn't react. His mouth hung half-open. It was as if time–

'You're almost there.'

He turned at hearing the voice behind him, and now something was there. Not the monster.

'How did *you* get here?' he asked the Morrigan.

She was standing amidst the rubble and the detritus of what had once been a neat, if rather cramped, little home, looking incongruous in her usual green-tinged finery amongst the wreckage. She looked around at the results of their battle and raised an eyebrow.

'Been working out a few issues?'

'I thought that … thing was my own self-doubt. What the hell was it?'

'What you're up against. A small taste of it. Nobody's fucking about here, Danny,' she said, her voice diamond hard. 'When this is over, when you're back in the Otherworld, there'll be no more stalling. It'll be you versus the best she has to throw at you, and if you manage to best *them*, it'll come down to you and her. It doesn't matter how much you think you're starting to get your head around this, to understand the power you have – understand *this*; she has *thousands of years* of experience behind her. You need to wake up and realise that.'

'So all this is a test? A training ground? What?'

'Yes. No. Both. It's all part of the Ordeal, Danny. When you go into the Cauldron, you don't automatically spring back fully-formed. You have to *earn* your resurrection. That's why it doesn't work for the Low Folk, for the faeries. They go in, they come out, but they come out wrong. Twisted. For us, for the Tuatha, it's different. It *has* to be, otherwise what's the difference between them and us?'

He sighed and turned away, not able to look at her. How did she expect him to handle all of this? A few days ago the biggest crisis in his life had been putting the bin out and stepping in a suspiciously solid, brown and squeaky puddle.

'I didn't bring you here, you know,' she told him. 'You did that. You chose this place as your third stage.'

'Third stage?'

'Think of the Cauldron as a sped-up model of your entire existence, except it's a little out of sequence. To gain entry, you have to go through death, which you did–'

'Thanks, I'd almost forgotten,' he said, knowing full well that every time he closed his eyes for the rest of his life – however long that might be – the sensation of being literally ripped apart wasn't likely to be lurking very far away.

'And after death,' she continued as if he hadn't spoken, 'you have to negotiate your birth. Your emergence from nothing.'

He thought back to the indeterminate amount of time he'd spent in that formless void. Was that the magical equivalent of the womb?

'How long was I ...?'

'It doesn't work like that there. Minutes. Millennia. It's all in the perception. The important thing is, you had the strength to pull yourself together, to reform yourself. Have you any idea how difficult that is?'

He thought back to the endless cycle of thought. The utter unshakeable conviction that he was in hell, and that it was going to last for all eternity ... and the feeling that in some ways, as the Morrigan had hinted, it *had* lasted an eternity.

'Yeah,' he said, with feeling. 'Yeah, I have.'

'And from death, to birth, to childhood,' she said, and waved a hand to indicate the cottage in which they stood.

Danny began to understand. 'I came here ... to grow up?'

'Yes.'

'So this, this really happened? I really came here, to this place, twelve years ago?'

'Yes.'

'But won't that, I don't know, fuck up the timeline or something? My dad's going to remember me–'

She smiled a brittle smile and looked at him, not unkindly, until he understood what was going to happen.

What had to happen.

'He's not, is he?'

'No.'

'But the cottage …'

'Fix it.'

He blinked. 'Excuse me?'

'Fix it.'

'What, like Mary Poppins? Sing a wee song and watch all the plates jump back on the shelves and the table legs un-splinter themselves?'

'Sing a wee song?' she said. 'Jesus, I hope not. Danny, tidying up a cottage is not beyond you. Wasn't *that* long ago you created a universe.'

'Fair point,' he said, and closed his eyes.

Okay. You can do this. Remember back to the blackness. You took that blackness and made light. This is the same principle, surely, except it's not blackness. Remember back to how the cottage looked before. Now overlay that with how it looks now, like … like you're putting a tablecloth on a table. Except it's a shitty tablecloth.

He exhaled and tasted the faint but unmistakable tang of magic in the air around him. *Now … grip the tablecloth. Good solid hold. Fuck, where did those all plates come from?*

'From me,' the Morrigan's voice butted in, laced liberally with amusement. 'Just wanted to make this a bit more challenging.'

'Thanks *so* much,' he hissed.

Grip it. Come on you've seen this trick done before. Jesus they look expensive. Okay. Pull—

Anyone walking past the cottage would have seen the interior lit by a pulse of blindingly powerful white-blue light, a single heartbeat of force. Thankfully, the nearest living witness larger than a beetle was an elderly badger, who merely put the sight down to experience and wandered off.

Danny opened his eyes.

'Well done,' the Morrigan said.

It had worked. He couldn't believe it. Not a plate smashed, not an ornament out of place. The fireplace, the table, the kitchen, all were back in one piece. It looked as if the place had been hit by a twister with Asperger's.

Danny staggered. The walls of the cottage were suddenly transparent; looking down, he could see himself phase almost completely out of existence.

'Almost time to go,' the Morrigan said urgently.

'Go? Where?'

'No time,' she said taking his hand and placing it on his father's forehead. Danny had the extremely odd sensation of his fingers phasing slightly *into* his father's brain. The effect was electric. Images, sounds, smells, sensations, all of them pulsed up through his arm into his own cerebrum through the conduit.

'Make him forget,' the Morrigan said. 'Quickly. You must.'

A thousand objections raised themselves in Danny's mind, but there was something more, some higher power – his own intuition, the synaesthesia … *something* – that told him unequivocally that this was non-negotiable. He plunged on into the melting pot that was his father's consciousness and was momentarily overwhelmed.

Memories rushed at him like speeding cars on an insanely busy motorway and Danny felt sure he'd be taken out by some of the sixteen-wheelers – not least of which was the lumbering behemoth of James Morrigan's death, the monster in the closet of his father's tortured past; although running a close second was the image of his own ten-year-old self, waving cheerily at his father for what, unbeknownst to him, would be the final time for a decade.

He saw the recent memories, from tonight, from Danny's arrival. Good memories. They came to him like puppies, all yapping and excited barking, making the painful memories much less powerful.

You know what you have to do, the Morrigan's voice sounded in his head. *Do it. Now.*

He reached out for those new, happy memories, and he murdered them all.

When it was done, he removed himself from his father's mind, recoiling from the horror of what he'd just done. Feeling a hand on his shoulder, he looked into the Morrigan's face and saw respect on her face.

'One more stop,' she said.

They had faded from existence before he got a chance to ask her where.

*

Something was different.

Tony Morrigan couldn't quite figure out what it was. Wandering around the cottage aimlessly for the last ten minutes (after having found himself asleep fully clothed and slumped over on the kitchen table) had failed to turn up any answers.

Drink? Had to be. He checked his watch. Jesus Christ. He'd have sworn it was the 17th, but his watch claimed it was the 18th. Somehow, he'd lost a day. Well, that explained the *incredible* fucking headache he was nursing. Felt like someone had stuck ice-cold fingers into his brain and had a good old rummage around.

He moaned softly, cradling his head as two soluble painkillers fizzed softly into nothingness in a tumbler on the table before him. This couldn't go on. He'd always been fond of a drink, and obviously Christ knew with all he'd been through recently there was ample temptation to indulge himself, but losing *days*? Much more of this and he'd develop a full-blown problem with the stuff.

Moments later, the rest of the JD was glugging softly down the sink as he stood and looked over the Wexford vista through his kitchen window. It was a beautiful day, a glorious day, and he would have given anything to have shared it with his son.

His jaw set.

Cupboards opened and closed. Items were fetched.

He sat at the kitchen table and began to write, the words seeming to come from somewhere deep within him. Words he didn't even know he had.

Meanwhile, testimony to Danny's less-than-perfect skills of

recollection, but as yet unnoticed and unseen, a thirty-two inch LCD TV gleamed in the corner of the cottage.

THE OTHERWORLD, NOW

Something was different.

Wily was not a being who dealt in *different*. For longer than he could remember he had performed a solitary function; to stalk, to hunt, to kill. Long, long ago, he had been free to roam the lands above, brighter lands where a shining disc others called 'the Sun' rose and set. He had been set loose across the country, able to track and kill as he pleased.

Things had changed. Most of his kin had perished in a war he could barely recall. The remainder, led by the queen, had been led down here, to a dark and shadowy place where, if you ran too far in one direction, you found yourself coming from the other direction, a place wrapped up around itself. The queen called it home, but they all knew it for what it really was.

A prison.

Caged, restless, he had taken to endlessly prowling until the passage of time had become meaningless. His only saving grace had been that the queen continued to breed, so the numbers of his kin were continually replenished. Some were strong and took their place as hunters. Some were not, and they quickly became the prey. He had chased down and killed more of his kin than he could count, participating in a culling exercise until he and the others that remained were the best of the best.

Not long ago – perhaps only a few hundred years, if he could still remember the concept of such a thing as a year – a hole had been opened, albeit briefly, and some of his pack had been released into the lands above before it closed once more. Unable to reach the portal in time to take his place amongst them he could only imagine the sport they had enjoyed ever since.

But now ...

Since the human ...

He felt different. He felt *reduced* somehow. Less sure of himself. Less sure of everything. His 'name' for example. The king had spoken the truth when he had said that such as he did not need a name. In all the thousands of years he had existed, he had never once felt the need for one. How would having a name assist in killing?

And yet ...

He *liked* having a name.

He had been ordered to speak to his kin. There were few, perhaps none, so senior amongst the wolf-faerie ranks left in the Otherworld, so when he howled for them to gather around him, they had heeded his call in great numbers. He stood on the crest of a hill with the circle of standing stones a distant light perhaps eight miles east, with hundreds of his kind surrounding him in all directions.

He had been ordered to tell them everything.

He did. He told them of the human, of the naming, and of the things the human had said. Of the way the human had spoken to him.

At first his words were met with growls. After a while, as he continued to speak, the great wolves around him had one by one fallen silent as they absorbed what he had to say.

When he had finished, the clamouring began. The demands. It only took one wolf, hesitantly at first, to begin the process and before long the rest had adopted it also, as it spread between them like wildfire. Like a virus.

The Naming of the Wolves had begun.

High above, under the blood-red skies, a solitary crow circled.

LIRCOM TOWER, BELFAST, NOW

'Nothing ever changes.'

Those were the first words that filtered through to Tony Morrigan's bewildered mind, as the world slid back from blissful oblivion to horrible, painful reality. He cursed each returning sense as it brought with it a world of pain.

Blobs became shapes, and shapes became people.

When the memories flooded back, they made the pain that had accompanied the gradual return of his consciousness look pitiful.

'Ellie?' he said weakly, sitting upright. He was seated on a luxurious black lounger in a room with enormous windows, The Belfast panorama spread below him. There was only one building in the city that tall.

Ellie, lying on a companion lounger about three feet to his right, chose that moment to come to herself. She sat bolt upright and began to scream.

He moved to her, not without some difficulty – he had been fighting for his life only hours before and was still feeling the effects – and by the time he reached her, Dermot was already there. She continued to scream, over and over and over and over.

'Daddy! Daddy! *Daddy!*'

'I know,' Tony tried to comfort her, repeating the two words with each utterance she made. He reached out a tentative hand and placed it on her shoulder. She reacted slightly to the touch, glanced at him with eyes full of bottomless despair, and he felt almost ashamed at the inadequacy of his gesture.

Eventually, Ellie could keep it up no longer. She collapsed into Tony, her entire body shaking with sobs. He held her to him, not saying a word, knowing that anything he could say would be pointless. As he held her, shushing her with nonsense words, he shifted his attention from the heartbroken girl in his arms to the demon whose voice had jerked him from unconsciousness.

Sitting behind his desk, Dother regarded them dispassionately. Little wonder he didn't look impressed. Ellie was a mess. Dermot looked like shit. Tony knew he himself must look even worse. And Steve …

'*Steve?* Where's Steve?' he asked urgently.

'Who?' Dother replied with a frown. 'Oh yes, Danny's great friend. Not really involved in any of this, though, is he? Not really his concern. I've spared him the worry.'

'Where is he?' Tony asked again, dread rising within him.

'Left early. In mid-transit, to be specific. I think the road broke his fall, and his legs, and his arms, and most likely his neck.'

Tony closed his eyes, grieving for the young man who he knew had meant more to his son than he himself did. Dermot looked as if it was taking every ounce of effort he had not to curl up in a foetal position and quietly expire from sheer terror. He kept shifting his gaze from the man coolly observing them from behind the desk to the various hulking great brutes scattered around the office, including – hard to miss – the two standing directly in front of the door.

'What do you want?' Tony demanded.

Dother laughed. 'I was merely observing that nothing ever changes. It seems that we,' and he gestured theatrically to himself and his henchmen, 'we *villains* are contractually obliged to bring the heroes to our lairs and, once there, explain our schemes to them in detail. Accept my apologies for the lack of piranha tank or go-go dancers, won't you?'

Amazingly, it was Ellie who spoke next. Even more amazingly, when she did so, emerging from Tony's embrace as if from a protective cocoon, it wasn't with sobs or screams. She had, it seemed, no more of either to give. What she did have, however, in plentiful supply, was anger. Cold, hard anger that did not threaten, was not hysterical, was expressed in simple point of fact statements.

'This is *funny* to you?' she said.

Dother fixed her with a stare. If he was as surprised by the transformation as the rest of them were, he showed absolutely no outward sign of it.

'You killed my daddy.'

'He killed my,' and there was an almost imperceptible pause, 'my daughter. Be thankful I didn't return the favour.'

'That spider freak? It was your daughter?'

'Ellie …' Tony said warningly. Dermot's terror level had

ratcheted up another few notches as he looked from Ellie to Dother, and back to Ellie. He looked like he had mid-court seats at the Men's Singles Final in hell.

Neither Dother nor Ellie took a blind bit of notice. For all that the rest of them mattered, they could have been performing a conga line across the office floor.

'I created her. I loved her. For longer than you can imagine.'

Ellie's voice did not waver. 'She begged for death. Can you *imagine* that?'

Finally, Dother did react. In one motion he was up and out of his chair and over the desk in a move that was over far too quickly to have been constrained by mundane considerations such as gravity.

His eyes ... how they burned. Tony half-expected Ellie to burst into flames on the spot.

'Hardly surprising that she begged,' Dother replied. 'Considering the messy death your father gave her. The quick end I gave him was a mercy by comparison.'

He was rattled. Tony could see it. The jibe was clumsy compared to his self-assured composure only moments before.

'Kill me. Save me. That's what she said,' Ellie continued. She may as well have been discussing the shopping list for all the care her voice betrayed.

'You are *lying!*'

Ellie began to laugh.

Tony steeled himself to spring. It'd be a suicidal move, of course, but he was determined that, should Dother make a move to get to Ellie, he would have to get past him first. Besides, completely fuckin' crazy as her fearless taunting of this lunatic was, on some level he couldn't help but admire the sheer brass *balls* of it.

Dother made no move. Tony went unsprung. Dermot, for his part, looked as if he'd been planning to spring too, albeit in the opposite direction.

There was no explosion of murderous rage from the man before them. Only a smile, faint at first, that kept growing in manic intensity until it became unsettling in the extreme to behold.

'Excellent,' Dother murmured. 'Here I am thinking that nothing ever changes, and you prove me wrong. How fortunate for you that your presence may be required at the big event.'

'The Network,' Dermot breathed, before he could stop himself. He shrank back as Dother's attention turned to him and the demon's smile took on an even more predatory quality.

'Yes,' Dother nodded. '*Insert evil speech here* and all that, with a liberal sprinkling of explaining my scheme to you in minute detail.'

'Danny's coming,' Tony said with quiet confidence. 'You're not ready for him. He'll stop your Network.'

Dother made a grand show of checking his watch. 'How does this go,' he said, his voice still dripping with boredom, 'let's see if I've got it right. Network's due to come online in ... six hours. Does that give brave Danny enough time to survive the trials of the Otherworld? Reclaim his heritage? Seize his inner power?' and he mimed sticking two fingers down his throat. 'Rescue his girlfriend? Rebuild his relationship with his father, make sure Greedo shoots first ... probably duel with me while the countdown ticks down behind us, slay me with a mighty thrust of the silver sword and deactivate the Network with ...' he looked to them with a shrug, 'what's traditional? Four seconds on the clock? Two? It's been ages since I've seen a Bond film.'

No one replied. His cocky assurance had returned, the brief crack in his façade had disappeared. He walked toward the wall on the far side of the office, behind his desk, and began to manipulate something there. Something in the way he had moved told Tony that, whatever this change of plans was, it was not something to be greeted joyously.

Silver light bathed the office interior.

'I think,' Dother said softly, as they shielded their eyes from the majesty of the Sword of Nuada, 'to *hell* with the way the story's supposed to go. Let's do this right now, shall we?'

He reached out and grasped the Sword.

Ireland vanished from the face of the earth.

Acknowledgements

As Keanu Reeves would no doubt say – whoa. It's been an eventful few months since *Folk'd* was launched in a blaze of nerdy glory and I'd like to take a mo to thank some of the kind people who have made it possible.

Firstly, to Michelle, who I'm 100 per cent sure has spoiled me rotten in terms of what editors are really like. I dread the first time I work with anyone else to be honest – who will I write wee nerdy in-jokes in comment boxes to then? Sob.

Secondly, to everyone at Blackstaff, particularly Stuart or 'Hawkeye' as he is now to be known. Don't mess with him or you'll find an arrow quivering in your back door (and no, that is not a metaphor).

Thirdly, to everyone who came to the launch night for *Folk'd* at Forbidden Planet in October 2013 – words cannot express how grateful and humbled I am by your support. To all the staff at Forbidden Planet itself, particularly John and of course the incomparable Malachy Coney, an actual living Belfast legend who, if there is any justice, will have a walk-on part in a Belfast-set, Donaghy-penned episode of *Doctor Who* sometime in the future.

Finally, as ever, to my friends and my family, and to Kath and my boys most of all. My character Danny shares in my joys but his sadnesses are, thank God, mostly all manufactured from my imagination, and that's down to how wonderful you guys are. I love you dearly.

READ ON FOR AN EXCERPT FROM

Completely Folk'd
Book Three of the *Folk'd* trilogy

by Laurence Donaghy

Published by Blackstaff Press

The Change

The 9.15 from Newark, poised to touch its wheels onto the tarmac of the Belfast International Airport, found itself gliding not over land, but nothingness.

Captain Lansing, the pilot, was a trained and seasoned professional. Only two years before he had single-handedly landed a plane with two engines out of commission, an action that had earned him a modest amount of media attention.

He panicked.

The co-pilot, Peters, was a novice, not long out of training. He had endured Lansing's arrogance all the way across the Atlantic, listening to umpteen speeches about how he still had a long way to go and a lot of things to learn – he dimly suspected the man was a big fan of the movie *Training Day* – so for the last hour he'd taken to glumly staring at the instruments.

Now, on seeing the pilot panic, Peters indulged in a quarter-second of vicious glee before his flight school training kicked in and he remembered the emergency protocols for landing in poor visibility with inaccurate altitude readings.

He aborted the landing procedure, trying desperately to hail a ground control that was no longer present (impossible) and tell the plane's computers that contrary to readings the plane was *not* taxiing down a runway but still descending into empty space (even more impossible).

Dimly he heard himself scream at Lansing to pull himself to-fucking-gether, then at one of the flight attendants to get the passengers to brace for impact, brace for an emergency landing, brace for *something*–

The plane fought him, but the most impossible thing about all of this (the complete and utter lack of terra firma below) was the thing that was saving them – there was no ground to crash into. The plane continued to descend. According to their instrumentation, they were now at minus 400 feet. Minus 500. Minus 600.

'Where is the fucking ground?' he heard Lansing gibber beside him. 'Where the fuck has the fucking ground gone? What the fuck is going on?'

Peters nudged the nose up, got the plane stabilised. The windows showed only blackness outside. All kinds of half-assed theories were going through his mind. He found himself fervently wishing he hadn't read Stephen King's 'The Langoliers' as a teenager: he half-expected to see those nightmarish creatures assembling outside the cockpit window, gobbling up pieces of reality …

Keep it together, he told himself sternly, feeling his entire body convulse in fear. He didn't want to crumble like the oh-so heroic Captain Lansing alongside him.

He swallowed, hard. 'I'm taking us back up,' he said, his voice level.

'We need to find the ground!' Lansing insisted. 'It's gotta fucking be there! It can't just vanish, Peters! A whole fucking city can't just up and vanish!'

'Captain, we're already six hundred feet below the surface!' Peters returned. 'The ground is gone. Impossible, *tell* me about it, but it's gone. Do you hear me?'

'So why are we going up? Why go up?' Lansing whined.

Peters spared a second to stare directly at Lansing. 'Do you want to be six hundred feet below if it comes *back*?' was all he said.

He'd been afraid that this would push the captain over the edge altogether, but it seemed to do the opposite. Lansing exhaled, straightened his shoulders, and, with a nod at Peters, grabbed the controls. Together they angled the plane upwards and the altimeter began to climb towards zero. When it span into positive numbers both men felt like they could suck in three lungfuls of air.

'What the *hell* is going on?' the Inflight Supervisor demanded from behind them. 'I've got a hundred and fifty people scared out of their fuckin' minds back there ... hundred fifty-one if you include me.'

'We–' Peters began.

'Tell them there's been a power cut,' Lansing broke in. He was all smoothness again. 'We need to go back up, circle awhile, make sure they're ready to have us come in. Nothing to worry about, have a drink on us, sorry for the inconvenience.'

The Inflight Supervisor was a career woman, with the airline twenty-seven years. Frankly she scared the hell out of Peters – his first flight, she'd given a look that could have withered Jack's beanstalk.

'Fine,' she said, fairly vibrating with indignation. 'But you tell me, you tell me right fucking now what's *really* going on.'

The plane banked left. Peters started in surprise; he hadn't initiated the manoeuvre.

'That,' Lansing said, taking one hand off the controls to point. His finger shook. His voice was little more than a whisper. 'That is what's *really* going on.'

The Irish Sea had been halted, as if by the hand of God, in an irregular line. The waters swirled and rebounded off an invisible wall, preventing tens of millions of gallons of seawater from rushing in and filling a great nothingness – a vast void where the island of Ireland had been.

Ireland was gone. Lock, stock and barrel, it was gone.

'Get me Heathrow. Get me Glasgow. Get me *anyone*,' Lansing said softly.

Screams sounded from behind them.

'That'll be the passengers,' the Inflight Supervisor said calmly, as though in a dream. She stared directly at Peters, all traces of her former fearsomeness wiped away. 'I better give them those drinks ...'

'Don't let them up here,' Peters told her retreating back. He hated himself for saying it, but it was necessary. Panicking passengers storming the cockpit wasn't going to solve anything, unless you counted the question 'What's the quickest way to get us all killed?'

The door closed. He fumbled for the radio to raise Heathrow, feeling a cavernous pit open in his stomach that threatened to dwarf the Ireland-shaped one hundreds of feet below. What if no one was out there? What if this plane was all that was left, doomed to fly the empty skies looking down at nothing but ocean and former landmasses now removed as simply and effectively as a child might pluck a jigsaw piece from a completed puzzle, until their fuel ran dry and they were forced to pitch into the raging sea ...

Fuck you, Stephen King, he thought, and made the call.

DUBLIN, NOW

We're packed in like bloody sardines, Tom Beckett thought, glaring daggers at the rear spoiler of the people carrier in front of him and trying to ignore the the six-year-old brat in the back seat who was pulling the most ludicrously annoying face Tom had ever seen a child perform. This was the same kid who'd spent 90 per cent of the voyage over running pell-fucking-mell across the fucking ship while his useless fat parents had sat struggling to breathe as they choked down burgers and fries.

Still. Another few minutes and the ship would be fully unloaded and he could leave that people carrier behind and start winding his way to Mullingar, where even now (according to the last text he'd received, anyway) Suzie his fiancée was currently browsing her extensive selection of Ann Summers lingerie, choosing the outfit she'd be wearing to greet him when he arrived at her door.

His hands tightened on the wheel. Somehow, that thought wasn't doing much to relieve his impatience with the unloading process ...

Ah! The cars were moving! He thanked God and edged forward, moving slowly from the massive ferry's interior and into the Dublin night, greeted immediately by a spray of water from the wind whipping up the waters below.

That little *bastard* ahead of him flicked him the V-sign. Tom debated whether to return the favour.

It was then that the cars started moving faster. For a whole second, perhaps two, Tom thought that his ship had quite literally come in. He actually smiled.

And then the screaming began.

The people carrier in front of him vanished, allowing Tom to see what lay ahead.

There was nothing beyond the exit ramp.

He slammed on the brakes and the car stopped, briefly, but the untethered exit ramp, no longer anchored securely to the Dublin harbour, was swinging freely and he was unable to stop the vehicle's forward momentum for long. As if to underline this, the white van behind him slammed into his back bumper, forcing him forward. He screamed as his car was pushed over the edge.

He fell into the abyss.

THE FIRST INSTALMENT IN THE
BRILLIANT *FOLK'D* TRILOGY

eBook
EPUB ISBN 978-0-85640-239-5
KINDLE ISBN 978-0-85640-240-1

Paperback
ISBN 978-0-85640-9J'

www.blackstaffp